Ford M

FORD MADOX FORD (the nam ... ... originally Ford Hermann Hueffer) ... ... in Merton, Surrey, in 1873. His mother, Catherine, was the daughter of the Pre-Raphaelite painter Ford Madox Brown. His father, Francis Hueffer, was a German emigré, a musicologist and music critic for *The Times*. Christina and Dante Gabriel Rossetti were his aunt and uncle by marriage. Ford published his first book, a children's fairy tale, when he was seventeen. He collaborated with Joseph Conrad from 1898 to 1908, and also befriended many of the best writers of his time, including Henry James, H.G. Wells, Stephen Crane, John Galsworthy and Thomas Hardy. He is best known for his novels, especially *The Fifth Queen* (a trilogy about Henry VIII; 1906–8), *The Good Soldier* (1915) and *Parade's End* (his tetralogy about the First World War). He was also an influential poet and critic, and a brilliant magazine editor. He founded the *English Review* in 1908, discovering D.H. Lawrence, Wyndham Lewis and Ezra Pound, who became another close friend. Ford served as an officer in the Welch Regiment 1915–19. After the war he moved to France. In Paris he founded the *transatlantic review*, taking on Ernest Hemingway as a sub-editor, discovering Jean Rhys and Basil Bunting, and publishing James Joyce and Gertrude Stein. In the 1920s and 1930s he moved between Paris, New York and Provence. He died in Deauville in June 1939. The author of over eighty books, Ford is a major presence in twentieth-century writing.

PAUL SKINNER took his first degree at the University of the West of England as a mature student, and later completed a PhD on Ford Madox Ford and Ezra Pound at the University of Bristol. He has since taught at both universities, and published articles on Ford, Pound and Rudyard Kipling. His edition of Ford's *No Enemy* was published by Carcanet in 2002. In 2007 he edited *Ford Madox Ford's Literary Contacts*, volume 6 of International Ford Madox Ford Studies. He was a bookseller for many years and now works in publishing.

Also by Ford Madox Ford from Carcanet Press

Critical Essays
England and the English
The English Novel
The Ford Madox Ford Reader
The Good Soldier
It Was the Nightingale
Ladies Whose Bright Eyes
A Man Could Stand Up –
No Enemy
No More Parades
Provence
The Rash Act
Return to Yesterday
Selected Poems
Some Do Not . . .
War Prose

FORD MADOX FORD

Parade's End

VOLUME IV

Last Post
A Novel

Edited by Paul Skinner

CARCANET

For my sister, Penny Levy,
too suddenly gone, May 2011

Last Post was first published in Great Britain in 1928 by Duckworth & Co.

This edition first published in Great Britain in 2011 by
Carcanet Press Limited
Alliance House
Cross Street
Manchester M2 7AQ

A CIP catalogue record for this book is available from the British Library

ISBN 978 1 84777 015 8 (*Last Post*)
ISBN 978 1 84777 021 9 (*Parade's End* volumes I–IV)

The publisher acknowledges financial assistance from Arts Council England

Supported by
ARTS COUNCIL
ENGLAND

Typeset by XL Publishing Services, Tiverton
Printed and bound in England by SRP Ltd, Exeter

CONTENTS

ACKNOWLEDGEMENTS

This has been a collaborative project from first to last, so my primary acknowledgements and thanks go to my fellow editors, Max Saunders, Joseph Wiesenfarth and Sara Haslam, who have read and commented on successive drafts, providing information, suggestions and encouragement. I feel privileged to have enjoyed their company (both in person and in correspondence) and remain profoundly impressed by their enthusiasm for the work, the high standards of their scholarship and the tolerance and good humour they have shown along the way.

It's impossible not to single out Max Saunders for the extraordinary contribution he has made, tirelessly drafting and re-drafting statements of principle and editorial practice, while always demonstrating a Fordian mastery of both the smallest detail and the largest view of the entire project. Personally, I owe him a substantial debt of gratitude for innumerable suggestions, invaluable criticism and an unfailing readiness to answer distress calls.

I'd like to acknowledge with gratitude the staff at the Division of Rare and Manuscript Collections at the Carl A. Kroch Library, Cornell University, who have been helpful and prompt in their responses. Thanks are also due to Cornell University (again), to Michael Schmidt and the estate of Janice Biala for permission to quote from Ford's and Biala's letters.

Special thanks go to our editor at Carcanet, Judith Willson, and, of course, to Michael Schmidt, as both director of Carcanet and Ford's executor, for supporting and facilitating this project.

For various instances of help, advice and information, I'd like to thank: Ashley Chantler for reading sample chapters and affording us the benefit of his editorial experience; Peter Clasen for generously offering the results of his research; and Brian Groth for racehorse tips.

Working on this edition has been inexhaustibly interesting and often exhilarating. Among those who have sometimes felt the effects of the resultant obsessive interest in horse-racing, agricultural implements or variants of fairy tales, I should acknowledge with thanks Nick Nile, Laney Nile, my daughters Jo and Kim, and Andrew Gilman.

My greatest acknowledgement remains to Naomi.

LIST OF ILLUSTRATIONS

LIST OF SHORT TITLES

Ancient Lights   *Ancient Lights and Certain New Reflections:*
                      Being the Memories of a Young Man (London:
                      Chapman & Hall, 1911)
Between St. Dennis *Between St. Dennis and St. George* (London:
                      Hodder & Stoughton, 1915)
Country   *The Heart of the Country* (London: Alston
                      Rivers, 1906)
England   *England and the English*, ed. Sara Haslam
                      (Manchester: Carcanet, 2003) (collecting
                      Ford's trilogy on Englishness: see also under
                      Country and *People*)
English Novel   *The English Novel from the Earliest Days to the
                      Death of Joseph Conrad* (1930) (Manchester:
                      Carcanet, 1983)
Fifth Queen   trilogy consisting of *The Fifth Queen*
                      (London: Alston Rivers, 1906); *Privy Seal*
                      (London: Alston Rivers, 1907); and *The
                      Fifth Queen Crowned* (Eveleigh Nash, 1908)
Ford/Bowen   *The Correspondence of Ford Madox Ford and
                      Stella Bowen*, ed. Sondra Stang and Karen
                      Cochran (Bloomington and Indianapolis:
                      Indiana University Press, 1994)
Joseph Conrad   *Joseph Conrad: A Personal Remembrance*
                      (London: Duckworth, 1924)
Letters   *Letters of Ford Madox Ford*, ed. Richard M.
                      Ludwig (Princeton, NJ: Princeton Univer-
                      sity Press, 1965)
March   *The March of Literature* (London: Allen &
                      Unwin, 1939)
Mightier   *Mightier Than the Sword* (London: Allen &
                      Unwin, 1938)

Mister Bosphorus	*Mister Bosphorus and the Muses or a Short History of Poetry in Britain. Variety Entertainment in Four Acts... with Harlequinade, Transformation Scene, Cinematograph Effects, and Many Other Novelties, as well as Old and Tried Favourites* (London: Duckworth, 1923)
Nightingale	*It Was the Nightingale* (1933), ed. John Coyle (Manchester: Carcanet, 2007)
People	*The Spirit of the People* (London: Alston Rivers, 1907)
Pound/Ford	*Pound/Ford: the Story of a Literary Friendship: the Correspondence between Ezra Pound and Ford Madox Ford and Their Writings About Each Other*, ed. Brita Lindberg-Seyersted (London: Faber & Faber, 1982)
Provence	*Provence: From Minstrels to Machine* (1935), ed. John Coyle (Manchester: Carcanet, 2007)
Reader	*The Ford Madox Ford Reader*, with Foreword by Graham Greene, ed. Sondra J. Stang (Manchester: Carcanet, 1986)
Return	*Return to Yesterday* (1931), ed. Bill Hutchings (Manchester: Carcanet, 1999)

Last Post

Ford Madox Ford

(Ford Madox Hueffer)

The Fourth and Final Volume of
THE "TIETJENS" NOVELS

"Tietjens is one of the few
truly original characters
which have appeared in
modern English fiction."—
The Times Literary Supplement.

DUCKWORTH

INTRODUCTION

> A song new to us was heard, 'What shall we be
> when we aren't what we are?' It foretold one of the many
> tragedies of Peace.
> Mrs C.S. Peel recalling Armistice Night in
> *How We Lived Then* (1929)

The Great War ended at 11:00 a.m. on 11 November 1918. Many
people felt both huge relief and uneasiness. '[T]hank the Lord
that's over [...] we have to face the perils of Peace now', Augustus
John wrote to John Quinn, while D.H. Lawrence harangued
David Garnett: 'The crowd outside thinks that Germany is
crushed forever. But the Germans will soon rise again. Europe is
done for; England most of all...'[1] In early December Aldous
Huxley wrote to Ottoline Morrell: 'It is certainly very curious the
way almost everybody has become extremely depressed at the
arrival of peace. One could regard the War as a nightmare and
unreal; but with peace one must look at facts as though they were
real – and they are extremely unpleasant.'[2]

Ford Madox Ford, then stationed at Redcar in Yorkshire,
where he was lecturing to the troops, wrote to Stella Bowen on
Armistice Day: 'Just a note to say I love you more than ever. Peace
has come, & for some reason I feel inexpressibly sad.' Yet to free
his beloved France from German occupation was 'like a fairy tale',
he told her.[3] In June 1919, when the Treaty of Versailles was

---

1 Stanley Weintraub, *A Stillness Heard Round the World. The End of the Great War:
   November 1918* (Oxford: Oxford University Press, 1987), 286; for other expressions
   of conviction that another war was already inevitable, see 325, 381, 394 fn.
2 Ottoline Morrell, *Ottoline at Garsington: Memoirs of Lady Ottoline Morrell 1915–1918*,
   ed. Robert Gathorne-Hardy (London: Faber & Faber, 1974), 210.
3 *The Correspondence of Ford Madox Ford and Stella Bowen*, ed. Sondra J. Stang and Karen
   Cochran (Bloomington and Indianapolis: Indiana University Press, 1994), 32, 35.

signed, or when, as Ford put it, peace was declared, he wrote to Charles Masterman: 'It's like a fairy world.'[4] How seriously should we treat such statements? Ford was not alone in making them, or statements very like them, and it's hardly necessary to point to the extreme contrast between the trenches of Flanders and the streets of central London or the fields of Sussex to grasp that there was a widespread sense of *unreality* among many returnees. Nor were such feelings restricted to those who had been to the war: 'Unreal city [...] I had not thought death had undone so many.'[5]

Biography

Ford's post-war life in West Sussex began at Red Ford, Hurston, Pulborough, in the spring of 1919, after his demobilisation. From the beginning of September 1920 he and his partner, the Australian painter Stella Bowen, lived at Coopers Cottage in Bedham, near Fittleworth. Their daughter, Esther Julia (Julie), was born three months later on 29 November. Ford and Bowen moved to France in late 1922; their relationship faltered under the impact of Ford's affair with Jean Rhys and failed in the face of his extended visits to the United States from 1926 onwards, and his further romantic entanglements there.

Bowen is central to the story of *Parade's End*, both personally and artistically. She provided indispensable practical and emotional support but also served as the primary model for the character of Valentine Wannop; other models were Stella's close friend Margaret Postgate (who married the Socialist historian and economist G.D.H. Cole) and, in Ford's own telling, the actress Dorothy Minto (*Nightingale*, 191).[6]

4 *No Enemy*, ed. Paul Skinner (Manchester: Carcanet, 2002), 46; *It Was the Nightingale*, ed. John Coyle (Manchester: Carcanet, 2007), 106, 116; *Letters of Ford Madox Ford*, ed. Richard M. Ludwig (Princeton, NJ: Princeton University Press, 1965), 94.

5 T.S. Eliot, *The Waste Land*, ll.60–63, in *Collected Poems 1909–1962* (London: Faber & Faber, 1965), 65. Vivien Eliot wrote to her brother-in-law Henry in November 1918 about the difficulty of *realising* Peace: 'I must say it is difficult to feel anything at all. One is too stunned altogether.' Valerie Eliot and Hugh Haughton (eds), *The Letters of T.S. Eliot. Volume I: 1898–1922* (London: Faber & Faber, rev. edn, 2009), 303.

6 Stella wrote to Ford (8 February 1927): 'But if they don't like Valentine, – what is the use of my ever coming to America??!' See *Ford/Bowen* 315. Katherine Hueffer, Ford's younger daughter by his wife Elsie, also saw herself in Valentine: see Max Saunders, *Ford Madox Ford: A Dual Life*, 2 vols (Oxford: Oxford University Press, 1996), II 597 n.46.

From the outset, *Last Post* draws heavily upon the material
details of their life together in Sussex. Bedham, Stella wrote, was
'on a great wooded hill [...] There was an immense view.'[7]
Douglas Goldring, Ford's friend and editorial assistant on the
English Review a dozen years earlier, wrote admiringly that 'the
views from hereabouts are unrivalled in Sussex',[8] and Ford later
remembered: 'They said locally that it looked over twelve counties, and I daresay we really could see three from the west window'
(*Nightingale* 117). The context of that memory was one of isola-
tion from the outer world (though Ford and Stella had numerous
visitors), 'being hidden in a green – a far too green – corner of
England, on a hill-top that was almost inaccessible to motor
traffic, under an immense screen of giant beeches' (*Nightingale*
138).

One constant concern in Ford's post-war work, not always
obvious or rendered in obvious ways, is a profound sense of loss,
of grief, of mourning. This was, of course, an inextricable feature
of the cultural landscape of that time: among the major combatants, Jay Winter has commented, 'it is not an exaggeration to
suggest that every family was in mourning'.[9] In addition to the
numerous deaths inextricable from his war service, Ford had lost
many close friends in recent years, including Arthur Marwood,
W.H. Hudson and Joseph Conrad, while the death of the painter
Juan Gris in May 1927 was closely followed by that of Ford's
mother, just three weeks later.[10]

All these and other deaths and vanishings lie behind his asking
of Isabel Paterson in *Last Post*'s 'Dedicatory Letter' if she does not
find that 'in the case of certain dead people' she 'cannot feel that
they are indeed gone from this world'. He goes on to say that, for
him, 'the world daily becomes more and more peopled with such

7 See Stella Bowen, *Drawn From Life* (London: Virago, 1984 [1941]), 69.
8 Douglas Goldring, *Nooks and Corners of Sussex & Hampshire* (London: Eveleigh Nash,
   n.d. [1920]), 115.
9 Jay Winter, *Sites of Memory, Sites of Mourning: The Great War in European Cultural
   History* (Cambridge: Cambridge University Press, 1995), 2. 'The post-war world',
   Juliet Nicolson writes, 'was in large part a world paralysed by grief': *The Great Silence
   1918–1920: Living in the Shadow of the Great War* (London: John Murray, 2009), 4.
10 Janice Biala believed that Marie Léonie was based on Juan Gris's wife Josette: see Alan
   Judd, *Ford Madox Ford* (London: Collins, 1990), 61, where he also mentions, as a
   possible model, Dora, the wife of Stephen Crane. Ford certainly described Dora Crane
   as 'large, fair and placid': see *Return to Yesterday*, ed. Bill Hutchings (Manchester:
   Carcanet, 1999), 48.

revenants and less and less with those who still walk this earth'.[11]

Remembrance of the dead and their resurrection in the pages of his books is, then, a crucial and constant feature of Ford's post-war writings. He was, as John Coyle remarks, 'a compulsive ghost-seer' (*Nightingale* viii). More immediately, perhaps, the setting of *Last Post* is itself a shadowing of Ford's life in Sussex. Fifteen years before, he had written of literary impressionism's rendering of 'those queer effects of real life that are like so many views seen through bright glass', when you see, in addition to the view through that glass, the reflection upon it of a face or person behind you.[12] That is often true of *Last Post*, with its overlaid images of alternative lives and disparate histories, its crowding of voices and memories into the spaces left by Mark's determined silence and Marie Léonie's absorption in her work. The novel is haunted by the unspoken or, at least, the understated: the war, as it is lived with in this 'after-war world',[13] and what is gone from the lives of not only the characters but their author also. It is this haunting that may bring before the reader a sharp and unsettling sense of the short, almost invisible step between 'last post' and 'lost past'.

The Title

The novel's title lends itself to multiple interpretations.[14] The *OED* offers a bewildering array of meanings for 'post' (as it does for 'last'): half a dozen headings as a verb and a dozen as a noun. Those merely of obvious relevance to Ford's novel are plentiful enough: support, boundary marker, horse-racing, the act of recording an entry in a ledger, the point at which a soldier is

---

11 In *Last Post* I.vii, Marie Léonie is fearful of encountering such ghosts, but the *revenants* would crowd ever more insistently into Ford's books of the 1930s.

12 'On Impressionism', usefully reprinted in *Critical Writings of Ford Madox Ford*, ed. Frank MacShane (Lincoln, NE: University of Nebraska Press, 1964), 41.

13 'The world before the war is one thing and must be written about in one manner; the after-war world is quite another and calls for quite different treatment': Ford to T.R. Smith (27 July 1931), quoted in Saunders, *Dual Life* II [iii].

14 I have discussed several of these in 'The Painful Processes of Reconstruction: History in *No Enemy* and *Last Post*', in *History and Representation in Ford Madox Ford's Writings*, ed. Joseph Wiesenfarth, International Ford Madox Ford Studies, 3 (Amsterdam and New York: Rodopi, 2004), 65–75. Mark Tietjens uses 'last post' twice in the course of the book, once quite explicitly as 'a grim joke' (I.v, I.vi).

stationed when on duty, and the Latin word for 'after' or 'since', as in 'post-war'. Yet the most immediately striking fact about the occurrences of 'post' in the novel is that more than half are specifically focused on beds and shelters. These are noticeably grouped towards the beginning and the end of the book. They relate particularly to the bed in which Mark lies and the shelter that contains it; but also the bed in which the pregnant Valentine Wannop lies and in which she expects and hopes that her child will be born.

The 'last post' is the bugle call sounded at the end of the military day, signalling the order to retire for the night. It is also sounded at military funerals and at services of remembrance, and this context is undoubtedly far more familiar to civilian ears, certainly since 1919 and the establishing of annual ceremonies on Armistice Day. Ford wrote of this – but also, tellingly, of what follows:

> At a British military funeral, after the Dead March in Saul, after the rattling of the cords from under the coffin, the rifle-firing and the long wail of the last post, suddenly the band and drums strike up "D'ye ken John Peel?" or the "Lincolnshire Poacher" – the unit's quickstep. It is shocking until you see how good it is as a symbol. (*Nightingale* 19–20)

That 'long wail' is heard several times in *Last Post*, both in the novel's present, in which a neighbour's sons (one of whom has been a bugler) play or attempt to play it, and in the memories of Armistice Night – variously painful for Mark Tietjens, Valentine, Marie Léonie and even Sylvia Tietjens – that such playing prompts.

The Novel

Last Post is set during a few hours of a June day, in the years following the First World War. Christopher Tietjens now makes his living as a dealer in old furniture. He and Valentine Wannop share a cottage in West Sussex with Christopher's older brother Mark and Mark's wife, Marie Léonie.

Much of the novel is presented from Mark's point of view as
he lies, mute and immobile, in an outdoor shelter; other sections
are presented from the viewpoints of Marie Léonie and Valentine. The narrative also dips in and out of the consciousnesses of
Christopher's estranged wife Sylvia, their son, Mark Junior, and
several minor characters. These interior monologues traverse the
past, speculate on the future, illuminate details of the present and
offer alternative perspectives on some of the events that have
occurred earlier in the sequence, particularly 'that infernal day'
and 'that dreadful night' of the Armistice, around which their
memories circle obsessively.

The tensions of the novel centre, domestically, on Valentine's
advanced pregnancy in the context of her, and Christopher's,
financial precariousness. Mark is wealthy but a feud between the
brothers, brought about by Sylvia's promotion of scurrilous
rumours about her husband, which were initially believed by
Mark and, consequently, by their father, has made it impossible
for Christopher to accept, either by gift or by inheritance, money
or property from his brother. The threats to the Tietjens ménage
derive directly or indirectly from the continued malicious
scheming of Sylvia Tietjens, who has tried to turn their neighbour and landlord against them, and manoeuvred an American
tenant of Groby (the Tietjens ancestral home) into cutting down
Groby Great Tree, 'the symbol of Tietjens' (I.iv).[15] Christopher
has flown to York in an attempt to avert this threat. The invasion of the Tietjens domain by the American tenant and the
Tietjenses' son, by Sylvia and by other figures from earlier in the
tetralogy closes with Sylvia's retreat and change of heart. The
novel's fine and poignant ending focuses on the death of Mark
Tietjens.

15 There is a Groby Old Hall in the Leicestershire village of Groby, built by the Grey
family, whose members included both Elizabeth Woodville, Queen Consort of Edward
IV, and Lady Jane Grey. But Ford probably based his idea of Groby (and its Great
Tree) on the Marwood family seat, Busby Hall, near Stokesley (and close to Redcar):
Saunders, *Dual Life* II 51, 565 n.16. At Bedham he was also very close to other great
houses, notably Parham and Petworth.

The Literary Context

The literary decade in which Ford published the four Tietjens volumes was a famously rich one. Those years saw Lawrence's *Women in Love* and Pound's *Hugh Selwyn Mauberley* in 1920, then *The Waste Land*, *Ulysses*, the early *Cantos*, several major volumes by Yeats, *The Great Gatsby*, *Mrs Dalloway*, *A Passage to India*, *The Sun Also Rises*, *To the Lighthouse* and *The Apes of God*. Ford knew most of the writers of these works and had himself published Lawrence, Lewis, Pound, Yeats, Joyce and Hemingway.

Ford later cited the example of Proust as an influence on the conception of *Parade's End* (though he had not at that stage read Proust's work: *Nightingale* 179–80); and he was certainly familiar with the novels of Woolf and Joyce, as he was with the poems of Pound, Yeats and Eliot. It was surely the case that such examples and such literary company as he enjoyed in both Paris and New York encouraged his confidence in the immense project he was embarked upon, strengthening his belief that he was producing some of the best and most significant work of his life. Ford had enjoyed some critical successes (and one or two commercial ones) but it was with *Some Do Not . . .* and its successors that he was reviewed and discussed with the same seriousness and with the same recognition of literary significance as were the other major Modernists.

The constituent volumes of *Parade's End* are usually – and, I think, quite rightly – viewed as closely, even inextricably, connected parts, though *Last Post*, as I discuss later, is sometimes not so regarded.[16] Their initial publications were, though, interspersed with half a dozen other titles, including *A Mirror to France* in 1926 and two books of essays, *New York is Not America* and *New York Essays*, both published in 1927.

That international flavour is certainly significant. Perhaps, though, the books by Ford most closely related to *Last Post* – apart from the earlier volumes of *Parade's End* – fall outside this period

---

16 Ford himself refers to 'the first part of my book', 'my large work' and 'my long book' (*Nightingale* 223, 326, 344). See *Letters* 204, on reading 'the Tietjens books as one novel in which case the whole design appears'.

and the real context is not purely chronological. *No Enemy* shares many similarities of setting and post-war mood, as well as numerous echoes of both image and phrasing, while *The Heart of the Country*, though twenty years earlier – and, obviously, pre-war – foreshadows several elements of *Last Post*.[17] There are echoes in the novel of two volumes of poetry, *A House* (1921) and *Mister Bosphorus and the Muses* (1923), and the later *It Was the Nightingale* has been described as 'a companion volume to *Parade's End*, reiterating the concerns of the tetralogy with renewed urgency' (*Nightingale* xiv). In fact, though the war was a huge and transformative event in Ford's life, as in countless others', many of his preoccupations, manifested in his writing, long pre-dated it and continued to engage him later. The war did not invalidate them: rather, it added urgency, depth and a stronger sense of the fragility of our lives and their surrounding darkness.

'Like a Fairy World'

Ford's writing to Masterman that 'Peace' was 'like a fairy world' surely hints at the grounds on which a few critics of *Last Post* have described the novel as 'retreating from history' and existing in its own time – though other readers and commentators have regarded this element altogether more positively. 'It is into the overgrown but still unblocked tunnels to dialect and faery England that the dying Mark Tietjens glimpses', Hugh Kenner wrote, 'it is from them that he extracts his legacy for the living.'[18]

Ford's publishing history begins with fairy tales and many of his later books draw on elements of this tradition: the possibilities of transformation, the frequent instability of 'reality', the subtle tug of archetypes, the pressure of conflicting narratives.[19] And fairy tale, like an undercurrent barely disturbing the surface

17 *The Heart of the Country* (London: Alston Rivers, 1906), reprinted, together with *The Soul of London* (1905) and *The Spirit of the People* (1907), in *England and the English*, ed. Sara Haslam (Manchester: Carcanet, 2003).
18 Hugh Kenner, 'Remember That I Have Remembered', in *Gnomon: Essays on Contemporary Literature* (New York: McDowell, Obolensky, 1958), 160.
19 *No Enemy* repeatedly refers to Gringoire and the cottage where he lives with his partner, Madame Sélysette, in terms of fairy tales. In *Nightingale* Ford comments that 'to date, this fairy-tale has found its appropriate close' (xxi).

of the water, is one example of the means by which Ford achieves that characteristic effect of glimpses, of sounds not quite heard, of objects vanishing or shifting in the moment of their detection.

Consider Valentine Wannop, under the several stresses of anxiety over her unborn child, her home under siege, having just emerged from the upstairs room in which she had unintentionally locked herself, needing to reach the doctor who attends to Mark Tietjens. She gazes down 'her long room' as she holds the telephone to her ear, looking 'into the distant future' when things will spread out 'like a plain seen from a hill'. In the meantime, they have 'to keep all on going'. All these are tiny echoes of details from earlier in the sequence or, like Meary Walker, the Bonnington agricultural worker about whom he wrote on several occasions, of recurring figures in Ford's work. Valentine asks the doctor to come quickly: 'Sister Anne! Sister Anne! For God's sake, Sister Anne! If she could get a bromide into her it would pass like a dream. / It was passing like a dream' (II.iii).

'Sister Anne' points us to Charles Perrault's story, 'Bluebeard', in which the wife's sister looks out from the top of the tower for their two brothers, who are riding towards them while Bluebeard calls his wife to meet her death at his hands.[20] Within *Parade's End* that in turn points back to the late pages of *A Man Could Stand Up –*, in which Valentine waits in the empty house while the 'madman', Tietjens, is coming up the stairs. 'He was carrying a sack. [...] A sack was a terrible thing for a mad man to carry. [...] It was a heavy sack. Bluebeard would have had in it the corpse of his first wife' (III.i). It is, of course, a sack of coal. Even carried by a madman, a sack may be benign. It is not always so. In an earlier passage, marked by high anxiety and hallucination preceding an expected enemy attack, Tietjens sees a pile of wet sacks and notes their appalling resemblance to 'prostrate men'. A few pages later:

---

20 *The Annotated Classic Fairy Tales* (New York and London: W.W. Norton and Co., 2002), edited with an introduction by Maria Tatar, who points out that the story is 'unique in the way that it begins with marriage and moves its protagonist back to her first family, a reversal of the conventional trajectory of fairy-tale heroes and heroines' (155).

Noise increased. The orchestra was bringing in *all* the brass, *all* the strings, *all* the wood-wind, all the percussion instruments. The performers threw about biscuit tins filled with horseshoes; they emptied sacks of coal on cracked gongs, they threw down forty-storey iron houses. It was comic to the extent that an operatic orchestra's crescendo is comic. Crescendo! ... Crescendo! CRRRRRESC ... The Hero *must* be coming! He didn't! (*A Man Could Stand Up* – II.i)

In *Some Do Not* . . . , when Valentine learns from Mark Tietjens that her mother will be provided for under the terms of Mr Tietjens' will, she reflects that it is 'as if a novel had been snatched out of her hand so that she would never know the end'. Ford adds: 'Of the fairytale she knew the end' – that is, tailors and goose-girls. 'But she would never know whether they, in the end, got together all the blue Dutch tiles they wanted to line their bathroom' (II.v). We need both novels and fairy tales (which are, Ford wrote, 'a prime necessity of the world'),[21] though the question of degrees of separation lingers. In *A Man Could Stand Up* – that 'small company' of the Rag-Time Army that Tietjens currently commands, 'men of all sorts of sizes, of all sorts of disparities and grotesquenesses of physique', including two music-hall comedians, is called to attention and 'positively, a dwarf concealed under a pudding basin shuffled a foot-length and a half forward'. It is 'like a blurred fairy-tale', Tietjens reflects (II.ii). So, of course, in many respects, is the entire experience of war. Blurred, senseless, incomprehensible, transforming fields into mud, houses into rubble and men into scraps, by turns deafening, terrifying and stupefyingly tedious. The fairy tale, in such conditions, can look unsettlingly like The Real Thing.

In *No Enemy*, when the poet (and Fordian persona) Gringoire relates the 'psychological anecdote which gives the note of this book', it concerns an envisioned landscape, or rather, 'not quite a landscape' but 'a nook' – 'with a gingerbread cottage out of Grimm'. 'A castle in Spain, in fact, only that it was in a southern country – the English country.'

---

21 Ford, *Portraits From Life* (Boston: Houghton Mifflin, 1937), 109.

'I ask to be believed in what I am now saying.' Gringoire uttered the words slowly. 'It is just the truth. If I wanted to tell fairy tales, I'd do better than this. Fairy tales to be all about the Earth shaking, and the wire, and the crumps, and the beef-tins … You know. And that would be true too. Anyway this is.… ' (33–4)

In *Last Post*'s teasing 'Dedicatory Letter' to his 'fairy godmother', Isabel Paterson, Ford reverts to the matter. He touches again on his attempt 'to project how this world would have appeared' to his friend Arthur Marwood 'to-day'. He recalls the many years during which he tended to ask himself what Marwood would have said and how he would have acted in certain situations.

And I do so still. I have only to say to my mind, as the child on the knees of an adult says to its senior: "Tell us a fairy tale!" – I have only to say: "Tell us what he would here have done!" and at once he is there.

Little wonder, perhaps, that Valentine Wannop reflects 'The age of fairy-tales was not, of course, past' (*Last Post* II.iii).[22] Little wonder, too, that something more is needed.

All this may simply enforce and emphasise the fact that, in practice, Ford's writing draws on many genres within a single work, which can unsettle some critics just as it enthuses many of Ford's readers. Is *Parade's End* historical novel, comedy, pantomime, fairy tale, romance or satire? Is it realistic or fantastic, concerned with 'public' or 'private' events? The temptation is simply to say 'yes, all of these', though risking some readers' inference that this means, necessarily, something unresolved, ungainly or untidy.

It does not.

22 In the typescript Ford had 'The age of windfalls' but changed this. 'Windfalls' now appears in the next sentence but in the pluperfect tense ('They had had windfalls'): one further back, in a sense.

Boundaries

If *Parade's End* is a novel, or novel-sequence, of both war and peace – or, at least, 'not-war' – where does the boundary lie? *Some Do Not . . .* often gives the impression of being pre-war – but half of it is not. *A Man Could Stand Up* – technically covers the post-war but it is, quite literally, Armistice Day; and the first and third sections bracket a much longer second section – exactly 60 per cent of the book – that deals most vividly with the war, specifically Ludendorff's great offensive of Spring 1918. The true post-war is limited to *Last Post*. And, though all four books were produced several years after the Armistice, *Last Post* is written, I believe, very much in the spirit of the *immediate* post-war: of that sense of fairy tale and of unreality, of wish-fulfilment, the rush of relief after the years of strain, but still a world turned upside-down, riddled with hazard and uncertainty. The trick of it was that Ford in 1927 was casting his mind back to the years in Sussex with Stella Bowen: their cottage then was the setting for 'Tietjens's' now. The tension, the tremendous effort of doing this, was heightened by the fact that his relationship with Bowen, so crucial to the conception, planning and production of *Parade's End*, was fracturing, now, as he wrote it.

The book is Ford's last, regretful, love letter to Stella Bowen, through which he is saying his farewells, and not only to her. He is in America, or rather in a ship off the coast of Canada taking him away from her – again – when he writes to say that his last 'English' novel is finished; she, the Australian, met and loved and lived with in England, then in France, to whom he dedicates not this last novel arising from their long intimacy (and, in a sense, the one rooted most deeply in their lives together) but a new edition of his *pre-war* masterpiece, *The Good Soldier*, written and published before he met her. That novel is about a divided Ford, about his portrait of the artist, the actor and the watcher. The actor cuts his throat and the watcher writes it down. Within a few months of its publication, Ford the actor was a soldier in uniform and the watcher could not write. And one version of how he came to be able to write again – or a parable of that – he set down at the beginning of their lives together, in a story called 'English Country', which was not published until a decade later, as *No Enemy*, after his life with Stella had ended.[23]

This is why, even within the fictional world of the novel, there are currents running towards the outside, the 'actual' world, sometimes of the early twenties soon after the war when there is a discernible rawness and fragility; but also a stronger current, I believe, running towards the writer's present, the transatlantic movement itself bridging (but deceptively, over the surface of the sea) two worlds, Europe and America, an author whose work was, increasingly, bridging those same two worlds, and whose life – or one version of it – was ending: his mother recently dead, the news of other deaths seeming to confront him at every turn, an essay just published in which he mourned for his lost fellow writers and said that it was like dying himself.[24] Lost, last.

Arts and Crafts

'Writing' is, in fact, a curious absence in *Last Post* – curious, in part, because it's so prevalent in the other volumes. *Some Do Not ...* opens with Macmaster correcting the proofs of his first book, though finding nothing to correct. Thereafter, as well as the many allusions to Fordian favourites (including Gilbert White, Christina Rossetti, Turgenev, Ezra Pound, James and Conrad), there are scores of instances of different arts and media: paintings and drawings, telegrams and telephone calls, military reports, the composition of music-hall sketches and sessions of *bout-rimés*. The many letters include those that Tietjens thinks of writing to Valentine and the one that he seems (to Levin) to be writing to her in his sleep, as well as those written by or about

---

23 Appearing in 1929 in the United States, *No Enemy* was not published in Britain in Ford's lifetime, nor, indeed, until the Carcanet edition of 2002. It is dedicated to Julie, Ford and Stella's daughter ('Très, très, chère petite Princesse').

24 Of Conrad, James and Crane, he wrote: 'They are all three now dead ... But it is only at this moment that for the first time in my life I have actually realized that they are all three dead, so vividly do I still see them and still feel their wonderful presences. I have known hitherto that, as it were, one of them was dead or then another – but never that all three were so, so that my intimate contact with artistic life is completely at an end with the death of the last of them. To realize that is like dying oneself.' See 'Stevie & Co.', in *New York Essays* (New York: William Edwin Rudge, 1927), 24–5. See also *Ford/Bowen* 273: 'This morning whilst I was writing the article I quite suddenly realised for the first time that Crane and Conrad and James are all three dead together and I just could not go on with the article.'

Sylvia. In *Last Post*, by contrast, the most significant letter
appears to be that written by Mrs de Bray Pape to Mark Tietjens
about her proposed cutting down of Groby Great Tree.

The foregrounding of the arts seems then to recede in *Last Post*
– yet this is not in fact the case. Ford had always taken a broader
view of 'the arts' than some of his contemporaries, and here the
cider-making, furniture-restoring, planting, keeping of chickens
and general maintenance, the multifarious tasks performed by
Gunning, are treated with seriousness and respect. That is to say
that the arts are less alluded to or described than *enacted*. Norman
Leer commented of *Last Post* that Christopher Tietjens is 'still the
central character, but he remains in the background, like an
accomplished fact'.[25] I would suggest that this context *is* what has
been accomplished; that Tietjens, through his ordeal at the hands
of Sylvia, obtuse or malevolent civilians, incompetent or
vengeful military superiors and the rest, has earned the right to
the imperfections, fallibilities and makeshifts of everyday life;
that he can now practise the arts of the ordinary processes of
living, as did the Ford of the early 1920s and the 1930s.

There are two main elements to this: Valentine's use of the
phrase 'keep all on going' is Ford's *hommage* to Meary Walker,
who could turn her hand to many things and whom Ford revisited several times. In retrospect, she gained in symbolic strength,
not only because of her honesty and sheer determination but also
because Ford saw her as exemplifying a vanishing and, in part,
regretted world (*England* 181).

The other element is the central positioning of Marie Léonie.
That she has her absurdities is an essential point about her; that
she possesses indispensable qualities is no less essential. The ideas
of frugality and the avoidance of waste were ones that Ford long
associated with the French, specifically, French women of a
certain type and age.[26] In the 1930s the Fordian *persona* of small
producer, eco-warrior and prophet would dominate such books as

25 Norman Leer, *The Limited Hero in the Novels of Ford Madox Ford* (East Lansing, MI:
   Michigan State University Press, 1967), 147.
26 See, for instance, *Between St. Dennis and St. George* (London: Hodder & Stoughton,
   1915), 195–6; *A Mirror to France* (London: Duckworth, 1926), 178–84. Cornelia
   Cook discusses Marie Léonie in her perceptive 'Last Post: "The Last of the Tietjens
   Series"', *Agenda*, 27:4–28:1, Ford Madox Ford special double issue (winter 1989–spring
   1990), edited by Max Saunders, 23–30.

Great Trade Route and *Provence*. But it was one of the foremost ideas he had brought away from the war, partly perhaps in reaction to what was now widely perceived as the wastefulness and over-consumption of the Edwardian upper and middle classes. *No Enemy*'s Gringoire noted of the war that 'it did teach us what a hell – what a hell! – of a lot we can do without' (52).[27] Then, too, it was *artistically* admirable. Ford would write of Izaak Walton's as an example of that kind of prose that is fresh 'because its author sought for the simplest words and the most frugally exact adjectives and similes, having the exact eye and the passion above all to make you see'.[28]

History and Fiction; or, Some Racehorses

Several commentators have attempted to clarify *Parade's End*'s chronology, sometimes listing inconsistencies and apparent contradictions of the sort almost inevitable in a long work written over several volumes and several years.[29] These and other analyses include the likely date at which *Last Post* is set. There is no obvious consensus here: some readers have assumed that the action of the novel takes place very soon after the war, with 1919 or 1920 the most popular suggestions; others have opted for the mid- or late-1920s or, more simply and broadly, 'post-war'.

Initially, the immediate post-war period seems entirely plausible. But what exactly does 'plausible' mean in this context?

27 Such qualities transcend nationality: so Valentine recognises that the things in Tietjens' room in *A Man Could Stand Up –* are not, in fact, 'sordid and forlorn': 'They looked frugal. And glorious!' The words – and the qualities – are then attached to the man: 'Frugal and glorious! That was he!' (II.i). In *Last Post* Valentine reflects that '[i]f the war had done nothing else for them—for those two of them—it had induced them, at least, to install Frugality as a deity' (II.iii).
28 Ford, *The March of Literature: From Confucius to Modern Times* (London: Allen & Unwin, 1939), 542. 'To make you see' is a reference to Conrad's 'Preface' to *The Nigger of the Narcissus* (1897). That 'exact eye' has occurred earlier, in *Some Do Not . . .*: 'Actually, this mist was not silver, or was, perhaps, no longer silver: if you looked at it with the eye of the artist ... With the exact eye! [...] The exact eye: exact observation: it was a man's work. The only work for a man' (I.vii).
29 See particularly Thomas Moser, *The Life in the Fiction of Ford Madox Ford* (Princeton, NJ: Princeton University Press, 1980), 217–18, 318–20; Arthur Mizener, *The Saddest Story: A Biography of Ford Madox Ford* (London: Bodley Head, 1972), 495, 506–07, 510–15; also his 'Afterword' to the two-volume Signet Classic edition of *Parade's End* (New York: New American Library, 1964), II, 337–50.

Ford's book, despite the continued presence and symbolic importance of Marie Léonie, is strongly rooted in England, in
considerations of the state of England. Yet most of his time after
1922 was spent in France and, increasingly, in the United
States.[30] He may well have seen English newspapers, of course,
and if he were the kind of writer who required historical 'accuracy' and wanted to anchor the action of his novel to particular
years, there were numerous candidates for such signposts. Clearly,
such precise historical alignment was not his concern.

There are very few unambiguous chronological clues in *Last
Post*. We know, for instance, that General Campion is now MP
for the West Cleveland Division. But the 'coupon election' in
December 1918 (candidates approved by the coalition between
Conservatives and Lloyd George's Liberals received a coupon)
was followed by three more elections in successive years, from
1922 to 1924. Ford may have deliberately obscured the date he
had in mind, not desiring to limit readers' interpretations, but it
seems now equally likely that he *had* no specific date in mind.

There are, however, two details in the novel that allow of only
one time period (plus a couple that point towards it); and at least
one other detail that contradicts it. We know that the novel
covers part of a day in June and we have a number of references
to horse races. The crucial one is not filtered through a character's consciousness but is presented in the context of the
newspaper that both Mark and Marie Léonie are reading: the
King's filly has won the Berkshire Foal Plate at Newbury and the
Seaton Delaval Handicap at Newcastle has been won by 'the
horse of a friend' (I.i).

At the beginning of the second chapter in both the English
and American first editions, the reference to 'Seattle' having won
a race was initially puzzling. Mr E. Gwilt's six-year-old, Seattle,
ran twice at Newbury, an also-ran in the Moderate Handicap
Hurdle on the 1st of the month while coming in last of seven
runners on the 30th! But that month was December 1921, not
June.

Ford's mother died on 3 June 1927. Ford was in London by the

30 'I am terribly out of touch with English affairs. I do not suppose I shall ever get into
touch with them again': Ford to Stella, 4–9 January 1927 (*Ford/Bowen* 286).

7th and Max Saunders writes that he stayed about a week (*Dual Life* II 316 and 613, n.2). The funeral took place on 15 June and a letter to Ezra Pound from Paris is dated the same day,[31] so Ford must have travelled back immediately after the ceremony if that date is correct. Was there another brief visit to London that month, perhaps in connection with the reading of his mother's will?

On leaf 42 of the typescript of *Last Post*, the word 'Thursday' is typed across the top left-hand corner. On Friday 24 June 1927 *The Times* carried the previous day's results from the Newbury summer meeting and from Newcastle. The Seaton Delaval Handicap was won by Carsebreck, owned by a Mr W.W. Hope.[32] The Berkshire Foal Plate was won by Scuttle, a filly owned by His Majesty George V.

The conversation at the beginning of I.ii follows on from that of the opening chapter. It is the King's filly, 'Scuttle', that is referred to and Ford's typescript error had been carried over to both UK and US editions, probably occurring at the outset because reading those 'endless, serried columns' in *The Times* did allow the strong possibility of *mis*reading one or two letters in a name – especially for a novelist who did not, as a rule, follow horse-racing.[33]

One other specific detail occurs in the course of young Mark Tietjens' comparison of his 'divinely beautiful' mother's athleticism with that of both Atalanta and Betty Nuthall. The same issue of *The Times* (Friday 24 June) carried a report of Miss Betty Nuthall's defeat of the American Anna Mallory in the Third Round at Wimbledon the previous day, by two sets to one. The paper included a photograph of the two players, taken just before the match. Nuthall is described as 'youthful', and no wonder: born on 23 May 1911, she was barely sixteen on her Wimbledon

---

31 *Pound/Ford: The Story of a Literary Friendship*, ed. Brita Lindberg-Seyersted (London: Faber & Faber, 1982), 89–90.

32 'The horse of a friend': conceivably, the 'real' owner, W.W. Hope, is connected with the 'Teddy Hope' mentioned in I.iv.

33 We know that both brothers read *The Times*, and that Mark had the old habit of 'airing' his newspaper, 'on a chair-back before the fire' (*No More Parades* II.ii). Cricket was, of course, a different matter (as were, in various contexts, golf and boxing) and heads the litany of personal predilections and habits designed to prove Ford's 'Englishness' to E.V. Lucas (*Nightingale* 57); see also *England* 125–7; *Great Trade Route* (London: Allen & Unwin, 1937), 246–9; *No Enemy*, Chapter VII and 'Envoi'.

début. Young Mark Tietjens' admiring reference would, then, make no 'historical' sense at all before 1927.

In *Some Do Not . . .* it emerges that Mark 'came up to town' at the age of twenty-five (II.iii). Knowing the difference in age between Mark and Christopher, and that Christopher was twenty-six in 1912, we can place that 'coming up to town' in 1897. In *Last Post* Mark reflects on the government department that he had entered, in the first British edition, 'thirty-five years before'. This points to a present of 1932, an obvious anachronism – but the reference in the US edition was 'corrected' to 'thirty years ago', which takes us back to 1927.[34] Perhaps one more detail does: in the 'Dedicatory Letter', Ford refers to Tietjens, tongue in cheek no doubt, 'at this moment': 'I here provide you with a slice of one of Christopher's later days so that you may know how more or less he at present stands.'

In that opening chapter, though, the racing reports already quoted evoke in Mark the reflection that:

> He had meant to go to the Newcastle meeting this year and give Newbury a by. The last year he had gone racing he had done rather well at Newbury, so he had then thought he would try Newcastle for a change, and, whilst he was there, take a look at Groby and see what that bitch Sylvia was doing with Groby. Well, that was done with. They would presumably bury him at Groby.

That 'was done with' because Mark is immobilised. The difficulties here are that, firstly, he is immobilised as a result of a stroke or a resolution on Armistice Night, that is to say, in November 1918.[35] 'He had meant to go to the Newcastle meeting this year' implies that, when the decision was made, he didn't know he would be immobilised, which means prior to November 1918. The decision to go to Newcastle could have been taken any time

34 There is also some slight inconsistency in the ages of the brothers. In *Some Do Not . . .* Mark is fifteen years older (I.vi), in *Last Post*, fourteen – though the typescript, before revision, had 'eighteen'. Mark's birth date of 1872 makes him just one year older than Ford.
35 Referring to Mark's silence in the novel, Max Saunders splendidly remarks: 'whether out of obstinate principle because he disapproves of the peace terms, or because of a stroke, or both, is left wonderfully uncertain' (Saunders, *Dual Life* II 251).

prior to 1918 but it would have centred on the next available racing year. In that context, 'this year' strongly implies 1919 and is thus wholly incompatible with other 'historical' data.

The typescript reading, 'Last year', makes it unmistakeably 1918, since he has been ill since that November and the latest he could have gone racing is that year. The US revision, 'During the last year when he had gone racing' merely elaborates the change in the UK edition ('The last year he had gone racing') but cannot remove the obstacle to rooting it in 1918–19.

And yet this 'incompatibility', in its peculiar way, is wholly in accord with my sense that Ford was precisely *not* focused on one time or, rather, was looking through the glass at 1927 and seeing, in addition to the view through that glass, the reflection upon it of – what behind him? Coopers Cottage, an orchard running up to the road at the top of the hill, the wood, the rough field. Stella, Julie. For Ford, in fact, the last of England.

The earlier volumes of *Parade's End* were more obviously concerned with 'such events as get on to the pages of history' (*No More Parades*, 'Dedicatory Letter'). Ford subsequently stressed the trouble he had taken to get details right, to check his memory, to affirm his Whitmanian power of witness ('I am the man, I suffered, I was there'), while also emphasising the fact that he was writing a novel (though, unusually for him, one with a purpose: that of obviating all future wars) and seeking to disentangle, in the minds of his readers, the opinions of his characters from those of their author.

What does occur, in all four volumes, I think, is the phenomenon of the historical 'fact' that is not quite there, that is *almost* 'right', that may be slightly misremembered, that may confuse or blur two or more details. These instances generally occur under the umbrella of characterisation, that is to say, within the thoughts or expressions of a fictional character. They raise, in any case, the old question of whether there can be factual 'mistakes' in a work of fiction, in which characters inhabit an invented world, or at least one that, though very similar to the 'real' world, is not identical with it.[36]

---

36 There is a highly diverting discussion of such 'mistakes' and related matters in Guy Davenport's 'Ernst Machs Max Ernst', in *The Geography of the Imagination* (Boston: David R. Godine, 1997), 373–84.

One example of this tendency, representative in its curious collusion of 'fact' and 'not quite fact', is precisely the matter of racehorses. A few pages into *Last Post*, Ford writes of Mark Tietjens, referring to the elder brother's great interest in horse-racing already alluded to in both *Some Do Not ...* and *No More Parades*: 'He knew the sire and dam of every horse from Eclipse to Perlmutter.' Eclipse was, of course, one of the most famous racehorses of all time, ancestor of 95 per cent of contemporary thoroughbreds and unbeaten in eighteen starts. But what of Perlmutter?

Montague Glass's highly successful stories about two Jewish business partners, 'Potash and Perlmutter', pre-date the First World War.[37] His play of the same title was first produced in Britain at the Queen's Theatre, Shaftesbury Avenue, on 14 April 1914. Further plays, then films, followed well into the 1920s. That 'Potash and Perlmutter' were fairly constant cultural references for at least a decade is confirmed by the fact that they were also the nicknames given to Charles John Green, cook, and Perce Blackborow, his assistant, on Shackleton's last Antarctic expedition.[38]

In 1922, the same year in which Ford moved to France, two Dutch sisters arrived in Paris. They became artists' models for Marie Laurencin and the photographer Berenice Abbott, among others. Tylia Perlmutter, born in 1904, died young. Bronja, two years her senior, became engaged to Raymond Radiguet, who died in 1923, and married the filmmaker René Clair two years later. Kay Boyle writes about them, in her revision of Robert McAlmon's memoir, as does Djuna Barnes.[39]

'Perlmutter', then, was part of a great many people's mental furniture for a decade or two, not only in London and New York but in Paris as well for those, like Ford, who moved in 'artistic'

---

37 'Potash and Perlmutter' was rhyming slang for butter from c.1910.

38 'These two, black as two Mohawk Minstrels with the blubber-soot, were dubbed "Potash and Perlmutter"': see Ernest Shackleton, *South: The Story of Shackleton's Last Expedition* (New York: Macmillan, 1920), 105 (there is an illustration of the two men facing 106).

39 Kay Boyle and Robert McAlmon, *Being Geniuses Together 1920–1930* (London: Michael Joseph, 1970), 114–16: the sisters appear under the names of 'Sari' and 'Toni'. Djuna Barnes, 'The Models Have Come to Town', collected in *I Could Never Be Lonely Without a Husband* (London: Virago, 1987), 297–303; also her story, 'The Grande Malade' (previously published in *This Quarter* in 1925 as 'The Little Girl Continues'), in *Collected Stories* (Los Angeles: Sun & Moon Press, 1996), 393–403.

circles. Was this a slip of the pen while intending to write, say, Persimmon? That *was* a famous horse: first Royal winner of the Derby (in 1896) for 108 years (the Prince of Wales' horse won both Derby *and* St Leger that year), later retired to stud at Sandringham. Persimmon died in 1908, nearly twenty years before Ford was writing *Last Post* – in Paris, then Avignon, then aboard ship en route to New York via Montreal. 'What was that damned horse's name?' Yet it could not have been mere forgetfulness, since Ford *does* mention Persimmon in *Last Post* (I.iv, I.vii). It seems impossible to say how much of this is misremembered in haste, how much, if any, is Fordian mischief – perhaps at the expense of Mark Tietjens of Groby.

Continuities and Contrasts

Last Post has sometimes been viewed as differing in kind from the tetralogy's three earlier volumes, perhaps because of the brevity of the time covered, shrinking here to part of a single afternoon, perhaps because of the shift in point of view from, primarily, Christopher Tietjens to a far more fluid and interior perspective, particularly that of Mark Tietjens, but also those of Marie Léonie and Valentine Wannop.

This apprehension of differences has sometimes tended to disguise the novel's continuities with those other volumes, a tendency strengthened by critics disposed to accept at face value Ford's complimentary address to Isabel Paterson, suggesting that it was at her insistence that *Last Post* was written.

It seems a very English novel or, rather, one reflecting a very particular vision of England. And as far as that vision is of Bedham, aligned with Ford's early post-war removal from the centre of things, *Last Post* is, in that sense, a novel of the periphery.

The metropolitan and the rural run curiously and characteristically through Ford's life and writerly preoccupations. Though strongly associated with London, with Paris and with New York, much of his time (and a good deal of his work) was devoted to Kent, to Sussex and to Provence, to fields and hedgerows, gardens and terraces. Ford was well aware of this doubleness, noting that the first thing he did on arrival in a city was to plant some seeds in a window-box.[40] Similarly, while he introduces 'peace' into 'war', assaulting his soldiers with domestic crises and anxieties, the reverse is also true. The assault on 'Tietjens's' curiously resembles a military campaign, and several phrases suggestive of more warlike contexts have bled into this outwardly peaceful setting in the course of the novel: 'mopping up', 'the air of a small army', 'surrendering his body', 'desultorily approaching cavalry'.[41] Reconnaissance is followed by the artillery barrage of Mrs de Bray Pape and son Mark, and that in turn by the heavy armour of Sylvia Tietjens, while Christopher's wartime nightmare of hearing voices beneath his bed – '*Bringt dem Hauptmann eine Kerze!*' – still recurs (II.iii).

As might be expected, there are innumerable echoes and allusions between the four volumes of *Parade's End*, and some of these are reflected in the notes. A few such echoes – or series of echoes – prompt and propose larger thematic or structural ones. Several commentators, for instance, have noted the comparison that is invited by the army hut in which *No More Parades* opens with Ford's 1921 poem 'A House', a comparison explicitly suggested by the description of the space as 'shaped like the house a child draws'. The poem begins: 'I am the House! / I resemble / The drawing of a child / That draws "just a house."'[42] But beyond this, all four novels can be seen as opening in comparable spaces, amid striking variations of greater or lesser threat.

Some Do Not . . . opens in a railway carriage, with many assurances of stability and power; yet the coming war, with its permanent destruction of such perfect assurance and confidence, is subtly inserted into this picture. The absolute terms applied to the pristine carriage cannot help but carry with them implications of imminent change, even subversion: 'perfectly appointed',

---

40 *Great Trade Route* 89. Robert Green notes the significance of the 'change in location' but is sceptical: 'Too much weight is being placed on the virtue of the countryside': *Ford Madox Ford: Prose and Politics* (Cambridge: Cambridge University Press, 1981), 164, 165. Ambrose Gordon explores the point, 'with respect to form', that 'it seems wrong to let the novel come to an end in London', in *The Invisible Tent: The War Novels of Ford Madox Ford* (Austin, TX: University of Texas Press, 1964), 133.

41 Cf. *No Enemy* 13, 'The plants in the garden wave in stiffness like a battalion on parade – the platoons of lettuce, the headquarters' staff, all sweet peas, and the colour company, which is of scarlet runners.'

42 Ford Madox Ford, *Selected Poems*, ed. Max Saunders (Manchester: Carcanet, 1997), 126.

'virgin newness', 'immaculate' and, more playfully, 'the train ran as smoothly [...] as British gilt-edged securities'. A muted threat is present in the German-designed upholstery pattern, and the 'bulging' of that upholstery is unsettling in the way that 'bend', 'swell' and 'o'erbrimm'd' are in Keats's ode 'To Autumn'.

That pristine railway carriage can be set against *No More Parades*' army hut, but may also be set beside the 'white-enamelled, wickerworked, be-mirrored lounge' of the Rouen hotel in which Sylvia and Perowne sit (II.i), discussing sexual morality and adultery, as did Tietjens and Macmaster on that earlier occasion. Against the carriage mirrors that had 'reflected very little', we can place the hotel mirror in which Sylvia sees Tietjens enter the lounge. The novel ends with General Campion's inspection of the cook-houses with, again, several subtle reminders of *Parade's End*'s very first scene ('spotless [...] mirrors that were the tops of camp-cookers').

The carriage in that first scene is surrounded by threatening forces, still distant but on an unimaginably vast scale. That same threat encloses the army hut but there is also a more immediate, direct danger, dramatised in its effects by the blood-soaked demise of O Nine Morgan. Around the hotel in Rouen hangs an air of insanity: in the midst of war, Sylvia Tietjens' inexhaustible appetite for the persecution of her husband has brought her, with the connivance of General Campion, into that 'theatre', where she functions for many onlookers, presumably, as an emblem of 'peace'.

At the beginning of *A Man Could Stand Up* – Valentine Wannop's immediate danger is a personal one: the re-emergence of the malicious and self-serving Edith Macmaster, formerly Duchemin. Valentine has been called to the telephone which, 'for some ingeniously torturing reason, was in a corner of the great schoolroom without any protection'. But the 'threat' beyond that is the peace that has broken out that day, its new dangers as yet undefined. At the end of the novel, in a symbolically stripped room, with the camp-bed 'against the wall', Valentine and Tietjens, dancing together within the – now – protective circle of khaki, celebrate their 'setting out'.

In *Last Post* the hut has no walls but is nevertheless safe within the ambience of an eccentric and unorthodox but still highly significant community, though the shelter is open to something more than mere weather.[43] Mark is accessible to invading Americans, to the Marxian Communist youth of Cambridge – and to his hated sister-in-law. He also – willingly – shares his space with a multitude of creatures, birds and dormice and tiny rabbits, and is sharply aware of others: night birds, foxes, stoats. He despises himself a little 'for attending to these minutiae' when it is 'really' those 'big movements' that have always interested him. But behind those musings stands an author who has mastered the art of the double view, of detail and map, of a finger's touch on a bare wrist or a man walking under elm trees as well as that westward shift of political and economic power that largely defined the twentieth century.

Mark's reflections on small mammals and big movements are set in the context of his recollection of 'a great night'. The multiplicity of creatures around him is a part of this but so is his sense of great spaces and the transcendence of ordinary time, the night as a fragment of eternity: 'The great night was itself eternity and the Infinite ... The spirit of God walking on the firmament.' The earlier volumes also have their great nights or, at least, their periods of stretched or fractured or recalibrated time. In *Some Do Not ...* it is Christopher's extraordinary night-ride with Valentine, through the dense mist, with time the object of intense speculation and calculation: 'He had not known this young woman twenty-four hours: not to speak to [...] Then break all conventions: with the young woman: with himself above all. For forty-eight hours.' *No More Parades* has its bizarre and farcical night in the Rouen hotel. What has occurred there, the actual sequence of events, the conflicting witnesses, the piecing together of muffled, partial and reluctant stories, all unfolds in slow motion: but the consequences for Tietjens are rapid and inexorable. In *A Man Could Stand Up* – the fantastic closing scene on Armistice Night is preceded by an even more extraordinary scene: the explosion in the trenches. Though this takes place in daylight, 'There was so much noise it seemed to grow dark. It was a mental darkness. You could not think. A Dark Age!

---

43 Ambrose Gordon comments on Ford's use of interiors as a structural principle, whereby each interior 'come to suggest all the rest', in *The Invisible Tent* 115.

The earth moved.' Again, time is stretched, curiously cinematic ('like a slowed-down movie'), the earth settles again, over dead and wounded men and those in mortal danger of suffocation. And Mark's own vigils, in those long, largely silent nights, fittingly in this post-war world, with their poignant sense of the vastness of the universe and the nearness of God, look back, perhaps, to the beginning of *The Young Lovell*, where the young knight rises from his knees, having kept his vigil from midnight until six in the morning.

For all his fabulous wealth and power, the Master of Groby is seen in *Last Post* only as master of a thatched shelter, a miniature Groby, overhung by apple boughs as Groby itself is overshadowed by its Great Tree. Ian Baucom has written of how the ruined country house can not only represent but actually define a dominant model of Englishness.[44] Groby is not a ruined country house but, in the pages of the first three volumes of *Parade's End*, it is certainly incomplete, removed and distanced. It is part of a title, 'Tietjens of Groby', a sign, a symbol that has no solidity. Nor has it, of course, in *Last Post* but it is noticeable that, though the shortest in extent, this last volume of *Parade's End* mentions Groby nearly twice as often as do the first three volumes together. By the end of it, Groby is, indeed, if not ruined, then certainly damaged, both materially – 'Half Groby wall is down. Your bedroom's wrecked' – and symbolically, with the Great Tree gone and 'the curse' (perhaps) lifted.

We see, in the course of *Parade's End*, many interiors but it is only 'Tietjens's' that is described in any extended way: its exterior and its context, its situation, its trees and outbuildings, as well as some details of its interior. The earlier drawing-rooms, army huts, hotel foyers and bedrooms have been the settings for 'incidents' and for the symbolic representations of power, class and money. The house in *Last Post* has a more extensive function: paradoxically, though the novel has sometimes been seen more in romantic or symbolic terms than the earlier volumes, its range of uses accords more with the tenets of realism; it must serve as the context in which these lives are set, not in any temporary

44 Ian Baucom, *Out of Place: Englishness, Empire, and the Locations of Identity* (Princeton, NJ: Princeton University Press, 1999), 4.

sense, but fully, daily, over years. Here people work, think, love, conceive.

A further theme, established on the first page of the tetralogy, that persists through many changes and in many guises to the last may be mentioned here: ostensibly 'foreignness' – but reaching beyond this and perhaps better called *difference*. The book begins with Tietjens, an Englishman, and Macmaster, a Scotsman, though this overt distinction is deceptive, a feint. There is a related difference, that Tietjens is 'Tietjens of Groby' while Macmaster is a son of the manse, yet while having his mother provide a little money for Macmaster to get through university would have left 'a sense of class obligation' had Macmaster been 'an English young man of the lower orders', with Macmaster being a Scot, 'it just didn't'. There are plenty of other apparent tensions between the English Tietjens (his absurdly un-English name so boldly foregrounded that its foreignness becomes quite invisible) and 'un-English' others, such as Levin, Aranjuez, and, at greatest length, Marie Léonie. Yet it is Tietjens and Valentine who are most obviously set apart: and this is not simply because they *care* – because their moral sense is not steered by expediency or pragmatism – but because they *notice*. Tietjens is 'an exact observer'; he notices not only the details of things, places, horses, people but also the direction in which history is tending ('Christopher was always right. Sometimes a little previous. But always right.') And Valentine Wannop, 'New Woman' and suffragette, while securely rooted in her own time, is also, as a classicist, well equipped for access to others.

The first novel begins with two men in an enclosed space, threatened but as yet in an abstract way, hinted at through the carriage's furnishings, friends and colleagues yet still foreign to one another in terms of class, connections, their sense of entitlement and expectations.

The second novel begins with men, most obviously four men in two pairs (the third pair, the sergeant-majors, play a lesser role), in an enclosed and threatened space, the two men on the ground clearly foreign to the two others by nationality, class and rank – and height; the two officers foreign to one another; the first cannot get the other's name right; the second has misunderstood the relationship of the first to General Campion.

The third novel begins with two women connected by a telephone and threatened by the peace that is now breaking out. One woman does not immediately realise that she knows the second: they are, in many ways, foreign to one another. One is a disembodied voice – in reality each would be so to the other but, in the novel, it is Valentine who is solid, athletic, bursting with health and vitality, listening to the disembodied and broken utterances of Lady Macmaster who is, indeed, insubstantial. Near the end of *Last Post*, Valentine observes that Edith Ethel is 'not much changed'.

The fourth novel begins with two men, one in an enclosed space but in a different sense; if threatened, also in a different sense. They differ in class but – differently. One speaks in dialect that the other understands; he himself does not speak. All power and authority is seemingly concentrated in him: yet he is powerless to move or speak.

Last Post is, in fact, largely dominated by two men: Mark and Christopher Tietjens, doubles, with that telepathic connection that Ford identified as existing between his brother Oliver and himself: 'when one of us broke the silence it was to say exactly what the other had been about to bring out' (*Nightingale* 255).[45] Mark serves, in fact, as a Fordian distancing device, enabling the confrontation with, and exploration of, intimate material, a role filled by 'the Compiler' in *No Enemy*. Nevertheless, unlike the Compiler, Mark is not there for that purpose: he is introduced for good reasons and earns his indispensability in the novel as in his government department. The similarities between the two brothers are rendered almost in order to accentuate their differences.[46]

Indeed, on a larger scale, consider these endings: *No More Parades* and *A Man Could Stand Up* – both end on a note of madness, the first threatening, the second more benign. On

---

45 Similar assertions are made of Tietjens and his father ('thinking so alike that there was no need to talk', in *Some Do Not . . .* I.i); ironically, it is the fact that 'the same qualities' in Valentine Wannop appeal to the father as to the son that helps convince Mr Tietjens that Christopher is guilty of the charges made against him by Ruggles (*Some Do Not . . .* II.iii).

46 One small example is the delay in identifying Mark by name at the beginning of *Last Post*; the naming of Christopher is similarly (though longer) delayed at the beginning of *No More Parades*.

either side of these two, *Some Do Not* ... contains the superb
derangement that is the Duchemin breakfast but ends with
Christopher, apparently alone,[47] in silence, reflecting on recent
events, while *Last Post* contains the smaller-scale irruption of
assorted characters into Tietjens's and ends with Mark's emergence *from* silence and sustained reflection on past events:
speaking to, and touching, the pregnant Valentine, before
returning into silence, finally and completely.

Endings and Un-endings

Just as *Parade's End* is concerned with both the end of the old
order and the emergence of a new, so *Last Post* is concerned with
both birth and death. That birth, not yet accomplished, is of the
child that Valentine carries, but the novel also engages with the
idea of *re*birth: the confirmed resurrection of Christopher Tietjens, pulled out of the mud – and then saving others – in *A Man
Could Stand Up* –; and the possible rebirth or reinvention of
'England', perhaps even that of Ford himself. He had lost and
recovered his memory; moved to France; presided over the birth
and death of a literary review; and was now engaged in another,
though partial, move to the United States. A double fording.
'Ford' is related, through its Germanic origin, to 'fare'. Ford
Madox Ford (né Hueffer, of Germanic origin) might have
savoured that.

War, as so many have attested, is hell: and it was very obviously so on the Western Front between 1914 and 1918. There
had been nothing comparable on earth, at least. But there had
been Homer, Dante, Virgil; epics, myths and legends. And hell
was increasingly preoccupying novelists, painters, autobiogra-
phers – and poets.

What was originally the second half of Ezra Pound's 'Third
Canto' became by 1925 the opening of his 'long poem including
history'. Based on Book XI of Homer's *Odyssey*, it recounts his
hero's journey to the underworld to consult the shade of the

---

47 In fact, as is subsequently made clear, Sylvia is waiting in the darkness at the far end
of the dining-room (*No More Parades* I.iii and see *Some Do Not* ..., Appendix).

soothsayer Tiresias: the sacrifice there of a sheep furnishes that
'blood for the ghosts' that became not only a familiar metaphor
for Pound's extraordinary translations but, in large part, his poetic
practice.⁴⁸ Ford and Pound exchanged letters about 'Canto VIII'
(later Canto II) in 1922, the year of Ford's move to France
(*Pound/Ford* 64–7). He was, of course, familiar with the classical
uses, in Virgil as well as Homer, of the underworld descent, but
Pound's (eventual) Canto I, together with the 'Hades' episode of
Joyce's *Ulysses*, would have kept the story vividly – and modernly
– before his eyes.⁴⁹

Ford is, then, hardly unusual in his references to Hell: but they
are remarkably many. Hell is there in the first chapter of *Some Do
Not . . .*, Dantescan and literary; theological in its second chapter,
in Sylvia's conversation with her mother and Father Consett;
grimly unavoidable, as Tietjens in the Wannops' cottage reflects
that he is going back to Sylvia, 'and of course to Hell!' In *No More
Parades*' first chapter Tietjens has a vision of McKechnie against
a background of hellfire, and when Dante's underworld reappears, it is in the context of Tietjens making a pact with destiny,
willingly 'to pass thirty months in the frozen circle of hell, for the
chance of thirty seconds' talking to Valentine Wannop. It is also
in the wry comment of the French soldier on the 'moving slime'
that is German deserters disconsolately passing: '*On dirait l'In-
ferno de Dante!*' As *A Man Could Stand Up –* begins, 'Hell' is a
matter of language, the sort of thing that Valentine must learn
again *not* to say, but in the mind and in memory it has lost neither
force nor relevance, as she reflects on the history of her relationship with Christopher Tietjens: 'But you don't seduce, as near as
can be, a young woman and then go off to Hell, leaving her, God
knows, in Hell.'

48 In 1935 Pound wrote to W.H.D. Rouse: 'The Nekuia shouts aloud that it is *older* than
the rest, all that island, Cretan, etc., hinter-time, that it is *not* Praxiteles, not Athens
of Pericles, but Odysseus': *Selected Letters 1907–1941*, ed. D.D. Paige (New York: New
Directions, 1971), 274. Praxiteles was an Athenian sculptor, fourth century BCE.
'Blood for the Ghosts' is the title of a classic essay by Hugh Kenner in Eva Hesse's
landmark volume, *New Approaches to Ezra Pound* (London: Faber & Faber, 1969),
331–48.
49 As would William Carlos Williams' *Kora in Hell: Improvisations* (1920). He was
'indebted to Pound for the title': *I Wanted to Write a Poem: The Autobiography of the
Works of a Poet* (New York: New Directions, 1978), 29.

Myth is a structural device in the works of Joyce and Pound but Ford's approach is typically more oblique. A recurrent classical allusion in *Parade's End* is to Euripides' *Alcestis*, which Ford referred to as his favourite of the Greek dramas and himself translated in 1918–19.[50] More than one aspect of the play is alluded to in *Last Post*. Marie Léonie refers to Apollo and Admetus, the god serving the man in expiation of a violent act; but more insistent are the references to the theme of sacrifice, of Admetus' wife Alcestis offering herself to Death in order that her husband may live, and of Hercules going down to the underworld to bring Alcestis back.

Tietjens' recurrent nightmare of a world quite literally undermined is one among several Fordian uses of the underworld motif. Sylvia remembers Tietjens plunging the feverish body of their critically ill son into a bath of split ice, risking the strain on his heart: 'She knew it was true: Christopher had been down to hell to bring the child back' (*No More Parades* II.ii).[51] In the trenches, Tietjens is temporarily buried, immersed in mud above his waist, Aranjuez swallowed up to his neck, and Lance-Corporal Duckett completely engulfed when their position is struck by a high-explosive shell.[52]

Characteristic of Ford's ironic use of mythic parallels, there is a neat reversal of the Orphean quest here, with Tietjens bringing back his Eurydice in a double sense: firstly, the young, fair Duckett, who reminds Tietjens so strongly of Valentine Wannop, is rescued and resuscitated; secondly, Tietjens himself begins to look decisively *forward*, primarily to his reunion with Valentine, emerging from his earthly encounter with an image of her as a woman to be lived with, rather than an image of renun-

---

50 *Alcestis* recurs in Ford's next published novel, A *Little Less Than Gods* (London: Duckworth, 1928), 110. The typescript of Ford's translation of *Alcestis* is at Cornell.

51 Tietjens has earlier remembered the same moment, in similar language (*No More Parades* I.i). The echoing of thoughts and images in the minds of different characters is a device that Ford uses often and with great skill.

52 C.E. Montague also has a character buried alive by a 'big shell' in *Rough Justice* (London: Chatto & Windus, 1926), 293; D.H. Lawrence's Captain Herbertson recalls being buried in an explosive shell in *Aaron's Rod* (1922), ed. Mara Kalnins (Cambridge: Cambridge University Press, 1988), 114–15; his Charles Eastwood is also buried (under snow) for twenty hours and then dug out in *The Virgin and the Gipsy*, written in 1926: *The Complete Short Novels* (Harmondsworth: Penguin, 2000), 531.

ciation, one of those who 'do not'.[53]

The closing of A Man Could Stand Up –, carnivalesque, a little drunk, a little unhinged, is wonderful. That's the ending that Graham Greene wanted. But it's not the ending we have. Nor should it be. 'I can remember seeing everyone looking happy,' Stella Bowen writes of Armistice Day, 'for the first time. And perhaps the last.' She comments of that day: 'I can't remember how we got home' (Drawn from Life 61).

Parades end – and the revellers go home. They must also remember, and live with what is remembered. 'It is not the horrors of war but the atrocities of peace that are impelling me to write this book in favour of pacifism', Ford wrote a few years later.[54] Last Post has a good deal to say about that Armistice Night and the ways in which wars do not end with signatures, salutes and handshakes.

Unsurprisingly, perhaps, given the sheer scale, as well as the complex materials, of the Tietjens novels,[55] Ford had difficulty with – or expended a good deal of trouble on – endings. As the notes to the earlier volumes indicate, he reworked material from the manuscript of Some Do Not ... and finally relocated some of it in No More Parades; the ending of that second novel was heavily revised, as was the conclusion of A Man Could Stand Up –. The ending of Last Post – and thus the ending of the entire sequence – must have presented a formidable challenge. Writing to Stella just after its completion, he remarked:

> I worked nearly night & day to finish it & I think it is all right. Crandall cried over the death of Mark – et moi aussi! It is short – but I found I had said all I had to say & thought it best to stop. I had planned another chapter – but felt it wd. come as an anti-climax.[56]

53 On the underworld motif, which is central to Parade's End, most explicitly in A Man Could Stand Up –, see the introduction and notes to that volume; also Saunders, Dual Life II 214, 569–70 n.24; Pound/Ford 104; Nightingale 131–4, and my '"Not the Stuff to Fill Graveyards": Joseph Conrad and Parade's End', in Inter-Relations: Conrad, James, Ford and Others, ed. Keith Carabine and Max Saunders (Boulder, CO: Columbia University Press, 2003), 169–70.

54 Great Trade Route 97.

55 The dust-jacket of Last Post uses this phrase ('the Tietjens novels'), simultaneously confirming the centrality of Christopher Tietjens and allowing the possibility that the series is, wholly or in part, about the family.

56 Ford to Stella, 24 Sept. 1927: Ford/Bowen 323.

We don't know what that 'planned' chapter would have contained, except that it would, presumably, have concerned events *after* Mark's death. Perhaps Ford had said all he needed to say because, though the futures of Christopher and Valentine and the unborn child are not assured, they are, to some extent, implicit in their natures, as well as their shared pasts, and in the terms of the present that they have made together.

One word, one idea that resounds throughout *Last Post* is that of change. But this is true of the whole tetralogy and has begun on the second page of *Some Do Not . . .*, with the information that Christopher ('a Tory') 'disliked changing his clothes', so sits in the train already attired in his golfing boots. In *No More Parades* Tietjens knows that 'The world was foundering' (I.iv), and Valentine in *A Man Could Stand Up* – acknowledges a 'World Turned Upside Down' (I.i) on Armistice Day. Christopher too thinks 'But to-day the world changed' (III.ii). In *Last Post* Mark Tietjens must acknowledge that 'times change', that 'The world was changing.' Ruminating on his father now, he exclaims inwardly: 'Great stretches of time! Great changes!' On Armistice Night, Valentine had interrupted his political rationale for there being more suffering 'to say that the world had changed'. And what has not? The land. Mark states, as does Christopher, as did Ford himself, that 'the land remains', while Valentine contemplates the procession of 'Gunnings' through the ages, the rocks on which the lighthouse is built.

Yet one of the most telling instances of such reflections comes in connection with Sylvia Tietjens: 'Her main bitterness was that they had this peace. She was cutting the painter, but they were going on in this peace; her world was waning. [. . .] In her world there was the writing on the wall.'

'They had this peace': the peace is not Sylvia's, nor Campion's, since their world is ending. It is not for Mark either, though this is presented more as a question of choice: a man who will not himself change but feels no bitterness towards those who are 'going on'. Ford touches on both Sylvia's retreat and this aspect of Mark's death in a letter to Stella:

Yes, I suppose the volte face in Sylvia surprised you – but I had thought of it a long time and it occurred to me that, after all she was a 'sport' and it takes a pretty unsporting woman to damage an unborn child. Besides *Mark could not have let himself die* if something of the sort had not happened ... And it would have been too melodramatic to kill Tietjens: he could not die whilst any worries remained for him. So I think I have done it right.[57]

This surely lies behind Mark's reflection, after Sylvia has appeared beside his bed, wet-eyed and swearing that she would never harm another woman's child, 'Well, if Sylvia had come to that, his, Mark's, occupation was gone. He would no longer have to go on willing against her; she would drop into the sea in the wake of their family vessel and be lost to view.'

It would, I think, take a dedicated optimist to find, in the marvellous conclusion of *Last Post*, an unambiguously serene and cloudless future. Most of the plot's uncertainties are 'resolved' only in the mind of Mark Tietjens, a man on his deathbed with, let us say, a vested interest in the settling of those questions that disturb him. It is articulating an answer to 'unanswerable' questions that frees Mark, just as his articulating the old song learned from his nurse may help to free Valentine Wannop, classicist and expectant mother, who has already told – to herself – the story of how futures evolve from pasts as well as presents. Marie Léonie would 'like to have had his last words', Valentine says to the doctor. 'But she did not need them as much as I.'

The real ending of Ford's novel, the unanswerable question, the abiding problem, as great as the mystery of how to engross the minds of the reading public with your stories of ordinary lives, is given to Valentine: 'How are we to live? How are we ever to live?' It is in response to this question that Mark finally speaks – and it is, too, this question that the whole novel seeks to answer.

The Writing of *Last Post*

On 22 September 1927 Ford wrote to Stella: 'I finished Last Post ten minutes ago.' Two days later he wrote again to say that his

---

57 *Ford/Bowen* 336, italics added. In a cancelled typescript passage (II.iii), Ford did indeed toy with the idea of killing Christopher in an aeroplane crash.

friend Charles Crandall, journalist and former editor of the Montreal *Daily Star*, 'will be posting you for the Last Post to-day, registered. <u>As soon as you have read it</u> forward it to D'worth [Duckworth]: I am writing to him to send you 50 quid on receipt. [...] Correct any obvious printer's errors, will you?' (*Ford/Bowen* 323).

Last Post was begun in Paris in the summer of 1927, worked on during a month's stay in Provence and continued to completion aboard the Canadian Pacific S.S. *Minnedosa*, off the coast of Labrador. It was Ford's sixty-sixth published book[58] and his twenty-sixth novel.

The dates of composition given in the British and American editions differ, though not hugely. Ford gives both an earlier commencement date and a later date of final completion, 12 November rather than 2 November,[59] in the British edition, thus making its stated period of composition nearly six weeks longer than that in the American edition. The date of the 'Dedicatory Letter' (13 October 1927) is, however, common to both.

On 6 October Ford planned to 'work a bit at revising *Last Post*' and five days later commented that he had 'done a certain amount of work – correcting up <u>Last Post</u> and so on'. Stella's letter of 14 October contained her initial reaction to the novel: 'But first let me say how splendid I think the "Last Post" is. (By the way, Duckworth has acknowledged receipt of MSS, so that's all safe.) [...] I let Bradley [Ford's literary agent in Paris] read the MSS before sending it to Duckworth' (*Ford/Bowen* 331).

Thus far, then, Ford finishes the novel and has it posted to Stella two days later. The bulk of the novel would have been completed before he set sail: we don't know for sure whether he was typing from a corrected manuscript or composing on the typewriter. The further 'correcting up <u>Last Post</u>' that he refers to would probably be a carbon copy of the typescript destined for his US publisher.

Ford had written to Bradley, of *No More Parades*, that 'I usually get Duckworth to print a set or two of proofs off right away and

---

58 This figure includes five collaborations (three with Conrad, two with Violet Hunt) and a translation (of Pierre Loti's wartime pamphlet, *L'Outrage des Barbares*).
59 12 November is the date specified by Ford as that on which he *received* the proofs of the UK edition.

thus save myself the bother and expense of typing'; he refers to both slip proofs and page proofs in a later letter and, in a third, asks Bradley of *A Man Could Stand Up* –: 'Would you just put this copy in your safe? It is incomplete but nearly complete. When I get towards the end of a book I always hate to have all the copies of a ms in one place for fear of fire.' And he adds: 'You have already had duplicates of the earlier chapters.'[60] It was not just the achingly sensible 'fear of fire', of course: 'until you have written the last word it is no more than a heap of soiled paper. I fear preposterous things – that one of the aeroplanes that are for ever soaring overhead here might drop a spanner on my head.... Anything' (*Nightingale* 254). The salient difference here was Ford's position – geographically, emotionally and financially – when he was revising and 'correcting up' *Last Post*: some of his usual procedures were simply not practicable and he may necessarily have had more recourse to carbon copies of his typescript.[61]

The next phase of the Ford/Bowen correspondence is primarily concerned with negotiations over both the US publication of *Last Post* and its selection by the Literary Guild, which would virtually guarantee a substantial sale: the figure of 37,696 subscribers was mentioned with the short extract from *Last Post* that the *Guild Annual* published.[62] In mid-October, the contract with Albert & Charles Boni had not been signed and Ford was not yet absolutely certain who was publishing his novel. And, while Carl Van Doren had recommended the novel to the Guild (of which this eminent critic and editor was one of the founders), there was some hesitation, largely due to *Last Post*'s being a

---

60 All quotations from letters in *The Ford Madox Ford Reader*, ed. Sondra J. Stang (Manchester: Carcanet, 1986), 487–90.

61 A letter from Gerald Duckworth to Ford, dated 3 November, confirms that two sets of proofs had been sent the previous day but, puzzlingly, adds that Duckworth is 'sending herewith a copy of the Last Post' (Cornell). This may be an extra set of proofs, perhaps a bound set for ease of handling. If Duckworth was returning Ford's typescript, he would presumably have referred to it as such ('your MS' or 'your TS').

62 The *Annual* extract runs from the beginning of I.vii to 'What the unfortunate *Elle* has not suffered!...', excising a page about the missing prints. The extract is identical with the US text, including the slightly eccentric punctuation, with the exception of one corrected spelling and two French words italicised (which they are not in the US text). The introductory note refers to Valentine as Christopher's wife, while the note on the author is quietly entertaining in its laconic way ('He was educated at Westminster School and studied at the Sorbonne. [...] In 1919 he changed his name, for family reasons, to Ford Madox Ford').

sequel. Eventually, on 8 November, a telegram confirmed that the Book Club sale was accomplished: 'GUILD PREND LAST POST SI CONTENT MILLE BAISERS, FORD.'

Three days later Ford reported to Bowen that he was 'doing the Mss. Proofs of Last Post' and on Wednesday 16 November he wrote to her: 'on Saturday [12 November, i.e., one day later than that given in the previous note] the English proofs of Last Post descended on me and on Monday the American one's [sic] and I literally could do nothing else as Boni's wanted the proofs back on Monday night. That however was impossible but I got them finished yesterday and then was too exhausted to do anything' (*Ford/Bowen* 353). The American proofs were, then, completed in less than two days. A letter from Caroline Gordon confirms that the English proofs had been sent to Duckworth 'by registered mail' on the Tuesday, 15 November.[63]

The publication date was fixed for 'early in January', and at the end of November Ford told Stella that 'both A & C Boni & Ginsberg [Harold J. Guinzburg of the Literary Guild] want me to stay over the publication of Last Post in January' (*Ford/Bowen* 360). On 21 December he sent off to her 'the first copy of the Last Post'. This was a copy of the Literary Guild edition rather than the Boni edition.[64] On 3 January 1928 Stella wrote to acknowledge Ford's letter and the copy of *Last Post*.

The Reception of *Last Post*

Due to its selection by the Literary Guild, and following a path prepared for it by the earlier volumes in the sequence, *Last Post* was the most commercially successful title of Ford's career. In a letter to Perceval Hinton in February 1928 he mentioned sales in the first two weeks of some 50,000 copies: a remarkable claim

---

63 Carolyn [sic] Gordon to Gerald Duckworth, letter of 16 November (Cornell). She began using 'Caroline' with the publication of her story 'Summer Dust' in November 1929: see Nancylee Novell Jonza, *The Underground Stream: The Life and Art of Caroline Gordon* (Athens, GA: University of Georgia Press, 1995), 71.

64 This copy was offered for sale in the Serendipity Books catalogue 189; information from Max Saunders.

but not impossible, given the figure of almost 40,000 Guild subscribers.[65]

Reviews were generally positive although some were a little uncertain, qualifying praise for the novel's technical qualities with regret that the war was no longer central to this concluding volume. The *Daily Telegraph* reviewer asserted that 'If the true art of writing were in the habit of receiving its legitimate reward, Mr. Ford Madox Ford would be one of the most widely read novelists in England', adding that *Last Post* was 'a perfect example of Mr. Ford's wayward, witty, allusive talent at its best'.[66]

L.P. Hartley wrote that 'of all the "Tietjens" novels "Last Post" is surely the greatest *tour de force*', a term also employed by the *English Review*, while the *Spectator* reviewer commented: 'Now that the magnificent war-passages no more transfigure the lives of the group into smoke and flame, the tone is naturally more quiet [...]. But one is left with a real sense of having lived through this surprising afternoon.'

Cyril Connolly, though claiming that the novel suffered from its being a sequel, acknowledged as Ford's great strength 'his ability to describe the quality of life, the bristling, tangled, harassed stream of consciousness as it flows through the minds of highly prejudiced, intelligent, and emotional people'.[67] Dorothy Parker's characteristic piece, in which she set Ford's novel against a recent newspaper story, expressed her reservations about the 'grave hardships for the reader' in the long interior monologues, 'a novel to be read with a furrow in the brow', but concluded that *Last Post* was:

a novel worth all its difficulties. There is always, for me, a vastly stirring quality in Ford's work. His pages are quick and true. I know of few other novelists who can so surely capture human bewilderment and suffering [...] all the books of the Tietjens

65 The letter is quoted and the figure mentioned by Douglas Goldring in *Trained for Genius: The Life and Writings of Ford Madox Ford* (New York: Dutton, 1949), 244, where he recalls Ford's comparison of UK and US sales.
66 'Books of the Day: New Novels', *Daily Telegraph* (10 Feb. 1928), 15 (review of *Last Post* and five others).
67 Extracts from these reviews are in David Dow Harvey, *Ford Madox Ford 1873–1939: A Bibliography of Works and Criticism* (New York: Gordian Press, 1972), 376.

saga have in them some of the same power, the same depth, the same rackingly moving honesty that makes *The Good Soldier* so high and fine a work.[68]

The *Times Literary Supplement* reviewer noted the novel's need to convey much of the sense of the preceding volumes for new readers. Though *Last Post* was 'less tumultuous and not lifted up by the tremendous war-passages of its predecessors', the reviewer expressed an admiration 'anything but diminished' and asserted of the whole series: 'this tetralogy has an originality, a robustness and a tragic vigour which make it worthy of inclusion in the great line of English novels'.[69]

Gerald Gould, though feeling that the 'accumulated oddity' of the characters gave 'the general impression of a nightmare in a lunatic asylum', nevertheless remarked on the success of Ford's method: 'the artist in Mr. Ford reaches out to the more difficult task of catching the untidiness, the blur, the jumble, the inconsequence, the this-way-and-thatness of experience'. The war, though, had been 'left behind' and he thought the incidents treated of in *Last Post* 'too commonplace to merit the treatment they receive'.[70]

Gould's review touches on two significant points. The timing, the marketing, the reviews of the constituent volumes of the tetralogy – and the considerable sales of the second and third volumes – together with Ford's best-known novel remaining *The Good Soldier* (reissued in the spring of 1927) had the unsurprising result of a strong emphasis upon the sequence as comprising a 'war novel'. In total, of course, a little over one-third of *Parade's End* is set at the Front. In 1928, though, among reviewers of *Last Post*, the war, or at least a related atmosphere of stress and nightmare, was never far away: 'at times [...] terribly like a psychopathic ward in some fabulous hospital for world-war wreckage'.[71]

As for 'commonplace' material, Ford himself was concerned

68 'A Good Novel, and a Great Story', in *The Collected Dorothy Parker* (Harmondsworth: Penguin, 1989), 487–91 (489).
69 Harvey, *Bibliography* 376.
70 Harvey, *Bibliography* 377. Three of the reviews excerpted in Harvey are included in *Ford Madox Ford: The Critical Heritage*, ed. Frank MacShane (London: Routledge, 1972), 110–16.
71 MacShane, *Critical Heritage* 113.

that the obvious 'importance' of the themes of the earlier volumes would be perceived as having fallen away with the 'post-war'. In *The English Novel* he says of the novel as a genre: 'It is, that is to say, the only source to which you can turn in order to ascertain how your fellows spend their entire lives. I use the words "entire lives" advisedly.'[72] He had always distrusted the Victorian (and later) use of 'the Strong Scene', commonly to meet the cliff-hanger demands of serialisation.[73] War, conventionally treated, holds out the promise of little else, while peacetime presents markedly different challenges and possibilities.

Ford's sense of those challenges surely reinforced his willingness to experiment stylistically in *Last Post* with his treatment of time and a striking freedom of movement within the interior monologues of his characters. As with the earlier volumes, much of the novel is necessarily retrospective, perhaps more noticeably so in *Last Post* because its structural importance is never diminished or drowned out by the clamour of war. And retrospection is hardly out of place: one of the major themes of both this volume and the sequence that it concludes is *memory*: what is recalled and what is lost, both in individual lives and in the collective life of a nation.

The more negative reactions to *Last Post* have tended to fall into two distinct but not unconnected groups: assertions that it was an afterthought and never originally planned as part of the sequence; and claims that the last novel does not belong with the other three, that its 'differences' somehow disqualify it. Notoriously, Graham Greene, not content with critical diagnosis, moved directly to surgery, publishing three-quarters of *Parade's End* in the Bodley Head edition, later reprinted in paperback.

Like Greene, a few critics have simply repeated one of Ford's several statements about the series, to the effect that he wanted it republished as a trilogy: 'I strongly wish to omit the *Last Post* from the edition. I do not like the book and have never liked it and always intended the series to end with *A Man Could Stand Up*.' So Ford wrote to his agent, Eric Pinker, in the summer of

---

72 Ford, *The English Novel: From the Earliest Days to the Death of Joseph Conrad* (Manchester: Carcanet, 1983), 8.
73 See *Return* 158–9; 'Literary Portraits – XX. Mr. Gilbert Cannan and "Old Mole"', *Outlook*, XXXIII (24 Jan. 1914): 'The fact is that the "strong scene" is the curse of the novel.'

1930 (*Letters* 196). Three years later, he referred to the series as his 'trilogy' (*Nightingale* 188) and maintained that position in a letter of 1937 (*Reader* 505). What is one to say to this?

The first and simplest answer is one made by Arthur Mizener and others: the book exists, and Ford's changing his mind does not affect that. Change it he did, several times – in 1932, he was again referring to it as a tetralogy (*Letters* 208) – though he is hardly the first or last writer to fluctuate in his opinion of a published work.

Secondly, it is evidently *not* the case that Ford 'always intended the series to end with *A Man Could Stand Up*'. His dedicatory letters to *No More Parades* and to *A Man Could Stand Up* – ('the series of books of which this is the third and penultimate') make it perfectly clear that (certainly by 1925) four books were planned, and Ford himself was enthusiastic about the book until some of the later reviews proved disappointing.

Thirdly, there are so many echoes and interconnections between all four volumes, as well as several passages in the first three that appear to point towards the fourth, that it seems frankly implausible that *Last Post* was 'a kind of afterthought, separate from the main design'.[74] These include many smaller details, such as the scene in *Some Do Not . . .* (I.vi) where Tietjens sits in the Wannop cottage, his reflections on his surroundings pointing in several particulars to the setting of *Last Post*; and those of more significance, such as Valentine's forgetting – and then remembering – the name 'Bemerton', as Tietjens does in a central passage of *A Man Could Stand Up* – (II.ii). The image of Herbert at Bemerton links Christopher, Valentine and Mark – but it also links the imagined or remembered past to the imagined futures of both individuals and, by extension, the country. The fact that the name is lost and recalled is highly suggestive in the context of a nation in danger of losing its memory.

An example of larger, more fundamental thematic continuities is the tetralogy's concern with furniture. Ford wrote to Ezra Pound in 1920:

---

74 John A. Meixner, *Ford Madox Ford's Novels: A Critical Study* (London: Oxford University Press, 1962), 217. Ford wrote – in 1924 – that he had 'seldom begun on a book without having, at least, the intrigue, the "affair," completely settled in his mind': *Joseph Conrad: A Personal Remembrance* (London: Duckworth, 1924), 173.

You are in fact bored with civilisation here – very properly –
and so you get bored with the *rendering* of that civilisation. It
is not a good frame of mind to get into – this preoccupation
with Subject rather than with rendering; it amounts really to
your barring out of artistic treatment everything and everyone
with whom you have not had personal – and agreeable –
contacts. There is the same tendency in your desire for the
STRONG STORY and in your objection to renderings of the
mania for FURNITURE [...] You might really, just as legiti-
mately, object to renderings of the passion of LOVE, with
which indeed the FURNITURE passion is strangely bound up.
(*Pound/Ford* 44–5)

This is both acute and suggestive about the two writers' differing
aesthetics. Eighteen months later, a revealing note in a letter
from Pound to Ford reads: 'Am not really interested in anything
that hasn't been there all the time' (*Pound/Ford* 66).

From the beginning, in *Some Do Not ...*, Tietjens' eye for
furniture is presented as an ability far transcending cabinets,
chairs and tables. The recurrent figure of Sir John Robertson is
introduced early in Part II, simultaneously with the notion of
wealthy and rapacious Americans: 'the Moiras had sold
Arlington Street stock, lock and barrel to some American'
(II.i).[75] More specifically, Tietjens' intention to enter the old
furniture trade is made explicit: 'Oh, I shall go into the old furniture business', he says to Valentine Wannop.

She didn't believe he was serious. He hadn't, she knew, ever
thought about his future. But suddenly she had a vision of his
white head and pale face in the back glooms of a shop full of
dusty things. He would come out, get heavily on to a dusty
bicycle and ride off to a cottage sale. (*Some Do Not ...* II.iv)

Clearly, Tietjens' creator *has* thought about his future.

75 See Douglas Goldring, *The Nineteen Twenties: A General Survey and Some Personal
   Memories* (London: Nicholson and Watson, 1945), 19, on 'a large number of owners
   of stately homes' forced to sell 'their estates, their pictures and their furniture' to
   'Canadian, American or native profiteers'. There are several other such references in
   novels of the period, including Violet Hunt's *The Last Ditch* (London: Stanley Paul,
   1918) and Aldous Huxley's *Crome Yellow* (London: Chatto & Windus, 1921).

In *No More Parades* Tietjens still receives the circulars of old furniture dealers (I.i); no other mail reaches him on this tour of duty but 'They never neglected him!'[76] In a deleted typescript passage, Ford allowed Tietjens to answer when General Campion asks what he will do after the war. Tietjens replies:

> "I, sir.... I shall make a living as an old furniture dealer ..." He continued into the general's speechlessness: "I've got a certain gift for it. I can detect fakes extraordinarily without knowing how. You needn't be alarmed sir. I know what I'm doing. Sir James Donaldson [Sir John Robertson in the published volumes][77] has offered to take me into partnership, he's been so impressed with my knack. It probably comes from my being in harmony with the seventeenth century to some extent. That's my period. In furniture, I mean...."

The continuity is maintained in *A Man Could Stand Up –* with the episode of Tietjens attempting to sell the model cabinet to Sir John Robertson, which connects to *Last Post*, but also with so marked a number of references to the fact of Tietjens having no furniture left – more than a dozen such allusions – that we may quite reasonably suspect some symbolic significance.[78]

As usual – I mean, particularly, as with gardening and cookery – Ford does not labour the connections between furniture and his primary art, nor that between furniture and, let us say, the ordinary processes of living. Valentine, in *A Man Could Stand Up –*, thinks that 'You do not run when you are selling furniture if you are sane' (III.i), while, on the telephone to her mother, Tietjens connects (in the same sentence) dealing in old furniture with a possible vice-consular post in Toulon (II.ii). This will also recur in *Last Post* where the impermanence of the furniture that fills the cottage and the significance of all that 'furniture' that Tietjens has relinquished (as, indeed, has Valentine) becomes

---

76 Sylvia is stopping all his personal letters, as we learn a little later (*No More Parades* II.i).
77 Sir John Robertson had already been mentioned four times in *Some Do Not ...* so this was presumably just a slip on Ford's part.
78 In the context of Ford's wife Elsie's removal from Winchelsea to Aldington, in 1908, Max Saunders comments: 'It was not to be the last time that Ford, like Tietjens, lost his furniture' (Saunders, *Dual Life* I 236).

apparent. Indeed, the image recalled by Mark of Christopher 'with a piece of furniture under his arm [...] his eyes goggling out at the foot of the bed' (I.iv) subtly prepares for the closing pages, when Christopher stands 'at the foot of [Mark's] bed', holding 'a bicycle and a lump of wood [...] his eyes stuck out' (II.iv). That 'piece of furniture', devalued by virtue of its owner having fought in the war, has become a mere lump of wood, a piece of debris, salvaged from the partial collapse of a great house.

The question of Ford's planned intention to include a fourth volume seems to me largely settled by the dedicatory letters to the second and third volumes, and reinforced by such internal evidence. But the burden of several more negative responses to *Last Post*, if not the specific charges, seems to be that Ford 'retreats' from history, that the novel is a pastoral or a fairy tale that does not connect with the 'real' world. Perhaps such a view implies that the war was *Parade's End*'s only authentic subject, and that the post-war could only be an anti-climax, a slackening of tension, an easing. But is that how Ford regarded it?

Though he recalled the days before the Great War as a lost world – 'London was adorable then at four in the morning' (*Return* 320) – Ford was often at pains to play down his own suffering in that conflict. Fifteen years after the Armistice he would write: 'War to me was not very dreadful' (*Nightingale* 205). *Joseph Conrad* was written closer to the war, though published at a time when Ford felt that he was 'able at last really to write again' (*Letters* 154), and there he remarked: 'A great many novelists have treated of the late war in terms solely of the war: in terms of pip-squeaks, trench-coats, wire-aprons, shells, mud, dust, and sending the bayonet home with a grunt.' But, he went on, 'had you taken part actually in those hostilities, you would know how infinitely little part the actual fighting took in your mentality' (*Joseph Conrad* 192). Ford wants to emphasise how much of the war was spent in waiting, in suspension, in boredom: 'that eternal "waiting to report" that takes up 112/113ths of one's time during war' (*No Enemy* 33). It is into just such spaces that worry, anxiety and the painful imagining of what is going on at home clamour and crowd, to the detriment of men's peace – and, not rarely, balance – of mind.

There were certainly times during Ford's war when it was 'very dreadful' indeed, yet, for the most part, he managed to maintain that double perspective, that precarious balance of participant and observer. And the problems of peace were, I think, exercising him quite as much as his experiences in the recent war, while he worked on successive volumes of *Parade's End*.

In an acutely challenging essay, Robert Caserio remarks: 'What is crystallized, of course, in *Last Post*'s pastoral world are the values that most can serve the public sphere.' Referring to Robert Green's justly admired book on Ford, Caserio cites Green's criticism as the kind that 'considers itself too tough to countenance the idea that public virtues can be kept alive in spheres of narrowed and hidden endeavour'.[79] We are, perhaps, more comfortable now with the idea of individual choices, actions and modes of living not only representing but, to varying degrees, affecting and shaping public discourse and eventually, in many cases, public policy. No doubt this is frequently for nega-tive reasons, in that elected public bodies are widely perceived to be failing to fulfil their intended functions, but it is in precisely this way that they were then perceived by Ford.

Ford's view of the true 'governing classes' was based neither on social status nor on money. In *No Enemy* he made this explicit, referring to

the *homines bonae voluntatis* [men – and, implicitly here, women – of goodwill] who must be preserved if the State is to continue.[80] They have rather abstracted expressions; they have aspects of fatigue, since the salvation of a world is a large order, and they bear on their backs the burden of the whole world; but they look at you directly, and in their glance is no expression of pride, ambition, profit, or renown. They have expressions of responsibility, for they are the governing classes. (139)

79 Robert L. Caserio, 'Ford's and Kipling's Modernist Imagination of Public Virtue', in *Ford Madox Ford's Modernity*, ed. Robert Hampson and Max Saunders, International Ford Madox Ford Studies, 2 (Amsterdam and New York: Rodopi, 2003), 175–90 (181).
80 Cf. Ford's 1907 review of a work by G.S. Street: 'He writes *hominibus bonae voluntatis* … And, after all, like Mr. Street, I, alas! write for a small circle of men of goodwill.' See 'Literary Portraits: XXII. London Town and a Saunterer', *Tribune* (21 Dec. 1907), 2. The Latin phrase, also with *hominibus* rather than *homines*, occurs in *The Cinque Ports* (Edinburgh and London: William Blackwood and Sons, 1900), ix, 184 and is used – now with *hominem*! – elsewhere in *No Enemy* (63).

They are, that is to say, the constructive spirits, the makers of gardens – the kitchen-gardeners who feed the world – and the makers of art. Ford was not unaware of the forces ranged against them. Sondra Stang remarks of the novel's ending that 'Ford cannot offer an ideal solution for Christopher and Valentine, and that is the point.'[81] It is true that Ford didn't know how things would turn out – and such uncertainty was not, of course, confined to his own immediate circumstances. He didn't know what England would become, or was in the process of becoming.[82] Inevitably, he was writing a good deal about death and endings.

Yet *Parade's End* is concerned not only with the end of an age but also with the beginning of another, or the evolution of one into another. *Last Post* (like *No Enemy*) is concerned with reconstruction, with the *process* of reconstruction, a man in process of being reconstructed. The apparent paradox here is that the man is not ostensibly 'present'. Yet Christopher Tietjens is everywhere in the book – because that 'everywhere' is the thoughts and memories of Mark, Valentine, Marie Léonie, Sylvia and Mark, Junior. And they, pre-eminently Mark but all of them, according to their lights, do 'reconstruct' Christopher and accord him a different kind of solidity than is derived directly from his actions. This reconstructive process is, then, not hidden but is everywhere apparent. It is almost indistinguishable from 'ordinary living' – though this is fiction, not life – but it is a life lived in the knowledge of terrible things having happened (and the enduring possibility that they may happen again). It is to live with – but not *in* – the past, in both personal and collective senses. And Ford, in almost everything he writes after the Great War, confronts and engages with such uncertainty, with the unresolved and the provisional. Indeed, they increasingly become his primary materials.

---

81 See Sondra J. Stang, *Ford Madox Ford* (New York: Frederick Ungar, 1977), 121.
82 He has Valentine reflect that 'she did not know what she wished, because she did not know what was to become of England or the world' (II.iii).

A NOTE ON THIS EDITION
OF *PARADE'S END*

   This edition takes as its copy-text the British first editions of the four novels. It is not a critical edition of the manuscripts, nor is it a variorum edition comparing the different editions exhaustively. The available manuscripts and other pre-publication materials have been studied and taken into account, and have informed any emendations, all of which are recorded in the textual notes.

   The British first editions were the first publication of the complete texts for at least the first three volumes. The case of *Last Post* is more complicated, and is discussed further below; but in short, if the British edition was not the first published, the US edition was so close in date as to make them effectively simultaneous (especially in terms of Ford's involvement), so there is no case for not using the British text there too, whereas there are strong reasons in favour of using it for the sake of consistency (with the publisher's practices, and habits of British as opposed to American usage).

   Complete manuscripts have survived for all four volumes. That for *Some Do Not . . .* is an autograph, the other three are typescripts. All four have autograph corrections and revisions in Ford's hand, as well as deletions (which there is no reason to believe are not also authorial). The typescripts also have typed corrections and revisions. As Ford inscribed two of them to say the typing was his own, there is no reason to think these typed second thoughts were not also his. The manuscripts also all have various forms of compositor's mark-up, confirming what Ford inscribed on the last two, that the UK editions were set from them.

   Our edition is primarily intended for general readers and students of Ford. Recording every minor change from manuscript to first book edition would be of interest to only a small number of textual scholars, who would need to consult the original manuscripts themselves. However, many of the revisions and deletions are highly illuminating about Ford's method of composition, and the changes of conception of the novels. While we have normally followed his decisions in our text, we have annotated the changes we judge to be significant (and of course such selection implies editorial judgement) in the textual notes.

There is only a limited amount of other pre-publication material, perhaps as a result of Duckworth & Co. suffering fires in 1929 and 1950, and being bombed in 1942. There are some pages of an episode originally intended as the ending of *Some Do Not . . .* but later recast for *No More Parades*, and some pages omitted from *Last Post*. Unlike the other volumes, *Last Post* also underwent widespread revisions differentiating the first UK and US editions. Corrected proofs of the first chapter only of *Some Do Not . . .* were discovered in a batch of materials from Ford's *transatlantic review*. An uncorrected proof copy of *A Man Could Stand Up –* has also been studied. There are comparably patchy examples of previous partial publication of two of the volumes. Part I of *Some Do Not . . .* was serialised in the *transatlantic review*, of which at most only the first four and a half chapters preceded the Duckworth edition. More significant is the part of the first chapter of *No More Parades* which appeared in the *Contact Collection of Contemporary Writers* in 1925, with surprising differences from the book versions. All of this material has been studied closely, and informs our editing of the Duckworth texts. But – not least because of its fragmentary nature – it didn't warrant variorum treatment.

The only comparable editing of Ford's work as we have prepared this edition has been Martin Stannard's admirable Norton edition of *The Good Soldier*.[83] Stannard took the interesting decision to use the text of the British first edition, but emend the punctuation throughout to follow that of the manuscript. He makes a convincing case for the punctuation being an editorial imposition, and that even if Ford tacitly assented to it (assuming he had a choice), it alters the nature of his manuscript.

83 *The Good Soldier*, ed. Martin Stannard (London and New York: W.W. Norton and Co., 1995).

A similar argument could be made about *Parade's End* too. Ford's punctuation is certainly distinctive: much lighter than in the published versions, and with an eccentrically variable number of suspension dots (between three and eight). However, there seem to us four major reasons for retaining the Duckworth punctuation in the case of *Parade's End*:

   1) The paucity of pre-publication material. The existence of an autograph manuscript for *Some Do Not ...* as opposed to typescripts for the other three raises the question of whether there might not have existed a typescript for *Some Do Not ...* or autographs for the others. Ford inscribed the typescripts of *A Man Could Stand Up –* and *Last Post* to say the typing was his own (though there is some evidence of dictation in both). The typescript of *No More Parades* has a label attached saying 'M.S. The property of / F. M. Ford'; although there is nothing that says the typing is his own, the typing errors make it unlikely that it was the work of a professional typist, and we have no reason to believe Ford didn't also type this novel. So we assume for these three volumes that the punctuation in the typescripts was his (and not imposed by another typist), and, including his autograph corrections, would represent his final thoughts before receiving the proofs. However, without full surviving corrected proofs of any volume it is impossible to be certain which of the numerous changes were or were not authorial. (Janice Biala told Arthur Mizener that 'Ford did his real revisions on the proofs – and only the publishers have those. The page proofs in Julies' [*sic*] and my possession are the English ones – no American publisher had those that I know of.'[84] However, no page proofs for any of the four novels are among her or Ford's daughter Julia Loewe's papers now at Cornell, nor does the Biala estate hold any.)

   2) Ford was an older, more experienced author in 1924–8 than in 1915. Though arguably he would have known even before the war how his editors were likely to regularise his punctua-

---

84 Biala to Arthur Mizener, 29 May 1964, Carl A. Kroch Library, Cornell University; quoted with the kind permission of the estate of Janice Biala and Cornell University.

tion, and had already published with John Lane, the first publisher of *The Good Soldier*, nevertheless by 1924 he certainly knew Duckworth's house style (Duckworth had published another novel, *The Marsden Case*, the previous year). More tellingly, perhaps, Ford's cordial relations with Duckworth would surely have made it possible to voice any concern, which his correspondence does not record his having done.

3) On the evidence of the errors that remained uncorrected in the first editions, the single chapter proofs for *Some Do Not . . .*, and Ford's comments in his letters on the speed at which he had to correct proofs, he does not appear to have been very thorough in his proofreading. Janice Biala commented apropos *Parade's End*:

> Ford was the worst proof reader on earth and knew it. Most of the time, the proofs were corrected in an atmosphere of [. . .] nervous exhaustion & exaperation [*sic*] with the publisher who after dallying around for months, would suddenly need the corrected proofs 2 hours after their arrival at the house etc, etc, you know.[85]

At the least, he was more concerned with style than with punctuation.

4) Such questions may be revisited should further pre-publication material be discovered. In the meantime, we took the decision to retain the first edition text as our copy-text, rather than conflate manuscript and published texts, on the grounds that this was the form in which the novels went through several impressions and editions in the UK and the US during Ford's lifetime, and in which they were read by his contemporaries and (bar some minor changes) have continued to be read until now.

---

85 Biala to Arthur Mizener, 29 May 1964, Carl A. Kroch Library, Cornell University; quoted with the kind permission of the estate of Janice Biala and Cornell University.

The emendations this edition has made to the copy-text fall into two categories:

1) The majority of cases are errors that were not corrected at proof stage. With compositors' errors the manuscripts provide the authority for the emendations, sometimes also supported by previous publication where available. We have corrected any of Ford's rare spelling and punctuation errors which were replicated in the UK text (the UK and US editors didn't always spot the same errors). We have also very occasionally emended factual and historical details where we are confident that the error is not part of the texture of the fiction. All such emendations of the UK text, whether substantive or accidental, are noted in the textual endnotes.

2) The other cases are where the manuscript and copy-text vary; where there is no self-evident error, but the editors judge the manuscript better reflects authorial intention. Such judgements are of course debatable. We have only made such emendations to the UK text when they are supported by evidence from the partial pre-publications (as in the case of expletives); or when they make better sense in context; or (in a very small number of cases) when the change between manuscript and UK loses a degree of specificity Ford elsewhere is careful to attain. Otherwise, where a manuscript reading differs from the published version, we have recorded it (if significant), but not restored it, on the grounds that Ford at least tacitly assented to the change in proof, and may indeed have made it himself – a possibility that can't be ruled out in the absence of the evidence of corrected proofs.

Our edition differs from previous ones in four main respects. First, it offers a thoroughly edited text of the series for the first time, one more reliable than any published previously. The location of one of the manuscripts, that of *No More Parades*, was unknown to Ford's bibliographer David Harvey. It was brought to the attention of Joseph Wiesenfarth (who edits it for this edition) among Hemingway's papers in the John Fitzgerald Kennedy Library (Columbia Point, Boston, Massachusetts). Its rediscovery finally made a critical edition of the entire tetralogy possible. Besides the corrections and emendations described above, the editors have made the decision to restore the expletives that are frequent in the typescript of *No More Parades*, set at the Front, but which were replaced with dashes in the UK and US book editions. While this decision may be a controversial one, we believe it is justified by the previous publication of part of *No More Parades* in Paris, in which Ford determined that the expletives should stand as accurately representing the way that soldiers talk. In *A Man Could Stand Up* – the expletives are censored with dashes in the TS, which, while it may suggest Ford's internalising of the publisher's decisions from one volume to the next, may also reflect the officers' self-censorship, so there they have been allowed to stand.[86]

Second, it presents each novel separately. They were published separately, and reprinted separately, during Ford's lifetime. The volumes had been increasingly successful. He planned an omnibus edition, and in 1930 proposed the title *Parade's End* for it (though possibly without the apostrophe).[87] But the Depression intervened and prevented this sensible strategy for consolidating his reputation. After Ford's death, and another world war, Penguin reissued the four novels as separate paperbacks.

The first omnibus edition was produced in 1950 by Knopf. This edition, based on the US first editions, has been reprinted exactly in almost all subsequent omnibus editions (by Vintage, Penguin

---

86 If the decision to censor the expletives in *No More Parades* is what led Ford to use euphemistic dashes in the typescript of *A Man Could Stand Up* –, that of *Last Post* complicates the story, containing two instances of 'bloody' and two instances of 'b——y'.

87 Ford wrote to his agent: 'I do not like the title *Tietjens Saga* – because in the first place "Tietjens" is a name difficult for purchasers to pronounce and booksellers would almost inevitably persuade readers that they mean the Forsyte Sage with great damage to my sales. I recognize the value of Messrs Duckworth's publicity and see no reason why they should not get the advantage of it by using those words as a subtitle beneath another general title, which I am inclined to suggest should be *Parades End* so that Messrs Duckworth could advertise it as PARADES END [TIETJENS' SAGA]'. Ford to Eric Pinker, 17 Aug. 1930: *Letters* 197. However, the copy at Cornell is Janice Biala's transcription of Ford's original. The reply from Pinkers is signed 'Barton' (20 Aug. 1930: Cornell), who says they have spoken to Messrs Duckworth who agree with Ford's suggested title; but he quotes it back as 'Parade's End' with the apostrophe (suggesting Biala's transcription may have omitted it), then gives the subtitle as the 'Tietjen's Saga' (casting his marksmanship with the apostrophe equally in doubt). These uncertainties make it even less advisable than it would anyway have been to alter the title by which the series has been known for sixty years.

and Carcanet; the exception is the new Everyman edition, for which the text was reset, but again using the US edition texts). Thus the tetralogy is familiar to the majority of its readers, on both sides of the Atlantic, through texts based on the US editions. There were two exceptions in the 1960s. When Graham Greene edited the Bodley Head Ford Madox Ford in 1963, he included *Some Do Not . . .* as volume 3, and *No More Parades* and *A Man Could Stand Up –* together as volume 4, choosing to exclude *Last Post*. This text is thus not only incomplete but also varies extensively from the first editions. Some of the variants are simply errors. Others are clearly editorial attempts to clarify obscurities or to 'correct' usage, sometimes to emend corruptions in the first edition, but clearly without knowledge of the manuscript. While it is an intriguing possibility that some of the emendations may have been Greene's, they are distractions from what Ford actually wrote. Arthur Mizener edited *Parade's End* for Signet Classics in 1964, combining the first two books in one volume, and the last two in another. Both these editions used the UK texts. Thus readers outside the US have not had a text of the complete work based on the UK text for over sixty years; those in the US, for forty-five years. Our edition restores the UK text, which has significant differences in each volume, and especially in the case of *Last Post* – for which even the title differed in the US editions, acquiring a definite article. This restoration of the UK text is the third innovation here.

With the exception of paperback reissues of the Bodley Head texts by Sphere in 1969 (again excluding *Last Post*), the volumes have not been available separately since 1948. While there is no doubt Ford intended the books as a sequence (there *is* some doubt about how many volumes he projected, as discussed above), the original UK editions appeared at intervals of more than a year. They were read separately, with many readers beginning with the later volumes. Like any writer of novel sequences, Ford was careful to ensure that each book was intelligible alone. Moreover, there are marked differences between each of the novels. Though all tell the story of the same group of characters, each focuses on a different selection of people. The locations and times are also different. In addition, and more strikingly, the styles and techniques develop and alter from novel to novel. Returning the

novels to their original separate publication enables these differences to be more clearly visible.

Parade's End in its entirety is a massive work. Omnibus editions
of it are too large to be able to accommodate extra material. A
further advantage of separate publication is to allow room for the
annotations the series now needs. This is the fourth advantage of
our edition. Though *Parade's End* isn't as difficult or obscure a
text as *Ulysses* or *The Waste Land*, it is dense with period references, literary allusions and military terminology unfamiliar to
readers a century later. This edition is the first to annotate these
difficulties.

To keep the pages of text as uncluttered as possible, we have
normally restricted footnotes to information rather than inter-
pretation, annotating obscurities that are not easily traceable in
standard reference works. English words have only been glossed
if they are misleadingly ambiguous, or if they cannot be found in
the *Concise Oxford Dictionary*, in which case the *Oxford English
Dictionary* (or occasionally Partridge's *Dictionary of Slang*) has
been used. *Parade's End* is, like Ford's account of *The Good Soldier*,
an 'intricate tangle of references and cross-references'.[88] We have
annotated references to works by other writers, as well as relevant
biographical references that are not covered in the introductions.
We have also included cross-references to Ford's other works
where they shed light on *Parade's End*. To avoid duplication, we
have restricted cross-references to other volumes of the tetralogy
to those to preceding volumes. These are given by Part- and
chapter-number: i.e. 'I.iv' for Part I, chapter IV. We have,
however, generally not noted the wealth of cross-references
within the individual volumes.

Works cited in the footnotes are given a full citation on first
appearance. Subsequent citations of often-cited works are by
short titles, and a list of these is provided at the beginning of the
volume. A key to the conventions used in the textual endnotes
appears on pp. 205–06.

88 'Dedicatory Letter to Stella Ford', *The Good Soldier* 5.

condition of ruin at home and foreign discredit to which the country must
almost immediately emerge under the conduct of the Scotch grocers, Frankfort
financiers, Welsh pettifoggers, Midland armament manufacturers and South
Country incompetents who during the later years ĩf the war had intrigued
themselves into office -- with that dreadful condition staring it in the face
the country must return to something like its old standards of North Country
commonsense and English probity. The old governing class to which he and his
belonged might never return to power but, whatever revolutions took place --
and he did not care! -- the country must ~~return to~~ exacting of whoever might
be its governing class some semblance of personal probity and public honouring
of pledges. He obviously was out of it or he would be out of it with the end
of the war, for even from his bed he had taken no small part in the directing
of affairs at his office..... ₴₴₴ A ₴₴₴₴₴₴ of war obviously favoured the
coming to the top of all kinds of devious storm petrels; that was inevitable
and could not be helped. But in normal times a country -- every country --
was true to itself.

    Nevertheless he was very content that his brother should in the interim
have no share in affairs. Let him secure his mutton chop, his pint of
claret, his woman and his umbrella and it mattered not into what obscurity
he retired. But how was that to be secured. There were several ways.

    He was aware, for instance, that ₴₴₴₴₴₴₴₴₴₴₴ Christopher was both a
mathematician of no mean order and a churchman. He might perfectly well take
orders, assume the charge of one of the three family livings that Mark had in
his gift and, whilst competently discharging the duties of his cure, ₴₴₴₴₴
pursue whatever are the occupations of a well-cared for mathematician.

    Christopher however, whilst avowing his predilection for such a life
-- which as Mark saw it was exactly fitted to his asceticism, his softness in
general and his private tastes -- Christopher admitted that there was an

A NOTE ON THE TEXT OF
LAST POST

This Carcanet text is based on the first UK edition, published by Gerald Duckworth in January 1928. It has been checked against the typescript held at Cornell University Library which, according to a handwritten note on the first leaf, was typed by Ford himself. Supplementary typescript leaves have also been consulted and one extensive and significant deletion included in an appendix.[89] The first American edition has been compared with the British edition and the more significant differences recorded.

The usual gap in publication dates between the UK and US versions of the first three novels, already diminished with successive volumes, has vanished altogether in the case of the fourth. Ford was clearly revising both editions simultaneously, possibly in both typescript and proof. But we encounter areas of uncertainty almost immediately, when Ford sends his typescript to Stella Bowen for her to forward to Duckworth, after correcting 'any obvious printer's errors'. We don't know precisely how many copies of the typescript existed, then or subsequently, nor what, if any, corrections Stella actually made. The most likely scenario, in any case, is that Ford was making revisions on more than one version of the eventual text, a procedure that was almost certainly suspended under the twin pressures of publishers' demands and postal deadlines. There is no doubt that emendations were not consistently recorded in both versions. But again, given the scarcity of pre-publication materials, we can't be sure what proportion of the resultant differences is accounted for by Ford revising on the proofs of both UK and US editions.

---

89 The Cornell University Library collection guide reads: 'Fragments of carbon copy of several versions of passages which appear between pages 183–234 of the first American edition of "The Last Post"'. I have described these pages in some detail in the appendix.

The LAST POST

FORD MADOX FORD

THE AVIGNON EDITION

A LITERARY GUILD BOOK

The
LAST POST

FORD MADOX FORD

The Literary Guild of America

Priority

The 'true' first edition of Last Post is still disputed. The Albert & Charles Boni edition now seems to have preceded the Literary Guild edition, previously assumed to have appeared first on the basis of reviews located by David Dow Harvey. The Guild Annual, when publishing the extract from Last Post, noted that the Boni edition was officially published on 5 January 1928. This may, in fact, have been when the Literary Guild edition was printed in bulk and available for dispatch: it is likely, though, that the Guild was contractually obliged to afford the Albert & Charles Boni edition priority.

This possibility is strengthened by the fact that, in other contexts, the official publication date for the Boni edition is given as 13 January 1928. Ford wrote to Stella a week earlier, confirming that date: 'I shall stay on a little longer as the Last Post comes out on the 13th and may help me towards serial work.' He wrote again on the actual date: 'Today is the publication day of the Last Post – Boni's having chosen a Friday and a thirteenth, everyone says, out of spite' (Ford/Bowen 374, 376). The earliest US review appears to be dated three days earlier.[90]

The composition dates in the two editions are as follows. The UK (Duckworth) edition has 'PARIS, 7th June–AVIGNON, 1st August–ST. LAWRENCE RIVER, 24th September–NEW YORK, 12th November.—MCMXXVII'. Both US versions (Boni and the Literary Guild) have 'PARIS 7th July—AVIGNON & S. S. MINNEDOSA—NEW YORK 2d NOVEMBER 1927'.[91]

The date of Stella Bowen's letter to Ford acknowledging his own letter and her copy of Last Post, 3 January 1928, is also the date of the first UK review: Perceval Hinton's 'The Week's Fiction: Tietjens of Groby', in the Birmingham Post.[92] David Dow Harvey, Ford's indefatigable bibliographer, remarked that the

---

90 Harry Hansen, 'The First Reader: The Ford Saga', World (New York) (10 Jan. 1928), 15: this is five days earlier than the first US review listed by Harvey.
91 As Arthur Mizener noted, the first date and place of the Duckworth details are not possible since Ford was in London on that day (Mizener, Saddest Story 585 n.1). For more detail on dates, see Saunders, Dual Life II 613 n.2.
92 Max Saunders, who located the review, bases the attribution on Hinton's letter to Ford of 4 February 1928 (Cornell), and Ford's letter to Hinton of 27 November 1931 (Letters 203–04).

Literary Guild edition was distributed to Guild members a little earlier than the Boni edition, thus 'probably' entitling it to the distinction of being the first American edition. Harvey bases his belief that the Duckworth edition was probably published in January 1928 'but later than the American edition' primarily on the fact that the first review he found was 26 January 1928 (in the *Times Literary Supplement*). Harvey also comments that:

> A few differences between the American and the English editions appear to indicate that Ford revised the former slightly before its English publication. His motive may have been simply to make the English edition 'different,' but most of the changes seem to be in the direction of greater clarity or stylistic improvement. Few simply adapt the novel for an English audience.[93]

Harvey then lists some half-dozen pages in the UK edition where the changes are 'so numerous that they can not be detailed here' and notes as '[o]ther interesting changes' nine more revisions between UK and US.[94]

A question that arises constantly from textual editing and textual comparison is that of 'significance'. Harvey's half-dozen pages where the differences between UK and US texts are 'so numerous' are recognisable enough. But there are, in fact, many hundreds of differences between the Duckworth and Boni editions. A substantial proportion of these variants, as with comparable variations between TS and UK, are arguably of little significance: details of punctuation that are often a matter of house style. But a good many are substantive: different wording, different word-order, whole sentences, even paragraphs, added or erased. And examination of these suggests that Harvey may have already decided, on the basis of review dates, that the US edition had preceded the UK edition, and viewed the revisions accord-

---

93 The practice of making editions 'different' which Harvey refers to is illuminated by the 'memorandum of proposals' that Ford gave to Douglas Goldring (then acting as agent for the New York publisher Thomas Seltzer), probably in the summer of 1923. These include 'author to make such revision or alteration of a published work as shall give publishers copyright'. See Goldring's *South Lodge* (London: Constable, 1943), 142.

94 Harvey, *Bibliography* 69, 70.

ingly. It appears equally, perhaps more, likely that the reverse is true, though the absence of both UK and US proofs as well as the typescript used to set up the US edition renders a definitive answer impossible.

On 13 February 1928, a month after the publication of *Last Post*, Ford wrote to Gerald Duckworth suggesting 'the ending of our agreement', remarking that 'it would really pay me not to publish in England, for the English editions coming out before the American ones really do skim the cream off the American market' (*Letters* 175–6). It was a thought he had voiced before but there is no indication that the very recent publication of *Last Post* had violated that order of priority, English preceding American.

Finally, it should be stressed that, almost certainly, the two editions appeared so close together that there was no possibility of either *published* text being drawn upon to correct errors or duplicate stylistic improvements prior to the publication of the other.

The Typescript of *Last Post*

The typescript of *Last Post* falls into two sections (three if we include a separate version of the brief 'Dedicatory Letter'). The first is a sequence of 200 leaves, essentially the text of the novel as we now have it. The second is a section of 47 leaves. This can be further divided into 22 leaves comprising a title sheet for the first chapter of Part II and leaves corresponding to pp. 136–54 of this edition, with the remaining 25 leaves consisting very largely of an extended scene between General Campion and Lord Fittleworth, excluded from the published version. This passage has been reproduced in the appendix to this volume.

Within these 25 leaves, there are 13 duplicates, two series of page numbers and two leaves that correspond to the end of I.vii, from halfway down p. 133 ('just before seemed to have a good deal of temperature') to the conclusion ('that young couple') on p. 135. Some of the duplicate leaves have later emendations and deletions, which have been noted in the appendix.

The published versions of the first three novels of the tetralogy were all subtitled 'A Novel'. The title leaf of this typescript reads

'LAST POST / \<A Novel\> / by / Ford Madox Ford'. Although this has been crossed through, the American (Boni) edition has on its title page 'A Novel by Ford Madox Ford'.

Ford has written (and signed with his initials) the statement that 'This is the original typescript – my own typing – from which the English edition was printed.' The lower right-hand corner carries his address: '84 rue Notre Dame des Champs / Paris VIe'.[95]

A query nevertheless remains as to whether this is literally the case. In comparison with, say, the typescript of *No More Parades*, that for *Last Post* is relatively tidy, with many pages having very few emendations. The variations in the quantity of revision suggests that some parts of the MS have been retyped, while there are several instances of misspellings that are in fact homophones, such as 'flower' corrected to 'flour', suggesting some element of dictation. The quality of the typing is never so good as to suggest a professional typist but it is certainly feasible that parts of the MS were typed again – perhaps by Caroline Gordon, who began assisting Ford in 1926 and was again giving secretarial help by late October 1927 (*Ford/Bowen* 340). In fact, considerable retyping accounts most plausibly for both the comparative neatness of the typescript we have and the complex and incomplete series of numbers on the leaves.

The majority of *typewritten* corrections in the *Last Post* TS render it impossible to decipher the words or letters overtyped. Ford's favoured method of deletion is to use the '@' key: a continuous line of these is, indeed, very effective in blacking-out whatever the writer wishes to obscure. In most cases, the type-written corrections do not affect the agreement between UK and US editions. I have only cited deleted words or phrases when I am sure, or at least reasonably confident, of the deleted words: most of these cases are of autograph deletions – these are generally decipherable

Though there are innumerable small differences between the three versions (UK, TS and US), there are, nevertheless, several sections of the TS in which, despite the typing errors (almost all

95 In August 1927 a friend of Jeanne Foster, the writer Jane Dransfield, spent some time with Ford and Stella and remembered him 'writing on his Corona (he was then writing *The Last Post*)' at a deal table in the attic of a small hotel in Villeneuve-les-Avignon (Saunders, *Dual Life* II 317).

corrected) and a small number of differences in the TS from Duckworth house style, there is little deviation.

The first two leaves of the typescript were clearly produced on a different typewriter from the bulk of the TS: the disparity is as marked as 10-pt and 12-pt on a modern word-processed document. The typeface is both larger and slightly less clear, though this may simply be due to worn carbon paper. There are several autograph emendations.

The rest of that first chapter shows clear signs of a change in procedure. Though there are autograph insertions, the deletions and some of the inserted words are typewritten. A clear majority of the revisions are corrections to misspellings or mistypings rather than second thoughts. This is, if anything, more the case with I.ii and I.iii. The early leaves of I.iv are slightly less clear but, again, show relatively few emendations. I.v is a little longer and a little messier. The revisions in I.vi and I.vii are also on a modest scale.

The shorter Part II (four chapters) is generally very different. II.i, one of the longer chapters in the book, consists of 21 leaves. The latter half of the chapter is fairly clean while the first half shows far more evidence of revision and uncertainty. This is the chapter of which the material now in the appendix would have been part. As that material makes evident, the conversation between Campion and Fittleworth would not only have cast in a different light the ways in which Sylvia is viewed, but, through the sympathetic depiction of Fittleworth, would have opened up a much broader review of the state and likely future of England. Ford clearly decided against this, intending to make the social and political points implicitly rather than explicitly.

Emendations in the final three chapters, with the exception of a few leaves that show a markedly higher incidence of autograph revisions, are again relatively few, the clear majority of them typewritten.[96]

---

96 Ford wrote to Jeanne Foster, very possibly referring to Part II, that he had 'got on rather slowly, owing to bothers and depressions with my novel': Janis and Richard Londraville, 'A Portrait of Ford Madox Ford: Unpublished Letters from the Ford-Foster Friendship', *English Literature in Transition*, 33:2 (1990), 181. (The letter is dated '[1925]' but this must be early September 1927: see Saunders, *Dual Life* II 614 n.7). See Londraville, 'Portrait', 194 for the possibility that Ford may have been using a typewriter given to him by Mrs Foster.

Any hopes that reference to Ford's 'usual practice' might yield definitive answers to some of the questions raised by this type-script do not long survive any examination of the matter. In *It Was the Nightingale* he discusses at length his dislike of writing with a pen but the advantages of doing so. He recounts an episode of correcting the typescript of a book finished some months earlier.[97] He is – again! – on board a ship: 'It was a horrible expe-rience. Partly I had typed the book; partly I had dictated it to a secretary who wrote longhand, partly to another who used a machine, and partly to a third who was a remarkable stenogra-pher' (*Nightingale* 221). In September 1920 Ford had written to Ezra Pound: 'Anyhow I'm a damn better typist than you!' (*Letters* 125) – which may be true but a large question mark hovers over 'better'. Is this 'quicker' or 'more accurate'?

There are, in total, some three thousand differences between TS, UK and US editions: as many as three hundred in a single chapter. Many of these fall under a few obvious headings, such as the absence of full stops after titles (Mr., Mrs.) and the fitful appearance of his French accents, Marie Léonie in particular moving half-naked through the pages of Ford's typescript on most occasions. Noting every point at which the UK edition differed from either US or TS would render the text almost unreadable, and this is not a variorum edition. The vast majority of these differences, however, are differences of punctuation and of publishing house style. Within these instances of punctuation, perhaps three-quarters concern commas: usually missing in Ford's typescript, often missing in the US printing, very rarely missing in the lavishly punctuated Duckworth edition, though there are occasions when Ford stirs himself to add an eccentric comma that Duckworth sternly ignores. Writing of the poet H.D., Catherine Zilboorg remarks that she 'frequently includes parenthetical or appositional material with only one of the required commas'.[98] This occurs very frequently in Ford's typescript. His relationship with the comma was a light-hearted and flirtatious one but, in the people who sub-edited, proofread and prepared texts for the

---

97 Quite likely *When the Wicked Man* (1931) – the composition dates specify completion aboard 'R. M. S. *Mauretania*, off the Scillies, 1st December, 1930'.
98 Caroline Zilboorg (ed.), *Richard Aldington and H.D.: Their lives in letters 1918–61. New Collected Edition* (Manchester: Manchester University Press, 2003), xiii.

firm of Duckworth, Ford came up against a tempered but sincere and substantial love, for the comma, in particular, but also for plenitude. The occasions on which the Duckworth text offers a longish sentence without punctuation strike the reader as aberrations.

There are, unavoidably, moments when an editor will reflect on just how representative of authorial intentions and decisions a text can be that rejects less a small fraction than a large proportion of an author's punctuation. How significant a part does punctuation play in a writer's style – or a writer's self? There is no obvious answer, though one can certainly say that Ford was not *that* sort of writer: he was concerned with the whole, with style, with word and image – far less so with comma and colon.[99] *Last Post* was, in any case, the fifteenth of Ford's books that Duckworth published and clearly he would have known not only Duckworth's house style but their general level of reliability and consistency.

Page Numbering

The 200-leaf sequence that provided the UK text of the novel has nearly two dozen oddities in numbering: duplications, gaps, alterations and a substantial number of handwritten figures, constituting a separate but erratic series, generally in the top left-hand corner of the leaf. Detailed examination confirms, however, that in every instance of numerical inconsistency or deviation the actual material is sequential.

Though several numerical sequences are discernible, they are too fragmentary to afford reliable insights into the development of the typescript. One example is the run of handwritten numbers in the top left-hand corner, apparently every third leaf, that peters out after leaf 89, having already ruptured that assumed sequence with several variations in the numbering. This may

---

99 In contrast to, say, James Joyce. My Viking Press edition of *Finnegans Wake* (New York: 4th printing, 1945) contains a list of corrections of misprints, made by Joyce: fifteen closely printed pages, in which such phrases as 'insert comma' and 'delete stop' abound. See, on Joyce 'adding commas', Richard Ellmann, *James Joyce* (Oxford: Oxford University Press, new edn, 1983), 731, 734.

have indicated division into proof pages, in which case the numbers would presumably have been inserted by Duckworth's printer, here the Chapel River Press in Kingston, Surrey (four different UK printers were used for the four volumes).

There are several instances of successive leaves bearing the same number – and several apparent gaps. What appears to be a second sequence begins with leaf 114: a number 22 or possibly 42, and again the sequence of pencilled numerals every third leaf. Once more, this is not consistent, but it continues almost to the end of the main section of the typescript (leaf 198 out of the total 200).

The supplementary batch of 47 leaves does carry an orderly sequence of pencilled numerals in the lower right-hand corners: these have been inserted by the librarian or archivist to ensure proper record-keeping.[100]

Some Examples of Revisions

The majority of revisions made to Ford's typescript are minor, more often handwritten, generally to remove obvious repetitions or assonances. Many emendations, though, are clearly intended to clarify the meaning, while some are second thoughts about phrases or whole sentences.

The early example of 'brushed by apple boughs' emended to 'brushed from above by apple boughs' confers, quite economically, a greater specificity. Almost immediately afterwards, the short sentence 'The hut had no sides' is written in, representative of apparently small revisions that are slightly – or, in this case, greatly – more significant in a larger context. Later in the novel, the change from 'the cheeks' to 'the bright red cheeks' of Mark Tietjens, Junior, when he first appears in the novel prepares for the several references to his high colour in his uncle's subsequent reflections.

If Ford's working procedure here comprised revising his type-script from the beginning, it is tempting to suggest that his work

---

100 Confirmed by Cornell's Division of Rare and Manuscript Collections, 8 December 2009.

on UK and US versions diverged at an early stage. The first chapter has several instances of autograph revisions in TS carried across to US; the revisions are minor and in the direction of greater clarity; and the differences are, in several cases, satisfactorily explained as errors by the US compositor. In the later parts of that first chapter, however, there are already whole sentences added to, or missing from, the US text; autograph revisions are transferred to UK but not to US; and examples begin to accumulate of corrections made on the TS appearing in neither UK or US texts: that is to say, evidence of decisions made only at the proof stage since there is nothing in the typescript's original or emended versions to account for such differences.

There are alterations – normally additions – that seem to have been made very much with Ford's American audience in mind. A minor example is the change from the original *bonne bouche* to *hors d'oeuvre* in US, plausibly because the latter phrase might be more familiar. Also in the opening chapter, the UK text reads: 'He only knew of Americans because of a book he had once read—a woman like a hedge-sparrow, creeping furtive in shadows and getting into trouble with a priest.' The beginning of the sentence is softened, becoming, in the US edition, 'Nearly all he knew of Americans came from a book he had once read', while American readers are given, after 'priest', the comforting assertion 'But no doubt there were other types.'

Given the gaps in the pre-publication evidence, some revisions stimulate speculation but elude definitive answers. An early chapter offers this:

UK the twilight; **TS** the <deep> twilight; **US** the deep twilight

The context is that of a bird 'that seldom sees the sun but lives in the deep twilight of deep hedges' (in the American text). The deletion made in the typescript, presumably to avoid the repetition of 'deep', and reflected in the UK text, did not carry across to the US edition. The US compositor is unlikely to have missed it if the typescript from which the US edition was set had the word similarly crossed out: that is to say, overtyped, the original 'deep' barely legible. Presumably, then, the typescript for the US edition did not show this deletion. So Ford did not copy that change on to the second typescript; or, as an afterthought, let it stand, then or in proof; or inserted it (or re-inserted it) at proof stage. Indeed, the repetition ('deep twilight of deep hedges') is *so* obvious that he could hardly have overlooked it. One might, then, be led into a digression about exploring the possibilities of 'repetition' – or rejecting the need to avoid it at all costs – as a recognisable feature of work by writers as varied as Lawrence, Joyce, Hemingway, Beckett and, of course, Gertrude Stein.

Another example of economical and effective revision is Sylvia's reference to Marie Léonie as a 'French hairdresser's widow' altered to 'French prostitute', reflecting not only Sylvia's franker and harsher verbal assaults upon those to whom she is opposed but also offering a pleasing irony, given that 'whore' is a word applied to Sylvia by at least three – male – characters in the course of the tetralogy.[101]

There are points at which Ford is clearly rethinking, even arguing with himself on the page: the closing pages of II.iii, for example, where there are innumerable changes, including the brief consideration of Christopher's accidental death. That Ford considered this hints, I suspect, at the central importance with which he regarded Valentine Wannop at this juncture. But he – surely correctly – resists the temptation.

Editorial Principles in Practice

The points at which this edition has departed from the first UK edition have, with a very few exceptions, always had the authority of at least one witness. One of those exceptions is the name of the racehorse, 'Scuttle', which has been 'corrected' and which I discuss in the Introduction. The Duckworth edition of *Last Post* appears, on the whole, to be fairly accurate. Such obvious lapses as the misprint 'nirls' for 'girls' (I.vi) are rare. There are some occasions on which I have opted for US over UK, gener-

---

101 She is thus referred to by Mark Tietjens, by Christopher himself, and by General Campion in a deleted typescript passage of *No More Parades*. The same epithet is applied to Mrs Duchemin by Christopher and by Valentine, while Campion remarks of 'the wild women' (suffragettes): 'They say they're all whores' – Valentine, of course, is a suffragette.

ally but not always on matters of punctuation. All departures
from UK are noted.

There are some recurring issues that may be best dealt with
here:

1) Ford, in almost every instance, omits the full stop after titles:
Mr., Mrs., Dr. These are inserted in line with Duckworth house
style but not noted.

2) With relatively few exceptions, Ford omits the acute accent
on the second part of Marie Léonie's name; other accents occur
fitfully in the TS, as does the underlining intended to italicise
foreign words not generally anglicised. We are used to inserting
symbols or even using shortcut keys: in the 1920s, of course,
Ford needed to remember to go through and mark all accents
manually on every copy of his manuscript, then on the various
proof pages where necessary. I have treated these variations as
minor punctuation and so not exhaustively catalogued them.

3) Names. In this volume, as in others of the series, Ford's use
of his characters' names is not always consistent. Sometimes
they are changed in the TS and adhered to, as in the case of
Cammie Fittleworth. Helen Lowther, though, remains Helen
Luther throughout the TS. Both the UK and US first editions
use 'Lowther' and this seems a clear case of the missing proofs
containing the authority for the change. Since there is no
inconsistency on either side, I have followed the UK text,
which has been authorised by Ford and confirmed by the US
text. Where there are only one or two inconsistencies, such as
'Wolstonmark' for 'Wolstonemark', the variants are simply
noted; in such cases as that of 'Luther' and 'Lowther', not every
instance is recorded in the textual notes, though mention is
made of that fact.

4) Variants in spelling and hyphenation abound. One oddity
is the reversal of the contemporary (or, at least, my) assump-
tion that the '-ize' suffix is characteristic of American English.
Both TS and US generally use the '-ise' suffix while the Duckworth edition uses '-ize'. The UK edition is the copy-text used,

so this text conforms in that respect too, printing 'agonized', 'demoralized' and 'naturalized'. On the same basis, the acceptance of old-fashioned forms of familiar words has followed the Duckworth conventions. (Such forms are, of course, highly appropriate to a man like Mark Tietjens.) So this text of *Last Post* has 'to-day' but does not follow Ford's 'gaol' or his frequent use of 'shew', 'shewn' and 'shewed'. Again, not every instance of this has been noted. The variations in hyphenation arise either from US usage or US following TS very closely. Generally, UK hyphenates far more: 'hard-headed' rather than 'hardheaded', 'school-room' rather than 'schoolroom', 'last-minute' rather than 'last minute'. The present text again adheres to the UK edition in this respect.

5) There is frequent confusion and inconsistency in the plural and possessive form of the name and family 'Tietjens', particularly in TS. UK is generally consistent and more accurate, and has been adhered to, even in the odd case that seems debatable. The usual convention is that Tietjens's is the house; Tietjens' the possessive singular; Tietjenses the plural; Tietjenses' the possessive plural.

6) There is some variation in the assumptions made about which foreign words (usually French) should be italicised and which assumed to be sufficiently anglicised to obviate the need to do so. Again, I have tended to follow the generally reliable UK edition. One curious exception is the marked inconsistency in the form of the word 'ménage'. This is accented and italicised every time in the US edition, only twice in UK, three times in TS, having neither accent nor italics three times in UK and twice in TS. My initial impression had been that Ford's typescript set out to accent the word when it occurs in Marie Léonie's thoughts or conversation but not otherwise. I now think, reviewing the details of the inconsistencies, that the word should be regularised to the degree that it is accented (its conventional English form) on all occasions but italicised only in Marie Léonie's thoughts (all witnesses agree on this last point). I suspect that Ford may have viewed this as a tiny contribution, together with the larger factors of syntax and

vocabulary, to the differentiation of Marie Léonie's language from that of the other characters. This impression of literal translation (confirming that a character must be understood to be speaking in a foreign language) is familiar, of course, from Ford's own *No Enemy* and from other novels too: R. H. Mottram's *The Spanish Farm* ('They regretted deranging her, but had the hunger of a wolf')[102] and, later and probably more familiar, Hemingway's *For Whom the Bell Tolls*.

---

102 R.H. Mottram, *The Spanish Farm Trilogy* (London: Chatto & Windus, 1927), 12. The individual novels, published in 1924, 1925 and 1926, were precisely contemporary with the first three volumes of Ford's tetralogy.

LAST POST

A NOVEL

By
FORD MADOX FORD

"Oh, Rokehope is a pleasant place
If the fause thieves would let it be."
BORDER BALLAD*

* This is the opening of 'Rookhope Ryde', included in Francis James Child's classic *The English and Scottish Popular Ballads* (1889). The version he prints there begins: 'Rookhope stands in a pleasant place, / If the false thieves wad let it be' (New York: Dover, 2003), III, 439. In Ford's *The Young Lovell* (London: Chatto & Windus, 1913) the monk Francis speaks of 'the false thieves of Rokehope and Cheviot' (108; see also 178), while, in *Between St. Dennis and St. George*, Ford alludes to 'Rokehope' as 'a pleasant place if the false thieves would let it be' (41). In October 1927, having just read the typescript of *Last Post*, Stella Bowen wrote to Ford: 'You ought to have had "Rokehope" as a sub-title!' Ford responded: 'Yes, I shall put O Rokehope is a pleasant place on the title page' (*Ford/Bowen* 331, 336). The first of 'Two Songs' that Ford contributed to the *Imagist Anthology 1930* (London: Chatto & Windus, 1930), 118, was headed 'To the Tune of *Rokehope*', while the second mentioned 'Rokehope Hills'. The ballad refers to a foray into Rookhope, Durham, by marauders from Thirl-wall in Northumberland and Williehaver (or Willeva) in Cumberland, in December 1569.

DEDICATORY LETTER

To ISABEL PATERSON*

MADAME ET CHER CONFRÈRE,†

I have for some years now had to consider you as being my[1] fairy godmother in the United States—though[2] how one can have a godmother junior to oneself I have yet to figure out. Perhaps godmothers of the kind that can turn pumpkins into glass coaches can achieve miracles in seniority. Or, when I come to think of it, I seem to remember that, for a whole tribe of Incas converted who knows how and simultaneously, in the days of the Conquistadores, an Infanta of Spain went to the font, she being, whatever her age, of necessity junior to the elders at least of the tribe.[3] That, however, is all a trifle—except for my gratitude!— compared with your present responsibility.

For, but for you, this book would only nebularly‡ have existed—in space, in my brain, where you will, so it be not on paper and between boards. Save,[4] that is to say, for your stern, contemptuous and almost virulent insistence on knowing "what became of Tietjens" I never should have conducted this chronicle to the stage it has now reached. The soldier, tired of war's alarms,§ it has always seemed[5] to me, might be allowed to rest

---

* Paterson (1886–1961), born in Ontario, was a journalist, novelist, literary critic and – later – political philosopher, who reviewed many of Ford's books and became a friend. From 1921 she was assistant to Burton Rascoe on what became the *New York Herald Tribune*, for which she wrote a 'Books' column from 1924 to 1949. (Ford knew Rascoe well and published more than two dozen items in that paper and in *The Bookman*, which Rascoe also edited.) In a 1926 article on the first three volumes of *Parade's End*, Paterson remarked that 'There may be a fourth volume, but for the present that is immaterial' (Harvey, *Bibliography* 367). In her 'Turns with a Bookworm' column shortly afterwards, however, she asserted that: 'All will be revealed in two or three years, when the fourth volume appears' (21 Nov. 1926: see Harvey, *Bibliography* 369).

† Colleague, fellow-member of a profession, associate (French).

‡ A stranger to the *OED*, which offers 'nebulously', but the meaning – hazily, formlessly – is clear enough.

§ 'War's alarms' occurs in Chaucer's *The Knight's Tale* and in many works since, ranging from William Collins through Thomas Hood and Tennyson to Gilbert and Sullivan, and was most memorably used in Yeats's late, brief poem, 'Politics'. But 'the soldier, tired of war's alarms' is the title of a song, subsequently performed to great acclaim by many sopranos (including Joan Sutherland), from the 1762 opera *Artaxerxes* by

beneath bowery vines. But you would not have it so.

You—and for once you align yourself with the Great Public— demand an ending: if possible a happy ending.* Alas, I cannot provide you with the end of Tietjens for a reason upon which I will later dwell—but I here provide you with a slice of one of Christopher's later days so that you may know how more or less he at present stands. For in this world of ours though lives may end Affairs† do not. Even though Valentine and Tietjens[6] were dead the Affair that they set[7] going would go rolling on down the generations—Mark junior and Mrs. Lowther, the unborn child and the rest will go on beneath the nut-boughs or over the seas— or in the best Clubs. It is not your day nor mine that shall see the end of them.

And think: How many people have we not known intimately and seen daily for years! Then they move into another township, and, bad correspondents as we all are[8] and sit-at-homes as Fate makes most of us, they drop out of our sights. They may—those friends of yours—go and settle in Paris. You may see them for fort-nights at decennial intervals, or you may not.

So I would have preferred to let it be with Tietjens, but you would not have it. I have always jeered at authors who senti-mentalised over their characters, and after finishing a book

---

Thomas Arne (1710–78), who also composed 'Rule, Britannia!' Ford mentions *Artax-erxes* in *Thus to Revisit* (London: Chapman & Hall, 1921), 15, but he is probably attributing this to Madeleine de Scudéry, as he does in *March* 571, 717. He may be misremembering de Scudéry's *Artamène*.

* This echoes the 'Epistolary Epilogue' of Ford's 1910 novel, *A Call* (Manchester: Carcanet, 1984), addressed to (an unnamed) Violet Hunt: 'you, together with the great majority of British readers, insist upon having a happy ending, or, if not a happy ending, at least some sort of an ending' (161).

† In *A Call*'s 'Epistolary Epilogue' Ford expresses the view that a novel is, to him, 'the history of an "affair"', adding that: 'There is in life nothing final. So that even "affairs" never really have an end as far as the lives of the actors are concerned' (161). He often plays on this double meaning of 'affair', connoting both sexual liaison and, more gener-ally, a complex of human (and literary) interconnections. In *Thus to Revisit* he remarks that 'no one will deny that his life is really a matter of "affairs"; of minute hourly embar-rassments; of sympathetic or unsympathetic personal contacts; of little-marked successes and failures of queer jealousies, of muted terminations – a tenuous, fluttering, and engrossing fabric. And intangible!' (36). The 'germ' of *The Good Soldier* – an instance of extreme repression of emotions in order to avoid 'a scene' – is recounted in *The Spirit of the People*. Excluding 'the silence of the parting', Ford refers to it as 'the otherwise commonplace affair' (*England* 313–14). See also 'Techniques', in *Critical Writings* 68; and 'A Haughty and Proud Generation' (1922) in *Critical Essays*, ed. Max Saunders and Richard Stang (Manchester: Carcanet, 2002), 208–17 (210).

exclaim like, say, Thackeray: "Roll up the curtains; put the
puppets in their boxes; quench the tallow footlights" . . . something like that.* But I am bound to say that in certain moods in
Avignon this year† it would less have surprised me to go up to the
upper chamber of the mill where I wrote and there to find that
friend of mine than to find you. For you are to remember that for
me Tietjens is the re-creation of a friend I had—a friend so vivid
to me that though he died many years ago I cannot feel that he
is yet dead.‡ In the dedicatory letter of an earlier instalment of
this series of books§ I said that in these volumes I was trying to
project how this world would have appeared to that friend to-day
and how, in it, he would have acted—or you, I believe, would say
re-acted. And that is the exact truth of the matter.

Do you not find—you yourself, too—that, however it may be
with the mass of humanity, in the case of certain dead people you
cannot feel that they are indeed gone from this world? You can
only know it, you can only believe it. That is, at any rate, the case
with me—and in my case the world daily becomes more and more
peopled with such *revenants* and less and less with those who still
walk this earth. It is only yesterday that I read of the death of
another human being who will for the rest of time have[9] for me
that effect.** That person died thousands of miles away, and

---

* Cf. *March* 587: 'But what must Mr. Thackeray do but begin or end up his books with
  paragraphs running: "Reader, the puppet play is ended; let down the curtain; put the
  puppets back into their boxes..."' Earlier, in *The English Novel*, he remarks of Thackeray that he 'must needs write his epilogue as to the showman rolling up his
  marionettes in green baize and the rest of it' (7). Thackeray's *Vanity Fair* (1847–8)
  ends 'Come, children, let us shut up the box and the puppets, for our play is played
  out.'
† Ford includes 'Avignon 1st August' among the dates and places of composition listed
  at the end of the novel. He and Bowen spent the month in Provence: see Saunders,
  Dual Life II 317–18 and 613–14 n.5. Albert & Charles Boni published *New York Is
  Not America*, the 1927 edition of *The Good Soldier* and *The Last Post* in their 'Avignon
  Edition'.
‡ Arthur Marwood, mentioned many times in Ford's writings, most relevantly in
  Nightingale 188–207, was a partial model for Christopher Tietjens. He died in May
  1916, though Ford referred to him as having died 'several years before the war' (*Return*
  281).
§ In *No More Parades*, dedicated to William Bird.
** The dedicatory letter in both UK and US editions is dated 13 October 1927. Jane
  Wells died on 6 October and her obituary appeared in *The Times* two days later. Ford
  mentioned it to Bowen in a letter dated 11 October, adding 'I have been a good deal
  distressed' (*Ford/Bowen* 329). See *Return* 278: 'There are three people in whose deaths
  I have never been able to believe. They are Conrad and Arthur Marwood and Mrs
  H.G. Wells.'

yesterday it would have astonished me if she had walked into my
room here in New York. To-day it would no longer. It would have
the aspect of the simplest thing in the world.

So then, for me, it is with Tietjens. With his prototype I set
out on several enterprises—one of them being a considerable
periodical publication of a Tory kind*—and for many years I was
accustomed as it were to "set" my mind by his comments on
public or other affairs. He was, as I have elsewhere said,† the
English Tory—the last English Tory, omniscient,[10] slightly
contemptuous—and sentimental in his human contacts. And for
many years before I contemplated the writing of these books—
before the War even—I was accustomed to ask myself not merely
what he would[11] have said of certain public or private affairs, but
how he would have acted in certain positions. And I do so still.
I have only to say to my mind, as the child on the knees of an
adult says to its senior: "Tell us a fairy tale"—I have only to say:
"Tell us what he would here have done" and at once he is there.

So, you see, I cannot tell you the end of Tietjens, for he will
end only when I am beyond pens and paper. For me at this
moment he is, oddly enough, in Avignon, rather disappointed in
the quality of the Louis Seize furniture‡ that he has found there,
and seated in front of the Taverne Riche under the planes he is
finding his Harris tweeds oppressive. Perhaps he is even mopping
the whitish brow under his silver-streaked hair. And I have a
strong itch to write to him that if he wants to find Louis Treize
stuff of the most admirable—perfectly fabulous armoires and
chests—for almost nothing, he should go westward into the
Limousin to ... But nothing shall make me here write that
name....

And so he will go jogging along with ups and downs and plenty
of worries and some satisfactions,[12] the Tory Englishman, running
his head perhaps against fewer walls, perhaps against more, until
I myself cease from those pursuits.... Perhaps he will go on even

*   Ford refers here to *The English Review*, which he edited for fifteen issues from its launch
     in December 1908 to February 1910.
†   'Thus to Revisit—III. The Serious Books', *Piccadilly Review* (6 Nov. 1919), 6: 'for, in
     essence, he was the last of the Tories'; see *Critical Essays* 192–7 (193).
‡   From the period of Louis XVI (1754–93), predominantly neoclassical, a reaction
     against the rococo style of the preceding period.

longer if you, as Marraine,* succeed in conferring upon these works that longevity.... [13]

But out and alas, now you can never write about me again: for it would, wouldn't it? look too much like: You scratch my back and I'll scratch yours![†]

So don't write about Tietjens: write your own projections of the lives around you in terms of your delicate and fierce art. Then you will find me still more

Your grateful and obedient
F. M. F.

New York,
October 13th, 1927.

---

* Godmother (French).
† In fact, Paterson reviewed five more of Ford's books, including the revised version (1935) of his 1911 novel, *Ladies Whose Bright Eyes*.

PART I[1]

CHAPTER I

HE lay staring at the withy binders[*] of his thatch; the[2] grass was infinitely green; his view embraced four counties;[†] the roof was supported by six small oak sapling-trunks, roughly trimmed and brushed from above by apple boughs. French crab-apple![‡] The[3] hut had no sides.[4§]

The Italian proverb says: He who allows the boughs of trees to spread above his roof, invites the doctor daily.[**] Words to that effect. He would have grinned, but that might have been seen.[††]

For a man who never moved, his face was singularly walnut-coloured; his head, indenting the skim-milk white of the pillows should have been a gipsy's,[‡‡] the dark, silvered hair cut extremely

---

* Flexible willow, perhaps the crack-willow.
† Presumably Surrey, Hampshire, East Sussex and West Sussex are meant, since the novel's setting is clearly the area around Bedham, where Ford and Stella lived from September 1920, as discussed in the Introduction.
‡ The French for crab-apple is *pomme sauvage*. The fruit is noted for its astringent or sour flavour. The noun *sauvage* can mean a recluse, an unsociable type, while the adjective crops up in, for instance, Edmund Gosse's description of Siegfried Sassoon to Ottoline Morrell, which she also employed after her first meeting with Sassoon in 1916: 'not exactly farouche [sullen, shy] ... he was more *sauvage*'. See *Ottoline at Garsington* 121.
§ Mark's accommodation recalls that of Ford's wife, Elsie Martindale, when recovering from illness, who wrote in an essay of the 'little shanty' in which she sleeps. Roofed with thatch, it has its sides open, with 'sails, that can be let down as a shelter from wind and rain and snow': 'The Art of Dining', *English Review*, II.i (August 1909), 88–92.
** There is a Corsican proverb which says, in effect, that the doctor comes to the house that the sunlight does not reach. In George Borrow's *The Romany Rye* (London: Dent, 1969) the narrator says to a stranger whom he has awakened: 'I was fearful [...] that you might catch a fever from sleeping under a tree' (134).
†† The first reference to the ambiguous nature of Mark's condition.
‡‡ Cf. the penultimate page of *A Man Could Stand Up –*: 'Gipsies break glasses at their weddings.' It continues 'The bed was against the wall. She did not like the bed to be against the wall. It had been brushed by....' Here, there are no walls, and the roof is

close, the whole face very carefully shaven and completely immobile. The eyes moved, however, with unusual vivacity, all[5] the life of the man being concentrated in them and their lids.

Down the path that had been cut in swathes from the knee-high grass, and came[6] from the stable to the hut, a heavy elderly peasant rolled in his gait. His over-long, hairy arms swung as if he needed an axe or a log or a full sack to make him a complete man. He was broad-beamed, in cord breeches, very tight in the buttock; he wore black leggings, an unbuttoned blue[7] waistcoat, a striped flannel shirt, open at the perspiring neck, and a square, high hat of black felt.

He said:

"Want to be shifted?"

The man in the bed closed his eyelids slowly.

"Ave a droper cider?"

The other again similarly closed his eyes. The standing man supported himself with an immense hand, gorilla-like, by one of the oaken posts.[8*]

"Best droper cider ever I tasted," he said. "Is Lordship give me. Is Lordship sester me: 'Gunning,' e ses, . . . 'the day the vixen got into keeper's coop enclosure . . .'"

He began and slowly completed a very long story, going to prove that English noble landlords preferred foxes to pheasants. Or should! English landowners of the right sort.

Is[9] Lordship would no more ave that vixen killed or so much as flurried, she being gravid like than.... Dreadful work a gravid vixen can do among encoops with pheasant poults.... Have to eat fer six or seven, she have! All a-growing.... So is Lordship sester Gunning....

And then the description of the cider.... Ard! Thet cider was

---

'brushed from above by apple boughs'. Earlier in *A Man Could Stand Up –* Ford alluded to gipsies twice, once to describe a deserter, 'a gipsyfied black-eyed fellow with an immense jeering mouth' (II.ii); and once to stress the need for Valentine to make her own decisions and trust her own judgment. Recalling George Borrow's assertion that 'the gipsies say: "Never trust a young man with grey hair!"' she argues that Christopher 'had only half-grey hair and he was only half-young' (III.i). Third-hand wisdom cannot be allowed to trump that direct and longed-for contact.

* 'Oaken' is isolated and discussed in Ford's *Joseph Conrad* as an example of those English words that connote 'innumerable moral attributes', in this case 'stolidity, resolution, honesty', as well as meaning simply 'made of oak' (214).

arder than a miser's art or'n ole maid's tongue. Body it ad.
Strength it ad. Stans to reason. Ten year cider. Not a drop was
drunk in Lordship's ouse under ten years in cask. Killed three
sheep a week fer his indoor and outdoor servants. An three
hundred pigeons.* The pigeon-cotes is a hundred feet high, an
the pigeons' nesteses in oles in the inside walls. Clap-nets[10†] a ole
wall at a go an takes the squabs. Times is not what they was, but
is Lordship keeps on. An always will!

The man in the bed—Mark Tietjens—continued his own
thought.

Old[11] Gunning lumbered slowly up the path towards the stable,
his hands swinging. The stable was a tile-healed, thatched affair,
no real stable in the North Country sense—a place where the old
mare sheltered among chickens and ducks. There was no tidiness
amongst South Country folk. They hadn't it in them, though
Gunning could bind a tidy thatch and trim a hedge properly. All-
round man.‡ Really an all-round man; he could do a great many
things. He knew all about fox-hunting,[12] pheasant-rearing, wood-
craft, hedging, dyking,§ pig-rearing and the habits of King
Edward** when shooting. Smoking endless great cigars! One
finished, light another, throw away the stub....

---

* A considerable number: still, the largest surviving dovecote, at Culham Manor in
  Oxfordshire, had nesting holes for three thousand pairs of pigeons. In the seventeenth
  century there were said to be some 26,000 dovecotes in Britain, each containing 500–
  1000 birds. See Eric S. Wood, *Historical Britain* (London: The Harvill Press, 1995),
  102.
† A 'clap-net' is a kind of net so constructed that it can be suddenly shut by pulling a
  string, used by both entomologists and fowlers. *OED* cites Fielding's *Joseph Andrews*
  on bird-catching. A large version of this device would be placed over one wall or
  section of a dovecote (in circular buildings, the nest boxes were reached by means of
  a revolving ladder, or potence) and the squabs – unfledged pigeons – taken in large
  numbers.
‡ Ford wrote several times of Ragged Ass Wilson (Ragged Arse in the US edition),
  whose nickname arose from 'the frailty of his nether garments'. 'There was nothing
  he could not do, patiently and to perfection' (*Return* 118). 'Here is, in short, a very
  proper man, an all-round one' (*England* 191). In Bedham Ford and Stella had a helper
  called Standing, 'with his old dialect that was just half Anglo-Saxon and half forgotten
  French words' (*Nightingale* 143).
§ Making – or cleaning out – a dyke or ditch.
** Edward VII (1841–1910), eldest son of Queen Victoria and Prince Albert, succeeded
  to the throne in 1901 and was crowned the following year. A Francophile, he played
  a significant role in securing the Entente Cordiale (1904) and the Anglo-Russian
  agreement of 1907. As Prince of Wales, he was devoted to horse-racing, yachting and
  shooting.

Fox-hunting, the sport of kings with only twenty per cent. of
the danger of war!* He, Mark Tietjens, had never cared for
hunting; now he would never do any more; he had never cared
for pheasant-shooting. He would never do any more. Not
couldn't; wouldn't. *From henceforth*.... [13] It annoyed him that he
had not taken the trouble to ascertain what it was Iago said,
before he had taken Iago's resolution.... *From henceforth he never
would speak word*.... † Something to that effect: but you could not
get that into a blank verse line.

Perhaps Iago had not been speaking blank verse when he had
taken his, Mark Tietjens', resolution.... *Took by the throat the
circumcisèd*[14] *dog and smote him*.... ‡ Good man, Shakespeare! All-
round man in a way, too.§ Probably very like Gunning. Knew
Queen Elizabeth's habits when hunting; also very likely how to
hedge, thatch, break up a deer or a hare or a hog, and how to serve
a writ and write bad French. Lodged with a French family** in
Crutched Friars[15] or the Minories. Somewhere.

The ducks were making a great noise on the pond up the hill.
Old Gunning in the sunlight lumbered between the stable-wall
and the raspberry canes,[16] up-hill. The garden was all up-hill.††
He[17] looked across the grass up at the hedge. When they turned
him round he looked down-hill at the house. Rough, grey stone!

Half-round, he[18] looked across the famous four counties;[19] half-
round,[20] the other way on, he could see up the grass-slope to the
hedge on the road-side. Now[21] he was looking up-hill across the
tops of the hay-grass, over[22] the raspberry canes at the hedge that
Gunning was going to trim. Full of consideration for him, they
were, all the lot of them. For ever thinking of developing his

---

* See R.S. Surtees, *Handley Cross* (1843), Chapter 7: 'it's the sport of kings, the image
of war without its guilt, and only twenty-five per cent of its danger'. See also William
Somerville, 'The Chase' (1735), I.13: 'the sport of kings; / Image of war, without its
guilt.'

† In *Othello* where Iago says, 'Demand me nothing, what you know, you know,/ From
this time forth I never will speak word' (V.ii.309–10).

‡ In V.ii.364–5 Othello speaks these words: 'I took by th' throat the circumcisèd dog, /
And smote him thus.' At this point, he stabs himself and dies almost immediately.

§ Ford also invoked Shakespeare in connection with Ragged Ass Wilson, who was dark
with 'a little beard like Shakespeare's and that poet's eyes' (*Return* 118).

** The Huguenot Mountjoy family with whom Shakespeare lodged between 1603 and
1605: see Charles Nicholl's *The Lodger: Shakespeare on Silver Street* (London: Allen
Lane, 2007).

†† 'Up-Hill' is one of the best-known poems by Christina Rossetti, Ford's aunt.

possible interests. He[23] didn't[24] need it. He had interests enough.

Up the pathway that was above and beyond[25] the hedge on a grass-slope went the Elliott children, a lanky girl of ten, with very long, corn-coloured hair, a fat boy of five, unspeakably[26] dirty. The girl too long and thin in[27] the legs and ankles, her hair limp. War-starvation in early years. . . . * Well, that was not his fault.[28] He had given the nation the transport it needed; they should have found the stuff. They[29] hadn't, so the children had long, thin legs and protruding wrists on pipe-stem arms.[30] All that generation!. . . † No fault of his. He had managed the nation's transport[31] as it should be managed. His department had. His own Department, made[32] by himself from junior temporary clerk to senior permanent official, from[33] the day of his entrance thirty years ago[34] to the day of his resolution never more to speak word.

Nor yet stir a finger. He had to be in this world, in this nation. Let them care for him; he[35] was done with them. . . . He knew the sire and dam of every horse from Eclipse to Perlmutter.‡ That was enough for him. They let him read all[36] that could be read about racing. He had interests enough!§

The ducks on the pond up the hill continued[37] to make a great noise, churning boisterously the water[38] with their wings and squawking. If they had been hens there would have been something the matter—a dog chasing them. Ducks did not signify; they went mad, contagiously. Like nations and[39] all the cattle of a county.

Gunning, lumbering past the raspberry canes, took a bud or so and squeezed the pale things between finger and thumb, then

---

* There were, inevitably, shortages of transport and shipping and a rise in food prices for the working class estimated at 60 per cent in the first two years of the war. Bread rationing was introduced in February 1917, sugar rationing in December 1917, while rationing of meat and fats began in February 1918. Some historians maintain that nutritional levels rose even though the total food supply declined in the war years. For a useful contemporary account, see C.S. Peel, *How We Lived Then, 1914–1918* (London: John Lane The Bodley Head, 1929), Chapters VI–VII and appendices.

† Pushkin, 'Poltava' (1829). Cf. Ford's poem, 'The Three-Ten', in *Songs from London* (1910) and the epigraph to *Ancient Lights* (London: Chapman & Hall, 1911), ascribed to Pushkin, 'Sardanapalus'. See Anat Vernitski, 'The Complexity of Truth: Ford and the Russians', in *Ford Madox Ford's Literary Contacts*, ed. Paul Skinner (Amsterdam and New York: Rodopi, 2007), 101–11 (109–10).

‡ Eclipse was one of the most famous racehorses of all time; Perlmutter . . . was not. This may be a misremembering of Persimmon: see the Introduction.

§ In *Some Do Not . . .* I.iv Christopher Tietjens too has sometimes passed afternoons in golf clubhouses 'studying the pedigrees and forms of racehorses'.

examined his thumb. Looking[40] for maggots, no doubt.[41] Pale
green leaves the raspberry had; a fragile plant amongst the
robuster rosaceae. That was not war-starvation[42] but race. *Their*
commissariat* was efficient enough, but they were presumably
not[43] gross feeders. Gunning began to brush the hedge, sharp,
brushing blows with[44] his baggin hook.† There was still far too
much bramble amongst the quickset; in a week the hedge would
be unsightly again.

That was part of their consideration again! They[45] kept the
hedge low so that he should be amused by passers-by[46] on the
path, though they would have preferred to let it grow high so[47]
that the passers-by should not see into the orchard.... Well, he
had seen passers-by. More than they knew.... [48] What the[49] hell
was Sylvia's game? And that old ass Edward Campion's?... Well,
he was[50] not going to interfere. There was, however, undoubtedly
something up!... Marie Léonie—formerly Charlotte!—knew[51]
neither of them[52] by sight, though she had undoubtedly seen
them peering[53] over the hedge!

They—it was more of their considerateness—had contrived a
shelf[54] on the left corner-post of his shelter. So that birds should
amuse him! A[55] hedge-sparrow,‡ noiseless and quaker-grey,§
ghost-like, was on this shelf. A thin, under-vitalized being that
you never saw. It[56] flitted, hiding itself deep in hedge-rows. He
had always thought[57] of it as an American bird: a[58] voiceless

---

* A department, especially military, for the supply of provisions, particularly food. By
  the mid-1920s, the Soviet usage – more generally, a government department – would
  also have been increasingly familiar. 'The Soviet Republic loomed enormously large
  in the Paris of those days [early 1920s]' (*Nightingale* 301).
† To bag or badge is to cut wheat, peas or beans with a reaping-hook (Ford presumably
  mimics Sussex dialect pronunciation, though the later Knopf edition changes 'baggin'
  to 'bagging'). There is some slight doubt as to whether this would be strong enough to
  cut the woodier parts of a hedge, which may have required a billhook.
‡ Not in fact a member of the sparrow family, the dunnock or hedge sparrow has an
  unusually complicated private life, its mating system marked by a good deal of partner
  swapping. See Mark Cocker and Richard Mabey, *Birds Britannica* (London: Chatto &
  Windus, 2005). In *Some Do Not . . .* I.iv Tietjens is straightfacedly referred to as being
  'interested in the domestic affairs of the cuckoo'.
§ 'Quaker' or 'quakerish' usually signifies subdued colours and there is a term, 'quaker-
  bird', applied to various birds with partly or wholly grey or brown plumage. James Joyce
  uses the term 'quakergrey' in the 'Circe' chapter of *Ulysses* (London: The Bodley Head,
  rev. edn, 1969), 626, which Ford read (and reviewed) in 1922: *Critical Essays* 218–27.
  Ford himself used it in *Mister Bosphorus and the Muses* (London: Duckworth, 1923),
  12, 22.

nightingale, thin,[59] long, thin-billed, almost without markings as becomes a bird that seldom sees the sun but lives in the twilight[60] of deep hedges. American because it ought to wear a scarlet letter. He only knew of Americans because of a book he had once read— a[61] woman like a hedge-sparrow, creeping furtive in shadows and getting into trouble with a priest.*

This[62] desultory, slim bird, obviously Puritan,[63] inserted its thin bill into the dripping that Gunning had put on the shelf for the tom-tits. The riotous tom-tit, the bottle-tit, the great-tit,[64] all that family love dripping. The hedge-sparrow obviously did not; the dripping on that warmish June day had become oleaginous; the hedge-sparrow, its bill all greased, mumbled its upper and lower mandible[65] but took no more dripping. It looked at Mark's eyes. Because these regarded it motionlessly, it uttered a long warning note and flitted, noiseless, into[66] invisibility. All hedge things ignore you whilst you move on and do not regard them.† The moment you stay still and fix your eyes on them they warn the rest of the hedge and flit off. This hedge-sparrow no doubt had its young within earshot. Or the warning might have been just co-operative.

Marie Léonie, *née* Riotor, was coming up the steps and then the path. He could hear her[67] breathing. She stood beside him, shapeless in her long pinafore of figured[68] cotton, and breathed heavily, holding[69] a plate of soup and saying:

"*Mon pauvre homme! Mon pauvre homme! Ce qu'ils ont fait de toi!*"[70]‡

She began a breathless discourse in French. She was of the large, blond, Norman type; in the middle forties, her extremely fair hair very voluminous and noticeable. She had lived with Mark Tietjens for twenty years now, but she had always refused to speak a word of English, having an invincible scorn for both language and people of her adopted country.[71]

---

*   In Nathaniel Hawthorne's *The Scarlet Letter*; Ford is probably referring to Chapters XVI–XIX, where Hester and Pearl go into the 'primeval forest', 'beyond the pale of Puritan law', as Brian Harding phrases it in his 1990 Oxford World Classics edition.
†   Cf. Ford, 'The Work of W.H. Hudson', *English Review*, II.i (April 1909); reprinted in *Critical Essays*, 65–71 (65).
‡   Translated a little later in the text: 'My poor man! My poor man! What they have made of you!' (French).

Her discourse poured on. She had set the little tray with the plate of reddish-yellowish soup on a flat shelf of wood that turned out on a screw from underneath the bed; in the soup was a shining clinical thermometer that she moved and regarded from time to time, beside the plate a glass syringe, graduated. She said that Ils—*They*—had combined to render her soup of vegetables uneatable. They would not give her *navets de Paris* but round ones, like buttons; they contrived that the carrots should be *pourris** at their bottom ends; the leeks were of the consistency of wood. They were determined that he should not have vegetable soup because they wanted him to have meat juice. They were anthropophagi. Nothing but meat, meat, meat! That girl!...

She had always in the Gray's Inn Road[†] had Paris turnips from Jacopo's in Old Compton Street.[‡] There was no reason why you should not grow *navets de Paris* in this soil. The Paris turnip was barrel-shaped, round, round, round like an adorable little pig till it turned into its funny little tail. That was a turnip to amuse you; to change and employ your thoughts. *Ils*—he and she—were incapable of having their thoughts changed by a turnip.

Between sentences she ejaculated from time to time:

"My poor man! What they have made of you!"

Her volubility flowed over Mark like a rush[72] of water over a grating, only a phrase or so now and then coming to his attention. It was not unpleasant; he liked his woman. She had a cat that she made abstain from meat on Friday. In[73] the Gray's Inn Road that had been easier, in a large room decorated with innumerable miniatures and silhouettes representing members of the Riotor family and its branches. Mme Riotor *mère* and Mme Riotor *grand'mère* too had been miniature painters, and Marie Léonie possessed some astonishingly white statuary by the distinguished sculptor Monsieur Casimir-Bar,[74§] a lifelong friend of her

---

* Rotten (French).

† '[A]n important but unattractive thoroughfare' according to the 1900 Baedeker, running from Holborn to Euston Road. At the beginning of *Some Do Not* ... Tietjens and Macmaster are living in Gray's Inn Road.

‡ Probably fictional. In 1895 there were three importers of foreign produce in Old Compton Street and, twenty years later, the Italian Produce Co. Ltd. and Edouard Robinson (A.O. Morandi, Proprietor) could be found there. Further afield, in Cross Lane, Hugo Salvarelli offered 'Paris mushrooms and other vegetables'.

§ Rather than a specific figure, 'Casimir-Bar' seems to represent a familiar kind of uninspired, pseudo-classical statuary common in nineteenth-century France. As far as the

family who had only never been decorated because of a conspiracy. So he had a great contempt for decorations and the decorated. Marie Léonie had been accustomed to repeat the voluminous opinions of Monsieur Casimir-Bar on the subject of decorations at great length on occasion. Since he, Mark, had been honoured by[75] his sovereign she had less frequently recited them. She admitted that the democracy of to-day had not the sterling value that had distinguished democrats[76] of the day of her parents, so it might be better to *caser* oneself—to find a niche amongst those whom the State distinguished.

The noise of her voice, which was deep-chested and not unpleasing, went on. Mark regarded her with the ironic indulgence that you accord to a child, but indeed, when he had been still in harness, it had rested him always to come home to her as[77] he had done every Thursday and Monday, and not infrequently on a Wednesday when there had been no racing. It had rested him to come home from a world of incompetent imbeciles and to hear this brain comment on that world. She had views on virtue, pride, downfalls, human careers, the habits of cats, fish, the clergy, diplomats, soldiers, women of easy virtue, Saint Eustachius,[*] President Grévy,[†] the purveyors of comestibles, custom-house officers, pharmacists, Lyons silk weavers, the keepers of boarding-houses, garotters, chocolate-manufacturers, sculptors other than M. Casimir-Bar, the lovers of married women, housemaids. . . . Her mind, in fact, was like a cupboard, stuffed, packed with the most incongruous materials, tools, vessels and debris.[78] Once the door was opened you never knew what would tumble out or be followed by what. That was restful to Mark as foreign travel might have been—only he had never

---

actual name is concerned, a 'Casimir's bar' is mentioned in Emil Zola's *Germinal* (1885), ed. and trans. Peter Collier (Oxford: Oxford University Press, 1993), 152.

[*] Or Saint Eustace, originally a Roman general named Placidus, said to have been converted by a vision of a stag with a crucifix between its antlers, the subject of a famous painting by Antonio Pisanello (?1440, National Gallery). The patron saint of hunters and of those in difficult situations, his saint's day is 20 September.

[†] François Paul Jules Grévy (1807–91) opposed Napoleon III and was elected President of the Republic in 1879; he resigned in 1887 after a financial scandal. Ford wrote of him in *A History Of Our Own Times*, ed. Solon Beinfeld and Sondra J. Stang (Manchester: Carcanet, 1989), that he was 'almost the model of what the president of the French Republic or the sovereign of any constitutional monarchy should be' (67–8).

been abroad except when his father, before his accession to
Groby, had lived in Dijon* for his children's education. That was
how he knew French.

Her conversation had another quality that continually amused
him: she always ended it with the topic with which she had
chosen to begin. Thus, to-day having chosen to begin with *navets
de Paris*, with Paris turnips she would end, and it amused him to
observe how on each occasion she would bring the topic back.
She might be concluding a long comment on ironclads and have
to get back suddenly to custards because the door-bell rang while
her maid was out, but accomplish the transition she[79] would
before she answered the bell. Otherwise she was frugal, shrewd,
astonishingly cleanly[80] and healthy.

Whilst she was giving him his soup, inserting the glass syringe
in his lips at half minute intervals which she timed by her wrist-
watch, she was talking about furniture.... *Ils* would not let her
apply to the species of rabbit-hutches in the salon a varnish that
she imported from Paris; Monsieur her brother-in-law had really
exhibited[81] when she had actually varnished a truly discreditable
chair—had exhibited a distraction that had really filled her with
amusement. It was possible that the fashion of the day was for
furniture of decrepitude, or gross forms. That *they* would not let
her place in the salon the newly-gilt arm-chair of her late mother
or the sculptural group representing Niobe† and some of her
offspring by the late Monsieur Casimir-Bar, or the overmantel
clock that was an exact reproduction in bronze of the Fountain
of the Médicis in the gardens of the Luxembourg at Paris—that
was a matter of taste. *Elle* might very well feel umbrage that she,
Marie Léonie, should possess articles of such acknowledged prestige. For what could be more unapproachable than a Second
Empire fauteuil newly gilt and maintained, she could assure the
world, at such a pitch of glitter as dazzled the eyes? *Elle* might very

---

* '[W]here magic cookery begins', in *Provence*, ed. John Coyle (Manchester: Carcanet,
   2009), 84, or 'reaches its Mecca' (*Provence* 305). In *A Mirror To France* it had been
   'Toulouse and Périgord for cookery, Dijon and the Côte du Rhône for wines' (86). In
   Some Do Not . . . II.iii the stay in Dijon is a critical factor in the discussion of whether
   Valentine could be Mr Tietjens' daughter.
† In mythology, wife to Amphion and mother of (usually) six sons and six daughters,
   who boasted that her fecundity placed her on a par with the Titaness Leto, where-
   upon Leto's children, Artemis and Apollo, killed all of Niobe's children.

well feel umbrage when you considered that the skirt that she wore when gardening was ... Well, in short was what it was! Nevertheless, in that skirt she allowed herself to be seen by the clergyman. But why did *Il*, who was admittedly a man of honour and sensibility and reputed[82] to know all the things of this world and perhaps of the next—why did *He* join in the infinitely stupid conspiracy against the work of the great genius Casimir-Bar? She, Marie Léonie, could understand that He, in his difficult situation, would not wish to give permission to install in the salon works at which Elle[83] took umbrage because her possessions did not include objects of art which all the world acknowledged to be of classic rank, not to mention the string of pearls which she, Marie Léonie, Riotor by birth, owed to the generosity of him, Mark, and her own economies. And other objects of value and taste. That was reasonable. If your woman is poorly *dot*-ed ... Let us call it *dot*-ed ... because certainly she, Marie Léonie, was not one to animadvert upon those in situations of difficulty.... It would ill become her so to do. Nevertheless, a great period of years of honesty, frugality, regularity of life and cleanliness.... And she asked Mark if he had ever seen in *her* parlour traces of mud such as on wet days she had certainly observed[84] in the salon of a certain person.... And certain revelations she could make as to the condition[85] of a cupboard under the stairs and the state to be observed behind certain presses in the kitchen. But if you have not had experience in the control of domestics, what would you?... Nevertheless, a stretch of years passed in the state of housewifeliness such as she had already adumbrated upon gave one the right to comment—of course with delicacy—upon the *ménage* of a young person even though her delicate situation might avert from her comment of an unchristian nature as to certain other facts. It did, however, seem to her, Marie Léonie,[86] that to appear before a clergyman in a skirt decorated with no less than three visible *taches* of petrol, wearing gloves encrusted with mud as you encrust a truffle with paste before baking it under the cinders—and holding, of all implements, a common gardening-trowel.... And to laugh and joke with him!... Surely the situation called for a certain—let them call it, retirement of demeanour. She was far from according to the Priest as such the[87] extravagant privileges to which he[88] laid claim. The late

Monsieur Casimir-Bar was accustomed to say that, if we accorded to our *soi-disant* spiritual advisers all that they would take, we should lie upon a bed that had neither sheets, *eidredons*, pillows, bolsters, nor settle. And she, Marie Léonie, was inclined to agree with Monsieur Casimir-Bar, though, as one of the heroes of the barricades in 1848,* he was apt to be a little extreme in his tenets. Still a vicar is in England a functionary of the State and as such should be received with a certain modesty and reserve. Yet she,[89] Marie Léonie, formerly Riotor, her mother having been born Lavigne-Bourdreau[†] and having in consequence a suspicion of Huguenot blood, so that she, Marie Léonie, might be expected to know how the Protestant clergy should be received—she then, Marie Léonie, from the little window on the side of the stairs, had distinctly seen *Elle* lay one hand on the shoulder of that cler-gyman and point—point, mind you, with the *trowel*—to the open front door and say—she had distinctly heard the words: "Poor man, if you have hunger you will find Mr. Tietjens in the dining-room. He is just eating a sandwich. It's hungry weather!" . . . That was six months ago, but Marie Léonie's ears still tingled at the words and the gesture. A trowel! To point with a *trowel*; *pensez y*! If a trowel why not a *main de fer*, a dust-pan? Or a vessel even more homely! . . . And Marie Léonie chuckled.

Her grandmother Bourdreau remembered a crockery-merchant of the ambulating sort who had[90] once filled one of those implements—a *vase de nuit*[‡]—but of course new, with milk and had offered the whole gratuitously to[91] any passer-by who would drink the milk. A young woman called Laborde accepted his challenge there in the market-place of Noisy-Lebrun. She had[92] lost her fiancé, who found the gesture exaggerated. But he was a farceur, that crockery-dealer!

---

* The 'Year of Revolutions' saw the abdication of Louis-Philippe, France's 'Citizen King' (who escaped to England under the name of 'Mr Smith' and died in Surrey two years later). During the night of 24 February some 1500 barricades were erected in Paris, according to Victor Hugo, a Deputy at that time and an active participant.

† Lavigne was the name of the couple who ran Le Negre de Toulouse, a favourite Mont-parnasse café; Ford and Bowen's large Alsatian was named Toulouse and was a present from M. Lavigne. The Lavignes and their staff were portrayed in a notable painting by Stella Bowen completed in 1927: see Joseph Wiesenfarth, *Ford Madox Ford and the Regiment of Women* (Madison, WI: University of Wisconsin Press, 2005), Plate 5.

‡ Chamber pot (French).

She drew from the pocket of her pinafore several folded pages of a newspaper and from under the bed a double picture-frame—two frames hinged together so that they would close. She inserted a sheet of the paper between the two frames and then hung the whole on a piece of picture wire that depended from the roof-tree beneath the thatch. Two braces of picture-wire, too, came from the supporting posts, to right and left. They held the picture-frames motionless and a little inclined towards Mark's face. She was agreeable to look at, stretching up her arms. She lifted his torso with great strength and infinite solicitude, propped it a little with the pillows and looked to see that his eyes fell on the printed sheet. She said:

"You can see well, like that?"

His eyes took in the fact that he was to read of the Newbury Summer Meeting and the one at Newcastle. He closed them twice to signify Yes! The tears came into hers. She murmured:

"Mon pauvre homme! Mon pauvre homme! What they have done to you!" She drew from another pocket in her pinafore a flask of eau-de-Cologne and a wad of cotton wool. With that, moistened, she wiped even more solicitously his face and then his thin, mahogany hands, which she uncovered. She had the air of women in France when they change the white satin clothes and wash the faces of favourite Virgins at the church doors in August.

Then she stood back and apostrophized him. He took in that the King's filly had won the Berkshire Foal plate and the horse of a friend the Seaton Delaval Handicap, at Newcastle.* Both might have been expected. He had meant to go to the Newcastle meeting this year and give Newbury a by. The last year he had gone racing he[93] had done rather well at Newbury, so he had then thought he would try Newcastle for a change, and, whilst he was there, take a look at Groby and see what that bitch Sylvia was doing with Groby.[94] Well, that was done with. They would presumably bury him at Groby.

She said in deep, rehearsed tones:

---

* On Thursday 23 June 1927, at Newbury, the Berkshire Foal Plate was won by George V's filly, Scuttle, ridden by Joseph Childs, at 4/5. (The same horse and rider triumphed in May the following year in the One Thousand Guineas at Newmarket, the king's first and only Classic winner.) The Seaton Delaval Handicap was won by Carsebreck. For more on this, see the Introduction.

"My Man!"—she might almost have well said: "My Deity!"—
"What sort of life is this we lead here? Was there ever anything
so singular and unreasonable? If we sit to drink a cup of tea, the
cup may at any moment be snatched from our mouths; if we
recline upon a divan—at any moment the divan may go. I do not
comment on this that you lie by night as by day for ever here in
the open air, for I understand that it is by your desire and consent
that you lie here and I will never exhibit aversion from that which
you desire and that to which you consent. But cannot you bring
it about that we should inhabit a house of some reason, one more
suited to human beings of this age, and one that is less of a procession of goods and chattels? You can bring that about. You are
all-powerful here. I do not know what are your resources. It was
never your habit to tell me. You kept me in comfort. Never did I
express a desire that you did not satisfy, though it is true that my
desires were always reasonable. So I know nothing, though I read
once in a paper that you were a man of extravagant riches, and
that can hardly all have vanished, for there can have been fewer
men of as great a frugality, and you were always fortunate and
moderate in your wagers. So I know nothing and I would scorn
to ask of these others, for that would imply doubt of your trust in
me. I do not doubt that you have made arrangements for my
future comfort, and I am in no uncertainty of the continuance of
those arrangements. It is not material fears that I have. But all
this appears to be a madness. Why are we here? What is the
meaning of all this? Why do you inhabit this singular erection? It
may be that the open air is of necessity for your malady. I do not
believe that you lived in perpetual currents of air in your chambers, though I never saw them. But on the days you gave to me
you had everything of the most comfortable and you seemed
contented with my arrangements. And your brother and his
woman appear so mad in all the other affairs of life that they may
well be mad in this also. Why then will you not end it? You have
the power. You are all-powerful here. Your brother will spring
from one corner to the other of this lugubrious place in order to
anticipate your slightest wish. Elle, too!"

Stretching out her hands, she had the air of a Greek woman
who[95] invoked a deity, she was so large and fair and her hair was
so luxuriantly blond. And indeed, to her, in his mystery and

silence he had the air of a deity who could discharge unthinkable darts and vouchsafe unimaginable favours. Though all their circumstances had changed, that had not changed, so that even his immobility enhanced his mystery. In all their life together, not merely here, he had been silent whilst she had talked. On the two regular days of the week on which he had been used to visit her, from the moment when she would open her door exactly at seven in the evening and see him in his bowler hat with his carefully rolled umbrella and with his[96] racing glasses slung diagonally across him to the moment when, next morning at half-past ten, she would brush his bowler and hand him that and his umbrella, he would hardly speak a word—he would speak such few words as to give the idea of an absolute taciturnity,* whilst she entertained him with an unceasing flow of talk and of comments on the news of the Quartier—of the French colonists of that part of London, or on the news in the French papers. He would remain seated on a hard chair, bending slightly forward, with, round the corners of his mouth, little creases that suggested an endless, indulgent smile. Occasionally he would suggest that she should put half a sovereign upon a horse; occasionally he would bring her an opulent present, heavy gold bangles floridly chased and set with large emeralds, sumptuous furs, expensive travelling trunks for when she had visited Paris or went to the seaside in the autumn. That sort of thing. Once he had bought her a complete set of the works of Victor Hugo† bound in purple morocco and all the works that had been illustrated by Gustave Doré, in green calf;‡ once a hoof of a racehorse, trained in France, set in silver

---

*   The notion of 'absolute taciturnity' will shortly be applied to Christopher also – with a slight qualification – 'at least as self-contained if not as absolutely taciturn as Mark himself' (I.ii) – as it has been earlier, in *Some Do Not* ... (I.i); Christopher's laconic response to questions also serves to remind Mark, after thirty years in 'the vociferous south', that 'there were taciturnities still' (*Some Do Not* ... II.iii). In *The Good Soldier*, when Edward receives the fatal telegram from Nancy Rufford, he regards it 'without emotion', handing it to Dowell 'in complete silence' (162).

†   Perhaps the Hetzel-Quantin edition of 1880–92, in 46 volumes, limited to a hundred sets. The binding of a set recently offered for sale was described as '3/4 red crushed levant', a kind of morocco leather.

‡   Gustav Doré illustrated dozens of books but, in 1870, Cassell, Petter & Galpin published *The Doré Gallery*, in two folio volumes, with 249 plates from works including the Bible, Milton's poems, *Don Quixote*, La Fontaine's *Fables* and all three volumes of Dante's *Divine Comedy*.

in the form of an inkstand.* On her forty-first birthday—though
she had no idea how he had ascertained that it was her forty-first
birthday—he had given her a string of pearls and had taken her
to a hotel at Brighton kept by an ex-prize-fighter.† He had told
her to wear the pearls at dinner, but to be careful of them because
they had cost five hundred pounds. He asked her once about her
investment of her savings,[97] and when she had told him that she
was investing in French *rentes viagères*‡ he had told her that he
could do better than that for her, and afterwards from time to
time he had told her of odd but very profitable ways of investing
small sums.

In this way, because his gifts[98] filled her with rapture on
account of their opulence and weightiness, he had assumed for
her the aspect by degrees of a godhead who could bless—and
possibly blast§—inscrutably. For many years after he had first
picked her up in the Edgware Road outside the old Apollo** she
had regarded him with suspicion, since he was a man and it is the
nature of men to treat women with treachery, lust and meanness.
Now she regarded herself as the companion of a godhead, secure
and immune from the evil workings of Fortune—as if she had
been seated on the shoulder of one of Jove's eagles, beside his
throne. The Immortals had been known to choose human

---

* In *No More Parades* II.ii Sylvia recalls her visit to Mark's apartment: 'it had for its chief
  decoration the hoofs of several deceased race-winners, mounted as ink-stands, as pen-
  racks, as paper-weights'.
† An earlier ex-prizefighter in a domestic setting is, of course, Parry, 'the Bermondsey
  light middle-weight' detailed to keep the Reverend Duchemin within (physically
  violent) bounds in *Some Do Not* . . . , while all three of Duchemin's curates have 'the
  physiques rather of prize-fighters than of clergy' (I.v). Brighton has also been
  mentioned in connection with Sir John Robertson, who 'had a harem, so it was said,
  in an enormous house at Brighton or somewhere' (*Some Do Not* . . . II.i).
‡ Life annuities (French).
§ Generally used by Ford as a cue for Wyndham Lewis, the Vorticist movement and its
  organ, *Blast: A Review of the Great English Vortex* (June 1914), which famously listed
  those to be blessed or blasted, mainly individuals, though France – and England – were
  both blessed *and* blasted. Ford reviewed both issues of *Blast*, and part of his 'The
  Saddest Story' (later *The Good Soldier*) was published in the first issue. In *A Man Could
  Stand Up* – Valentine, trying to hear who is on the telephone, 'got back a title. . . . Lady
  something or other. . . . It might have been Blastus' (I.i.).
** Possibly alluding to the Metropolitan Theatre at 207 Edgware Road. Originally a
  public house dating from 1524, it was rebuilt in 1836 as a concert room, and again in
  1862. On Easter Monday 1864 it reopened as the Metropolitan Music Hall. Rebuilt
  again in 1897, it survived until demolition in 1963. Mark's memory would, then, pre-
  date 1897.

companions: when they had so done fortunate indeed had been the lot of the chosen. Of them she felt herself to be one.

Even his seizure had not deprived her of her sense of his wide-spreading and inscrutable powers, and she could not rid herself of the conviction that if he would, he could talk, walk and perform the feats of strength of a Hercules. It was impossible not to think so; the strength[99] of his glance was undiminished, and it was the dark glance[100] of a man, proud, vigorous, alert[101] and commanding. And the mysterious nature and occurrence of the seizure itself only confirmed her subconscious conviction. The fit had[102] come so undramatically that although the several pompous and, for her, nearly imbecile, English physicians who had been called in to attend on him, agreed that some sort of fit must have visited him as he lay in his bed, that had done nothing to change her mind. Indeed, even when her own Doctor, Drouant-Rouault,* asserted with certitude and knowledge that this was a case of fulminant hemiplegia† of a characteristic sort, though her reason accepted his conclusion, her subconscious intuition remained the same. Doctor Drouant-Rouault was a sensible man; that he had proved by pointing out the anatomical excellence of the works of sculpture by Monsieur Casimir-Bar and agreeing that only a conspiracy of rivals could have prevented his arriving at the post of President of the École des Beaux Arts.‡ He was, then, a man of sense and his reputation amongst the French tradesmen of the Quarter stood very high: she[103] had never herself needed the attentions of a doctor. But if you needed a doctor, obviously

* Probably pure invention, though Charles Drouant, a native of Alsace, opened his restaurant in Place Gaillon in 1880. It was patronised by Zola, Renoir, Rodin, Monet, Toulouse-Lautrec and others. The winner of the Prix Goncourt has been decided at an annual dinner upstairs since 1914. Ford mentions the restaurant in 'Boston', one of his 'Portraits of Cities' essays, first published in *Ford Madox Ford and the City*, ed. Sara Haslam (Amsterdam and New York: Rodopi, 2005), 217. The painter Georges Rouault concentrated mainly on graphic art between 1917 and 1927. 'Rouault' was also the maiden name of Emma Bovary: Ford's admiration for Flaubert remained constant, not least because it was inextricably entwined with his memories of Joseph Conrad. He claimed to have read Flaubert's *Education Sentimentale* fourteen times: *Henry James* (London: Martin Secker, 1914), 136; *Thus To Revisit* 159; 'Pont...ti...pri...ith', in *War Prose*, ed. Max Saunders (Manchester: Carcanet, 1999), 35.
† A paralysis of one side of the body that comes on very rapidly, a stroke.
‡ School of fine arts. In 1863 the Académie Royale school was renamed the École des Beaux Arts. The basis of the teaching was the art of ancient Greece and Rome. Many illustrious figures passed through the École up to the period of early Impressionism.

you went to a Frenchman and acquiesced in what he said.

But although she acquiesced in words to others, and indeed to herself, she could not convince herself in her *for intérieur*,* nor indeed had she arrived at that amount of exterior conviction without some argument at least. She had pointed out, not only to Doctor Drouant-Rouault, but she had even conceived it to be her duty to point out to the English practitioners to whom she would not otherwise have spoken, that the man lying there in her bed was a North-countryman, from Yorkshire, where men were of an inconceivable obstinacy. She had asked them to consider that it was not unusual for Yorkshire brothers and sisters or other relatives to live for decades together in the same house and never address a word to each other, and she had pointed out that she knew Mark Tietjens to be of an unspeakable determination. She knew it from their lifelong intimacy. She had never, for instance, been able to make him change his diet by an ounce in weight, or the shaking of a pepper-pot as to flavour—not once in twenty years during which she had cooked for him. She pleaded with these gentlemen to consider as a possibility that the terms of the Armistice were of such a nature as to make a person of Mark's determination and idiosyncrasies resolve to withdraw himself for ever from all human contacts, and that if he did so determine nothing would cause him to change his determination. The last word he had spoken had been whilst one of his colleagues at the Ministry had been telephoning to tell her, for Mark's information, what the terms of the Armistice were. At the news, which she had had to give him over her shoulder, he had made from the bed some remark.—He had been recovering from double pneumonia at the time.—What the remark had been she could not exactly repeat; she was almost certain that it had been to the effect—in English—that he would never speak again. But she was aware that her own predilection was sufficient to bias her hearing. She had felt herself, at the news that the Allies did not intend to pursue the Germans into their own country—she had felt herself as if she could say to the High Permanent Official[104] at the other end[105] of the telephone that she would never speak word to him and his race again. It was the first thing that had come into her

* Innermost space, heart of hearts (French).

mind, and no doubt it had been the first thing to come into Mark's.

So she had pleaded with the doctors. They had paid practically no attention to her, and she was aware that that was very likely due to her ambiguous position as the companion for long, without[106] any legal security, of a man whom they considered as now in[107] no position to continue his protection of her. That she in no way resented; it was in the nature of English male humanity. The Frenchman had naturally listened with deference, bowing even a little. But he had remarked with a sort of deaf obstinacy: Madame must consider that the occasion of the stroke only made more certain that it *was* a stroke. And that argument to her, as Frenchwoman, must seem almost incontrovertible. For[108] the betrayal of France by her Allies at the supreme moment of triumph had been a crime, the news of which might well cause the end of the world to seem desirable.

CHAPTER II

SHE continued to stand beside him and to apostrophize him until it should be time to turn round the framed newspaper so that he could read the other side of the sheet. What he read first contained the remarks of various writers on racing. That he took in rapidly, as if it were a mere *bonne bouche*.[1]* She knew that he regarded with contempt the opinions of all writers on racing, but the two who wrote in this particular sheet with less contempt than the others. But the serious reading began when she turned the page. Here were endless, serried columns of the names of race-horses, their jockeys and entrants at various race-meetings, their ages, ancestries, former achievements. That he would peruse with minute attention that would[2] cost him just under an hour. She would have liked to stay with him whilst he read it, for the intensive study of matters connected with race-horses had[3] always been their single topic of communion. She had spent almost sentimental hours leaning over the back of his armchair reading news of the turf simultaneously with himself, and the compliments he had been used to pay her over her predictions[4] of Form, if they were the only compliments he ever paid her, had filled her with the warm pleasure and confusion that she might have felt had he addressed the same compliments to her on the subject of her person. She did not indeed need compliments from him as to her person; his complete contentment with her sufficed—but she had rejoiced in, and now missed, those[5] long, quiet times of communing. She remarked to him indeed that Scuttle[6] had won her race as she had several days ago predicted because there had been no other competitors in any way of the same class as the filly, but there had been no answering, half-contemptuous grunt of acquiescence such as in the old days had been hers.

---

* A tasty morsel, a titbit (French). Ford uses the phrase also in *The Good Soldier* 30; *No Enemy* 52; and *Some Do Not . . .* II.iv.

An aeroplane had droned overhead[7] and she had stepped out to look up at the bright toy that, shone upon by the sun, progressed slowly across the pellucid sky. When she went in, in answer to the double closing of his lids that meant that he acquiesced in the turning of his news-sheet, she unhitched one brace from the oaken post to his right and, walking round his bed, attached the brace on the post to his left, doing the reverse with[8] the brace that had gone to the left. In that way the picture-frames turned completely round and exhibited the other side of the newspaper-frame.[9]

It was a contrivance that daily excited[10] her annoyance and, as usual, she expressed herself. This was another instance of the madness of They—of her brother-in-law and his woman. Why had they not obtained one of those ingenious machines, like an arm of bright brass supporting a reading-shelf of agreeably varnished mahogany, that you clamped to a bedstead and could adjust at any angle? Why indeed had They not procured one of those huts for the tuberculous that she had seen depicted in a catalogue?[11] Such huts could be painted in agreeable stripes of green and vermilion, thus presenting a gay appearance, and they could be turned upon a pivot so as to meet the rays of the sun or avoid the currents of air caused by the wind?* What could be the explanation of this mad and gross structure? A thatched roof supported on posts without walls![12] Did they desire him to be blown out of his bed by the draughts? Did They merely desire to enrage her? Or could it be that their resources were of such exiguity that they could not afford the conveniences of modern civilization?

She might well have thought that to be the case. But how could it, in[13] face of the singular behaviour of Monsieur her *beau-frère* in the matter of the statuary of Casimir-Bar the great sculptor?[14] She had offered to contribute to the expenses of the establishment even at the cost of the sacrifice[15] of what she held most dear, and how singular had been his[16] behaviour. During their absence on the occasion of the great sale at Wingham

---

* Such as those at Pendyffryn Hall in Caernarvonshire, opened in 1900. See Linda Bryder, *Below the Magic Mountain: A Social History of Tuberculosis in Twentieth-Century Britain* (Oxford: Clarendon Press, 1988), 51, for a photograph of the open-air shelters at Papworth Village Settlement, founded in 1917.

Priory* she had ordered the amiable if gross Gunning and the semi-imbecile carpenter to descend from her room to the salon that admirable *Niobe* and the admittedly incomparable *Thetis informing Neptune of the death of a Son-in-law*, not to mention her newly re-gilt Second Empire fauteuil. And[17] in that gloomy wilderness how had they not shone in their respective whiteness and auriference!† The pose of the *Niobe* how passionate, the action of the *Thetis* how spirited and how at the same time pathetic! And she had seized the opportunity to varnish with a special preparation imported from the City of the Arts the only chair in the salon that was not too rough to be susceptible of varnish even though it came from Paris herself. A clumsy affair at that—of the epoch of Louis the Thirteenth of France, though heaven knew whose epoch that was here. Without doubt that of Cromwell the regicide!‡

And Monsieur must needs seize the moment of his entry on this thus enlivened scene to exhibit the only display of emotion that she had ever known him vouchsafe. For otherwise Monsieur had the pose of being at least as self-contained if not as absolutely taciturn as Mark himself. She asked Mark: was that the moment for what was after all if you analysed it a manifestation of attachment for his young woman? What else could it be? *Il*—Monsieur their relative, passed for a man of unbounded knowledge. He knew all knowledge. He could not but be aware of the supreme value of the work of Casimir-Bar who, but for the machinations of his rival Monsieur Rodin and his confrères, must have attained to the highest honours in France. But not only had Monsieur with hisses and tut-tuts of anger ordered Gunning and the carpenter at once to remove the statuary and the fauteuil from the salon where she had exhibited them—with heaven knew how much reluctance—with a view to their attracting the attention of a chance customer—for chance customers did come in Their

---

* The lands belonging to Dover Priory passed, after the dissolution of the monasteries, to a cleric called Richard Thornden or Thornton, then to Archbishop Cranmer who, in December 1538, leased them out to Henry Bingham of Wingham, gentleman, on a 999-year lease.

† Not in *OED* but the noun is clearly assumed here to derive from the adjective, 'auriferous', containing or yielding gold.

‡ Louis XIII died in 1643, the year following the outbreak of the English Civil War but six years before the execution of Charles I.

absence without rendezvous. . . . Not only that, but Monsieur, to gratify the[18] perhaps not unnatural envy of Elle, had cast mere-tricious doubts on the pecuniary value of the works of Casimir-Bar themselves. Every one knew how the Americans to-day were stripping the unfortunate land of France of her choicest art treasures; the enormous prices they paid; the avidity they showed. Yet that man had tried to persuade her that her statues were worth no more than a few shillings apiece. It was incom-prehensible. He was in want of money to the extent of turning their house into a mere depot for dilapidated objects in rough wood and battered brass. He had contrived to obtain singular prices for these forlorn objects from insane Yankees who came great distances to purchase these debris[19] from him. Yet when he was offered pieces of the utmost beauty in the most perfect condi-tion he just simply turned the objects down with scoffing.

For herself, she respected passion—though she could have imagined an object of passion more calculated to excite that feeling than Elle, whom for convenience she would call her *belle-sœur*. She at least was broad-minded, and moreover she understood the workings of the human heart. It was creditable for a man to ruin himself for the object of his affections. But this at least she found exaggerated.

And what, then, was this determination to ignore the devel-opments of modern genius? Why would they not purchase for Mark a reading-desk with a brass arm that should indicate to the neighbours and dependents that at least he was a person of condi-tion? Why no revolving hut? There were certain symptoms of that age that were disquieting. She would be the first to acknowl-edge that. They had only to read in the papers of the deeds of assassins, highway robbers, of the subversive and the ignorant who everywhere seized the reins of power. But what was to be said against such innocent things as the reading-desk, the revolving hut and the aeroplane. Yes, the aeroplane!

Why did they ignore the aeroplane? They had told her that the reason why they had been unable to provide her with *navets de Paris* was that the season was becoming too advanced for the sowing of the seeds of those admirable and amusing vegetables which, seen advancing through the[20] pale electric lights of the early hours of the morning, piled symmetrically as high as the first

floors of the hotels, on the market-carts, provided one of the
gayest spectacles of the night-life of la Ville Lumière.* They had
said that to procure the seeds from Paris would demand at least a
month. But supposing they had sent a letter by aeroplane,
requesting the dispatch of the seeds equally by aeroplane, to
procure them, as all the world knew, would be a matter merely of
a few hours. And, having thus brought the matter back to turnips
again, she concluded:

"Yes, mon pauvre homme, they have singular natures, our relatives—for I will include the young woman in that category. I, at
least, am broad-minded enough for that. But they have singular
natures. It is a singular[21] affair!"[22]

She departed up the path towards the stable, speculating on
the nature of her man's relatives. They were the relatives of a
godhead—but godheads had relatives of a singular nature. Let
Mark figure as Jupiter; well, Jupiter had a son called Apollo who
could not be regarded as exactly *fils de famille*. His adventures had
been of the most irregular. Was it not known that he had spent
a long space of time with the shepherds of King Admetus, singing
and carousing?† Well, Monsieur Tietjens might for convenience
be regarded as a sort of Apollo, now amongst the shepherds of
Admetus and complete with female companion. If he did not
often sing, he also concealed the tendencies that had brought
about his downfall. He was quiet enough about the house,
extraordinary as the house might be. Elle also. If their relationship was irregular it presented no aspects of reprehensible
festivity. It was a sufficiently serious *collage*. That at least ran in
the family.

She came round the rough balks of the side of the stable upon
Gunning, seated on the stone-sill of the door, cutting with a
broad-bladed clasp-knife considerable chunks out of a large meat
pasty. She surveyed his extended leggings, his immense be-mired
boots and his unshaven countenance and remarked in French
that the shepherds of Admetus were probably differently dressed.

---

*   The City of Light, 'as they call Paris because of the expenditure of a few beggarly
    candles', Assheton Smith comments drily in *A Little Less Than Gods* 6.
†   Banished for a time from Heaven for killing the Cyclopes who made Zeus's thunder-
    bolts, Apollo was forced to serve a mortal, Admetus (husband of Alcestis), who
    employed Apollo to care for his horses and cattle.

They certainly were in all the performances of the *Alceste** that she had seen. But perhaps he served his turn.

Gunning said that he supposed he had to go on duty again. She, he supposed, was going to bottle off the cider or she would not have had him bring down that ere cask. She was to be careful to tie the carks tight; it would get itself a ed proper.

She said that if she, a Norman of a hundred generations, did not know how to handle cider it would be a strange thing, and he said that it would be a pity if that cider went wrong after all the trouble they ad ad.

He brushed the crumbs of his demolished pie[23] off the cords of his breeches, carefully picking up the larger fragments of crust and inserting them into his mouth between his broad red lips. He asked if er Ladyship knew whether the Cahptn wanted the mare that afternoon. If not e might's well turn er on the Common. She said that she did not know; the Captain had said nothing to her about it. He said he supposed e might 's well. Cramp said e would not have the settee ready to go to the station fore mornin. If she would wait there he would go git some tepid water and they would moisten the eggs. She did not ask better.

He scrambled to his feet and lumbered down the stone path towards the house. She stood in the bright day regarding the long grass of the orchard, the gnarled, whitened trunks of the fruit trees, the little lettuces like aligned rosettes in the beds, and the slope of the land towards the old stones of the house that the boughs of the apple-trees mostly hid. And she acknowledged that, in effect, she did not ask better. A Norman, if Mark had died in the ordinary course, she would no doubt have gone back to the neighbourhood either of Falaise or Bayeux, from which places[24] came the families of her grand-father and grand-mother[25] respectively. She would probably have married a rich farmer or a rich grazier, and, by choice, she would have pursued a life of bottling

---

* Marie Léonie presumably refers to the opera by Gluck (1767), based on Euripides' tragedy. Ford wrote that his favourite plays by Euripides were the *Alcestis* and the *Bacchae*, which he had re-read 'constantly ever since he was at school', and his 'favourite passage of all Greek drama' was from the *Alcestis* (*March* 117, 118). He translated the play himself after the war, though it was not published or performed: see Saunders, *Dual Life* II 78–9. Gluck's opera and excerpts from it occurred frequently on London concert programmes in the 1920s; on 23 June 1927 a radio station in Paris (Petit Parisien) broadcast *Alceste*.

off cider and moistening the eggs of sitting hens. She had had her training as a *coryphée** at the Paris opera, and no doubt if she had not made her visit to London with the Paris opera troupe and if Mark had not picked her up in the Edgware Road where her lodgings had been, she would have lived similarly with[26] some man in Clichy or Auteuil until with her economies she would have been able, equally, to retire to one or other of the *pays* of her families, and marry a farmer, a butcher, or a grazier. She acknowledged, for the matter of that, that she would probably not have raised more succulent *poulets au grain*[†] or more full-bodied cider than came from the nest-boxes and the presses here, and that she was leading no other life than that which she had always contemplated. Nor, indeed, would she have wanted any other henchman than Gunning who, if you had given him a blue blouse with stitchery and a *casquette*[‡] with a black leather peak, would have passed for any peasant in Caen market.

He swung up the path, carrying gingerly a large blue bowl, just as if his blouse bellied out round him; he had the same expression of the mouth; the same intonation. It was nothing that she obstinately spoke French to him.[§] On his subjects he could tell by intuition what her answers to his questions were and she[27] understood him well enough.

He said that he had better take the ens off the nesteses fer fear they peck er ands, and giving her the bowl, brought out from the shadows a protesting, ruffled and crooning hen, before which he dropped a handful of bran paste and a lettuce leaf. He came out with another and yet others.[28] Then he said she could go in and sprinkle the eggs. He said that it always bothered him to turn the eggs; his clumsy ol ands bruk em 's often as not. He said:

"Wait whilst I brings out ol mare. Bit o grass wunt do er much mischief."

The hens, swollen to an enormous size, paraded hostilely against one another about her feet; they clucked; crooned; pecked at lumps of paste; drank water eagerly from an iron dog-

---

* A leading dancer in a corps de ballet (French).
† *Poulets de grain* (French) are corn-fed or free-range chickens.
‡ Cap (French).
§ Cf. the conversation between Rosalie Prudent and the orderly in *No Enemy*: 'She spoke Flemish, and he, Wiltshire, but they understood each other' (129).

trough. With an exaggerated clatter of hoofs old mare emerged from the stable. She was aged nineteen, obstinate, bitter, very dark bay, extremely raw-boned. You might fill her with oats and mash five times a day but she would not put on flesh. She emerged into the light from the door with the trot of a prima-donna, for she knew she had once been a famous creature. The hens fled; she bit into the air, showing immense teeth. Gunning opened the orchard gate, just at hand; she went out at a canter; checked; crumpled her knees together; fell on her side and rolled and rolled; her immense lean legs were incongruous, up in the air.

"Yes," Marie Léonie said, "pour moi-même je ne demanderais pas mieux!"[29]*

Gunning remarked:

"Don't show er age, do she? Gambolling like a five day lamb!" His voice was full of pride, his grey face joyful. Is Lordship once sed thet[30] ol mare had orter be put in the Orse Show up to Lunnon. Some yeers ago that was!

She went into the dark, warm, odorous depths of the hen-house-stable shed; the horse-box being divided off from the hen half by wire netting, nest-boxes, blankets extended on use-poles.[†] She had to bend down to get into the hen-half. The cracks of light between the uprights of the walls blinked at her. She carried the bowl of tepid water gingerly, and thrust her hand into the warm hay hollows. The eggs were fever-heat or thereabouts; she turned them and sprinkled in the tepid water; thirteen, fourteen, fourteen, eleven—That hen was a breaker!—and fifteen. She emptied out the tepid water and from other nests took out egg after egg. The acquisition gratified her.

In an upper box a hen brooded low. It crooned menacingly, then screamed with the voice of poultry disaster as her hand approached it. The sympathetic voices of other hens outside

---

* Variants of this phrase occur at least nine times in *Last Post*, used by Marie Léonie and by Valentine with reference to Marie Léonie. Ford had used it in non-fictional contexts too: *New York Essays* 95; *New York Is Not America* (London: Duckworth, 1927), 168; and (in translation) in *A Mirror to France*, as he would in *Nightingale* 84. See also Macmaster's reflection at the Duchemin breakfast in *Some Do Not* ... I.v: 'He asked nothing better!'

† 'A pole thicker than a hop-pole and strong enough to use for other purposes.' See Joseph Wright, *The English Dialect Dictionary* (London: Henry Frowde, 1905), Vol. VI. The origin is cited as 'Kentish', thus pointing back to an earlier period in Ford's life – and to an earlier volume in *Parade's End*, *Some Do Not* ...

came to her, screaming with poultry disaster—and other hens on the Common. A rooster crowed.

She repeated to herself that she did not demand a better life than this. But was it not self-indulgence[31] to be so contented? Ought she not to be, still, taking steps for her future—near Falaise or Bayeux? Did one not owe that to oneself? How long would this life last here? And, still more, when it broke up, *how* would it break up? What would *Ils*—the strange people, do to her, her savings, her furs, trunks, pearls, turquoises, statuary, and newly-gilt Second Empire chairs and clocks? When the Sovereign died what did the Heir, his concubines, courtiers and sycophants do to the Maintenon* of the day? What precautions ought she not to be taking against that wrath to come? There must be French lawyers in London. . . .

Was it to be thought that *Il*—Christopher Tietjens, clumsy, apparently slow-witted but actually gifted with the insight of the supernatural. . . . Gunning would say: The Captain, he never says anything, but who knows what he thinks? He perceives everything. . . . Was it to be thought then that, once Mark was dead and he actual owner of the place called Groby and the vast stretch of coal-bearing land that the newspaper had spoken of, Christopher Tietjens would maintain his benevolent and frugal dispositions of to-day? It was truly thinkable. But, just as he appeared slow-witted and was actually gifted with the insight of the supernatural, so he might well now maintain this aspect of despising wealth and yet develop into a true Harpagon† as soon as he held the reins of power. The rich are noted for hardness of heart, and brother will prey upon brother's widow sooner than on another.

So that, certainly, she ought to put herself under the protection of the Authorities. But then, what Authorities? The long arm of France would no doubt protect one of her nationals even in this remote and uncivilized land. But would it be possible to

---

* Madame de Maintenon (1635–1719), married to the poet Paul Scarron; later mistress and then second wife of Louis XIV. Encouraging piety and dignity at court, she founded a home for destitute noblewomen at Saint-Cyr to which she herself retired after the death of Louis in 1715. Mrs de Bray Pape, introduced in I.iii, believes that she is 'descended, not by blood, but by moral affinity from Madame de Maintenon'.
† Leading character in Molière's 1668 play *L'Avare* (*The Miser*).

put that machinery in motion without the knowledge of Mark—
and what dreadful steps might Mark not take in his wrath if he
thought that she had set machinery in motion?

There appeared nothing for it but to wait, and that side of her
nature being indolent, perhaps being alone indolent, she was
aware that she was contented to wait. But was such a course right?
Was it doing justice to herself or to France? For it is the duty of
the French citizen, by industry, frugality and vigilance, to accumulate goods; and it was above all the duty of the French citizen
to carry back accumulated hoards to that distressed country,
stripped bare as she was by the perfidious* Allies. She might
herself rejoice in these circumstances, these grasses, orchards,
poultry, cider-presses, vegetable-gardens—even if the turnips
were not of the Paris *navet* variety! She might not ask for better.
But there might be a little *pays*, near Falaise, or, in the alternative, near Bayeux, a little spot that she might enrich with these
spoils from the barbarians. If every inhabitant of a *pays* in France
did the same would not France again be prosperous, with all its
clochers† tolling out contentment across smiling acres? Well,
then!

Standing gazing at the poultry, whilst Gunning with a hone
smoothed out some notches from his baggin hook, previous to
again going on duty,[32] she began to reflect on the nature of
Christopher Tietjens, for she desired to estimate what were her
chances of retaining her furs, pearls and gilt articles of vertu. . . .
By the orders of the doctor who attended daily on Mark—a dry,
sandy, no doubt perfectly ignorant person—Mark was never to
be left out of sight. He was of opinion, this doctor, that one day
Mark might move—physically. And there might be great danger
if ever he did move. The lesions, if lesions there were[33] in his
brain, might then be re-started with fatal effects.—Some such
talk.‡ So they must never let him out of their sight. For the night

---

* Often used specifically in the phrase 'perfidious Albion'. This faithless or treacherous
  England ('la perfide Albion') has been traced back to the French Revolutionary verses
  of Augustin, Marquis de Ximénèz. The phrase recurs (in English) in Ford's next novel:
  see *A Little Less Than Gods* 48.
† Bell-towers, church towers (French).
‡ 'Lesions' have cropped up once before in connection with Christopher's 'complex'
  about the bloody death of O Nine Morgan and its after-images: 'It might mean that
  there was a crack in his, Tietjens', brain. A lesion.' See *No More Parades* III.ii.

they had an alarm that was connected by a wire from his bed to hers. Hers was in a room that gave onto the orchard. If he so much as stirred in his bed the bell would ring in her ear. But indeed she rose every night, over and over again, to look from her window into his hut; a dim lantern illuminated his sheets. These arrangements appeared to her to be barbarous, but they met the views of Mark and she was thus in no position to question them. . . . So she had to wait whilst Gunning honed out his sickle-shaped, short-handled blade.[34]

It had all then begun—all the calamities of the world had begun[35] amidst the clamours and intoxications of that dreadful day. Of Christopher Tietjens till then she had known little or nothing. For the matter of that of Mark himself she had known little or nothing until a very few years ago. She had known neither his name, nor how he occupied himself, nor[36] yet where he lived. It had not been her business to inquire,[37] so she had never made inquiries.[38] Then one day—after thirteen years—he had awakened one morning with an attack of bronchitis after a very wet Newmarket Craven Meeting.[*] He had told her to go to his Office with a note addressed to his chief clerk, to ask for his letters and to tell them to send a messenger to his chambers to get some clothes and necessaries.

When she had told him that she did not know what his Office was nor where were his chambers, nor even his surname, he had grunted. He had expressed neither surprise nor gratification, but she knew that he had been gratified—probably with himself for having chosen a woman companion who displayed no curiosity rather than with her for having displayed none. After that he had had a telephone installed in her rooms, and not infrequently he would stay later of a morning than had been his habit, letting a messenger from the Office bring letters or fetch documents that he had signed. When his father had died he had put her into mourning.

By that date, gradually, she had learned that he was Mark Tietjens of Groby, an immense estate somewhere in the North. He employed himself at an Office of the Government's[39] in White-hall—apparently with questions of railways. She gathered,

---

[*] One of the first meetings of the year, usually in April, regarded by some as marking the start of the flat-racing season.

chiefly from ejaculations of the Messenger, that he treated his
Ministry with contempt, but was regarded as so indispensable
that he never lost his post.* Occasionally, the Office would ring
up and ask her if she knew where he was. She would gather from
the papers afterwards that that was because there had been a great
railway accident. On those occasions he would have been absent
at a race-meeting. He gave the Office, in fact, just as much of his
time as he chose, no more and no less. She gathered that, with
his overpowering wealth, it was of no account to him except as
an occupation of leisure time between meetings, and she gathered that he was regarded as an occult power amongst the rulers
of the nation. Once, during the war when he had hurt his hand,
he dictated to her a note of a confidential nature to one of the
Cabinet Ministers. It had concerned itself with Transport and its
tone had been that of singular, polite contempt.

For her he was in no way astonishing. He was the English Milor
with *le Spleen*.† She had read of him in the novels of Alexander
Dumas, Paul de Kock, Eugene Sue and Ponson du Terrail.‡ He

---

* So indispensable an elder brother is bound to recall Mycroft Holmes, seven years the
senior of Sherlock Holmes (there are fourteen years between the Tietjens brothers),
introduced in 'The Greek Interpreter' (1893), where he 'audits the books in several
Government departments', and reappearing in 'The Bruce-Partington Plans' (1908),
in which Sherlock remarks that Mycroft is not only 'under the British Government'
but, occasionally, 'is the British Government'. See Arthur Conan Doyle, *The New
Annotated Sherlock Holmes*, ed. Leslie S. Klinger, 2 vols (New York and London: W.W.
Norton and Co., 2005), I 639 and II 1302.

† 'Spleen' has a complicated literary history but ideas of melancholy and grumpiness are
fairly constant. Cf. *The Marsden Case* (London: Duckworth, 1923), 151 ('An English
Lord: "*Avec un spleen!*"'). See also *Joseph Conrad* 64, 121; *No More Parades* II.ii. In *A
Little Less Than Gods* Assheton Smith is the 'famous *milor* whose glories, spleen and
disdain were the talk of the world' (10). On the subject of national stereotypes, see
No Enemy 71. Iain Pears noted in 1992 that 'in France the milord has only recently
been challenged by the football hooligan as the abbreviated quintessence of English-
ness': 'Wellington and Napoleon', in *Myths of the English*, ed. Roy Porter (Cambridge:
Polity, 1992), 216–36 (233 n.1).

‡ Either Alexandre Dumas (père) – *Le Comte de Monte-Cristo, Les Trois Mousqetaires* –
or Alexandre Dumas (fils) – *La dame aux camellias, Le demi-monde*; Charles Paul de
Kock (1793–1871), immensely popular and successful writer of bawdy, sentimental
novels of Paris life ('Nice name he has', Molly Bloom remarks: *Ulysses* 78); Eugène
Sue (1804–57) was another hugely successful and prolific novelist, who began with
seafaring stories but turned to novels of crime and the Paris underworld; Ponson du
Terrail, another popular writer, his name inscribed as the last words of Ford's *Joseph
Conrad* (256). The 'Appendix', in French, ends with the reflection that a writer can
never really know whether he or she is the greatest genius in the world or 'le dernier,
le plus infecte descendant de … Ponson du Terrail …' See also *Portraits From Life* 223.

represented the England[40] that the Continent applauded—the
only England that the Continent applauded. Silent, obstinate,
inscrutable, insolent but immensely wealthy and uncontrollably
generous. For herself, *elle ne demandait pas mieux*. For there was
about him nothing of the unexpected. He was as regular as the
Westminster Chimes;* he never exacted the unexpected of her
and he was all-powerful and never in the wrong. He was, in short,
what her countrywomen called *sérieux*. No Frenchwoman asks
better than that of lover or husband. It was the serious *collage par
excellence*:[41†] they as a *ménage* were[42] sober, honest, frugal, indus-
trious, immensely[43] wealthy, and seriously saving. For his dinner,
twice a week, she cooked him herself two mutton chops with all
but an eighth of an inch of the fat pared off, two mealy potatoes,
as light and as white as flour, an apple-pie with a very flaky crust
which he ate with a wedge of Stilton and some pulled bread and
butter.‡ This dinner was[44] never varied once in twenty years,
except during the season of game, when on alternate weeks a
pheasant, a brace of grouse or of partridges would come from
Groby. Nor in the twenty years had they once been separated for
a whole week except that every late summer he spent a month at
Harrogate. She always had his dress-shirts washed for him by her
own laundress in the Quartier. He spent almost every week-end
in one country house or another, using at most two dress-shirts
and that only if he stayed till Tuesday. English people of good
class do not dress for dinner on Sundays. That is a politeness to
God, because theoretically you attend evening service and you
do not go to church in the country in evening dress. As a matter
of fact you never go to evening service—but it is complimentary
to suggest by your dress that you might be visited by the impulse.
So, at least, Marie Léonie Tietjens understood the affair.

---

* i.e., the pattern of chimes struck at successive quarters by Big Ben in the Palace of
Westminster (*OED*).
† Ideal relationship (French).
‡ Cf. 'He ate daily the same English food wherever he found himself—mutton chops
grilled without condiments, potatoes boiled without sauce, a slice of apple pie, some
Stilton with pulled bread' (*Return* 180). Ford was writing of René Byles, manager of
the firm called Alston Rivers, which published seven of Ford's books between 1905
and 1907. The passage (179–85) is an affectionate testimonial to a man important to
Ford as a personal friend as well as publisher of several of his most significant books.
Byles was later editor of the *Throne* magazine when Elsie Hueffer sued it for libel: Saunders, *Dual Life* I 366, 372–3.

She was looking out on the Common that sloped up to beech trees, at the poultry—bright chestnut birds, extremely busy on[45] the intense green of the browsed grass. The great rooster reminded her of the late Monsieur Rodin, the sculptor who had conspired against Casimir-Bar.* She had once seen him[46] in his studio, conducting some American ladies round his work, and he had precisely resembled a rooster kicking its leg back and drooping its wings in the dust round a new hen. Only round a new one. Naturally!... This rooster was a tremendous Frenchman. *Un vrai de la vraie*.[47]† You could imagine nothing more unlike Christopher Tietjens!... The backward-raking legs on the dancing toes; the gait of a true master of deportment at an academy of young ladies! The vigilant clear eye cocking up every minute.... Hark! A swift shadow ran over the ground: the sparrow-hawk! The loud, piercing croon of that Father of his Country. How the hens all re-echoed it; how the chickens ran to their mothers and all together to the shadow of the hedge. Monsieur the[48] hawk would have no chance amidst that outcry. The hawk flits silent and detests noise. It will bring the poultry-keeper with his gun!... All is discovered because of the vigilance of Milord Chantecler.... ‡ There are those who reprove him because his eyes are always on the sky, because he has a proud head. But that is his function—that and gallantry. Perceive him with a grain of corn; how he flies upon it; how he invites with cries! His favourite—the newest—hens run clucking joyously to him. How he bows, droops and prances, holding the grain of corn in his powerful bill, depositing it, pecking to bruise it and then depositing it before his sultana of the moment. Nor will he complain if a little ball of fluff runs quickly and pecks the grain from his bill before Madame Partlet§ can take it from him. His

---

* Rodin died in 1917.
† The real thing, the genuine article (French).
‡ Aesop's fable, 'The Cock and the Fox', was also featured in the collection of fables by Jean de la Fontaine; Chantecler appears in Chaucer too: see next note on 'Partlet'. More recent was the February 1910 premiere of Edmond Rostand's *Chantecler* in Paris, with Lucien Guitry in the title role (Mme. Simone played the pheasant). It was his determination to see Guitry in this drama, two months later, that resulted in Edward VII catching the cold (in an overheated theatre) that precipitated his final illness. He died on 6 May.
§ The hen in the series of tales featuring Reynard the fox, occurring in many guises, including Aesop's *Fables* and Chaucer's 'The Nun's Priest's Tale'.

gallantry has been wasted, but he is a good father!... Perhaps there is not even a grain of corn when he issues his invitations; perhaps he merely calls his favourites to him that he may receive their praise or perform the act of Love....

He is then the man that a woman desires to have vouchsafed her. When he smites his wing feathers behind his back and utters his clarion cry of victory over the hawk that now glides far away down the hill, his hens come out again from the shadows, the chickens from beneath their mothers' wings. He has given security to his country and in confidence they can return to their avocations. Different, indeed, from that Monsieur Christopher who, even when he was still a soldier, more than anything resembled a full, grey, coarse meal-sack short in the wind and with rolling, hard-blue eyes. Not hard eyes, but of a hard blue! And yet, curiously, he too had some of the spirit of Chantecler beneath his rolling shoulders of a farmyard boar. Obviously you could not be your brother's brother and not have some traces of the Milor.... The spleen too. But no one could say that her Mark was not a proper man, *Chic* in an eccentric manner, but, oh yes, *chic*! And that was his brother.

Naturally he might try to despoil her. That is what brother does to brother's widow and children....[49] But, on occasion, he treated her with a pompous courtesy—a parade. On the first time he had seen her—not so long ago that; only during that period of the war that had been without measurable time—he had treated her to heavy but expressive gestures of respect and words of courtesy in an old-fashioned language that he must have learned at the Théatre Français while they still played *Ruy Blas*.* French was a different thing now, that she must acknowledge. When she went to Paris—which she did every late summer whilst her man went to Harrogate—the language her nephews spoke was a different affair—without grace, courtesy, intelligibility. Certainly without respect! Oh, là, là! When they came to divide up her inheritance that would be a sharper kind of despoilment than ever Christopher Tietjens'! Whilst she lay on her bed of death those young fellows and their wives would be all through her

---

* A drama by Victor Hugo, first performed in 1838. On Christopher's 'old-fashioned French with an atrocious English accent', see *No More Parades* II.ii and note.

presses and armoires like a pack of wolves. . . . * *La famille!* Well, that was very proper. It showed the appropriate spirit of acquisition. What was a good mother for if not to despoil her husband's relatives in the interests of their joint children![50]

So Christopher had been as courteous as a well-trained mealsack of the *dix-huitième*. Eighteenth century. Older still, *période Molière!* When he had come into her room that had been dimly lit with a *veilleuse*—a night-light; they are so much more economical than shaded electric lights!—he had precisely suggested to her a lumbering character from Molière as presented at the Comédie Française; elaborate of phrase and character but protuberant in odd places. She might in that case have supposed that he entertained designs on her person; but with his eyes sticking out in elaborate considerateness, he had only come to break to her the news that his brother was about to make an honest woman of her. That had been Mark's phrase. It is of course only God that can do that. . . . But the enterprise had had the full concurrence of Monsieur the Heir-Apparent.

He had indeed been active whilst she had slumbered[51] in a hooded-chair after four days and three nights on her feet. She would have surrendered the body of Mark to no human being but his brother. Now the brother had come to tell her not to be alarmed—panting with nervousness and shortness of breath. . . . Bad lungs both the brothers had! Panting he had come to tell her not to be alarmed at finding in her man's room a priest, a lawyer and a lawyer's clerk. . . .[52] These black-robed people attend on death, bringing will-forms and the holy oils. The doctor and a man with oxygen cylinders had been there when she had gone to repose herself. It was a pretty congregation of the vultures that attend on us during life.

She had started at once to cry out. That undoubtedly was what had made him nervous—the anticipation that she would cry out sharply in the black, silent London that brooded between airraids. In that silence, before sleep had visited her peignoir-enveloped, and therefore clumsyish form, she had been aware of Christopher's activities on the telephone in the passage.

---

* This is not merely a conventional phrase. Ford uses the image of wolves or refers to the proverb *homo homini lupus* (man is a wolf to his fellow-men) at least a dozen times in his published work.

It had struck her that he might have been warning the Pompes Funèbres!...* So she had begun to scream: the sound that irresistibly you make when death is about to descend. But he had agitated himself to soothe her—for all the world like Monsieur Sylvain† on the boards of Molière's establishment! He spoke that sort of French, in a hoarse whisper, in the shadows of the night-light ... assuring her that the priest was for marriage, with licence of the Archevêque de Cantorbéri such as in London you got in those days from Lambeth Palace for thirty pounds sterling. That enabled you to make any woman honest at any hour of the day or night. The lawyer was there to have a will re-signed. Marriage in this singular country invalidates any previous will. So Tietjens (Christophère) assured her.

But then, if there was that haste, there was danger of death. She had often speculated as to whether he would or would not marry her as an act of deathbed contrition. Rather contemptuously as great lords with *le spleen* make their peace with God. She screamed. In silent, black London. The night-light wavered in its saucer.

He crepitated out that his brother was doubling, in this new will, his posthumous provision for her. With provision for the purchase of a house in France if she would not inhabit the Dower House at Groby. A Louis Treize dower-house. It was his idea of consolation. He affected to be business-like.... These English. But then, perhaps they do not go through your presses and wardrobes whilst your corpse is still warm!

She screamed out that they might take away their marriage papers and will-forms, but to give her her man again. If they had let her give him her tisanes instead of ...

With her breast heaving, she had cried into that man's face:

"I swear that my first act when I am Madame Tietjens and have the legal power will be to turn out all these men and give him infusions of poppy-heads and lime-flowers." She expected to see him recoil, but he had said:

---

* Funeral directors, morticians (French).
† There is a notice of a performance of Molière's *Femmes Savantes*, featuring the 'young aspirant' M. Sylvain, at 'The Comédie Française at the Gaiety' in *The Times* of 10 July 1879.

"In heaven's name do, my dear sister. It might save him and the nation."

It was silly of him to talk like that. These fellows had too much pride of family. Mark did no more than attend to Transport. Well, perhaps transport in those days had its importance. Still, probably Tietjens, Christopher, overrated the indispensableness of Tietjens, Mark. . . . That would have been a month[53] before the Armistice. They were black days. . . . A good brother, though. . . .

In the other room, whilst papers were signing, after the *curé* in his *calotte** and all had done reading from his book, Mark had signed to her to bend her head down to him and had kissed her. He whispered:

"Thank God there is one woman-Tietjens who is not a whore and a bitch!" He winced a little; her tears had fallen on his face. For the first time, she had said:[54] "Mon pauvre homme, ce qu'ils ont fait de toi!" She had been hurrying from the room when Christopher had stopped her. Mark had said:

"I regret to put you to further inconvenience . . . " in French. He had never spoken to her in French before. Marriage makes a difference. They speak to you with ceremony out of respect for themselves and their station in life. You also are at liberty to address them as your *pauvre homme*.

There had to be another ceremony. A man looking like a newly dressed jail-bird[55] stepped out with his book like an office register. With a blue-black jowl. He married them over again. A civil marriage this time.

It was then that, for the first time, she had become aware of the existence of another woman-Tietjens, Christopher's wife. . . . She had not known that Christopher had a wife. Why was not she there? But Mark with his labouring politeness and chest had told her that he exaggerated the formality of the marriage because if both he and Christopher died, she, Marie Léonie Tietjens, might have trouble with a certain Sylvia. The Bitch!. . . Well, she, Marie Léonie, was prepared to face her sister-in-law.[56]

* Skullcap (French).

CHAPTER III

THE little maid, Beatrice, as well as Gunning, regarded Marie Léonie with paralysed but bewildered obedience. She was Er Ladyship, a good mark; a foreign Frenchy, bad; extraordinarily[1] efficient about the house and garden and poultry-yard, a matter for mixed feelings. She was fair, not black-avised,* a good mark; she was buxom, not skinny, like the real Quality. A bad mark because she was, then, not real Quality; but a qualifiedly good mark because, if you as to ave Quality all about you in the ouse, tis better not to ave real Quality.... But on the whole the general feeling was favourable, because like themselves she was floridly blond. It made er uman like. Never you trust a dark woman, and if you marries a dark man e will treat you bad. In the English countryside it is like that.

Cabinet-maker Cramp, who was a remnant of the little dark persistent race that once had peopled Sussex,† regarded Marie Léonie with[2] distrust that mingled with admiration for the quality of the varnish that she imported from Paris. Proper French Polish that were. He lived in the cottage just across the path on the Common. E couldn' say as ow e liked the job the Governor[3] give im. He had to patch up and polish with beeswax—not varnish—rough stuff such s is granf'er ad ad. An ad got rid of. Rough ol truck. More 'nundred yeers[4] old. N more!

He had to take bits of old wood out of one sort of old truck and fit it into missing bits of other old truck. Bought old Moley's pig-pound boards that had been Little Kingsworth church stalls. The

---

* Dark-complexioned. Fairly uncommon, though Ford has used it earlier in *No More Parades* I.ii.

† Meeting in Paris a man called Evans, who had been in the same regiment, Ford wrote of him: 'He was, of course, Welsh—one of the little, dark, persistent race....' (*Nightingale* 175). Writing to the novelist Richard Hughes (of Welsh descent), Ford remarked on Hughes's 'foreignness from things Anglo-Saxon', adding: 'The little dark persistent race might see better where you get it from but they couldn't admire more' (*Letters* 306). See also 'Pont...ti...pri...ith', in *War Prose* 33, and *Ford/Bowen* 10, where Ford, still at Redcar, mentions teaching 'the mechanism of the Lewis gun' to 'little, dark, foreign speaking Welch devils'.

Cahptn ad ad im, Cramp,[5] use'm for all manner of patchin's up. The Captain had bought, too, ol Miss Cooper's[*] rabbit utch. Beautifully bevelled the panels was, too, when cleaned up n beeswaxed. Cramp would acknowledge that. Made him match the bevelling in the timber from Kingsworth Church stalls for one of the missing doors, an more of the timber for[6] the patching. Proper job, he, Cramp, had made of it, too; he would say that. N it looked proper when it was finished—a long, low press, with six bevelled doors; beautiful purfling on the edges. Like some of the stuff Is Lordship ad in the Tujer Room at Fittleworth House.[†] More'n a undred yeers old. Three undred. Four.... There's no knowin.

N no accountin fer tastes. E would say e ad n eye—the Cahptn ad. Look at a bit of ol rough truck, the Cahptn would, n see it was older than the Monument to Sir Richard Atchison[7] on Tadworth Ill that was set up in the year 1842 to celebrate the glorious[8] victory of Free Trade.[‡] So the Monument said. Lug a bit of rough ol truck out of the back of a cow-house where it had been throwed—the Cahptn would. And his, Cramp's, heart would sink to see the ol mare come back, some days, the cart full of encoops, n leaden pig-truffs, n pewter plates that ad been used to stop up oles in cow-byres.

N off it would all go to Murrikay. Queer place Murrikay must be—full of the leavins of ol England. Pig-troughs, hen-coops, rabbit-hutches, wash-house coppers that no one now had any use for. He loaded em, when he'd scrubbed, and silver-sanded and bees-waxed-n-turpentined em, onto the ol cart, n put to ol mare, n down to station, n on to Southampton n off to New York. Must be a queer place, yon! Hadn't they no cabinet-makers or ol rough truck of ther own?

Well, it took all sorts to make a world n thank God fer that.

---

[*]   Perhaps a nod to Cooper's Cottage, Ford and Stella's home in Bedham.

[†]   Fittleworth is three miles south-east of Petworth, and also, as Stella herself recalled, three miles from Bedham (*Drawn From Life* 76).

[‡]   This presumably refers to the repeal of the Corn Laws, which occurred in 1846 (the Royal assent was given in June). In *A History of Our Own Times* 46, Ford refers to 'the passing of the Corn Laws in 1842' and the editors point out that 'The repeal, not the passage, of the Corn Laws took place in 1846' (235 n.3). Ford's misdating was, then, consistent and occurred in both fictional and non-fictional contexts. In *Some Do Not ... I.*vii Valentine remarks that Tenterden market 'was abolished in 1845—the effect of the repeal of the Corn Laws'.

He, Cramp, had a good job likely to last im is lifetime because some folks wus queer in the ed. The ol lumber went out yon and his, Cramp's missus, was gettin together a proper set of goods. A tidy treat their sittin room looked with aspidistras in mahogany tripods, n a Wilton carpet n bamboo cheers n mahogany what-nots. A proper woman Missus Cramp was if sharp in the tongue.

Miss's Cramp she didn' give so much fer Er Ladyship. She was agin Foreigners. All German spies they wus. Have no truck with them, she wouldn't. Oo noo if they wus s much s married. Some says they wus, some says they wusn. But you couldn' take in Miss's Cramp.... N Quality! What was to show that they were real Quality? Livin how they did wasn' Quality manners. Quality wus stuck up n wore shiny clothes n had motor-cars n statues n palms n ball-rooms n conservatories. N didn bottle off the cider n take the eggs n speak queer lingo to th handy-man. N didn' sell the cheers they sat on. The four younger children also didn't[9] like Er Ladyship. Never called em pretty dears, she didn't,[10] nor give em sweeties nor rag-dolls nor apples. Smacked[11] em if she found em in the orchard. Never so much s give em red flannel capes in the winter.

But Bill, the eldest, liked Er Ladyship. Called er a proper right un. Never stopped tarkin of er. N *she* ad statues in er bedroom, n fine gilt cheers, n clocks, n flowerin plants. Bill e'd made fer Er Ladyship what she called n eightyjare.* In three stories, to stand in a corner n hold knick-nacks[12] out of fretwork to a pettern she'd give im. Varnished proper, too. A good piece of work if he shouldn't say so.... But Miss's Cramp she'd never been allowed in er Ladyship's bedroom. A proper place it was. Fit fer a Countess! If Miss's Cramp could be allowed to see it she'd maybe change her opinions.... But Miss's Cramp she said: Never you trust a fair woman, bein dark.

The matter of the cider, however, did give him to think. Proper cider it was, when they was given a bottle or two. But it wasn't Sussex cider. A little like Devonshire cider, more like Hereford-shire. But not the same as any. More head it had n was sweeter, n browner. N not to be drunk s freely! Fair scoured you it did if you drunk s much s a quart!

---

* An étagère is an ornamental stand with several shelves.

The little settlement was advancing furtively to the hedge. Cramp put his bald poll out of his work-shed and then crept out. Mrs. Cramp, an untidy, dark, very thin woman emerged over her door-sill, wiping her hands on her apron. The four Cramp children at different stages of growth crept out of the empty pig-pound.—Cramp was not going to buy his winter pigs till next fortnightly fair at Little Kingsworth.[13]—The Elliott Children, with the milk-can, came at a snail's pace down the green path from the farm; Mrs. Elliott, an enormous woman with untidy hair, peered over her own hedge, which formed a little enclosure on the Common; Young Hogben,* the farmer's son, a man of forty, very thick-set, appeared on the path in the beech-wood, ostensibly driving a great black sow. Even Gunning left his brushing and lumbered to the edge of the stable. From there he could still see Mark in his bed, but also, looking downwards between the apple-trunks he could see Marie Léonie bottle the cider, large, florid and intent, in the open dairying-shed where water ran in a V-shaped wooden trough.

"Runnin t'cider out of cask with a chube!" Mrs. Cramp[14] screamed up the hill to Mrs. Elliott. "Ooever eered!" Mrs. Elliot rumbled huskily back at Mrs. Cramp. All these figures closed in furtively; the children peering through tiny interstices in the hedge and muttering one to the other: "Ooever eered.... Foreign ways, I call it.... A glass chube.... Ooever eered." Even Cramp, though, wiping his bald head with his carpenter's apron, he admonished Mrs. Cramp to remember that he had a good job— even Cramp descended from the path to the hedge-side and stood so close—peering over—that the thorns pricked his perspiring chest through his thin shirt. They said to the baker who wearily

---

* Too similar for coincidence, surely, to Hobden ('Hobden the hedger'), Rudyard Kipling's archetypal Sussex countryman in both *Puck of Pook's Hill* (1906) and *Rewards and Fairies* (1910); also the poem, 'The Land', included in *A Diversity of Creatures* (1917). Andrew Lycett mentions that the character was based on William Isted, Kipling's 'main source about country lore'. He was an excellent hedger and knew about poaching, 'from the days when it was possible to pick up a fallow deer in Lord Ashburnham's woods towards Battle': *Rudyard Kipling* (London: Weidenfeld & Nicolson, 1999), 436. There is a 'Nicholas Hogben', a Lincolnshire man, in Ford's *Privy Seal* (1907): *The Fifth Queen*, ed. Graham Greene (London: The Bodley Head, 1962), 311ff. But see *Some Do Not ...* I.v and textual note on the occurrences of 'Haglen' and 'Hogben': Max Saunders points out that the latter was a name also known to Ford from the farmhouse at Aldington that the Conrads had rented in 1908: Hogben House.

followed his weary horse up the steep path, coming from the deep woods below: It had ought to be stopped. The police had ought to know. Bottling cider by means of a glass tube. And standing the cider in running water. Where was the excise? Rotting honest folks guts! Poisoning them. No doubt the governor could tell them a tale if[15] he could speak or move. The police had ought to know.... Showing off, with cider in running water—to cool it when first bottled! Ooever eered! Just because they ad a Ladyship to their tail. N more money than better folks. Not so much money either. Reckon they'd come to smash n be sold up like Igginson at Fittleworth. Set isself up fer Quality, e did too!... N not so much of a Ladyship, neither. Not so much more of a Ladyship as us if the truth was known. Not an Earl or a Lord, only a baronite-ess at that, supposin we all ad our rights.... The police had ought to be brought into this affair!

A number of members of the Quality,* on shining horses, their leathers creaking beautifully, rode at a walk up the path. They were the real Quality. A fine old gentleman, thin as a lath, clean face, hooky nose, white moustache, lovely cane, lovely leggings. On Is Lordship's favourite hack. A bay mare. A fine lady, slim as a boy, riding astride as they do to-day though they did not use to. But times change. On the Countess's own chestnut with white forehead. A bad-tempered horse. She must ride well that lady. Another lady, grey haired, but slim too, riding side-saddle in[16] a funny sort of get-up. Long skirt with panniers and three-cornered hat like the ones you see in pictures of highwaymen in the new pub in Queen's Norton. Sort of old-fashioned, she looked. But no doubt it was the newest pattern. Things is so mixed up nowadays. Is Lordship's friends could afford to do as they pleased. A boy, eighteen maybe. Shiny leggings too: all their clothes is shiny. Rides well, too, the boy. Look how his legs nip into Orlando†— the chief whip's horse. Out for an airing. Is Lordship's groom of

---

*   In *The Cinque Ports* 179, Ford had written of 'the villager of these parts' being 'intensely suspicious of what he calls "the quality" ...'
†   Virginia Woolf's *Orlando* was not published until October 1928, but Orlando is also the name of one of the three sons of Sir Rowland de Boys in Shakespeare's *As You Like It*. It was performed at the Old Vic in 1923–4 and again in 1925–6. Ford had alluded to the play in the title of *No Enemy*. There was also, of course, Ariosto's *Orlando Furioso*, and Luigi Pulci's *Morgante* (which took as model an anonymous poem entitled *Orlando*), certainly known to Ford if only from Borrow's *The Romany Rye* 325.

the stud only too glad if the horses can get exercise in hay-cutting time. The real Quality.

They reined in their horses and sat staring, a little further up the road, down[17] into the orchard. They had ought to be told what was going on down there. Puts white powder into the cider along o the sugar. The Quality ought to be told. . . . But you do not speak to the Quality. Better if they do not notice you. You never know. They sticks together. Might be friends of Tietjenses for all you know. You don't know Tietjenses ain't Quality. Better git a move on or something might appen to you. You hear!

The boy in the shiny leggings and clothes—bare-headed he was, with shiny fair hair and shiny cheeks—exclaimed in a high voice:

"I say, mother, I don't like this spying!" And the horses started and jostled.

You see. They don't like this spying. Get a move on. And all that peasantry got a move on whilst the horses went slowly up hill. Queer things the Gentry can do to you still if they notice you. It is all very well to say this is a land fit for whatever the word is that stands for simple folk. They have[18] the police and the keepers in their hands and your cottages and livings.

Gunning went out at the garden gate beside the stable and shouted objurgations at Young Hogben.

"Hey, don't you drive that sow. She's as much right on Common as you."

The great sow was obstinately preceding the squat figure of Young Hogben, who hissed and squeaked behind her. She flapped her great ears and sniffed from side to side, a monument of black imperturbability.

"You keep your ogs out of our swedes!" Young Hogben shouted amidst objurgations. "In our forty-acre she is all day n all night too!"

"You keep your swedes outen our ogs," Gunning shouted back, swinging his gorilla arms like a semaphore. He advanced on to the Common. Young Hogben descended the slope.

"You fence your ogs in same's other folks as to do," Young Hogben menaced.

"Folks as abuts on Commons as to fence out, not fence in," Gunning menaced. They stood foot to foot on the soft sward menacing each other with their chins.

"Is Lordship sold Tietjens's to the Cahptn without Common rights," the farmer said. "Ask Mr. Fuller."

"Is Lordship could no more sell Tietjens's 'thout Common rights n you could sell milk[19] without drinking rights. Ast Lawyer Sturgis!" Gunning maintained. Put arsenic in among is roots, Young Hogben maintained that he would. Spend seven years up to Lewes Jail if e did, Gunning maintained. They continued[20] for long the[21] endless quarrel that obtains between tenant-farmer who is not Quality but used to brutalizing his hinds and gentlemen's henchman who is used to popularity amongst his class and the peasantry. The only thing upon which they agreed was that you wouldn't think there adn't been no war. The war ought to have given tenant-farmers the complete powers of local tyrants; it should have done the same for gentlemen's bailiffs. The sow grunted round Gunning's boots, looking up for grains of maize that Gunning usually dropped. In that way sows come to heel when you call them however far away they may be on the Common.[22]

From the[23] hard road up the hill—Tietjens's went up the slope to the hedge there—descended the elderly lady who was singularly attired in the eyes of the country people. She considered that she was descended, not by blood, but by moral affinity from Madame de Maintenon, therefore she wore a long grey riding skirt with panniers, and a three-cornered, grey felt hat, and carried a riding switch of green shagreen. Her thin grey face was tired but authoritative, her hair which she wore in a knot beneath her hat was luminously grey, her pince-nez rimless.

Owing to the steepness of the bank on which the garden rose, the path of sea-pebbles zigzagged across most of its width, orange-coloured because it had been lately sanded. She went furtively between quince-trunks, much like the hedge-sparrow, flitting a stretch and then stopping for the boy with the shining leggings stolidly to overtake her.

She said that it was dreadful to think that the sins of one's youth could so find one out. It ought to make her young companion think. To come at the end of one's life to inhabiting so remote a spot. You could not get there with automobiles. Her own Delarue-Schneider* had broken down on the hill-road in the attempt to get there yesterday.

The boy, slim in the body, but heavy in the bright red cheeks,[24] with brown hair, truly shiny leggings and a tie of green, scarlet and white stripes, had a temporarily glum expression. He said, nevertheless, with grumbling determination, that he did not think this was playing the game. Moreover hundreds of motors got up that hill; how else would people come to buy the old furniture? He had already told Mrs. de[25] Bray Pape that the carburetters[26] of Delarue-Schneiders were a wash-out.

It was just that, Mrs. Pape maintained, that was so dreadful a thought. She went swiftly down another zigzag of the path and then faltered.

It was that that was dreadful in these old countries, she said. Why could they never learn? Take example? Here were the descendants of a great family, the Tietjens of Groby, a haunt of ancient peace,[†] the one reduced to a no doubt dreadful state by the sins of his youth, the other to making a living by selling old furniture.

The youth said she was mistaken. She must not believe all that his mother hinted to her. His mother was all right, but her hints went further than facts warranted. If he wanted to let Groby to Mrs. de Bray Pape it was because he hated swank. His uncle also hated swank.... He mumbled a little and added: "And ... my father!" Moreover it was not playing the game. He had soft brown eyes that were now clouded and he was blushing.

He mumbled that mother was splendid, but he did not think she ought to have sent him there. Naturally she had her wrongs. For himself he was a Marxist-Communist. All Cambridge was.[‡] He therefore of course approved of his father's living with whom he wished. But there were[27] ways of doing things. Because you

---

*   There was a leading car manufacturing company called Rochet-Schneider formed in 1894. Another company was founded in the same year by Emile Delahaye. This might be a Fordian near-miss, combining the two and slightly misremembering 'Delahaye'.

†   The Poet Laureate (1896–1913) Alfred Austin's immensely successful *Haunts of Ancient Peace* (1902) was based on his travels through the country in 1901 in search of 'Old England'. In *The Spirit of the People* Ford had referred to 'the spirit of the home of ancient peace' (*England* 260), while Dowell, in *The Good Soldier*, recalls having mistakenly trusted in 'the tranquillity of ancient haunts of peace' (130).

‡   Not only Cambridge: Valentine's brother, who attended Magdalen College, Oxford, 'was a Communist!' (*Some Do Not ...* II.iv).

were advanced you did not have to treat women with discourtesy. The reverse, rather. He was painfully agitated by the time he overtook the tired lady at the corner of the next zigzag.

She wanted him not to misunderstand her. No discredit attached in her eyes to the pursuit of selling old furniture. Far from it. Mr. Lemuel of Madison Avenue might be called a dealer in old furniture. It was, of course, Oriental, which made a difference. But Mr. Lemuel was a most cultivated man. His country house at Crugers[28]* in the State of New York was kept up in a style that would have done credit to the grands seigneurs of pre-Revolutionary France. But from that to this . . . what a downfall!

The house—the cottage—was by now nearly below her feet, the roof extremely high, the[29] windows sunk very deep in grey stone and very small. There was a paved semi-circular court before the door, the space having been cut out of the orchard bank and walled with stones. It was extravagantly green, sunk in greenery, and the grass that came nearly to Mrs. Pape's middle was filled with hiding profusions of flowers turning[30] to seed. The four counties swept away from under her, hedges like string going away, enclosing fields, to the hills on the very distant horizon. The country near at hand wooded. The boy beside her took a deep breath as he always did when he saw a great view. On the moors above Groby, for instance. Purple they were.

"It *isn't* fit for human habitation!" the lady exclaimed with the triumphant intonation of one who sees a great truth confirmed. "The homes[31] of the poor in these old countries beggar even pity. Do you suppose they so much as have[32] a bath?"

"I should think my father and uncle were personally *clean*!" the boy said. He mumbled that this was supposed to be rather a show place. He could trust his father indeed to find rather a show place to live in. Look at the rock plants in the sunk garden! He exclaimed: "Look here! Let's go back!"

Mrs. Pape's perturbation gave way to obstinacy. She exclaimed: "Never!" She had a mission from the poor boy's injured mother. She would never look Sylvia Tietjens in the face if she flinched. Sanitation went before anything. She hoped to leave the world a better place before she passed over. She had

---

* Hamlet in Cortlandt, Westchester County, New York State.

Authority conferred on her. Metempsychosistically.* She
believed that the soul of Madame de Maintenon, the companion
of Lewis[33] the Fourteenth, had passed into her. How many
convents had not the Maintenon set up and how rigidly had she
not looked after the virtue and the sanitation of the inhabitants?
That was what she, Mrs. Millicent de Bray Pape, looked to. She
had in the South of France—the Riviera—a palace, erected by
Mr. Behrens,† the celebrated architect—after the palace of the
Maintenon at Sans Souci.‡ But sanitated! She asked the young
man to believe her. The boudoir appeared to be only a panelled
boudoir; very large because of the useless vanity of le Raw Solale.§
Madame de Maintenon would have been content without such
vanity. . . . But only touch a spring in the panels and every sort
of bathing arrangement presented itself to you hidden in the wall.
Sunken baths; baths above ground; douches with sea-water extra-
iodized; lateral douches with and without bath-salts dissolved in
the water. That was what she called making the world a little
better.** Impossible not to be healthy with all that. . . .[34]

The boy mumbled that he was not in principle against the old
tree's coming down. He was, indeed, in principle against his
uncle's and his father's adoption of the peasant life. This was an
industrial age. The peasant had always spoilt every advance in
the ideas of the world. All the men at Cambridge were agreed as
to that. He exclaimed:

"Hi! You can't do that. . . . Not go through standing *hay*!"[35]††

---

* 'Metempsychosis' is the word that Molly consults Bloom about in James Joyce's *Ulysses*
77: 'from the Greek. That means the transmigration of souls. —O, rocks! she said. Tell
us in plain words.' As 'met him pike hoses' (with variations), the word reappears
several times thereafter. Ford alluded to *Ulysses* very positively in July 1922 and
reviewed it enthusiastically in December (*Critical Essays* 217, 218–27). Thomas Hardy
had also used the word thirty years before in *The Well-Beloved* (serialised 1892; 1897).

† The architect Peter Behrens (1868–1940) included Mies van der Rohe, Le Corbusier
and Walter Gropius among his students and assistants between 1907 and 1912. He
was later involved in Hitler and Speer's utopian plans for Berlin.

‡ Sans Souci is the name of Frederick the Great's estate near Potsdam, and of a famous
French racehorse. The home for poor noblewomen that Madame de Maintenon
founded was at Saint-Cyr.

§ i.e. Le Roi Soleil, the Sun King, Louis XIV.

** In *The Good Soldier* Florence 'always wanted to leave the world a little more elevated
than she found it' (17). Tellingly, Ford found in Henry James 'little trace [...] of a
desire to leave humanity any better than he found it' (*Henry James* 23).

†† In Ford's 1913 novel, *The Young Lovell*, Lovell is described as going 'decently by round-
about ways and paths from landmark to landmark that he might not trample down the
long grass of which his bondsmen were making their hay all about him' (102).

Every fibre of his country boy landowner's soul was outraged as he saw the long trail of satiny grey that followed Mrs. de Bray Pape's long skirts. How were his father's men to cut hay that had been trampled like that? But, unable to bear any longer the suspense of the spectacular advance towards Mark Tietjens along those orange zigzags, Mrs. de Bray Pape was running straight down the bank towards the unwalled, thatched hut. She could see it through the tops of the apple-tree.

The boy, desperately nervous, continued to descend the zigzag paths that would take him into the very purlieus of his father's house—onto the paved court where there were rock plants between the interstices. His mother *ought* not to have forced him to accompany Mrs. de Bray Pape. His mother was splendid. Divinely beautiful: athletic as Atalanta* or Betty Nuthall,† in spite of her sufferings. But she ought not to have sent Mrs. de Bray Pape. It was *meant* as a sort of revenge. General Campion had not approved. He could see that, though he had said: "My boy, you ought always to obey your dear mother! She has suffered so much. It is your duty to make it up to her by fulfilling her slightest whim. An Englishman always does his duty to his mother!"

Of course it was the presence of Mrs. de Bray Pape that forced the General to say that. Patriotism. General Campion was deadly afraid of mother. Who wasn't? But he would hardly have enjoined upon a son to go and spy upon his father and his father's . . . companion if he had not wanted to show Mrs. de Bray Pape how superior English family ties were to those of her country. They ragged each other about that all day long.

And yet he did not know. The dominion of women over those of the opposite sex was a terrible thing. He had seen the old General whimper like a whipped dog and mumble in his poor white moustache. . . . Mother was splendid. But wasn't sex a terrible thing. . . . His breath came short.

* In Greek mythology, Atalanta agreed to marry only a suitor who could outrun her. Milanion did so with the aid of three golden apples, the gift of Venus, which he dropped during the race and which Atalanta stopped to pick up. Atalanta has occurred in *Some Do Not* . . . , in a significant conversation between Mrs Duchemin and Valentine (I.v) and recurred during Valentine's walk with Tietjens: 'She didn't waste time looking round: she wasn't a fool like Atalanta in the egg race. She picked up her heels and sprinted' (I.vi).

† A British tennis player, Nuthall (1911–83) was ranked in the world's top ten in 1927 and lost the US singles championship to Helen Wills Moody that year.

He covered two foot of pebbles with the orange sand rolled into them. A tidy job it must be rolling on that slope! Still, the actual gradient was not so steep on the zigzags. One in sixteen perhaps. He covered another two foot[36] of pebbles with orange sand rolled in. How could he? How could he cover another two? His heels were trembling!

Four counties ran out below his feet. To the horizon! *He showed him the kingdoms of the earth.** As great a view as above Groby, but not purple and with no sea. Trust father to settle where you could see a great view by going up hill. *Vox adhæsit....* "His[37] feet were rooted to the earth." ... No, *vox adhæsit faucibus*† meant that his voice stuck to his jaws. Palate rather. His palate was as dry[38] as sawdust! How *could* he do it!... A terrible thing! They called it Sex!... His mother had coerced him into this dry palate and trembling heels by the force of her sex fever. Dreadful good-nights they had had in her boudoir, she forcing and forcing and forcing him[39] with arguments to go. To come here. Beautiful mother!... Cruel! Cruel!

The boudoir all lit up. Warm! Scented! Mother's shoulders! A portrait of Nell Gwynn by Sir Peter Lely.‡ Mrs. de Bray[40] Pape wanted to buy it. Thought she could buy the earth, but Lord Fittleworth only laughed.... How had they all got forced down there? By mother.... To spy on father. Mother had never set any store by[41] Fittleworth—good fellow Fittleworth, good land-lord!—till last winter when she had got to know that father had bought this place. Then it was Fittleworth, Fittleworth, Fittle-worth! Lunches, dinner, dances at the Ambassadors. Fittleworth wasn't saying no. Who could say no to mother with her figure in the saddle and her hair?

If he had known when they came down to Fittleworth's last winter what he knew now! He knew now that his mother, come down for the hunting, though she had never taken much stock in hunting ... Still, she could ride. Jove, she could ride. He had gone queer all over again and again at first in taking those leaps that she took laughing. Diana, that's what she was.... Well, no,

---

* Matthew 4:8 and Luke 4:5 ('kingdoms of the world' in the King James Bible).

† Virgil, *Aeneid* II.774 and III.48.

‡ There is a portrait of Nell Gwynn 'from the studio of Sir Peter Lely', dated around 1675, in the National Portrait Gallery, where there are also several portraits 'after Sir Peter Lely' by Peter van Bleeck, Gerard Valck, James Macardell and others.

Diana was ... His mother, come down for the hunting, was there to torment father and his ... companion. She had told him. Laughing in that way she had.... It must be sex cruelty!... Laughing like those Leonardi-do-da.... Well, Vinci women. A queer laugh, ending with a crooked smile....* In correspondence[42] with Father's servants.... Dressing up as a housemaid and looking[43] over the hedge.

How *could* she do it? *How?* How could she force him to be here? What would Monty, the Prime Minister's son, Dobles, Porter— fat ass because his father was too beastly rich—what would his set think at Cambridge? They were all Marxist-Communists to a man. But still ...

What would Mrs. Lowther think if she *really* knew?... If she could have been in the corridor one night when he came out from his mother's boudoir! He would have had the courage to ask her then. Her hair was like floss silk, her lips like cut pomegranates.† When she laughed she threw up her head.... He was now warm all over, his eyes wet and warm.

When he had asked if he ought to—if *she* wanted him to—do whatever his mother wanted whether or no he approved.... If his mother asked him to do what he thought was a mean action.... But that had been on the Peacock Terrace with the famous Fittleworth Seven Sister Roses.... How she went against the roses.... In a yellow ... No, moth-coloured ... Not yellow, not yellow. Green's forsaken, but yellow's forsworn.‡ Great pity filled him at the thought that Mrs. Lowther might be forsaken. But she must not be forsworn ... moth-coloured silk. Shim-

---

* This, and the reference to Botticelli's Venus below, strongly evoke Ford's novel *The Young Lovell*, in which the envisioned figure of the goddess Venus has a 'crooked and voluptuous mouth' (47).

† Dante Gabriel Rossetti's 1874 painting, *Proserpine*, for which Jane Morris modelled, contrasts the red of the woman's lips and the flesh of the pomegranate that she holds with cooler, more subdued colours. Ford much admired this painting: see his *Rossetti* (London: Duckworth [1902]), 174. In *Some Do Not ...* Mrs Macmaster's beauty has been defined, from Valentine's point of view, partly by means of her 'pomegranate lips', though Tietjens, recalling the final Macmaster party, alludes to the pre-Raphaelite paintings from the rectory study: 'A fair blaze of bosoms and nipples and lips and pomegranates' (II.iv, II.vi). On Armistice Day the idea of 'eating pomegranates' on the shores of the Mediterranean represents to Valentine the transformative nature of the ending of the war (*A Man Could Stand Up* – I.i).

‡ The old rhyme (one of many applied to the choice of colours worn by a bride) runs 'Oh, green is forsaken, and yellow forsworn, / But blue is the prettiest colour that's worn.'

mering. Against pink roses. Her fine, fine hair, a halo. She had looked up and sideways. She had been going to laugh with her lips like cut pomegranates.... She had told him that as a rule it was a good thing to do what one's mother wanted when she was like Mrs. Christopher Tietjens. Her soft voice.... Soft Southern voice.... Oh, when she laughed at Mrs. de Bray Pape.... How could she be a friend of Mrs. de Bray Pape's?...

If it hadn't been sunlight.... If he had come on Mrs. Lowther as he came out of his mother's boudoir! He would have had courage. At night. Late. He would have said: "If you are really interested in my fate tell me if I ought to spy upon my father and his ... companion!" She would not have laughed, late at night. She would have given him her hand. The loveliest hands and the lightest feet. And her eyes would have dimmed....[44] Lovely, lovely pansies! Pansies are heartsease....*

Why did he have these thoughts: these wafts of intolerable ... oh, desire. He was his mother's son.... His mother was ... He would kill anyone who said it....

Thank God! Oh, thank God! He was down on the crazy paving level with the house. *AND there was another path went up to Uncle Mark's shed.* The Blessed Virgin—who was like Helen Lowther!—had watched over him. He had not to walk under those little deep, small-paned windows.

His father's ... companion might have been looking out. He would have fainted....

His father was a good sort of man. But he, too, must be ... like Mother. If what they said was true. Ruined by dissolute living. But a good, grey man. The sort of man to be tormented by Mother. Great spatulate fingers. But no one had ever tied flies like Father. Some he had tied years ago were the best he, Mark Tietjens junior of Groby, had yet. And Father loved the wine-coloured moor. *How* could he stifle under these boughs! A house overhung by trees is unsanitary. Italians say[45] that....

But what a lovely glimpse under the trees! Sweet-williams along the path. Light filtered by boughs. Shadow. Gleams in the little window-panes. Wall-stones all lichen. That's England. If he

---

* Usually applied to the wild pansy (viola tricolour), though, at least up to the sixteenth century, also to the wallflower.

could spend a while here with Father. . . .

Father had been matchless with horses. Women, too. . . .
What an inheritance was his, Mark Tietjens, junior's! If he could
spend a while here. . . . But his Father slept with. . . . If she came
out of the door. . . . She must be beautiful. . . . No they said she
was not a patch on mother. He had overheard that at Fittleworth's. Or Helen Lowther. . . . But his father had had his
pick!. . . [46] If he chose then to sleep with . . .

If she came out of the door he would faint. . . . Like the Venus
of Botti . . . A crooked smile. . . . No, Helen Lowther would
protect. . . . He might fall in love with his Father's . . . What do
you know of what[47] will happen to you when you come in contact
with the Bad Woman. . . . Of advanced views. . . . They said she
was of Advanced Views. And a Latinist. . . . He was a Latinist.
Loved it!

Or his father might with Hel . . . Hot jealousy filled him. His
father was the sort of man . . . She might . . . Why did over . . .
People like mother and father beget children?

He kept his eyes fascinatedly fixed on the stone porch of the
cottage whilst he stumbled up the great stone slabs to the path.
The path led to Uncle Mark's wall-less thatched hut. . . . No form
filled the porch. What was to become of him? He had great
wealth; terrific temptation would be his. His mother was no
guide. His father might have been better. . . . Well, there was
Marxian-Communism. They all looked to that now, in his set at
Cambridge. Monty, the Prime Minister's son, with black eyes;
Dobles, Campion's nephew, lean as a rat; Porter, with a pig's
snout, but witty as hell. Fat ass.

CHAPTER IV

MARK TIETJENS thought that a cow or a hog must have got into the orchard, there was such a rushing in the grass. He said to himself that that damn Gunning was always boasting about his prowess as a hedger; he might see that his confounded hedges kept out the beasts from the Common. An unusual voice— unusual in its intonation—remarked:

"Oh, Sir Mark Tietjens, this is dreadful!"

It appeared to be dreadful. A lady in a long skirt—an apparently elderly Di Vernon out of *Waverley*,[1]* which was one of the few novels Mark had ever read[2]—was making dreadful havoc with the standing grass. The beautiful, proud heads swayed and went down as she rushed knee-deep amongst it; stopped, rushed again across his view and then stopped apparently to wring her hands and once more explain that it was dreadful. A tiny rabbit, scared out by her approach, scuttered out under his bed and presumably down into the vegetable beds. Marie[3] Léonie's Mistigris† would probably get it and, since it was Friday, Marie Léonie would be perturbed.

The lady pushed through the remaining tall grass that stood between them and had the air of rising up at his bed-foot.‡ She was rather a faint figure—like the hedge-sparrow. In grey, with a grey short coat and a waistcoat with small round buttons and a three-cornered hat. A tired, thin face. . . . Well, she must be tired, pushing through that long grass with a long skirt. She had a switch of green shagreen. The hen-tomtit that lived in the old shoe they had tucked on purpose under his thatch uttered long warning cries. The hen-tomtit did not like the aspect of this apparition.

---

*   Diana Vernon is the heroine of Walter Scott's *Rob Roy* rather than *Waverley*.
†   This is Marie Léonie's – presumably Roman Catholic – cat, mentioned in the opening chapter: 'She had a cat that she made abstain from meat on Friday.'
‡   A curious echo of *The Good Soldier*, in which Dowell recalls Nancy Rufford 'appearing suddenly to Edward, rising up at the foot of his bed' (130). And later: 'That was the picture that never left his imagination—the girl, in the dim light, rising up at the foot of his bed' (154).

She was devouring his face with her not disagreeable eyes and muttering:

"Dreadful! Dreadful!" An aeroplane was passing close over-head. She[4] looked up and remarked almost tearfully:

"Hasn't it struck you that but for the sins of your youth you might be doing stunts round these good-looking hills? Now!"*

Mark considered the matter, fixedly returning her glance. For an Englishman the phrase, "the sins of your youth," as applied to a gentleman's physical immobility implies only one thing.† It never had occurred to him that that implication might be tacked on to him. But of course it might. It was an implication of a disagreeable, or at least a discrediting, kind, because in his class they had been accustomed to consider that the disability[5] was incurred by consorting with public women of a cheap kind. He had never consorted with any woman in his life but Marie Léonie, who was health exaggerated. But if he had had to do with women he would have gone in for the most expensive sort. And taken precautions! A gentleman owes that to his fellows!

The lady was continuing:

"I may as well tell you at once that I am Mrs. Millicent de Bray Pape. And hasn't it struck you that but for *his* depravity—unbridled depravity—your brother might to-day be operating in Capel Court‡ instead of peddling old furniture at the end of the world?"

She added disconcertingly:

"It's nervousness that makes me talk like this. I have always been shy in the presence of notorious libertines. That is my education."

Her name conveyed to him that this lady was going to occupy Groby. He saw no objection to it. She had, indeed, written to ask him if he saw any objection to it. It had been a queerly written letter, in hieroglyphs of a straggling and convoluted kind. . . . "I am[6] the lady who is going to rent your mansion, Groby, from my friend Mrs. Sylvia."

---

* That unappealing phrase, 'doing stunts', resurfaces – and is discussed – in *Portraits from Life* 205, 215.
† Venereal disease, most likely tertiary syphilis. The phrase is from Psalms 25:7: 'Remember not the sins of my youth.' Violet Hunt contracted syphilis many years before she and Ford became lovers: Joan Hardwick, *An Immodest Violet: The Life of Violet Hunt* (London: André Deutsch, 1990), 41–2.
‡ The location of the London Stock Exchange.

It had struck him then—whilst Valentine had been holding the letter up for him to read. . . . Pretty piece, Valentine, nowadays. The country air suited her—that this woman must be an intimate friend of his brother's wife Sylvia. Otherwise she would have said "Mrs. Sylvia Tietjens," at least.

Now he was not so certain. This was not the sort of person to be an intimate friend of that bitch's. Then she was a cat's-paw. Sylvia's intimates—amongst women—were all Bibbies and Jimmies and Marjies. If she spoke to any other woman it was to make use of her—as a lady's maid or a tool.

The lady said:

"It must be agony to you to be reduced to letting your ancestral home. But that does not seem to be a reason for not speaking to me. I meant to ask the Earl's housekeeper for some eggs for you, but I forgot. I am always forgetting. I am so active. Mr. de Bray Pape says I am the most active woman from here to Santa Fé."

Mark wondered: why Santa Fé? That was probably because Mr. Pape[7] had olive-tree plantations in that part of California.* Valentine[8] had told him over Mrs. Pape's letter[9] that Mr. Pape[10] was the largest olive-oil merchant in the world. He cornered all the olive-oil and all the straw-coloured flasks in Provence, Lombardy, California, and informed his country that you were not really refined if you used in your salads oil that did not come out of a Pape Quality flask.[11] He showed ladies and gentlemen in evening dress starting back from expensively laid dinner-tables, holding their noses and exclaiming: "Have you no *Papes!*" Mark wondered where Christopher got his knowledges,[12] for naturally Valentine had the information from him. Probably Christopher had looked at American papers. But why should one look at American papers? Mark himself never had. Wasn't there the *Field*?. . .† He was a queer chap, Christopher.

The lady said:

"It *isn't* a reason for not speaking to me! It isn't!"

Her greyish face flushed slowly. Her eyes glittered behind her rimless pince-nez. She exclaimed:

---

* Santa Fé is the capital of New Mexico. This is presumably designed to further emphasise Mark's lack of knowledge of, and interest in, the United States.

† *The Field* was first published in 1853 and continues today, catering for enthusiasts of country sports and pursuits.

"You are probably too haughtily aristocratic to speak to me, Sir Mark Tietjens. But I have in me the soul of the Maintenon; you are only the fleshly descendant of a line of chartered libertines. That is what Time and the New World have done to redress the balance of the Old. It is we who are keeping up the status of the grands seigneurs of old in your so-called ancestral homes."

He thought she was probably right. Not a bad sort of woman: she would naturally be irritated at his not answering her. It was proper enough.

He never remembered to have spoken to an American or to have thought about America. Except, of course, during the war. Then he had spoken to Americans in uniform about Transport. He hadn't liked their collars,* but they had known their jobs as far as their jobs went—which had been asking to be provided with a disproportionate amount of transport for too few troops. He had had to wring that transport out of the country.

If he had had his way he wouldn't have. But he hadn't had his way. Because the Governing Classes were no good. Transport is the soul of a war: the spirit of an army had used to be in its feet, Napoleon had said.† Something like that. But those fellows had starved the army of transport; then flooded it with so much it couldn't move; then starved it again. Then they had insisted on his finding enormously too much transport for those fellows with queer collars[13] who used it for disposing of typewriters[14] and sewing machines that came over on transports.... It had broken his back. That and solitude. There had not been a fellow he could talk to in the Government towards the end. Not one who knew the difference between the ancestry of Persimmon and the stud form of Sceptre or Isinglass.‡ Now they were paying for it.

---

*   It's not clear whether Mark refers to the design of the collar or, more likely, the bronze collar service devices that indicated the enlisted man's affiliation, such as ordnance or medical departments, field artillery, trench mortar, engineers or quartermaster corps.

†   Cf. *No More Parades* II.i, where the newly promoted Second-Lieutenant Cowley tells Sylvia Tietjens: 'Madam! If the brains of an army aren't, the life of an army *is* ... in its feet.'

‡   In 1896 Persimmon (sired by St Simon) won both the Derby and the St Leger, together with the Eclipse Stakes and the Ascot Gold Cup. Sceptre was sired by Persimmon and won four classics in the 1902 season, retiring in 1904 with 13 victories. Isinglass won the triple crown (2000 Guineas, Derby and St Leger) in 1893. In *It's a Battlefield* (1934), Graham Greene would write: 'Behind the tall upper windows old ladies in silks spoke softly of meeting Mr Browning in Florence to old men with white mous-

The lady was saying to him that her spiritual affinity was probably a surprise to Sir Mark. There was none the less no mistake about it. In every one of the Maintenon's houses she felt instantly at home; the sight in any Museum of any knick-knack[15] or jewel that had belonged to the respectable companion of Louis Quatorze startled her as if with an electric shock. Mr. Quarternine, the celebrated upholder of the metempsychosistic school, had told her that those phenomena proved beyond doubt that the soul of the Maintenon had returned to earth in her body. What, as against that, were the mere fleshly claims of Old Family?

Mark considered that she was probably right. The old families of his country were a pretty inefficient lot that he was thankful to have done with. Racing was mostly carried on by English nobles from Frankfort-on-the-Main. If this lady could be regarded as speaking allegorically she was probably right. And she had had to get a soul from somewhere.

But she talked too much about it. People ought not to be so tremendously fluent. It was tiring; it failed to hold the attention. She was going on.

He lost himself in speculations as to her reason for being there, trampling on his brother's grass. It would give Gunning and the extra hands no end of an unnecessary job to cut. The lady was talking about Marie Antoinette. Marie Antoinette had gone sledging on salt in summer.* Trampling down hay-grass was really worse. Or no better. If every one in the country trampled on grass like that it would put up the price of fodder for transport animals to something prohibitive.

Why had she come there? She wanted to take Groby furnished. She might for him. He had never cared about Groby. His father had never had a stud worth talking about. A selling plater† or two.

---

taches, whose interest in racing had never survived the ecstatic moment of Persimmon's passing.' This was the novel that Greene sent to Ford when they first corresponded.

* In fact, popular tradition maintained that it was Maria Theresa, Empress of Austria and mother of Marie Antoinette, who, in the summer of 1751, prevailed upon her host, Count Grassalkovich, to have a year's supply of salt from the Felvidék mine spread on the road so that she could go sledging from Buda to Gödöllő.

† An inferior racehorse that competes chiefly in plate or prize races: here, a race in which the owners agree in advance to sell the horses. In *The Good Soldier* 'the name of the chap who rode a plater down the Khyber cliffs' is used as an illustrative example of the sort of thing that Edward Ashburnham thought – and talked – about (24).

He had[16] never cared for hunting or shooting. He remembered standing on Groby lawn watching the shooting parties take to the hills on the Twelfth* and feeling rather a fool. Christopher of course loved Groby. He was younger and hadn't expected to own it.

A pretty muck Sylvia might have made of the place—if[17] her mother had let her. Well, they would know pretty soon. Christopher would be back if the machine did not break his obstinate neck.... What, then, was this woman doing here? She probably represented a new turn of the screw that that unspeakable woman was administering to Christopher.

His sister-in-law Sylvia represented for him unceasing, unsleeping activities of a fantastic kind. She wanted, he presumed, his brother to go back and sleep with her. So much hatred could have no other motive.... There could be no other motive for sending this American lady here.

The American lady was telling him that she intended to keep up at Groby a semi-regal state—of course with due democratic modesty. Apparently she saw her way to squaring that circle!... Probably there are ways. There must be quite a lot of deucedly rich fellows in that country! How did they reconcile doing themselves well with democracy? Did their valets sit down to meals with them, for instance? That would be bad for discipline. But perhaps they did not care about discipline. There was no knowing.

Mrs. de Bray Pape apparently approved of having footmen in powder and the children of the tenants kneeling down† when she drove out in his father's coach and six. Because she intended to use his father's coach and six when she drove over the moors to Redcar or Scarborough.[18] That, Mrs. de Bray Pape had been told by Sylvia, was what his father had done. And it was true enough. That queer old josser his father had always had out that

---

* Twelfth of August, traditionally the start of the grouse-hunting season. In *Some Do Not ...* II.ii Tietjens views his ability to recall this date as a possible sign of recovery: 'He repeated these names and dates to himself for the personal satisfaction of knowing that, amongst the repairs effected in his mind, these two remained: Eton and Harrow, the end of the London season: 12th of August, grouse shooting begins.... It was pitiful....'

† Ford writes in *Heart of the Country*: 'The other day, in my own village, I heard a wealthy lady lamenting that the little girls did not curtsey to her: she had been in the place six months' (*England* 141).

monstrosity when he went justicing or to the Assizes. That was to keep up his state. He didn't see why Mrs. de Bray Pape shouldn't keep up hers if she wanted to. But he did not see the tenants' children kneeling to the lady! Imagine old Scutt's[19] children at it, or Long Tom o' th' Clough's!... Their grandchildren, of course. They had called his father "Tietjens"—some of them even "Auld Mark!" to his face. He himself had always been "Young Mark" to them. Very likely he was still. These things do not change any more than the heather on the moors. He wondered what the tenants would call her. She would have a tough time of it. They weren't her tenants; they were his and they jolly well knew it. These fellows who took houses and castles furnished thought they jolly well hired the family.[20] There had been before the war a fellow from Frankfort-on-the-Main took Lindisfarne or Holy Island or some such place and hired a bagpiper to play round the table while they ate. And closed his eyes whilst the fellow played reels. As if it had been a holy occasion.... Friend of Sylvia's friends in the Government. To do her credit she would not stop with Jews. The only credit she had to her tail!

Mrs. de Bray Pape was telling him that it was not undemocratic to have your tenants' children kneel down when you passed.

A boy's voice said:

"Uncle Mark!" Who the devil could that be? Probably the son of one of the people[21] he had week-ended with. Bowlby's maybe; or Teddy Hope's. He had always liked children and they liked him.

Mrs. de Bray Pape was saying that, yes, it was good for the tenants' children. The Rev. Dr. Slocombe, the distinguished educationalist, said that these touching old rites should be preserved in the interests of the young. He said that to see the Prince of Wales at the Coronation kneeling before his father and swearing fealty had been most touching.* And she had seen pictures of the Maintenon having it done when she walked out.

---

*　Ford wrote a piece about Edward VIII during the abdication crisis of 1936, which was broadcast on NBC. He had seen the coronation of George V in June 1911 and recalled Edward on that occasion, standing 'lonely, embarrassed and aloof'. Three days after the broadcast, Edward abdicated. 'Last Words About Edward VIII', unpublished manuscript: see Saunders, *Dual Life* II 502.

She was now the Maintenon, therefore it must be right. But for Marie Antoinette . . .

The boy's voice said:

"I hope you will excuse. . . . I *know* it isn't the thing. . . ."

He couldn't see the boy without turning his head on the pillow and he was not going to turn his head. He had a sense of someone a yard or so away at his off-shoulder. The boy at least had not come through the standing hay.

He did not imagine that the son of anyone he had ever week-ended with would ever walk through standing hay. The young generation were a pretty useless lot, but he could hardly believe they would have come to that yet. Their sons might. . . . He saw visions of tall dining-rooms lit up, with tall pictures and dresses, and the sunset through high windows over tall grasses in the parks. He was done with that. If any tenants' children ever knelt to him it would be when he took his ride in his wooden coat to the little church over the Moors. . . . Where his father had shot himself.

That had been a queer go. He remembered getting the news. He had been dining at Marie Léonie's. . . .

The boy's voice was, precisely, apologizing for the fact that that lady had walked through the grass. At the same time, Mrs. de Bray Pape was saying things to the discredit of Marie Antoinette, whom apparently she disliked. He could not imagine why anyone should dislike Marie Antoinette. Yet very likely she was dislike-able. The French, who were sensible people, had cut her head off, so *they*[22] presumably disliked her. . . .

He had been dining at Marie Léonie's, she standing, her hands folded before her, hanging down, watching him eat his mutton chops and boiled potatoes, when the porter from his Club had 'phoned through that there was a wire for him. Marie Léonie had answered the telephone. He had told her to tell the porter to open the telegram and read it to her. That was a not unusual proceeding. Telegrams that came to him at the Club usually announced the results of races that he had not attended. He hated to get up from the dinner-table. She had come back slowly, and said still more slowly that she had bad news for him; there had been an accident; his father had been found shot dead.

He had sat still for quite a time; Marie Léonie also had said nothing. He remembered that he had finished his chops, but had not eaten his apple-pie. He had finished his claret.

By that time he had come to the conclusion that his father had probably committed suicide, and that he—he, Mark Tietjens— was probably responsible for his father's having done that. He had got up, then, told Marie Léonie to get herself some mourning, and had taken the night train to Groby. There had been no doubt about it when he got there. His father had committed suicide. His father was not the man unadvisedly to[23] crawl through a quicken-hedge with his gun at full-cock behind him, after rabbits.... It had been purposed.*

There was, then, something soft about the Tietjens stock—for there had been no real and sufficient cause for the suicide. Obviously his father had had griefs. He had never got over the death of his second wife; that was soft for a Yorkshireman. He had lost two sons and an only daughter in the war; other men had done that and got over it. He had heard through him, Mark, that his youngest son—Christopher—was a bad hat. But plenty of men had sons who were bad hats.... Something soft then about the stock! Christopher certainly was soft. But that came from the mother. Mark's stepmother had been from the south of Yorkshire. Soft people down there:[24] a soft woman. Christopher had been her ewe-lamb and she had died of grief when Sylvia had run away from him!...[25]

The boy with a voice had got himself into view towards the bottom of the bed, near Mrs. de Bray Pape ... a tallish slip of a boy, with slightly chawbacony cheeks,† high-coloured, lightish hair, brown eyes. Upstanding but softish. Mark seemed to know him, but could not place him. The boy asked[26] to be forgiven for the intrusion, saying that he knew it was not the thing.

Mrs. de Bray Pape was talking improbably about Marie Antoinette, whom she very decidedly disliked. She said that Marie Antoinette had behaved with great ingratitude to Madame de Maintenon—which must have been difficult. Apparently, according to Mrs. de Bray Pape, when Marie Antoinette had been

---

* In *Some Do Not ...*, however, he reflects that 'Hundreds of men, mostly farmers, die from that cause every year in England....' (II.iii).

† Chawbacon is 'a ludicrous or contemptuous designation for a country clown; a bumpkin' (*OED*).

a neglected little girl about the Court of France, Madame de Maintenon had befriended her, lending her frocks, jewels and perfumes. Later Marie Antoinette had persecuted her benefactor. From that had arisen all the woes of France and the Old World in general.

That appeared to Mark to be to mix history, but he was not very certain.* Mrs. de Bray Pape said, however, that she had those little-known facts from Mr. Reginald Weiler, the celebrated professor of social economy at one of the Western Universities.

Mark returned to the consideration of the softness of the Tietjens stock, whilst the boy gazed at him with eyes that might have been imploring or that might have been merely moon-struck. Mark could not see what the boy could have to be imploring about, so it was probably just stupidity. His breeches, however, were very nicely cut. Very nicely, indeed;[27] Mark recognized the[28] tailor—a man in Conduit Street.† If that fellow had the sense to get his riding breeches from that man, he could not be quite an ass....

That Christopher was soft because his mother did not come from the north of Yorkshire or Durham might be true enough—but that was not enough to account for the race dying out. His, Mark's, father had no descendants by his sons. The[29] two brothers who had been killed had been childless. He himself had none. Christopher ... Well, that was debateable![30]

That he, Mark, had practically killed his own father he was ready to acknowledge. One made mistakes; that was one. If one made mistakes, one should try to repair them; otherwise, one must, as it were, cut one's losses. He could not bring his father back to life; he hadn't, equally, been able to do anything for Christopher.... Not much, certainly. The fellow had[31] refused his brass.... He couldn't really blame him.

The boy was asking him if he would not speak to them. He said he was Mark's nephew, Mark Tietjens junior.

Mark took credit to himself because he did not stir a hair. He had so made up his mind, he found, that Christopher's son was not his son that he had almost forgotten the cub's existence. But

* Madame de Maintenon died in 1719; Marie Antoinette was born in 1755.
† At the time of the First World War there were some three dozen tailors in Conduit Street, several of them listed separately as breeches-makers, including Jacob Dege and Sons, J.W. Reakes and Sandilands & Son.

he ought not to have made up his mind so quickly: he was astonished to find from the automatic working of his mind that he so
had. There were too many factors to be considered that he had
never bothered really to consider. Christopher had determined
that this boy should have Groby: that had been enough for him,
Mark. He did not care[32] who had Groby.

But the actual sight of this lad whom he had never seen before
presented the problem to him as something that needed solution.
It came as a challenge. When he came to think of it, it was a challenge to him to make up his mind finally as to the nature of
Woman. He imagined that he had never bothered his head about
that branch of the animal kingdom. But he found that, lying
there, he must have spent quite a disproportionate amount of his
time in thinking about the motives of Sylvia.

He had never spoken much with any but men—and then
mostly with men of his own class and type. Naturally you
addressed a few polite words to your week-end hostess. If you
found yourself in the rose-garden of a Sunday before church with
a young or old woman who knew anything about horses, you
talked about horses, or Goodwood, or Ascot to her for long
enough to show politeness to your hostess's guests. If she knew
nothing about horses you talked about the roses or the irises, or
the weather last week. But that pretty well exhausted it.

Nevertheless, he knew all about women. Of that he was confident. That is to say, that when in the course of conversation or
gossip he had heard the actions of women narrated or commented
on, he had always been able to supply a motive for those actions
sufficient to account for them to his satisfaction, or to let him
predict with accuracy what course the future would take. No
doubt, twenty years of listening to the almost ceaseless but never
disagreeable conversation of Marie Léonie had been a liberal
education.

He regarded his association with her with complete satisfaction—as the only subject for complete satisfaction to be found in
the contemplation of the Tietjens family. Christopher's Valentine was a pretty piece enough and had her head screwed
confoundedly well on. But Christopher's association with her had
brought such a peck of troubles down on his head that, except for
the girl as an individual, it was a pretty poor choice. It was a man's

job to pick a woman who would neither worry him nor be the cause of worries. Well, Christopher had picked two—and look at the results!

He himself had been completely unmistaken—from the first minute. He[33] had first seen Marie Léonie on the stage at[34] Covent Garden. He had gone to Covent Garden in attendance on his stepmother, his father's second wife—the soft woman. A florid, gentle, really saintly person. She had passed around Groby for a saint. An Anglican saint, of course.[*] That was what was the matter with Christopher. It was the soft streak. A Tietjens had no business with[35] saintliness in his composition! It was bound to get him looked on as a blackguard!

But he had attended Covent Garden as a politeness to his stepmother, who very seldom found herself in Town. And there, in the second row of the ballet, he had seen Marie Léonie—slimmer, of course, in those days. He had at once made up his mind to take up with her, and, an obliging commissionaire having obtained her address for him from the stage-door, he had, towards twelve-thirty next day, walked[36] along the Edgware Road towards her lodgings. He had intended to call on her; he met her, however, in the street. Seeing her there, he had liked her walk, her figure, her neat dress.

He had planted himself, his umbrella, his billycock hat and all, squarely in front of her—she had neither flinched nor attempted to bolt round him—and had said that, if at the end of her engagement in London, she cared to be placed "*dans ses draps*,"[†] with two hundred and fifty pounds a year and pin money to be deliberated on, she might hang up her cream-jug at an apartment that he would take for her in St. John's Wood Park, which was the place in which, in those days, most of his friends had establishments. She had preferred the neighbourhood of the Gray's Inn Road, as reminding her more of France.

But Sylvia was quite another pair of shoes. . . .

[*]　Ford begins a 1914 essay by remarking that a friend of his had said, 'in a matter-of-fact tone, "My mother was a saint!"' (*Critical Essays* 129). The friend sounds very much like Arthur Marwood and, in the same context, Ford mentions as 'his poets' Vaughan, Crashaw and George Herbert, whose 'Vertue' is quoted. In *The Marsden Case* Jessop's brother (apart from lying about his 'great view') is 'a saint – of the English variety' (135).

[†]　Between his sheets, i.e., as his mistress (French).

That young man was flushing all over his face. The young of the tomtit in the old shoe were getting impatient; they were chirruping in spite of the alarm-cries of the mother on the boughs above the thatch. It was certainly insanitary to have boughs above your thatch, but what did it matter in days so degenerate that even the young of tomtits could not restrain their chirpings in face of their appetites.

That young man—Sylvia's by-blow—was addressing embarrassed remarks to Mrs. de Bray Pape. He suggested that perhaps his uncle resented the lady's lectures on history and sociology. He said they had come to talk about the tree. Perhaps that was why his uncle would not speak to them.

The lady said that it was precisely giving lessons in history to the dissolute aristocracy of the Old World that was her mission in life. It was for their good, resent it how they might. As for talking about the tree, the young man had better do it for himself. She now intended to walk around the garden to see how the poor lived.

The boy said that in that case he did not see why Mrs. de Bray Pape had come at all. The lady answered that she had come at the sacred behest of his injured mother. That ought to be answer enough for him. She flitted, disturbedly, from[37] Mark's view.

The boy, swallowing visibly in his throat, fixed his slightly protruding eyes on his uncle's face. He was about to speak, but he remained for a long time silent and goggling. That was a Christopher Tietjens trick—not a Tietjens family trick. To gaze at you a long time before speaking. Christopher had it, no doubt, from his mother—exaggeratedly. She would gaze at you for a long time. Not unpleasantly, of course. But Christopher had always irritated him, even as a small boy. . . . It is possible that he himself might[38] not be as he was if he[39] hadn't gazed at him for a long time, like a stuck pig. On the morning of that beastly day. Armistice Day. . . . Beastly.

Cramp's eldest son, a bugler in the second Hampshires, went down the path, his bugle shining behind his khaki figure.* Now they would make a beastly row with that instrument. On Armistice Day they had played the Last Post on the steps of the

---

* Cf. Ford writing of life at Coopers, mentioning Hunt the carpenter, his wife, the laundress, 'their son, who was in the Royal Artillery' and 'his damnable bugle' (*Nightingale* 141).

church under Marie Léonie's windows. . . . The Last Post! . . . The
Last of England! He remembered thinking that. He had not by
then had the full terms of that surrender, but he had had a dose
enough of Christopher's stuck-piggedness! . . . A full dose! He
didn't say he didn't deserve it. If you make mistakes you must take
what you get for it. You shouldn't make mistakes.

The boy at the foot of the bed was making agonized motions
with his throat: swallowing his Adam's apple.[40]

He said:

"I can understand, uncle, that you hate to see us. All the same,
it seems a little severe to refuse to speak to us!"

Mark wondered a little at the breakdown in communications
that there must have been. Sylvia had been spying round that
property, and round and round and round again. She had had
renewed interviews with Mrs. Cramp. It had struck him as curious
taste to like to reveal to dependents——to reveal and to dwell
upon the fact that you were distasteful to your husband. If his
woman had left him he would have preferred to hold his tongue
about it. He certainly would not have gone caterwauling about it
to the carpenter of the man she had taken up with. Still, there
was no accounting for tastes. Sylvia had, no doubt, been so full
of her own griefs that very likely she[41] had not listened to what
Mrs. Cramp had said about his, Mark's, condition. On the one or
two interviews he had had with[42] that bitch she had been like
that. She had sailed in with her grievances against Christopher
with such vigour that she had gone away with no ideas at all as
to the conditions on which she was to be allowed to inhabit
Groby. Obviously it taxed her mind to invent what she invented.
You could not invent that sort of sex-cruelty stuff without having
your mind a little affected. She could not, for instance, have
invented the tale that he, Mark, was suffering for the sins of his
youth without its taking it out of her. That is the ultimate retri-
bution of Providence on those who invent gossip frequently.
They go a little dotty. . . . The fellow—he could not call his name
to mind, half Scotch, half Jew, who had told him the worst tales
against Christopher had gone a little dotty.* He had grown a

---

* Ruggles, who shared Mark's rooms and spread scurrilous rumours about Christopher.
Mentioned in *No More Parades*, he features mainly in *Some Do Not* . . . , particularly
II.iii.

beard and wore a top-hat at inappropriate functions. Well, in effect, Christopher was a saint, and Provvy invents retributions of an ingenious kind against those who libel saints.

At any rate, that bitch must have become so engrossed in her tale that it had not come through to her that he, Mark, could not speak. Of course, the results of venereal disease are not pleasant to contemplate, and, no doubt, Sylvia, having invented the disease for him, had not liked to contemplate the resultant symptoms. At any rate, that boy did not know—and neither did Mrs. de Bray Pape—that he did not speak. Not to them, not to anybody. He was finished with the world. He perceived the trend of its actions, listened to its aspirations, and even to its prayers, but he would never again stir lip or finger. It was like being dead—or being God.[43]

This[44] boy was apparently asking for absolution. He was of opinion that it was not a very sporting thing of himself and Mrs. Bray to come there....

It[45] was, however, sporting enough. He could see that they were both as afraid of him, Mark, as of the very devil. Its taste might, however, be questioned. Still, the situation was unusual—as all situations are.* Obviously[46] it was not in good taste for a boy to come to the house in which his father lived with a mistress, nor for the wife's intimate friend either. Still they apparently wanted, the one to let, the other to take, Groby. They could not do either if he, Mark, did not give permission, or, at any rate, if he opposed them. It was business, and business may be presumed to cover quite a lot of bad taste.

And, in effect, the boy was saying that his mother was, of course, a splendid person, but that he, Mark Junior, found her proceedings in many respects questionable. One could not, however, expect a woman—and an injured woman ... The boy, with his shining eyes and bright cheeks, seemed to beg Mark to concede that his mother was at least an injured woman.... One could not expect, then, a wronged woman to see things eye to eye

---

* Cf. Ford's discussion of the Englishman being 'curiously unable to deal with individual cases' and England thus being one of the worst places to suffer from mental distress, since 'every case of mental distress differs from any other': *England* 248. Cf. *Great Trade Route* 298–9: 'All laws are bad because they can never meet special cases, and every case is a special case.'

with . . . with young Cambridge! For, he hastened to assure Mark, his Set—the son of the Prime Minister, young Doble, and Porter, as well as himself, were unanimously of opinion that a man ought to be allowed to live with whom he liked. He was not, therefore, questioning his father's actions, and, for himself, if the occasion arose, he would be very glad to shake his father's . . . companion . . . by the hand.

His bright eyes became a little humid. He said that he was not in effect questioning anything, but he thought that he himself would have been the better for a little more of his father's influence. He considered that he had been too much under his mother's influence. They noticed it, even at Cambridge! That, in effect, was the real snag when it came to be a question of dissolving unions once contracted. Scientifically considered. Questions of . . . of sex attraction, in spite of all the efforts of scientists, remained fairly mysterious. The best way to look at it . . . the safest way, was that sex attraction occurred, as a rule, between temperamental and physical opposites, because Nature desired to correct extremes. No one, in fact, could be more different than his father and mother—the one so graceful, athletic and . . . oh, charming. And the other so . . . oh, let us say perfectly honourable, but . . . oh, lawless.[47] Because, of course, you can break certain laws and remain the soul of honour.

Mark wondered if this boy was aware that his mother habitually informed every one whom she met that his father lived on women. On the immoral earnings of women, she would infer[*] when she thought it safe. . . .

The soul of honour, then, and masculinely clumsy and damn fine in his way. . . . Well, he, Mark Tietjens junior, was not there to judge his father. His uncle Mark could see that he regarded his father with affection and admiration. But if Nature—he must be pardoned for using anthropomorphic expressions since they were the shortest way—if Nature, then, meant unions of opposite characters to redress extremes in the children, the process did not complete itself with . . . in short, with the act of physical union. For just as there were obviously inherited physical characteristics,

---

[*] 'This use is widely considered to be incorrect, esp. with a person as the subject' (OED). UK, US and TS all agree, however, on 'infer' rather than 'imply'.

and, no doubt, inherited memory, there yet remained the question of the influence of temperament by[48] means of personal association. So that for one opposite to leave the fruits of a union exclusively under the personal influence of the other opposite was very possibly to defeat the purposes of Nature. . . . [49]

That boy, Mark thought, was a very curious problem. He seemed to be a good, straight boy. A little loquacious; still, that was to be excused since he had to do all the talking himself. From time to time he had paused in his speech as if, deferentially, he wished to have Mark's opinion. That was proper. He, Mark, could not stand hobbledehoys—particularly the hobbledehoys of that age, who appeared to be opinionative and emotional beyond the normal in hobbledehoys. Anyhow, he could not stand the Young once they were beyond the age of childhood. But he was aware that, if you want to conduct a scientific investigation, if you want to arrive, for yourself, at the truth of an individual's parentage—you must set aside your likes and dislikes.

Heaven knew, he had found Christopher, when he had been only one of the younger ones in his father's[50]—he had found him irritating enough . . . a rather moony, fair brat, interested mostly in mathematics, with a trick of standing with those goggle eyes gazing bluely at you—years ago, in and around, at first the nursery, then the stables at Groby. Then, if this lad irritated him, it was rather an argument in favour of his being Christopher's son than Sylvia's by-blow by another man. . . . What was the fellow's name?* A rank bad hat, anyhow.

The probability was that he *was* the other fellow's son. That woman would not have trepanned† Christopher into the marriage if she hadn't at least thought that she was with child. There was nothing to be said against any wench's tricking any man into marrying her if she were in that condition. But once having got a man to give a name to your bastard you ought to treat him with some loyalty; it is a biggish service he has done you. That Sylvia had never done. . . . They had got this young fellow[51] into their—the Tietjenses'—family. There he was, with

---

* The name is 'Drake': mentioned later in II.ii, he occurs mainly in *Some Do Not . . .* (I.ii, II.i, II.iii) and is also referred to in *No More Parades* (II.ii).
† 'Trepan': to lure, beguile or ensnare. The *OED* now classifies this sense of the word as 'obsolete' or 'archaic'.

his fingers on Groby already.... That was all right. As great families as Tietjenses[52] had had that happen to them.

But what made Sylvia pestilential was that she should afterwards have developed this sex-madness for his unfortunate brother.

There was no other way to look at it. She had undoubtedly lured Christopher on to marry her because she thought, rightly or wrongly, that she was with child by another man. They would never know—she herself probably did not know!—whether this boy was Christopher's son or the other's. English women are so untidy—shame-faced—about these things. That was excusable. But every other action of hers from that date had been inexcusable—except regarded as actions perpetrated under the impulsion of sex-viciousness.

It is perfectly proper—it is a mother's duty to give an unborn child a name and a father. But afterwards to blast the name of that father is more discreditable than to leave the child nameless. This boy was now Tietjens of Groby—but he was also the boy who was the son[53] of a father who had behaved unspeakably according to the mother.... And the son of a mother who had been unable to attract her man!... Who advertised the fact to the estate carpenter! If we say that the good of the breed is the supreme law what sort of virtue was this?

It was all very well to say that every one of Sylvia's eccentricities had in view the sole aim of getting her boy's father to return to her. No doubt they might. He, Mark, was[54] perfectly ready to concede that even her infidelities, notorious as they had been, might have been merely ways of calling his unfortunate brother's attention back to her—of keeping herself in his mind. After the marriage Christopher, finding out that he had been a mere cat's-paw, probably treated her pretty coldly or ignored her—maritally.... And he was a pretty attractive fellow, Christopher. He, Mark, was bound nowadays to acknowledge that. A regular saint and Christian martyr and all that.... Enough to drive a woman wild if she had to live beside him and be ignored.

It is obvious that women must be allowed what means they can make use of to maintain—to arouse—their sex attraction for their men. That is what the bitches are for in the scale of things.

They have to perpetuate the breed. To do that they have to call attention to themselves and to use what devices they see[55] fit to use, each one according to her own temperament. That[56] cruelty was an excitant, he was quite ready, too, to concede. He was ready to concede anything to the woman. To be cruel is to draw attention to yourself; you cannot expect to be courted by a man whom you allow to forget you. But there probably ought to be a limit to things. You probably ought in this, as in all other things, to know what you can do and what you can't—and the proof of this particular pudding, as of all others, was in the eating. Sylvia had left no stone unturned in the determination to keep herself in her man's mind, and she had certainly irretrievably lost her man: to another girl. Then she was just a nuisance.

A woman intent on getting a man back ought to have some system, some sort of scheme at the very least. But Sylvia—he knew it from the interminable talk that he had had with Christopher on Armistice Night—Sylvia delighted most in doing what she called pulling the strings of shower-baths.* She did extravagant things, mostly of a cruel kind, for the fun of seeing what would happen. Well, you cannot allow yourself fun when you are on a campaign. Not as to the subject matter of the campaign itself! If then you do what you want rather than what is expedient, you damn well have to take what you get for it.† *Damn* well!

What would have justified Sylvia, no matter what she did, would have been if she had succeeded in having another child by his brother. She hadn't. The breed of Tietjens was not enriched. Then she was just a nuisance. . . .

An infernal nuisance. . . . For what was she up to now? It was perfectly obvious that both Mrs. de Bray Pape and this boy were here because she had had another outbreak of . . . practically Sadism. They were here so that Christopher might be hurt some more and she not forgotten. What, then, was it? What[57] the deuce was it?

---

*   A recurrent phrase in *No More Parades*, it was used by Violet Hunt in her diary ('A showerbath string pulled'); see Robert Secor and Marie Secor, *The Return of the Good Soldier: Ford Madox Ford and Violet Hunt's 1917 Diary* (Victoria, BC: University of Victoria, 1983), 76.

†   Ford often uses this 'Spanish proverb', frequently in the form of 'Do what you want and take what you get for it'. Cf. *A Call* 55, 119; *New York Is Not America* 188; *The English Novel* 93; *A Man Could Stand Up* – II.vi.

The boy had been silent for some time. He was gazing at Mark with the goggle-eyed gasping that had been so irritating in his father—particularly on Armistice Day. . . . Well, he, Mark, was apparently now conceding that this boy was probably his brother's son. A real Tietjens after all was to reign over the enormously long, grey house behind the fantastic cedar. The tallest cedar in Yorkshire. In England. In the Empire. . . . He didn't care. He who lets a tree overhang his roof calls the doctor in daily. . . . The boy's lips began to move. No sound came out. He was presumably in a great state!

He was undoubtedly like his father. Darker . . . Brown hair, brown eyes, high-coloured cheeks all flushed now. Straight nose; marked brown eyebrows. A sort of . . . scared, puzzled . . . what was it?. . . expression. Well, Sylvia was fair; Christopher was dark-haired with silver streaks, but fair-complexioned. . . . Damn it: this boy was more attractive than Christopher had been at his age and earlier. . . . Christopher hanging round the school-room door in Groby, puzzled over the mathematical theory of waves. He, Mark, hadn't been able to stand him or, indeed, any of the other children. There was sister Effie—*born* to be a curate's wife. . . . Puzzled! That was it!. . . That bothering woman, his father's second wife—the Saint!—had[58] introduced the puzzlement strain into the Tietjenses. . . . This was Christopher's boy, saintly strain and all. Christopher was probably born to be a rural dean in a fat living writing treatises on the integral calculus all the time except on Saturday afternoons. With a great reputation for saintliness. Well, he wasn't the one and hadn't the other. He was an old-furniture[59] dealer, who made a stink in virtuous nostrils. . . . Provvy works in a mysterious way. The boy was saying now:

"The tree . . . the great tree. . . . It darkens the windows. . . ."

Mark said: "Aha!"[60] to himself. Groby Great Tree was the symbol of Tietjens. For thirty miles round Groby they made their marriage vows by Groby Great Tree. In the other Ridings they said that Groby Tree and Groby well[61] were equal in height and depth one to the other. When they were really imaginatively drunk Cleveland villagers would declare—would knock you down if you denied—that Groby Great Tree was 365 foot high and Groby well 365 feet deep. A foot for every day of the year. . . .

On special occasions—he could not himself be bothered to remember what—they would ask permission to hang rags and things from the boughs. Christopher said that one of the chief indictments against Joan of Arc had been that she and the other village girls of Domrémy had hung rags and trinkets from the boughs of a cedar. Offerings to[62] fairies.... Christopher set great store by the tree. He was a romantic ass. Probably he set more store by the tree than by anything else at Groby. He would pull the house down if he thought it incommoded the tree.

Young Mark was bleating, positively bleating:

"The Italians have a proverb.... He who lets a tree overhang his house invites a daily call from the doctor.... I agree myself.... In principle, of course...."

Well, that was that! Sylvia, then, was proposing to threaten to ask to have Groby Great Tree cut down. Only to threaten to ask. But that would be enough to agonize the miserable Christopher. You couldn't cut down Groby Great Tree. But the thought that the tree was under the guardianship of unsympathetic people would be enough to drive Christopher almost dotty—for years and years.*

"Mrs. de Bray Pape," the boy was stammering, "is extremely keen on the tree's being.... I agree in principle.... My mother wished you to see that—oh, in modern days—a house is practically unlettable if ... So she got Mrs. de Bray Pape ... She hasn't had the courage though she swore she had...."

He continued to stammer. Then he started and stopped, crimson. A woman's voice had called:

"Mr. Tietjens.... Mr. Mark.... Hi ... hup!"

A small woman, all in white, white breeches, white coat, white wide-awake, was slipping down from a tall bay with a white star on the forehead—a bay with large nostrils and an intelligent head. She waved her hand obviously at the boy and then caressed the horse's nostrils. Obviously at the boy.... for it was obviously unlikely that[63] Mark Senior would know a woman who could make a sound like "Hi, hup!" to attract his attention.

---

* Sylvia has already made this threat to Christopher during the war: 'She warned him that, if he got killed, she should cut down the great cedar at the south-west corner of Groby' (*No More Parades* II.ii).

Lord Fittleworth, in a square, hard hat, sat on an immense, coffin-headed dapple-grey. He had bristling, close-cropped moustaches[64] and sat like a limpet. He waved his crop in the direction of Mark and[65] went on talking to Gunning, who was at his stirrup. The coffin-headed beast started forward and reared a foot or so; a wild, brazen, yelping sound had disturbed it. The boy was more and more scarlet and, as emotion grew on him, more and more like Christopher on that beastly day.... Christopher with a piece of furniture under his arm, in Marie Léonie's room, his eyes goggling out at the foot of the bed.

Mark swore painfully to himself. He hated to be reminded of that day. Now this lad and that infernal bugle that the younger children of Cramp had got hold of from their bugler-brother had put it back damnably in his mind. It went on. At intervals. One child had a try, then another.[66] Obviously then Cramp the eldest took it. It blared out.... Ta ... Ta ... Ta.... Ta ...[67] ti ... ta-ti ... Ta....[68] The Last Post. The b—y[69] infernal Last Post.... Well, Christopher, as that day Mark had predicted, had got himself, with his raw sensibilities, into a pretty b—y[70] infernal mess while some drunken ass had played the Last Post under the window.... Mark meant that whilst that farewell was being played he had had that foresight. And he hated the bugle for reminding him of it. He hated it more than he had imagined. He could not have imagined himself using profanity even to himself. He must have been profoundly moved. Deucedly and profoundly moved at that beastly noise. It had come over the day like a disaster. He saw every detail of Marie Léonie's room as it had been on[71] that day. There was, on the marble mantel-shelf, under an immense engraving of the Sistine Madonna,* a feeding-cup over a night-light in which Marie Léonie had been keeping some sort of pap warm for him.... Probably the last food to which he had ever helped himself....

---

* Raphael painted this Madonna in about 1513 for the church of San Sisto (Saint Sixtus) in Piacenza. It is now in the Gemäldegalerie, Dresden.

CHAPTER V

BUT NO . . . that must have been about twelve, or earlier or later, on that infernal day. In any case he could not remember any subsequent meal he had had then; but he remembered an almost infinitely long period of intense vexation. Of mortification in so far as he could accuse himself of ever having felt mortified. He could still remember the fierce intaking of his breath through his nostrils that had come when Christopher had announced what had seemed to him then his ruinous intentions. . . . It had not been till probably four in the morning that Lord Wolstonmark[1] had rung him, Mark, up[2] to ask him to countermand the transport that was to have gone out from Harwich*. . . . At four in the morning, the idiotic brutes.—His substitute had disappeared in the rejoicings, and[3] Lord Wolstonmark[4] had wanted to know what code they used for Harwich because the transport must at all costs be stopped. There was going to be no advance into Germany. . . . He had never spoken after that!

His brother was done for; the country finished; he was as good as down and out, as the phrase was, himself. In[5] his deep mortification—yes, mortification!—he had said to Christopher that morning—the 11th November, 1918—that he would never speak to him again. He hadn't at that moment meant to say that he would never speak to Christopher at all again—merely that he was never going to speak to him about affairs—the affairs of[6] Groby! Christopher might take that immense, far-spreading, grey bothersome house and the tree and the well and the moors and all the John Peel outfit. Or he might leave them. He, Mark, was never going to speak about the matter any more.

He remembered thinking that Christopher might have taken him to mean that he intended to withdraw, for what it was worth, the light of his countenance from the Christopher Tietjens

---

* The base for the British destroyer and submarine fleets during the Great War. After the Armistice, it was agreed that all remaining German submarines were to be surrendered at Harwich.

ménage.[7] Nothing had been further from his thoughts. He had a soft corner in his heart for Valentine Wannop. He had had it ever since sitting, feeling like a fool, in the anteroom of the War Office, beside her—gnawing at the handle of his umbrella. But, then, he had recommended her to become Christopher's mistress: he had, at any rate, begged her to look after his mutton chops and his buttons. So that it wasn't likely that when, a year or so later, Christopher announced that he really was at last going to take up with the young woman and to chance what came of it—it wasn't likely that he intended to dissociate himself from the two of them.

The idea had worried him so much that he had written a rough note—the last time that his hand had ever held a pen—to Christopher. He had said that a brother's backing was not of great use to a woman, but in the special circumstances of the case, he being Tietjens of Groby for what it was worth, and Lady Tietjens—Marie Léonie—being perfectly willing to be seen on all occasions with Valentine and her man, it might be worth something, at any rate with tenantry and such like.

Well, he hadn't gone back on that!

But once the idea of retiring, not only from the Office but the whole world, had[8] come into his head it had grown and grown, on top of his mortification and his weariness. Because he could not conceal from himself that he was weary to death—of the Office, of the nation, of the world and people.... People ... he was tired of them,[*] and[9] of the streets, and the grass, and the sky and the moors. He had done his job.—That was before Wolstonmark[10] had telephoned, and he still thought that he had done his job of getting things here and there about the world to some purpose.

A man is in the world to do his duty by his nation and his family.... By his own people first. Well, he had to acknowledge that he had let his own people down pretty badly—beginning with Christopher. Chiefly Christopher. But that reacted on the tenantry.

He had always been tired of the tenantry and Groby. He had been born tired of them. That happens. It happens particularly

---

[*]   As editor of the *transatlantic review*, Ford published William Carlos Williams' poem 'Last Words of my Grandmother', which ends: 'Trees? Well, I'm tired / of them and rolled her head away.' In a letter to Ezra Pound that year (1924) Ford wrote: 'I repeat: Trees, Well, I'm tired of them!' See *Pound/Ford* 76, 191–2, n.56. But see also Ford's letter to Ernest Rhys in April 1930 (*Letters* 195).

in old and prominent families. It was odd that Groby and the whole Groby business should so bore[11] him; he supposed he had been born with some kink. All the Tietjenses were born with some sort of kink. It came from the solitude maybe, on the moors, the hard climate, the rough neighbours—possibly even from the fact that Groby Great Tree overshadowed the house. You could not look out of the school-room windows at all for its great, ragged trunk, and all the children's wing was darkened by its branches. Black!... funeral plumes! The Hapsburgs were said to hate their palaces—that was no doubt why so many of them, beginning with Juan Ort,* had come muckers. At any rate, they had chucked the royalty business.

And at a very early age he had decided that he would chuck the country-gentleman business. He didn't see that he was the one to bother with those confounded, hard-headed beggars or with those confounded wind-swept moors and wet[12] valley bottoms. One owed the blighters a duty, but one did not have to live among them or see that they aired their bedrooms. It had been mostly swank that, always; since[13] the Corn Laws, it had been almost entirely swank. Still, it is obvious that a landlord owes something to the estate from which he and his fathers have drawn their incomes for generations and generations.

Well, he had never intended to do it, because he had been born tired of it. He liked racing and talking about racing to fellows who liked racing. He had intended to do that to the end.

He hadn't been able to.

He had intended to go on living between the Office, his chambers, Marie Léonie's and week-ends with race-horse owners of good family until his eyes closed.... Of course God disposes in the end, even of the Tietjenses of Groby! He had intended to give over Groby, on the death of his father, to whichever of his brothers had heirs and seemed likely to run the estate well. That would have been quite[14] satisfactory. Ted, his next brother, had had his head screwed on all right. If he had had children he would

---

* The Archduke John Salvator of Austria renounced his title as well as all connection to the Habsburg Imperial House in 1889 and adopted the name John (or Johann) Orth, after his castle, Schloss Ort, near Gmunden. The ship on which he was travelling disappeared between Montevideo and Valparaiso in 1890. An official decree of his death was finally published in Vienna in May 1911.

have filled the bill. So would the next brother. . . . But neither of
them had had children and both had managed to get killed in
Gallipoli. Even sister Mary, who was actually next to him and a[15]
maîtresse femme if ever there was one, had managed to get killed
as a Red Cross matron. *She* would have run Groby well enough—
the great, blowsy, grey woman with a bit of a moustache.

Thus God had let him down with a bump on Christopher. . . .
Well, Christopher would have run Groby well enough. But he
wouldn't. Wouldn't own a yard of Groby land; wouldn't touch a
penny of Groby money. He was suffering for it now.

They were both, in effect, suffering, for Mark could not see
what was to become of either Christopher or the estate.

Until his father's death Mark had bothered precious little
about the fellow. He was by fourteen years[16] the younger: there
had been ten children altogether, three of his own mother's children having died young and one having been soft. So Christopher
had been still a baby when Mark had left Groby for good—for
good except for visits when he had brought his umbrella and seen
Christopher mooning at the school-room door or in his own
mother's sitting-room. So he had hardly seen[17] the boy.

And at Christopher's wedding he had definitely decided that
he would not see him again—a mug who had got trepanned[18] into
marrying a whore. He wished his brother no ill, but the thought
of him made Mark sickish. And then, for years, he had heard the
worst possible rumours about Christopher. In a way they had
rather consoled Mark. God knows, he cared little enough about
the Tietjens family—particularly for the children by that soft
saint. But he would rather have any brother of his be a wrong un
than a mug.

Then gradually, from the gossip that went abroad, he had come
to think that Christopher was a very bad wrong un indeed. He
could account for it easily enough. Christopher had a soft streak,
and what a woman can do to deteriorate a fellow with a soft streak
is beyond belief. And the woman Christopher had got hold of—
who had got hold of him—passed belief too. Mark did not hold
any great opinion of women at all; if they were a little plump,
healthy, a little loyal and not noticeable in their dress that was
enough for him. . . . But Sylvia was as thin as an eel, as full of vice
as a mare that's a wrong un, completely disloyal and dressed like

any Paris cocotte. Christopher, as he saw it, had had to keep that harlot to the tune of six or seven thousand a year, in a society of all wrong uns[19] too—and on an income of at most two. . . . Plenty for a younger son. But naturally he had had to go wrong to get the money.

So it had seemed to him . . . and[20] it had seemed to matter precious little. He gave a thought to his brother perhaps twice a year. But then one day—just after the two brothers had been killed—their father had come up from Groby to say to Mark at the Club:

"Has[21] it occurred to you that, since those two boys are killed, that fellow Christopher is practically heir to Groby? You have no legitimate children, have you?" Mark replied that he hadn't any bastards either, and that he was certainly not going to marry.

At that date it had seemed to him certain that he was not going to marry Papist Marie Léonie[22] Riotor, and certainly he was not going to marry anyone else. So Christopher—or at any rate Christopher's heir—must surely come in to Groby. It had not really, hitherto, occurred to him. But when it was thus put forcibly into his mind he saw instantly that it upset the whole scheme of his life. As he saw Christopher then, the fellow was the last person in the world to have the charge of Groby—for you had to regard that as to some extent a cure of souls.* And he, himself, would not be much better. He was hopelessly out of touch with the estate, and, even though his father's land-steward was a quite efficient fellow, he himself at that date was so hopelessly immersed in the affairs of the then war that he would hardly have a moment of time to learn anything about the property.

There was, therefore, a breakdown in his scheme of life. That was already a pretty shaking sort of affair. Mark was accustomed to regard himself as master of his fate†—as being so limited in his ambitions and so entrenched behind his habits and his wealth that, if circumstances need not of necessity bend to his will, fate could hardly touch him.

---

*   OED gives for one meaning of 'cure': 'The spiritual charge or oversight of parishioners or lay people; the office or function of a curate. Commonly in phrase *cure of souls*.'

†   A highly literary phrase: W.E. Henley, 'Invictus' ('I am the master of my fate / I am the captain of my soul'); Tennyson, 'The Marriage of Geraint', *Idylls of the King* (Enid sings: 'For man is man and master of his fate'); Shakespeare, *Julius Caesar*, I.ii.140 (Cassius: 'Men at sometime were masters of their fates').

And it was one thing for a Tietjens younger son to be a bold sort of law-breaker—or at any rate that he should be contemptuous of restraint. It was quite another that the heir to Groby should be a soft sort of bad[23] hat whose distasteful bunglings led his reputation to stink in the nostrils of all his own class if[24] a younger son can be said to have a class.... At any rate in the class to which his father and eldest brother belonged. Tietjens was said to have sold his wife to her cousin the Duke at so contemptible a price that he was obviously penniless even after that transaction. He had sold her to other rich men—to bank managers, for instance. Yet even after that he was reduced to giving stumer* cheques. If a man sold his soul to the devil he should at least insist on a good price. Similar transactions were said to distinguish the social set in which that bitch moved—but most of the men who, according to Ruggles, sold their wives to members of the government obtained millions by governmental financial tips—or peerages. Not infrequently they obtained both peerages and millions. But Christopher was such a confounded ass that he had got neither the one nor[25] the other. His cheques were turned down for twopences. And he was such a bungler that he must needs get with child the daughter of their father's oldest friend, and[26] let the fact be known to the whole world....

This information he had from Ruggles—and it killed their father. Well, he, Mark, was absolutely to blame: that was that. But—infinitely worse—it had made Christopher absolutely[27] determined not to accept a single penny of the money that had become Mark's and that had been his father's. And Christopher was as obstinate as a hog.† For that Mark did not blame him. It was a Tietjens job to be as obstinate[28] as a hog.

He couldn't, however, disabuse his mind of the idea that Christopher's refusal of Groby and all that came from Groby was as much a manifestation of the confounded saintliness that he got

---

* A dud: during the First World War, a shell that failed to explode was called a 'stumer'. In *A Man Could Stand Up* – two men are mentioned as 'awaiting court-martial for giving stumer cheques' (II.iii).

† Though the Tietjens brothers are Yorkshiremen, this also alludes to the Sussex motto that Ford mentions in *The 'Half-Moon'* (London: Eveleigh Nash, 1909), 168; *Nightingale* 140, 143; and again in *Provence* 293: 'Her emblem, as I have reminded the reader, is a hog and her proud motto: "Wunt be druv".' In *No More Parades* General Campion articulates his own variation on Christopher's animal affinities: 'You are as conceited as a hog; you are as obstinate as a bullock.... You drive me mad....' (III.ii).

from his soft mother as of a spirit of resentment. Christopher *wanted* to rid himself of his great possessions. The fact that his father and brother had believed him to be what Marie Léonie would have called *maquereau** and had thus insulted him he had merely grasped at with eagerness as an excuse. He wanted to be out of the world. That was it. He wanted to be out of a disgustingly inefficient and venial world, just as he, Mark, also wanted to be out of a world that he found almost more fusionless† and dishonest than Christopher found it.

At any rate, at the first word that they had had about the heirship to Groby after their father's death, Christopher had declared that he, Mark, might take his money to the devil and the ownership of Groby with it. He proposed never to forgive either his father or Mark. He had only consented to take Mark by the hand at the urgent solicitation of Valentine Wannop. . . . ‡

That had been the most dreadful moment of Mark's life. The country was, even then, going to the devil; his brother proposed to starve himself; Groby, by his brother's wish, was to fall into the hands of that bitch. . . . And the country went further and further towards the devil, and his brother starved worse and worse . . . and as for Groby . . .

The boy who practically owned Groby had, at the first sound of the voice of the woman who wore white[29] riding-kit and called "Hi-hup!"—at the very first sound of her voice the boy had scampered off through the raspberry canes and was now against the hedge, whilst she leaned down over him, laughing, and her horse leaned over behind her. Fittleworth was smiling at them benevolently, and at the same time continuing his conversation with Gunning. . . .

The woman was too old for the boy, who had gone scarlet at the sound of her voice. Sylvia had been too old for Christopher: she had got him on the hop when he had been only a kid. . . . The world went on.

---

* A pimp or a ponce (French). Ford would use the word again in *When the Wicked Man* (London: Jonathan Cape, 1932), 288.

† Not in OED but it is in *Chambers English Dictionary* under the Scottish word 'foison', 'plenty', 'vitality', 'essential virtue'. 'Fusionless' means, then, lacking these qualities and is explained as deriving from the Latin for 'to pour forth'. Borrow uses the alternative version, 'fushionless', in *The Romany Rye* 357.

‡ See *Some Do Not . . .* II.v.

He was nevertheless thankful for the respite. He had to acknowledge to himself that he was not as young as he had been. He had a great deal to think of if he was to get the hang of—he was certainly not going to interfere with—the world, and having to listen to conversations that were mostly moral apophthegms had tired him. He had got[30] too many at too short intervals. If he had spoken he would not have, but, because he did not speak, both the lady who was descended from the Maintenon and that boy had peppered him with moral points of view that all required to be considered, without leaving him enough time to get his breath mentally.

The lady had called them a corrupt and effete aristocracy. They were probably not corrupt, but certainly, regarded as landowners, they were effete—both he and Christopher. They were simply bored at the contemplation of that terrific nuisance—and refusing to perform the duties of their post they refused the emoluments too. He could not remember that, after childhood, he had ever had a penny out of Groby. They would not accept that post; they had taken others. . . . Well this was his, Mark's, last post. . . . He could have smiled at his grim joke.

Of Christopher he was not so sure. That ass was a terrific sentimentalist. Probably he would have liked to be a great landowner, keeping up the gates on the estate—like Fittleworth, who was a perfect lunatic about gates. He was probably even now jaw-jawing Gunning about them, smacking his boot-top with his crop-handle. Yes—keeping up the gates and seeing that the tenants' land gave so many bushels of wheat to the acre or supported so many sheep the year round. . . . How many sheep would an acre keep all the year round,* and how many bushels of wheat, under proper farming, should[31] it give? He, Mark, had not the least idea. Christopher would know—with the difference to be expected of every acre of all the thousand acres of Groby. . . . Yes, Christopher had pored over Groby with the intentness of a mother looking at her baby's face!

So that his refusal to take on that stewardship might very well arise from a sort of craving for mortification of the spirit. Old

---

* Twenty years before, Ford had written of the 'clever man of the world set down in the country' being 'startled by such questions as: "How many sheep will an acre of marsh-land carry all the year round?"' (*England* 121).

Campion had once said that he believed—he positively believed with shudders—that Christopher desired to live in the spirit of Christ. That had seemed horrible to the General, but Mark did not see that it was horrible, *per se.* . . . He doubted, however, whether Christ would have refused to manage Groby had it been his job.* Christ was a sort of an Englishman, and Englishmen did not, as a rule, refuse to do their jobs. . . . They had not used to. Now, no doubt, they did. It was a Russian sort of trick. He had heard that even before the revolution great Russian nobles would disperse their estates, give their serfs their liberty, put on a hair shirt and sit by the roadside begging. . . . Something like that. Perhaps Christopher was a symptom that the English were changing. He himself was not. He was just lazy and determined—and done with it!

He had not at first been able to believe that Christopher was resolved—with a Yorkshire resolution—to have nothing to do with Groby or his, Mark's, money. He had, nevertheless, felt a warm admiration for his brother the moment the words had been said. Christopher would take none of his father's money; he would never forgive either his father or his brother. A proper Yorkshire sentiment, uttered coldly and, as it were, good-humouredly. His eyes, naturally, had goggled, but he had displayed no other emotion.

Nevertheless, Mark had imagined that he might be up to some game. He might be merely meaning to bring Mark to his knees. . . . But how could Mark be more brought to his knees than by offering to give over Groby to his brother? It is true he had kept that up his sleeve whilst his brother had been out in France. After all, there was no sense in offering a fellow who might be going to become food for powder† the management of great possessions. He had felt a certain satisfaction in the fact that Christopher *was* going out, though he was confoundedly sorry too. He really admired Christopher for doing it—and he imagined that it might clear some of the smirchiness that must attach

---

* Cf. *No More Parades* I.iv, where Christopher thinks of 'the Almighty as, on a colossal scale, a great English Landowner' and Christ as 'an almost too benevolent Land-Steward, son of the owner'.

† Shakespearean cannon-fodder. See *Henry IV, Part I*, IV.ii.65-7, where Falstaff says, 'Tut, tut, good enough to toss, food for powder, food for powder. They'll fill a pit as well as better. Tush, man, mortal men, mortal men.'

to Christopher's reputation, in spite of what he now knew to be his brother's complete guiltlessness of the crimes[32] that had been attributed to him. He had, of course, been wrong—he had reckoned without the determined discredit that, after the war was over, the civilian population would contrive to attach to every man who had been to the front as a fighting soldier. After all, that was natural enough. The majority of the male population was civilian, and, once the war was over and there was no more risk, they would bitterly regret that they had not gone. They would take it out of the ex-soldiers all right!*

So that Christopher had rather been additionally discredited than much helped by his services to the country. Sylvia had been able to put it, very reasonably, that Christopher was by nature that idle and dissolute thing, a soldier. That, in times of peace, had helped her a great deal.

Still, Mark had been pleased with his brother, and once Christopher had been invalided back, and had returned to his old-tin saving depot near Ealing, Mark had at once set wheels in motion to get his brother demobilized, so that he might look after Groby. By that time Groby was inhabited by Sylvia, the boy, and Sylvia's mother. The estate just had to be managed by the land-steward who had served his father, neither Sylvia nor her family having any finger in that; though her mother was able to assure him, Mark, that the estate was doing as well as the Agricultural Committees of grocers and stock-jobbers would let it. They insisted on wheat being sown on exposed moors where[33] nothing but heather had a chance, and active moorland sheep being fattened in water-bottoms full of liver fluke. But the land-steward fought them as well as one man could be expected to fight the chosen of a nation of small shop-keepers. . . .

And at that date—the date of Christopher's return to Ealing— Mark had still imagined that Christopher had really only been holding out for the possession of Groby. He was, therefore, disillusioned rather nastily. He had managed to get Christopher demobilized—without telling him anything about it—by just about the time when the Armistice came along. . . . And then he

---

* The distinctions – and divisions – between non-combatants and serving soldiers is a subject to which Ford returned several times in his post-war writings: see, for instance, *Nightingale* 50–4, 66–8.

found that he really had put the fat in the fire!

He had practically beggared the wretched fellow, who, counting on living on his pay for at least a year longer, had mortgaged his blood-money in order to go into a sort of partnership in an old-furniture business with a confounded American. And, of course, the blood-money was considerably diminished, being an allowance made to demobilized officers computed on the number of their days of service. So he had docked Christopher of two or three hundred pounds. That was the sort of mucky situation into which Christopher might be expected to be got by his well-wishers. . . . There he had been, just before Armistice Day, upon the point of demobilization and without an available penny! It appeared that he had to sell even the few books that Sylvia had left him when she had stripped his house.

That agreeable truth had forced itself on Mark at just the moment when he had been so rotten bad with pneumonia that he might be expected to cash in at any moment. Marie Léonie had indeed, of her own initiative, telephoned to Christopher that he had better come to see his brother if he wanted to meet him on this side of the grave.

They had at once started arguing—or, rather, each had started exposing his views. Christopher stated what he was going to do, and Mark his horror at what Christopher[34] proposed. Mark's horror came from the fact that Christopher proposed to eschew comfort. An Englishman's[35] duty is to secure for himself for ever reasonable clothing, a clean shirt a day, a couple of mutton chops grilled without condiments, two floury potatoes, an apple pie with a piece of Stilton and pulled bread, a pint of Club Médoc, a clean room, in the winter a good fire in the grate, a[36] comfortable armchair, a comfortable woman to see that all these were prepared for you, to[37] keep you warm in bed and to brush your bowler and fold your umbrella in the morning. When you had that secure for life, you could do what you liked provided that what you did never endangered that security. What was to be said against that?

Christopher had nothing to advance except that he was not going to live in that way. He was not going to live in that way unless he could secure that, or something like it, by his own talents. His only available and at the same time marketable talent was his gift for knowing genuine old furniture. So he was going to make a living out of old furniture. He had had his scheme perfectly matured; he had even secured an American partner, a fellow who had as great a gift for the cajolement of American purchasers of old stuff as he, Christopher, had for its discovery. It was still the war then, but Christopher and his partner, between them, had predicted the American mopping up of the world's gold supply and the consequent stripping of European houses of old stuff. . . . At that you could make a living.

Other careers, he said, were barred to him. The Department of Statistics, in which he had formerly had a post, had absolutely cold-shouldered him. They were not only adamant, they were also vindictive against civil servants who had become serving soldiers. They took the view that those members of their staffs who had preferred serving were idle and dissolute fellows who had merely taken up arms in order to satisfy their lusts for women. Women had naturally preferred soldiers to civilians; the civilians were now getting back on them. That was natural.

Mark agreed that[38] it was natural. Before he had been interested in his brother as a serving soldier, he had been inclined to consider most soldiers as incompetent over[39] Transport and, in general, nuisances. He agreed, too, that Christopher could not go back to the Department. There he was certainly a marked man. He could possibly have insisted on his rights to be taken back even though his lungs, being by now pretty damaged by exposure, might afford them a pretext for legally refusing him. H.M. Civil Service and Departments have the right to refuse employment to persons likely to become unfit for good. A man who has lost an eye may be refused by any Department because he may lose the other and so become liable for a pension.* But, even if Christopher forced himself on the Department, they would have their bad mark against him. He had been too rude to them during the war when they had tried to force him to employ himself in the faking of statistics that the Ministry had coerced the Department into supplying in order to dish the French, who demanded more troops.

With that point of view, Mark found himself entirely in

---

* Ford elsewhere referred to precisely such a case (*Nightingale* 51).

sympathy. His long association with Marie Léonie, his respect for
the way in which she had her head screwed on, the constant intimacy with the life and point of view of French individuals of the
petite bourgeoisie which her gossip had given him—all these
things, together with his despair for the future of his own country,
had given him a very considerable belief in the destinies and,
indeed, in the virtues of the country across the Channel. It would,
therefore, have been very distasteful to him that his brother
should take pay from an organization that had been employed to
deal treacherously with our Allies. It had, indeed, become
extremely distasteful to him to take pay himself from[40] a Government that had forced such a course upon the nation, and he
would thankfully have resigned from his Office if he had not
considered that his services were indispensable to the successful
prosecution of the war which was then still proceeding. He
wanted to be done with it, but, at the moment, he saw no chance.
The war was by then obviously proceeding towards a successful
issue. Owing to the military genius of the French, who, by then,
had the supreme command, the enemy nations were daily being
forced to abandon great stretches of territory. But that only made
the calls on Transport the greater, whilst, if we were successfully
and unwastefully to occupy the enemy capital, as at that date he
imagined that we obviously must, the demand for the provision
of Transport must become almost unmeasurable.

Still, that was no argument for the re-entry of his brother into
the service of the country. As he saw things, public life had
become—and must remain for a long period—so demoralized by
the members of the then Government, with their devious foreign
policies and their intimacies with a class of shady financiers such
as had never hitherto had any finger in the English political pie—
public life had become so discreditable an affair that the only
remedy was for the real governing classes to retire altogether from
public pursuits. Things, in short, must become worse before they
could grow better. With the dreadful condition of ruin at home
and foreign discredit to which the country must almost immediately emerge under the conduct of the Scotch grocers, Frankfort
financiers, Welsh pettifoggers, Midland armament manufacturers and South Country incompetents who during the later
years of the war had intrigued themselves into office—with that

dreadful condition staring it in the face, the country must return
to something like its old standards of North Country common
sense and English probity. The old governing class to which he
and his belonged might never return to power, but, whatever
revolutions took place—and he did not care!—the country must
reawaken to the necessity for exacting[41] of whoever might be its
governing class some semblance of personal probity and public
honouring of pledges. He obviously was out of it, or he would be
out of it with the end of the war, for even from his bed he had
taken no small part in the directing of affairs at his Office. . . . A
state of war obviously favoured the coming to the top of all kinds
of devious stormy[42] petrels; that was inevitable and could not be
helped. But in normal times a country—every country—was true
to itself.

Nevertheless, he was very content that his brother should, in
the interim, have no share in affairs. Let him secure his mutton
chop, his pint of claret, his woman and his umbrella, and it
mattered not into what obscurity he retired. But how was that to
be secured? There had seemed to be several[43] ways.

He was aware, for instance, that Christopher[44] was both a
mathematician of no mean order and a Churchman. He might
perfectly well take orders, assume the charge of one of the three
family livings that Mark had in his gift, and, whilst competently
discharging the duties of his cure, pursue whatever are the occupations of a well-cared-for mathematician.

Christopher, however, whilst avowing his predilection for
such a life—which, as Mark saw it, was exactly fitted to his asceticism, his softness in general and his private tastes—Christopher
admitted that there was an obstacle to his assuming such a cure
of souls—an obstacle of an insuperable nature. Mark at once
asked him if he were, in fact, living with Miss Wannop. But
Christopher answered that he had not seen Miss Wannop since
the day of his second proceeding to the front. They had then
agreed that they were not the sort of persons to begin a hidden
intrigue, and the affair had proceeded no further.

Mark was, however, aware that a person of Christopher's way
of thinking might well feel inhibited from taking on a cure of
souls if, in spite of the fact that he had abstained from seducing
a young woman, he nevertheless privately desired[45] to enter into

illicit relations with her, and that that was[46] sufficient to justify him in saying that an insuperable obstacle existed. He did not know that he himself agreed, but it was not his business to interfere between any man and his conscience in a matter of the Church. He was himself no very good Christian, at any rate as regards the relationships of men and women. Nevertheless, the Church of England was the Church of England. No doubt, had Christopher been a Papist he could have had the young woman for his housekeeper and no one would have bothered.

But what the devil, then, was his brother to do? He had been offered, as a sop in the pan, and to keep him quiet, no doubt, over the affair of the Department of Statistics, a vice-consulate in some Mediterranean port—Toulon or Leghorn, or something of the sort.* That might have done well enough. It was absurd to think of a Tietjens, heir to Groby, being under the necessity of making a living. It was fantastic, but if Christopher was in a fantastic mood there was nothing to be done about it. A vice-consulate is a potty sort of job. You attend to ships' manifests, get members of crews out of jail,[47] give old lady tourists the addresses of boarding-houses kept by English or half-castes, or provide the vice-admirals of visiting British squadrons with the names of local residents who should be invited to entertainments given on the flagship. It was a potty job; innocuous too, if[48] it could be regarded as a sort of marking time. . . . And at that moment Mark thought that Christopher[49] was still holding out for some sort of concession on Mark's part before definitely assuming the charge of Groby, its tenants and its mineral rights. . . . But there were insuperable objections to even the vice-consulate. In the first place, the job would have been in the public service, a fact to which, as has been said, Mark strongly objected. Then the job was offered as a sort of a bribe. And, in addition, the consular service exacts from[50] every one who occupies a consular or vice-consular post the deposit of a sum of four hundred pounds sterling, and Christopher did not possess even so much as four hundred shillings. . . . And, in addition, as Mark was well aware, Miss Wannop might

---

* In *A Man Could Stand Up* – III.ii Christopher told Mrs Wannop: 'I have also been recommended to apply for a vice-consulate. In Toulon, I believe.' That novel was begun in Toulon, while both *A Mirror to France* and *New York Is Not America* were completed there.

again afford an obstacle. A British vice-consul might possibly
keep a Maltese or Levantine in a back street and no harm done,
but he probably could not live with an English young woman of
family and position without causing so much scandal as to make
him lose his job....

It was at this point that Mark again, but for the last time, asked
his brother why he did not divorce Sylvia.

By that time Marie Léonie had retired to get some rest. She
was pretty[51] worn out. Mark's illness had been long and serious;
she had nursed him with such care that during the whole time
she had not been out into the streets except once or twice to go
across the road to the Catholic church, where she would offer a
candle or so for[52] his recovery, and once or twice to remonstrate
with the butcher as to the quality of the meat he supplied for
Mark's broths. In addition, on many days, she had worked late,
under Mark's directions, on papers that the Office had sent him.
She either could not or would not put her man into the charge
of any kind of night nurse. She alleged that the war had mopped
up every kind of available attendant on the sick, but Mark
shrewdly suspected that she had made no kind of effort to secure
an assistant. There was her national dread of draughts to account
for that. She accepted with discipline, if with despair, the English
doctor's dictum that fresh air must be admitted to the sick-room,
but she sat up night after night in a hooded chair, watching for
any change in the wind and moving in accordance a complicated
arrangement of screens that she maintained between her patient
and the open window. She had, however, surrendered[53] Mark to
his brother without a murmur, and had quietly gone to her own
room to sleep, and Mark, though he carried on almost every kind
of conversation with his brother, and though he would not have
asked her to leave them in order that he might engage on topics
that his brother might like to regard as private—Mark seized the
opportunity to lay before Christopher what he thought of Sylvia
and the relationships of that singular couple.

It amounted, in the end, to the fact that Mark wanted Christopher to divorce his wife, and to the fact that Christopher had not
altered in his views that a man cannot divorce a woman. Mark
put it that if Christopher intended to take up with Valentine, it
mattered practically very little whether after an attempt at a

divorce he married her or[54] not. What a man has to do if he means to take up with a woman, and as far as possible to honour her, is to make some sort of fight of it—as a symbol. Marriage, if you do not regard it as a sacrament—as, no doubt, it ought to be regarded—was nothing more than a token that a couple intended to stick to each other. Nowadays people—the right people—bothered precious little about anything but that. A constant change of partners was a social nuisance; you could not tell whether you could or couldn't invite a couple together to a tea-fight. And society existed for social functions. That was why promiscuity was no good. For social functions you had to have an equal number of men and women, or someone got left out of conversations, and so you had to know who, officially in the social sense, went with whom. Everyone knew that all the children of Lupus at the War Office were really the children of a Prime[55] Minister, so that presumably the Countess and the Prime Minister slept together most of the time, but that did not mean that you invited the Prime Minister and the woman to social-official functions, because they hadn't any ostensible token of union. On the contrary, you invited Lord and Lady Lupus together to all functions that would get into the papers, but you took care to have the Lady at any private, week-endish parties or intimate dinners to which the Chief was coming.

And Christopher had to consider that if it came to marriage ninety per cent. of the inhabitants of the world regarded the marriages[56] of almost everybody else as invalid. A Papist obviously could not regard a marriage before an English registrar[57] or a French *maire* as having any moral[58] validity. At best it was no more than a demonstration of aspirations after constancy. You went before a functionary publicly to assert that man and woman[59] intended to stick to each other. Equally for extreme Protestants a marriage by a Papist priest, or a minister of any other sect, or a Buddhist Lama, had not the blessing of their own brand of Deity. So that really, to all practical intents, it was sufficient if a couple really assured their friends that they intended to stick together, if possible, for ever; if[60] not, at least for years enough to show that they had made a good shot at it. Mark invited Christopher to consult whom he liked in his, Mark's, particular set and he would find that they agreed with his views.

So he was anxious that if Christopher intended to take up with the Wannop young woman he should take at least a shot at a divorce. He might not succeed in getting one. He obviously had grounds enough, but Sylvia might make counter-allegations, he, Mark, couldn't say with what chance of success. He was prepared himself to accept his brother's assertions of complete innocence, but Sylvia was a clever devil and there was no knowing what view a judge might take. Where there had been such a hell of a lot of smoke he might consider that there must be enough flame to justify refusing a divorce. There would no doubt be, thus—a beastly stink. But a beastly stink would be better than the sort of veiled ill-fame that Sylvia had contrived to get attached to Christopher. And the fact that Christopher had faced the stink and made the attempt would be at least that amount of tribute to Miss Wannop. Society was good-natured[61] and was inclined to take the view that if a fellow had faced his punishment and taken it he was pretty well absolved. There might be people who would hold out against them, but Mark supposed that what Christopher wanted for himself and his girl was reasonable material comfort with a society of sufficient people of the right sort to give them a dinner or so a week and a week-end or so a month in the week-ending season.

Christopher had acquiesced in the justness of his[62] views with so much amiability that Mark began to hope that he would get his way in the larger matter of Groby. He was prepared to go further and to stake as much as his assurance that if Christopher would settle down at Groby, accept a decent income and look after the estate, he, Mark, would assure his brother and Valentine of bearable social circumstances.

Christopher, however, had made no answer at all beyond saying that if he tried to divorce Sylvia it would apparently ruin his old-furniture business. For his American partner assured him that in the United States if a man divorced his wife instead of letting her divorce him no one would do any business with him. He had mentioned the case of a man called Blum, a pretty warm*

* 'Comfortably off, well to do; rich, affluent' (*OED*). Cf. 'I suppose Macmaster's a pretty warm man now' (*Some Do Not ...* II.iii); also *The Benefactor* (London: Brown, Langham & Co., 1905), 157: 'a warm man'; *True Love & a GCM*, in *War Prose* 84, 'warm city men'.

stock-exchange man, who insisted on divorcing his wife against the advice of his friends; he found when he returned to the stock market that all his clients cold-shouldered him, so that he was ruined. And as these fellows were shortly going to mop up every-thing in the world, including the old-furniture trade, Christopher supposed that he would have to study their prejudices.[63]

He had come across his partner rather curiously. The fellow, whose father had been a German-Jew but a naturalized American citizen, had been in Berlin mopping up German old furniture for sale in the American interior, where he had a flourishing busi-ness. So, when America had come in on the side that was not German, the Germans had just simply dropped on Mr. Schatzweiler in their pleasant way, incorporated him in their forces and had sent him to the front as a miserable little Tommy before the Americans had been a month in the show. And there, amongst the prisoners he had had to look after, Christopher had found the little, large-eyed sensitive creature, unable to speak a word of German but just crazy about the furniture and tapestries in the French châteaux that the prisoners passed on their marches. Christopher had befriended him; kept him as far as possible separated from the other prisoners, who naturally did not like him, and had a good many conversations with him.

It had appeared that Mr. Schatzweiler had had a good deal to do in the way of buying with Sir John Robertson, the old old-furniture millionaire,[64] who was a close friend of Sylvia's and had been so considerable an admirer[65] of Christopher's furniture-buying gifts that he had, years ago, proposed to take Christopher into partnership with himself. At that time Christopher had regarded Sir John's proposals as outside the range of his future; he had then been employed in the Department of Statistics. But the proposal had always amused and rather impressed him. If, that is to say, that hard-headed old Scotsman who had made a vast fortune at his trade made to Christopher a quite serious business proposition on the strength of Christopher's *flair* in the matter of old woods and curves, Christopher himself might take his own gifts with a certain seriousness.

And by the time he came to be in command of the escort over those miserable creatures he had pretty well realized that after the necessity for escorts was over he would jolly well have to consider how he was going to make a living for himself. That was certain. He was not going to reinsert himself amongst the miserable collection of squits who occupied themselves in his old Department; he was too old to continue in the Army; he was certainly not going to accept a penny from Groby sources. He did not care what became of him—but his not caring did not take any tragico-romantic form. He would be quite prepared to live in a hut on a hillside and cook his meals over three bricks outside the door—but that was not a method of life that was very practicable and even that needed money. Everyone who served in the Army at the front knew how little it took to keep life going—and satisfactory. But he did not see the world, when it settled down again, turning itself into a place fit for old soldiers who had learned to appreciate frugality. On the contrary, the old soldiers[66] would be chivvied to hell by a civilian population who abhorred them.[67] So that merely to keep clean and out of debt was going to be a tough job.

So, in[68] his long vigils in tents, beneath the moon, with the sentries walking, challenging from time to time, round the barbed wire stockades, the idea of Sir John's proposition had occurred to him with some force. It had gathered strength from his meeting with Mr. Schatzweiler. The little fellow was a shivering artist, and Christopher had enough of superstition in him to be impressed by the coincidence of their having come together in such unlikely circumstances. After all, Providence must let up on him after a time, so why should not this unfortunate and impressively Oriental member of the Chosen People be a sign of a covenant? In a way he reminded Christopher of his former protégé Macmaster—he had the same dark eyes, the same shape, the same shivering eagerness.

That he was a Jew and an American did not worry Christopher; he had not objected to the fact that Macmaster had been the son of a Scotch grocer. If he had to go into partnership and be thrown into close contact with anyone at all he did not care much who it was as long as it was not either a bounder or a man of his own class and race. To be in close mental communion with either an English bounder or an Englishman of good family would, he was aware, be intolerable to him. But, for a little shivering, artistic Jew, as of old for Macmaster, he was quite capable of feeling a real fondness—as you might for an animal. Their manners were not your manners and could not be expected to be, and whatever their intelligences,[69] they would have a certain little alertness, a certain exactness of thought. . . . Besides, if they did you in, as every business partner or protégé must be expected to do, you did not feel the same humiliation as you did if you were swindled by a man of your own race and station. In the one case it was only what was to be expected, in the other you were faced with the fact that your own tradition had broken down. And under the long strain of the war he had outgrown alike the mentality and the traditions of his own family and his own race. The one and the other were not fitted to endure long strains.

So he welcomed the imploring glances and the eventual Oriental gratitude of that little man in his unhappy tent. For, naturally, by communicating in his weighty manner with the United States Headquarters when he happened to find himself in its vicinity, he secured the release of the little fellow, who was by now safely back somewhere in the interior of the North American Continent.

But before that happened he had exchanged a certain amount of correspondence with Sir John, and had discovered from him and from one or two chance members of the American Expeditionary Force that the little man was quite a good old-furniture dealer. Sir John had by that time gone out of business and his letters were not particularly cordial to Tietjens—which was only what was to be expected if Sylvia had been shedding her charms over him. But it had appeared that Mr. Schatzweiler had had a great deal of business with Sir John, who had indeed supplied him with a great part of his material, and so, if Sir John had gone out of business, Mr. Schatzweiler would need to find in England someone to take Sir John's place. And that was not going to be extraordinarily easy, for what with the amount of his money that the Germans had mopped up—they had sold him immense quantities of old furniture and got paid for it, and had then enlisted him in the ranks of their Brandenburgers, where naturally he could do nothing with carved oak chests that had elaborate steel hinges and locks. . . . What then with that, and his prolonged absence from the neighbourhood of Detroit, where he had mostly found his buyers, Mr. Schatzweiler found himself extremely

hampered in his activities. It therefore fell to Christopher, if he
was to go into partnership with the now sanguine and charming
Oriental, to supply an immediate sum of money. That had not
been easy, but by means of mortgaging his pay and his blood-
money, and selling the books that Sylvia had left him, he had
been[70] able to provide Mr. Schatzweiler with enough to make at
least a start somewhere across the water.... And Mr.
Schatzweiler and Christopher had between them evolved an
ingenious scheme along lines that the American had long
contemplated, taking into account the tastes of his countrymen
and the nature of the times.

Mark had listened to his brother during all this with indulgence and even with pleasure. If a Tietjens contemplated going
into trade he might at least contemplate an amusing trade carried
on in a spirited manner. And what Christopher humorously
projected was at least more dignified than stock-broking or bill-
discounting. Moreover, he[71] was pretty well convinced by this
time that his brother was completely reconciled to him and to
Groby.

It was about then and when he had again begun to introduce
the topic of Groby that Christopher got up from the chair at the
bedside that he had been occupying and,[72] having taken his
brother's wrist in his cool fingers, remarked:

"Your temperature's pretty well down. Don't you think it is
about time that you set about marrying Charlotte? I suppose you
mean to marry her before this bout is finished; you[73] might have
a relapse."

Mark remembered that speech perfectly well, with the addition that if he, Christopher, hurried about it they might get the
job done that night. It must therefore then have been about one
o'clock of an afternoon about[74] three weeks before the 11th
November, 1918.

Mark had replied[75] that he would be much obliged to Christopher, and Christopher, having roused[76] Marie Léonie and told her
that he would be back in time to let her have a good night's rest,
disappeared, saying that he was going straight to Lambeth. In
those days, supposing you could command thirty pounds or so,
there was no difficulty in getting married at the shortest possible
notice, and Christopher had promoted too many last-minute

marriages amongst his men not to know the ropes.

Mark viewed the transaction with a good deal of satisfaction.[77] It had needed no arguing; if the proceeding had the approval of the heir-presumptive to Groby there was nothing more to be said against it. And Mark took the view that if he agreed to a proceeding that Christopher could only have counselled as heir-presumptive, that was an additional reason for Mark's expecting that Christopher would eventually consent to administer Groby himself.

CHAPTER VI

THAT would have been three weeks before the eleventh of November. His mind boggled a little at computing what the actual date in October must have been. With his then pneumonia his mind had not much registered the dates of that period; days[1] had gone by in fever and boredom. Still, a man ought to remember the date of his wedding. Say it had been the twentieth of October, 1918. The twentieth of October had been his father's birthday. When he came to think of it he could remember remembering hazily that it was queer that he should be going out of life on the date his father had entered it. It made a sort of full stop. And it made a full stop that, practically on that day, Papists entered into their own in Groby. He had, that is to say, made up his mind to the fact that Christopher's son would have Groby as a home even if Christopher didn't. And the boy was by now a full-fledged Papist, pickled and oiled and wafered and all. Sylvia had rubbed the fact in about a week ago by sending him a card for his nephew's provisional baptism and first communion about a week before. It had astonished him that he had not felt more bitter.

He had not any doubt that the fact had reconciled him to his marriage with Marie Léonie. He had told his brother a year or so before[2] that he would never marry her because she was a Papist, but he was aware that then he was only chipping at Spelden, the fellow that wrote *Spelden on Sacrilege*,[3]* a book that predicted all sorts of disaster for fellows[4] who owned former Papist Church lands or who had displaced Papists. When he had told Christopher that he would never marry Charlotte—he had called her Charlotte for reasons of camouflage before the marriage—he had

---

* Presumably Henry Spelman's *The History and Fate of Sacrilege*, written in the early seventeenth century but not published until 1698. It did indeed assert that those who profited from seized Catholic properties would come to a bad end. Ford had used the idea of such a curse in an earlier novel: 'it had been prophesied by a wise woman in those parts that no land that had been taken from the monks would prosper' (*Fifth Queen* 500).

been quite aware that he was chipping at Spelden's ghost—for Spelden must have been dead a hundred years or so. As it were, he had been saying grimly if pleasantly to that bogy:[5]

"Eh, old un. You see. You may prophesy[6] disaster to Groby because a Tietjens was given it over the head of one of your fellows in Dutch William's time. But you can't frighten me into making an honest woman—let alone a Lady of Groby—out of a Papist."

And he hadn't. He would swear that no idea of disaster to Groby had entered his head at the date of the marriage. Now, he would not say; but of what he felt then he was certain. He remembered thinking whilst the ceremony was going on of the words of Fraser of Lovat* before they executed him in the Forty-Five.[7] They had told him on the scaffold that if he would make some sort of submission to George II they would spare his body from being exhibited in quarters on the spikes of the buildings in Edinburgh. And Fraser had answered: "An the King will have my heid I care not what he may do with my—," naming a part of a gentleman that is not now mentioned in drawing-rooms. So, if a Papist was to inhabit Groby House, it mattered precious little if the first Lady Tietjens of Groby were Papist or Heathen.

A man as a rule does not marry his mistress whilst he has any kick in him. If he still aims at a career it might hinder him if[8] she were known to have been his mistress, or, of course, a fellow who wants to make a career might want to help himself on by making a good marriage. Even if a man does not want to make a career he may think that a woman who has been his mistress as like as not may cuckold him after marriage, for, if she has gone wrong with him, she would be more apt to go wrong elsewhere as well. But if a fellow is practically finished those considerations disappear, and he remembers that you go to hell if you seduce virgins. It is as well at one time or another to make your peace with your Creator. For ever is a long word and God is said to disapprove of unconsecrated unions.

---

* Simon Fraser, 11th Lord Lovat. A man of varying – professed – loyalties, he spent much time in France, some of it in prison, but supported the government in 1715 to obtain a full pardon for earlier crimes and to assume the title. Though also protesting loyalty to the government during the 1745 rebellion, he fled after Culloden, was captured, tried in London and beheaded. The narrator of George Borrow's *The Romany Rye* calls Fraser 'the prince of all conspirators and machinators' (25).

Besides, it would very likely please Marie Léonie, though she had never said a word about it, and it would certainly dish Sylvia, who was no doubt counting on being the first Lady Tietjens of Groby, and then, too, it[9] would undoubtedly make Marie Léonie safer. In one way and another he had given his mistress quite a number of things that might well be desirable to that bitch, and neither his nor Christopher's lives were worth much, whilst Chancery* can be a very expensive affair if you get into it.

And he was aware that he had always had a soft spot in his heart for Marie Léonie, otherwise he would not have provided her with the name of Charlotte for public consumption. A man gives his mistress another name if there is any chance of his marrying her, so that it may look as if he were marrying someone else when he does it. *Marie Léonie Riotor* looks different from a casual Charlotte. It gives her a better chance in the world outside.

So it had been well enough. The world was changing and there was no particular reason why he should not change with it. . . . And he had not been able to conceal from himself that he was getting on the way. Time lengthened out. When he had come in drenched from one of the potty local meetings that they had had to[10] fall back on during the war[†] he had known that something was coming to him because after Marie Léonie had tucked him up in bed he could not remember the strain of the winner of some handicap of no importance. Marie Léonie had given him a goodish tot of rum with butter in it and that might have made him hazy—but, all the same, that had never happened to him in his life before, rum or no rum. And[11] by now he had forgotten even the name of the winner and the meeting. . . .

He could not conceal from himself that his memory was failing, though otherwise he considered himself to be as sound a man as he had ever been. But when it came to memory, ever since that

* A division of the High Court of Justice, dealing with those disputes over legacies and trusts that had to be decided not on the grounds of Common Law but on those of Equity. The Court of Chancery existed as a separate institution until 1873 and was immortalised in Charles Dickens' *Bleak House* (1853).

† Horse-racing was not entirely suspended but there were severe restrictions, several of the major meetings being halted. The Grand National was run at Gatwick rather than Aintree, while racing at Brighton was halted from 1914 to 1917 because the stand was being used as an ammunition dump and food store. Part of the Grand Stand at Ascot became a hospital, which prompted 'an acrimonious correspondence between those who thought that, war or no war, racing should continue and those who did not': Peel, *How We Lived Then* 28.

day his brain had checked at times as a tired horse will at a fence.... A tired horse!

He could not bring himself to the computation of what three weeks back from the eleventh of November came to; his brain would not go at it. For the matter of that, he could remember precious little of the events of that three weeks in their due order. Christopher had certainly been about, relieving Marie Léonie at night and attending to him with a soft, goggle-eyed attentiveness that only a man with a saint for a mother could have put up. For hours and hours he would read aloud in Boswell's *Life of Johnson*,[12] for which Mark had had a fancy.

And Mark could remember drowsing off with satisfaction to the sound of the voice and drowsing with satisfaction awake again, still to the sound of the voice.* For Christopher had the idea that if his voice went droning on it would make Mark's slumbers more satisfactory.

Satisfaction.... Perhaps the last satisfaction that Mark was ever to know. For at that time—during those three weeks—he had not been able to believe that Christopher really meant to stick out about the matter of Groby. How could you believe that a fellow who waited on you with the softness of a girl built of meal-sacks was determined to ... call it, break your heart. That was what it came to.... A fellow, too, who agreed in the most astounding manner with your views of things in general. A fellow, for the matter of that, who knew ten times as much as you did. A damn[13] learned fellow....

Mark had no contempt for learning—particularly for younger sons. The country was going to the dogs because of the want of education of the younger sons, whose business it was to do the work of the nation. It was a very old North Country rhyme that, that when land is gone and money spent, then learning is most excellent.† No, he had no contempt for learning. He had never

---

* In *Return to Yesterday* Ford recalls how, when he was suffering from a breakdown in 1904, exacerbated by 'complete sleeplessness', his mother came out to Germany to join him. 'For four nights running she read to me from Boswell's *Johnson*—through the entire night. She read on even when I dozed off' (205).

† The immediate source for this rhyme appears to be *Taste*, a dramatic sketch of 1752 by Samuel Foote, 'the English Aristophanes' to many of his contemporaries, though the first line runs 'When house and land are gone and spent'. In George Eliot's *The Mill on the Floss* (III.iii) Mr Glegg quotes the rhyme in the version recalled by Mark here.

acquired any because he was too lazy: a little Sallust, a little
Cornelius Nepos,* a touch of Horace, enough French to read a
novel and follow what Marie Léonie said. . . . Even to himself he
called her Marie Léonie once he was married to her. It had made
her jump at first!

But Christopher was a damn learned fellow. Their father, a
younger son at the beginning, had been damn learned too.[14] They
said that even at his death he had been one of the best Latinists
in England—the intimate friend of that fellow Wannop, the
Professor. . . . A great age at which to die by his own hand, his
father's![†] Why, if that marriage had been on the 20th[15] October,
1918, his father, then dead, must have been born on the 20th[16]
October what?. . . 1834. . . . No, that was not possible. . . . No:
'44. *His* father, Mark knew, had been born in 1812—before
Waterloo!

Great stretches of time. Great changes! Yet Father had not
been an incult[‡] sort of a man. On the contrary, if he was burly
and determined, he was quiet. And sensitive. He had certainly
loved Christopher very dearly—and Christopher's mother.

Father was very tall; stooping like a toppling poplar towards
the end. His head seemed very distant as if he hardly heard you.
Iron-grey; short-whiskered! Absent-minded towards the end.
Forgetting where he had put his handkerchief and where his spectacles were when he had pushed them up on to[17] his forehead. . . .
He had been a younger son who had never spoken to his father
for forty years. Father's father[18] had never forgiven him for
marrying Miss Selby of Biggen . . . not because it was marrying
below him, but because his father had[19] wanted their mother for
his eldest son. . . . And they had been poor in their early childhood, wandering over the Continent, to settle at last in Dijon,
where they had kept some sort of state . . . a large house in the
middle of the town with several servants. He never could imagine
how their mother had done it on four hundred a year. But she

---

* Lived c. 99–24 BCE. Acquainted with Cicero and a friend of Catullus, who dedicated
  a volume to him. Writer of the first surviving biography in Latin, Nepos was the author
  of *De Viris Illustribus*, a title recalling that on which Sylvia Tietjens pauses as she moves
  along the bookshelves, *Vitare Hominum Notiss* (*Some Do Not . . .* II.i).
† At that date the average life expectancy for a man was a little over fifty.
‡ 'Wanting in culture or refinement; inelegant, rough, coarse' (*OED*, which notes that
  it is 'now *rare*').

had. A hard woman. But Father had kept in with French people and corresponded with Professor Wannop and Learned Societies. He had always regarded him, Mark, as rather a dunce.... [20] Father would sit reading in elegantly bound books, by the hour. His study had been one of the show-rooms of the house in Dijon.

Did he commit suicide? If so then Valentine Wannop was his daughter. There could not be much getting away from that, not that it mattered much. In that case Christopher would be living with his half-sister.... Not that it mattered much. It did not matter much, to him, Mark ... but his father was the sort of man that it might drive to suicide.

A luckless sort of beggar, Christopher!... If you took the whole conglobulation* at its worst—the father suiciding, the son living with his sister in open sin, the son's son not his son, and Groby going over to Papist hands.... That was the sort of thing that would happen to a Tietjens of the Christopher variety: to any Tietjens who would not get out or get under as he, Mark, had done. Tietjenses[21] took what they damn well got for doing what they damn well wanted to. Well, it landed them in that sort of post.... A last post, for, if that boy was not Christopher's, Groby went out of Tietjens hands. There would be no more Tietjenses.[22] Spelden might well be justified.

The grandfather of Father scalped by Indians in Canada in the war of 1812;[23]† the father dying in a place where he should not have been—taking what he got for it and causing quite a scandal for the Court of Victoria; the elder brother of Father killed drunk whilst fox-hunting; Father suicided; Christopher a pauper by his own act with a by-blow in his shoes. If then there were to be any more Tietjenses[24] by blood[25] ... Poor little devils! They would be their own cousins. Something like that.

And possibly none the worse off[26] for that.... Either Spelden or Groby Great Tree had perhaps done for the others. Groby Great Tree had been planted to commemorate the birth of Great-grand-father who had died in a whoreshop—and it had always been whispered in Groby, amongst the children and servants, that Groby Great Tree did not like the house. Its roots tore

---

* 'The act of forming a rounded or compact mass; such a mass' (*OED*: this is one of the two examples of the word's usage cited).

† The war between the United States and the British Empire (June 1812–March 1815).

chunks out of the foundations, and two or three times the trunk
had had to be bricked into the front wall. It[27] had been brought
as a sapling from Sardinia at a time when gentlemen still thought
about landscape gardening. A gentleman in those days consulted
his heirs about tree planting. Should you plant a group of copper
beeches against a group of white maples over against the ha-ha[28]
a quarter of a mile from the house so that the contrast seen from
the ball-room windows should be agreeable—in thirty years'
time? In those days thought, in families, went in periods of thirty
years, owner gravely consulting heir who[29] should see that development of light and shade that the owner never would.

Nowadays the heir apparently consulted the owner as to
whether the tenant who was taking the ancestral home furnished
might not cut down trees in order to suit the sanitary ideas of the
day.... An American day! Well, why not? Those people could
not be expected to know how picturesque a contrast the tree
would make against the roofs of Groby Great House when seen
from Peel's Moorside. They would never hear of Peel's Moorside,
or John Peel, or the coat so grey....[30]

Apparently that was the meaning of the visit of that young colt
and Mrs. de Bray Pape. They had come to ask his, Mark's, sanction as owner to cut down Groby Great Tree. And then they had
funked it and bolted. At any rate the boy was still talking
earnestly to the woman in white over the hedge. As to where Mrs.
de Bray Pape was, he[31] had no means of knowing; she might be
among the potato rows studying the potatoes of the poor for all
he knew. He hoped she would not come upon Marie Léonie,
because Marie Léonie would make short work of Mrs. de Bray
Pape and be annoyed on top of it.

But they were wrong to funk talking to *him* about cutting down
Groby Great Tree. He cared nothing about it. Mrs. de Bray Pape
might just as well have come and said cheerfully: "Hullo, old
cock, we're going to cut down your bally old tree and let some
light into the house ..." if that was the way Americans talked
when they were cheerful; he had no means of knowing. He never
remembered to have talked to an American.... Oh, yes, to
Cammie Fittleworth! She[32] had certainly been a dreadfully slangy
young woman before her husband came into the title. But then
Fittleworth was[33] confoundedly slangy too. They said he had to

give up in the middle of a speech he tried to make in the House of Lords because he could not do without the word "toppin," which upset the Lord Chancellor. . . . So there was no knowing what Mrs. de Bray Pape might not have said if she had not thought she was addressing a syphilitic member of an effete aristocracy mad about an old cedar tree. But she might just as well have cheerfully announced it. He did not care. Groby Great Tree had never seemed to like him. It never seemed to like anybody. They say it never forgave the Tietjenses[34] for transplanting it from nice warm Sardinia to that lugubrious climate. . . . That was what the servants said to the children and the children whispered to each other in the dark corridors.

But poor old Christopher! He was going to go mad if the suggestion were made to him. The barest hint! Poor old Christopher, who was now probably at that very minute in one of those beastly machines overhead, coming back from Groby. . . . If Christopher *had* to buy a beastly South Country show-cottage, Mark wished he would not have bought it so near a confounded air-station. However, he had expected,[35] probably, that beastly Americans would come flying in the beastly machines to buy the beastly old junk. They did indeed do so—sent by Mr. Schatzweiler, who was certainly efficient except[36] in the sending of cheques.

Christopher had nearly jumped out of his skin—that is to say, he had sat as still as a lump of white marble—when he had gathered that Sylvia and, still more his own heir, wanted to let Groby furnished. He had said to Mark, over Sylvia's first letter: "You won't let 'em?" and Mark knew the agony that was behind his tallowy mask and goggle eyes. . . . Perfectly white around the nostrils he went—that was the sign!

And it had been as near to[37] an appeal as he had ever come—unless the request for a loan on Armistice Day could be regarded as an appeal. But Mark did not think that that could be regarded as a score. In their game neither of them had yet made a real score. Probably neither of them ever would; they were a stout pair of North Countrymen whatever else could be said against them.

No: it hadn't been a score when Christopher had said: "You won't let 'em let Groby?" the day before yesterday: Christopher had been in an agony, but he was not *asking* Mark not to let Groby be let; he was only seeking information as to how far Mark would let the degradation of the old place go. Mark had let him pretty well know that Groby might be pulled down and replaced by a terra-cotta hotel before he would stir a finger. On the other hand, Christopher had only to stir a finger and not a blade of grass between the cobbles in the Stillroom Yard could be grubbed up.... But by the rules of the game neither of them could give an order. Neither. Mark said to Christopher: "Groby's yours!" Christopher said to Mark: "Groby's yours!" With perfect good-humour and coldness. So probably the old place would fall to pieces or Sylvia would turn it into a bawdy-house.... It was a good joke! A good, grim Yorkshire joke!

It was impossible to know which of them suffered more. Christopher, it is true, was having his heart broken because the house suffered—but, damn it, wasn't Mark himself pretty well heart-broken because Christopher refused to accept the house from him?... It was impossible to know which!

Yes, his confounded heart had been broken on Armistice Day in the morning—between the morning and the morning after.... Yes: after Christopher had been reading Boswell aloud, night after night for three weeks.... Was that playing the game? Was it playing the game to get no sleep if you had not forgiven your brother.... Oh, no doubt it was playing the game. You don't forgive your brother if he lets you down in a damn beastly way.... And of course it *is* letting a fellow down in a beastly—a beastly!—way to let him know that you believe he lives on the immoral earnings of his wife.... Mark had done that to Christopher. It was unforgivable all right. And equally of course you do not hurt your brother except[38] on the lines circumscribed by the nature of the offence: you are the best friend he has—except on the lines circumscribed by the offence; and you will nurse him like a blasted soft worm[39]—except in so far as the lines circumscribed by the offence do not preclude your ministrations.

For, obviously, the best thing Christopher could have done for his brother's health would have been to have accepted the stewardship of Groby—but his brother could die and he himself could die before he would do that. It was nevertheless a pretty cruel affair.... Over Boswell the two brothers had got as thick as thieves with an astonishing intimacy—and with an astonishing

similarity. If one of them made a comment on Bennet[40] Langton[*]
it would be precisely the comment that the other had on his lips.
It was what asses call telepathy nowadays ... a warm, comfortable feeling, late at night with the light shaded from your eyes,
the voice going on through the deep silence of London that
awaited the crashes[41] of falling bombs.... Well, Mark accepted
Christopher's dictum that he himself was an eighteenth-century
bloke and was only forestalled when he had wanted to tell
Christopher that he was more old-fashioned still—a sort of
seventeenth-century Anglican who ought to be strolling in a
grove with the Greek[42] Testament beneath the arm and all....[43]
And, hang it all, there was room for him! The land had not
changed.... There were still the deep beech-woods making
groves beside the ploughlands and the rooks rising lazily as the
plough came towards them. The land had not changed....[†]
Well, the breed had not changed.... There was Christopher....
Only, the times ... they had changed.... The rooks and the
ploughlands and the beeches and Christopher were there still....
But not the frame of mind in the day.... The sun might rise and
go above the plough till it set behind the hedge, and the
ploughman went off to the inn settle; and the moon could do the
same. But they would—neither sun nor moon—look on the spit
of Christopher in all their journeys. Never. They might as well
expect to see a mastodon.... And he, Mark, himself was an old-
fashioned buffer. That was all right. Judas Iscariot himself was an
old-fashioned ass, once upon a time!

But it was almost on the edge of not playing the game for
Christopher to let that intimacy establish itself and all the time
to cherish that unforgivingness.... Not quite not playing the
game: but almost. For hadn't Mark held out feelers? Hadn't he
made concessions? Hadn't his very marrying of Marie Léonie
been by way of a concession to Christopher? Didn't Christopher,
if the truth was to be known, want Mark to marry Marie Léonie

---

[*] Friend of Samuel Johnson. Though there were occasional disagreements between
     them, Johnson said of him: 'I know not who will go to Heaven if Langton does not.
     Sir, I could almost say, *Sit anima mea cum Langtono* [May my soul be with Langton].'
     See James Boswell, *Life of Johnson*, ed. R.W. Chapman, rev. J.D. Fleeman (Oxford:
     Oxford University Press, 1980), 1282.

[†] This passage relates very closely to *A Man Could Stand Up* – II.ii and Christopher's
     similar reflections.

because he, Christopher, wanted to marry Valentine Wannop and hadn't a hope? If the truth were known.... Well, he had made that concession to Christopher, who was a sort of a parson[44] anyhow. But ought Christopher to have exacted—to have tele-pathically willed—that concession if he wasn't himself going to concede something? Ought he to have forced him, Mark, to accept his mooning womanly services when the poor devil was already worn out with his military duties of seeing old tins cleaned out day after day, if he[45] meant to become a beastly old-furniture dealer and refuse Groby? For, upon his soul, till the morning of Armistice Day, Mark had accepted Christopher's story of Mr. Schatzweiler as merely a good-humoured, grim threat.... A sort of a feint at a threat.

Well, probably it was playing the game all right: if Christopher thought it was jonnock,* jonnock it was!

But ... a damn beastly shock.... Why, he had been practi-cally convalescent, he had been out of bed in a dressing-gown and had told Lord Wolstonmark[46] that he could pile in as many papers as he liked from the Office.... And then Christopher, without a hat and in a beastly civilian suit of light mulberry-coloured Harris tweed, had burst into the room with a beastly piece of old furniture under his arm.... A sort of inlaid toy writing-desk. A model. For cabinet-makers! A fine thing to bring into a conva-lescent bedroom, to a man quietly reading Form T.O. LOUWR, 1962, E 17 of the 10/11/18, in front of a clean fire.... And chalk-white about the gills the fellow was—with an awful lot of silver in his hair.... What age was he? Forty? Forty-three? God knew![†]

Forty.... He wanted to borrow forty quid on that beastly piece of furniture. To have an Armistice Day Beanfeast and set up house with his gal! Forty quid! My God! Mark felt his bowels turning over within him with disgust.... The gal—that fellow's half-sister as like as not—was waiting in an empty house for him to go and seduce her. In order to celebrate the salvation of the world by seven million deaths!

If you seduce a girl you don't do it on forty pounds: you accept

---

*   Straightforward, genuine. Borrow uses it in *The Romany Rye* 186. In *A Man Could Stand Up* – III.i it occurs in Valentine's reflections as 'jannock'.

†   In the opening chapter of *Some Do Not ...*, generally agreed to be set in 1912, Christo-pher is twenty-six: he would, then, be thirty-two on Armistice Day.

Groby and three, seven, ten thousand a year. So he had told
Christopher.

And then he had got it. Full in the face.* Christopher was not
going to accept a penny from him. Never. Not ever!... No doubt
about that, either. That fact had gone into Mark as a knife goes
into the[47] stag's throat. It had hurt as much, but it hadn't killed!
Damn it, it might as well have! It might as well have.... Does a
fellow do that to his own brother just because his own brother has
called him ... what is the word? *Maquereau*!... Probably a
maquereau is worse than a pimp.... The difference between a flea
and a louse, as Dr. Johnson said.[†]

Eh, but Christopher was bitter!... Apparently he had gone
round first to Sir John Robertson's with that[48] jigamaree. Years
before, Sir John had[49] promised to buy it for a hundred pounds. It
was a special sort of model signed by some duke of a Bath cabinet-
maker in 1762.... Wasn't that the year of the American
Rebellion?[‡] Well, Christopher had bought it in a junk-shop of
sorts for a fiver and Sir John had promised him a hundred quid.
He collected cabinet-makers' models: extraordinarily valuable
they were. Christopher had spat out that this was worth a thousand dollars.... Thinking of his old-furniture customers!

When Christopher had used that word—with the blue pebbles
sticking out of his white-lard head—Mark had felt the sweat
break out all over him. He had known it was all up.... Christopher had gone on: you expected him to spit electric sparks but his
voice was wooden. Sir John had said to him:

"Eh, no, mon. You're a fine soldier now, raping half the girls[50]
in Flanders and[51] Ealing and asking us to regard you as heroes.
Fine heroes. And now you're safe.... A hundred pounds is a price
to a Christian that is faithful to his lovely wife. Five pounds is as
much as I'll give you for the model, and be thankful it is five, not
one, for old sake's sake!"

---

*   In *The Good Soldier* Dowell receives the news that his wife had been Edward's mistress
    'full in the face' (73). Florence herself, eavesdropping on Edward and Nancy, had
    herself 'got it in the face, good and strong' (77).
†   Pressed to choose between Derrick and Smart as the better poet, Johnson 'at once felt
    himself roused; and answered, "Sir, there is no settling the point of precedency
    between a louse and a flea."' See Boswell, *Life of Johnson* 1214.
‡   The War of American Independence (1775–83). Mark's knowledge of American
    matters shows little sign of improving.

That was what Sir John Robertson had said to Christopher: that was what the world was like to serving soldiers in that day. You don't have to wonder that Christopher was bitter—even to his brother with the sweat making his under-linen icy. Mark had[52] said:

"My good chap. I won't lend you a penny on that idiotic jiga-maree. But I'll write you a cheque for a thousand pounds[53] this minute. Give me my cheque-book from the table. . . ."

Marie Léonie had come into the room on hearing Christopher's voice. She liked to hear the news from Christopher. And she liked Christopher and Mark to have heated discussions. She had observed that they did Mark good: on the day when Christopher had first come there, three weeks before, when they certainly had heatedly discussed she had observed that Mark's temperature had fallen from ninety-nine point six to ninety-eight point two. In two hours. . . . After all, if a Yorkshire man can quarrel he can live. They were like that, those others, she said.

Christopher had turned on her and said:

"Ma belle amie m'attend à[54] ma maison; nous voulons célébrer avec mes camarades de régiment.[55] Je n'ai pas le sous. Prêtez moi quarante livres, je vous en prie, madame!"* He had added that he would leave his cabinet as a pledge. He was as stiff as a sentry outside Buckingham Palace. She had looked at Mark with some astonishment. After all, she might well be astonished. He himself had made no sign and suddenly Christopher had exclaimed:

"Prêtez les moi, prêtez les moi, pour l'amour de Dieu!"

Marie Léonie had gone a little white, but she had turned up her skirt and turned down her stocking and took out the notes.

"Pour le dieu d'Amour, monsieur, je[56] veux bien," she had said. . . . You never knew what a Frenchwoman would not say. That was out of an old song.[57†]

But the sweat burst out all over his face at the recollection: great drops of sweat.

---

*   'My lover is waiting for me at my house; we want to celebrate with friends from my regiment. I'm penniless. Lend me forty pounds, I beg you, madame' (French).
†   Perhaps 'Au clair de la lune', an eighteenth-century folk song that includes the line 'Au dieu de l'amour' and, in one variant, 'Ouvrez votre porte pour le dieu d'amour'.

CHAPTER VII

MARIE LÉONIE, a strong taste of apples in her mouth, strong savours[1] of apples on the air, wasps around her and as if a snow-drift of down descending about her feet, was frowning seriously over Burgundy bottles into which ran cider[2] from a glass tube that she held to their necks. She frowned because the task was serious and engrossing, because the wasps annoyed her and because she was resisting an impulse inside herself. It told her that something ailed Mark and urged her to go and look at him.

It annoyed her because, as a rule—a rule so strong that it had assumed the aspect of a regulation—she[3] felt presages of some-thing ailing Mark only at night. Only at night. During the day usually she felt in her *for intérieur* that Mark was like what he was only because he wanted so to be. His glance was too virile and dominant to let you think otherwise—the dark, liquid, direct glance! But at nightfall—or at any rate shortly after supper when she had retired to her room terrible premonitions of disaster to Mark visited her. He was dying where he lay; he was beset by the spectral beings[4] of the countryside; robbers, even, had crept upon him, though that was unreasonable. For all the countryside knew that Mark was paralysed and unable to store wealth in his mattress.... Still, nefarious strangers might see him and imagine that he kept his gold repeater watch beneath his pillow.... So she would rise a hundred times in a night and, going to the low, diamond-casement window, would lean out and listen. But there would be no sound: the wind in the leaves; the cry of water-birds over head. The dim light would be in the hut, seen unmoving through the apple-boughs.

Now, however, in broad daylight, towards the hour of tea, with the little maid on a stool beside her plucking the boiling-hens that were to go to market next day, with the boxes of eggs on their shelves, each egg wired to the bottom of its box, waiting till she had time to date-stamp it—in the open potting-shed in the quiet, broad light of a summer day she was visited by a presage of something ailing Mark. She resented it, but she was not the woman to resist it.

There was, however, nothing to warrant it. From the corner[5] of the house to which she proceeded she could see quite well the greater part of Mark's solitary figure. Gunning, being talked to by the English lord, held a spare horse by the bridle and was looking at Mark over the hedge. He[6] exhibited no emotions. A young man was walking along the inside of the hedge between it and the raspberries. That was no affair of hers: Gunning was not protesting. The head and shoulders of a young woman—or it might be another young man—were proceeding along the outside of the hedge nearly level with the first one. That was equally no affair of hers. Probably they were looking at the bird's nest. There was some sort of bird's nest, she had heard, in that thick hedge. There was no end to the folly of the English in the country as in the town: they would waste time over everything. This bird was a bottle ... bottle-something,* and Christopher and Valentine and the parson and the doctor and the artist who lived down the hill were crazy about it. They walked on tiptoe when they were within twenty yards. Gunning was allowed to trim the hedge, but apparently the birds knew Gunning.... For Marie Léonie, all birds were "moineaux"; as who should say "sparrers"; in London they called them that—just[7] as all flowers were "giroflées"—as you might say wall-flowers....† No wonder this country[8] was going to rack and ruin when it wasted its time over preserving the nests of sparrers and naming innumerable wall-flowers! The country was well enough—a sort of suburb of Caen; but the people!... No[9] wonder William, of Falaise, in

---

* Probably the long-tailed tit (*Parus caudatus*), so-called from the shape of its nest. See *Birds Britannica* 385–7, where now obsolete 'linguistic invention' is recalled, its names including 'bum barrel', 'bush oven', 'jack in a bottle' and 'pudding bag'. The 'bottle-tit' has been mentioned earlier (I.i). In a letter of 1933 Ford asked: 'Why should a London public like my works?' His answer, in part, was that they contained 'nothing about British birds' nests, wildflowers or rock-gardens' (*Letters* 222).
† In *Nightingale* 115 Ford writes of the 'burden of nature quotation' falling from his shoulders when he walked with two French friends in Provence. 'For the Provençal every wild flower is "quelque giroflé" – "some sort of wallflower" and every wild bird: "Quelque moineau" – "some sort of sparrow"....' Marie Léonie is from the north of France but the principle clearly still applies. 'Sparrer' can be traced back at least as far as *The Heart of the Country* (*England* 159). Cf. the key scene in *Some Do Not ...* I.vi in which Christopher and Valentine 'walk through Kentish grass fields'.

Normandy* subjugated them with such ease.

Now she had wasted five minutes, for the glass tubes, hinged on rubber, that formed her siphon from barrel to bottle had had perforce to be taken out of the spile-hole; the air had entered into it, and she would have to put it back and suck once more at the tube until the first trickle of cider entered her mouth. She disliked having to do that; it wasted the cider and she disliked the flavour in the afternoon when one had lunched. The little maid also would say: "A-oh, meladyship, Ah *du* call thet queer!" ... Nothing would cure that child of saying that though she was otherwise *sage et docile*. Even Gunning scratched his head at the sight of those tubes.

Could these savages never understand that if you want to have *cidre mousseux*—foaming—you must have as little sediment as possible? And that in the bottom of casks, even if they had not been moved for a long time, there will always be sediment— particularly if you set up a flow in the liquid[10] by running it from a tap near the bottom. So you siphon off the top of the great casks for bottling *mousseux*, and drink the rest from the cask,[11] and run the thickest into little thin-wood casks[12] with many hoops for freezing in the winter.... To make *calvados* where you cannot have alembics because of the excise.... In this unhappy country you may not have alembics for the distilling of applejack, plum- brandy or other *fines*—because of the excise! *Quel pays! Quel gens!*

They lacked industry, frugality—and, above all, spirit! Look at that poor Valentine, hiding in her room upstairs because there were people about whom she suspected of being people from the English Lord's house.... By rights that poor Valentine should be helping her with the bottling and ready to sell that lugubrious old furniture to visitors whilst her lord was away buying more old rubbish.... And she was distracted because she could not find some prints. They represented—Marie Léonie was well aware because she had heard the facts several times—street criers of ambulant wares in London years ago. There were only eight of these to be found. Where were the other four? The customer, an

* William the Conqueror, who ruled as William I of England from 1066, the year of his invasion, until 1087, when he died at Rouen from injuries sustained when he fell from his horse.

English lady[13] of title, was anxious for them. As[14] presents for an immediate wedding! Monsieur my brother-in-law had come upon the four that were to make up the set at a sale two days before. He had recounted with satisfaction how he had found them on the grass.... It was supposed that he had brought them home; but they were not in the warehouse at Cramp the carpenter's, they were not to be found left in the cart. They were in no drawer or press.... What was to prove that *mon beau-frère* had brought them home from the sale? He was not there: he was gone for a day and a half. Naturally he would be gone for a day and a half when he was most needed.... And where was he gone, leaving his young wife in that nervous condition?[15] For a day and a half! He had never before been gone for a day and a half.... There was then something brewing; it was in the air; it was in her bones.... It was like that dreadful day of the Armistice when this miserable land betrayed the beautiful *pays de France*!... When monsieur had borrowed forty pounds of her.... In the name of heaven why did not he borrow another forty—or eighty—or a hundred, rather than be distracted and distract Mark and his unhappy girl?...

She was not unsympathetic, that girl. She had civilization. She could talk of Philémon and Baucis.* She had made her *bachot*, she was what you would call *fille de famille*.... But without *chic*.... Without ... Without ... Well, she neither displayed enough erudition to be a *blas bleu*—though she had enough erudition!— nor enough *chic* to be a *femme légère*—a *poule* who would *faire la noce*† with her gallant. Monsieur the brother-in-law was no gay spark. But you never know with a man.... The cut of a skirt; a twist of the hair.... Though to-day there was no hair to twist: but there is the equivalent.

And it was a fact that you never knew a man. Look at the case of Eleanor Dupont, who lived for ten years with Duchamp of the Sorbonne.... Eleanor would never attend scrupulously to her

---

* The husband and wife who offer hospitality to the disguised gods, Jupiter and Mercury, in Ovid's *Metamorphoses* viii, and are spared the punishment meted out to the rest of their neighbourhood. Granted their wish to die together, they are transformed into trees. Cf. the Belgian couple in the 'gingerbread cottage out of Grimm' on the top of Mt Vedaigne (*No Enemy* 37–42).

† Baccalauréat; girl of good family; blue-stocking; a loose woman; a tart; live it up (French).

attire because her man wore blue spectacles and was a *savant*. . . .
But what happened. . . . There came along a little piece with a
hat as large as a cart-wheel[16] covered with green-stuff and sleeves
up above her ears—as the mode was then. . . .

That had been a lesson to her, Marie Léonie, who had been a
girl at the time. She had determined that if she achieved a *collage
sérieux* with a monsieur of eighty and as blind as a bat she would
study the modes of the day right down to the latest perfume.
These messieurs did not know it, but they moved among *femmes
du monde* and the fashionable cocottes, and however much she at
home might be the little brown bird of the domestic hearth, the
lines of her dresses, her hair, her personal odour, must conform.
Mark did not imagine; she did not suppose he had ever seen a
fashionable journal in her apartments that were open to him, or
had ever suspected that she walked in the Row on a Sunday when
he was away. . . . But she had studied these things like another.
And more. For it is difficult to keep with the fashion and at the
same time appear as if you were a serious *petite bourgeoise*. But she
had done it; and observe the results. . . .

But that poor Valentine. . . . Her man was attached enough:
and well he ought to be,[17] considering the affair in which he had
landed her. But always there comes the *pic des tempêtes*,* the Cap[18]
Horn, round which you must go. It is the day when your man
looks at you and says: "H'm, h'm," and considers if the candle is
not more valuable than the game! Ah, then. . . . There are wise
folk who put that at the seventh year; other wise ones, at the
second; others again, at the eleventh. . . . But in fact you may put
it at any day on any year—to the hundredth. . . . And that poor
Valentine with four spots of oil on her only skirt but two. And
that so badly hung, though the stuff no doubt was once good. One
must concede that! They make admirable tweeds in this country:
better certainly than in Roubaix. But is that enough to save a
country—or a woman dependent on a man who has introduced
her into a bad affair?

A voice behind her said:

"I see you have plenty of eggs!"—an unusual voice of a sort of
breathless nervousness. Marie Léonie continued to hold the

* The height of the storm (French).

mouth of her tube into the neck of a burgundy bottle; into this she had already introduced a small screw of sifted sugar and an extremely minute portion of a powder that she got from a pharmacist of Rouen.* This, she understood, made the cider of a rich brownness. She did not see why cider should be brown, but it was considered to be less fortifying if it were light golden. She continued also to think about Valentine, who would be twittering with nerves at the window whose iron-leaded casement was open above their heads. She would have put down her Latin book and have crept to the window to listen.

The little girl beside Marie Léonie had risen from the three-legged stool and held a dead, white fowl with a nearly naked breast by its neck. She said hoarsely:

"These ere be er Ladyship's settins of prize Reds." She was blonde, red-faced and wore on her dull fair hair a rather large cap, on her thin body a check blue cotton gown. "Arf a crownd a piece the heggs be or twenty-four shillings a dozen if you takes[19] a gross."

Marie Léonie heard the hoarse voice with some satisfaction. This girl whom they had only had for a fortnight seemed to be satisfactory mentally; it was not her business to sell the eggs but Gunning's; nevertheless she knew the details. She[20] did not turn round: it was not *her* business to talk to anyone who wanted to buy eggs and she had no curiosity as to customers. She had too much else to think about. The voice said:

"Half a crown seems a great deal for an egg. What is that in dollars? This must be that tyranny over edibles by the producer of which one has heard so much."

"Tiddn nothing in dollars," the girl said. "Arf a dollar is two bob. Arf a crownd is two n six."

The conversation continued, but it grew dim in Marie Léonie's thoughts. The child and the voice disputed as to what a dollar was—or so it appeared, for Marie Léonie was not familiar with either of the accents of the disputants. The child was a combative

---

* Probably a reference to Homais, the apothecary in Flaubert's *Madame Bovary*. It is also, perhaps, a nod to Joseph Conrad, who shared Ford's admiration for Flaubert and who, Ford noted in *Joseph Conrad* 91, had begun to write *Almayer's Folly* 'in the state-room of a ship moored in this very port' of Rouen, Flaubert's birthplace. According to Conrad, it was 'the tenth chapter' that was begun there: *A Personal Record* 3, in *The Mirror of the Sea and A Personal Record*, ed. Zdzisław Najder (Oxford: Oxford University Press, 1988). See also 'Pont…ti…pri…ith', in *War Prose* 35.

child. She drove both Gunning and the cabinet-maker Cramp[21] with an organ of brass. Of tin perhaps, like a penny whistle. When she was not grubbily working she read books with avidity—books about Blood if she could get them. She had an exaggerated respect for the Family, but none for any other soul in the world. . . .

Marie Léonie considered that, by now, she might have got down to the depth of the cask where you find sediment. She ran some cider into a clear glass, stopping the tube with her thumb. The cider was clear enough to let her bottle another dozen, she judged; then she would send for Gunning to take the spile-bung out of the next cask. Four sixty-gallon casks she had to attend to; two of them were done. She began to tire: she was not unfatiguable if she was indefatigable. She began at any rate to feel drowsy. She wished Valentine could have helped her. But that girl had not much backbone, and she, Marie Léonie, acknowledged that for the sake of the future it was good that she should rest and read books in Latin or Greek. And avoid nervous encounters.

She had tucked her up under an eiderdown on their four-post bed because They would have all the windows open and currents of air must, above all, be avoided by women. . . . *Elle* had smiled and said that it had once been her dream to read the works of Aeschyle[22] beside the blue Mediterranean. They had kissed each other. . . .

The maid beside her was saying that orfn n orfn[23] she'd eared er farver oo was a dealer wen a lot of ol ens, say, ad gone to three an nine, say "Make it two arf dollars!" They didn ave dollars in thet country but they did ave arf dollars. N Capt'n Kidd th' pirate: e ad dollars, n pieces of eight n moi-dors too!

A wasp annoyed Marie Léonie; it buzzed almost on her nose, retired, returned, made a wide circuit. There were already several wasps struggling in the glass of cider she had just drawn; there were others in circles round spots of cider on the slats of wood on which the barrels were arranged. They drew in their tails and then expanded, ecstatically. Yet only two nights before she and Valentine had gone with Gunning all over the orchard with a lantern, a trowel and a bottle of prussic acid,* stopping up holes

* In *The Good Soldier* Dowell is made to realise that during the whole of their married life, the 'little brown flask' that his wife Florence carried contained 'not nitrate of amyl, but prussic acid', with which she kills herself (75, 72).

along the paths and in banks. She had liked the experience; the darkness, the ring of light from the lantern on the rough grass; the feeling that she was out, near Mark, and that yet Gunning and his lantern kept spiritual visitors away.... What she suffered between the desire to visit her man in the deep nights and the possibility of coming up against *revenants*.... Was it reasonable? ... What women[24] had to suffer for their men! Even if they were faithful....

What the unfortunate *Elle* had not suffered....

Even on what you might call her *nuit de noces*.... At the time it had seemed incomprehensible. Marie Léonie[25] had had no details. It had merely seemed fantastic: possibly even tragic because Mark had taken it so hardly. Truly she believed he had become insane. At two in the morning, beside Mark's bed. They had—the two brothers—exchanged words of considerable violence whilst the girl shivered. And was determined. That girl had been determined. She would not go back to her mother. At two in the morning.... Well, if you refuse to go back to your mother at two in the morning you kick indeed your slipper over the mill!

The details of that night came back to her, amongst wasps and beneath the conversation of the unseen woman in the shed where the water ran in the trough. She had set the bottles in the trough because it is a good thing to cool cider before the process of fermentation in the bottles begins. The bottles with their shining necks of green glass were an agreeable spectacle. The lady behind her back was talking of Oklahoma.... The cowboy with the large nose that she had seen on the film at the Piccadilly Cinema had come from Oklahoma.* It was, no doubt, somewhere in America. She had been used to go to the Piccadilly Cinema on a Friday. You do not go to the theatre on a Friday if you are *bien pensant*, but you may regard the cinema as being to the theatre what a *repas maigre* is as against a meal with meat.... The lady speaking behind her came apparently from Oklahoma: she had eaten prairie chickens in her time. On a farm. Now, however, she was very rich. Or so she told the little maid. Her husband could buy

---

* A likely candidate is Will Rogers, who made over 70 movies between 1918 and the year of his death. He was born in 1879 near what would become Oologah, Oklahoma and died in a plane crash en route to Alaska in 1935.

half Lord Fittleworth's estate and not miss the money. She said that if only people here would take example. . . .

On Armistice[26] evening they had come thumping on her door. The bell had failed to wake her after all the noise in the street of that[27] day. . . . She had sprung into the middle of the floor and flown to save Mark . . . from an air raid. She had forgotten that it was the Armistice. . . . But the knocking had gone on on the door.

Before it had stood monsieur the brother-in-law and that girl in a dark blue girl-guide's[28] sort of uniform. Both chalk-white and weary to death. As if they leaned against one another. . . .[29] She had been for bidding them go away, but Mark had come out of the bedroom. In his nightshirt with his legs bare. And hairy! He had bidden them come in, roughly, and had got back into bed. . . . That had been the last time he had been on his legs! Now, he having been in bed so long, his legs were no longer hairy, but polished. Like thin glazed bones!

She had recalled his last gesture. He had positively used a gesture, like a man raving. . . . And, indeed, he was raving. At Christopher. And dripping with sweat. Twice she had wiped his face whilst they shouted at each other.

It had been difficult to understand what they said because they had spoken a sort of *patois*. Naturally they returned to the language they had spoken in their childhoods—when they were excited, these unexcitable people! It resembled the *patois* of the Bretons. Harsh. . . .

And, for herself, she had been all concerned for the girl. Naturally she had been concerned for the girl. One is a woman. . . . At first she had taken her for a little piece from the streets. . . . But even for a little piece from the streets. . . Then she had noticed that there had been no rouge; no imitation pearl necklace. . . .

Of course when she had gathered that Mark was pressing money on them she had felt different. Different in two ways. It could not be a little piece. And then her heart had contracted[30] at the idea of money being given away. They might be ruined. It might be these people instead of her Paris nephews who would pillage her corpse. But the brother-in-law pushed the thought of money away from him with both hands. If she—Elle—wanted to go with him she must share his fortunes. . . .[31] What a country! What people!

There had seemed to be no understanding them then. . . . It had appeared that Mark insisted that the girl should stop there with her lover: the lover, on the contrary, insisted that she should go home to her mother. The girl kept saying that on no account would she leave Christopher. He could not be left. He would die if he was left. . . . And, indeed, that brother-in-law had seemed sick enough. He panted worse than Mark.

She had eventually taken the girl to her own room. A little, agonized, fair creature. She had felt inclined to enfold her in her arms but she had not done so. Because of the money. . . . She might as well have. It was impossible to get these people to touch money. She would now give no little to lend that girl twenty pounds for a frock and some under-garments.

The girl had sat there without speaking. It had seemed for hours. Then some drunken man on the church steps opposite had begun to play the bugle. Long calls. . . . Tee . . . Teee . . . TEEEE. . . . Ta-heee. . . . To-hee. . . . Continuing for ever. . . .

Valentine[32] had begun to cry. She had said that it was dreadful. But you could not object. It was the Last Post they were playing. For the Dead. You could not object to their playing the Last Post for the Dead that night. Even if it was a drunken man who played and even if it drove you mad. The Dead ought to have all they could get.

If she had not made the necessary allowances[33] that would have seemed to Marie Léonie an exaggerated sentiment. The English bugle-notes could do no good to the French dead and the English losses were so negligible in quantity that it hardly seemed worth while to become *émotionnée* when their funeral call was played by a drunken man. The French papers estimated the English losses at a few hundreds: what was that as against the millions of her own people?. . . But she gathered that this girl had gone through something terrible that night with the wife, and being too proud to show[34] emotion over her personal vicissitudes she pretended to find an outlet because of the sounds of that bugle. . . . Well, it was mournful enough. She had understood it when Christopher, putting his face in at the crack of the door, had whispered to her that he was going to stop the bugle because its sound was intolerable to Mark.

The girl apparently had been in a reverie, for she had not heard him. She, Marie Léonie, had gone to look at Mark, and the girl sat there, on the bed. Mark was by then quite quiescent. The bugle had stopped. To cheer him she had made a few remarks about the inappropriateness of playing, for a negligible number of dead, a funeral call at three in the morning. If it had been for the French dead—or if her country had not been betrayed! It was betraying her country to have given those monsters[35] an armistice when they were far from their borders. Merely that was treachery on the part of these sham Allies. They should have gone right through those monsters slaying them by the million, defenceless, and then they should have laid waste their country with fire and sword. Let them, too, know what it was to suffer as France had suffered. It was treachery enough not to have done that, and the child unborn would suffer for it.

But there they waited, then, even after that treachery had been done, to know what were the terms of even that treachery. They might even now not intend to be going to Berlin. . . . What, then, was Life for?

Mark had groaned. In effect he was a good Frenchman. She had seen to that. The girl had come into the room. She could not bear to be alone. . . . What a night of movement and cross movement. She had begun to argue with Mark. Hadn't there, she had asked, been enough of suffering? He agreed that there had been enough of suffering. But there must be more. . . . Even out of justice to the poor bloody Germans. . . . He had called them the poor bloody Germans. He had said that it was the worst disservice you could do your foes not to let them know that remorseless consequences follow determined actions. To interfere in order to show fellows that if they did what they wanted they need not of necessity take what they got for it was in effect to commit a sin against God. If the Germans did not experience that in the sight of the world there was an end of Europe and the world. What was to hinder endless recurrences of what had happened near a place called Gemmenich* on the 4th of August, 1914, at six o'clock in

* In *Some Do Not . . .* Valentine weeps in 'the first moment of the lifting of strain that she had known since the day before the Germans crossed the Belgian frontier, near a place called Gemmenich' (II.iv). Ford returns to this place-name, usually with a date and time appended, repeatedly in both fictional and non-fictional contexts. See, for example, *No Enemy* 13, 36, 55; *Provence* 38, 68, 134–5, 217; *Great Trade Route* 266. Violet Hunt also uses the phrase in her 1918 novel, *The Last Ditch*, 14.

the morning? There was nothing to hinder it. Any other state from the smallest to the largest might . . .

The girl had interrupted to say that the world had changed, and Mark, lying back exhausted on his pillows, had said with a sort of grim sharpness:

"It is you who say it. . . . Then you may run[36] the world. . . . I know nothing about it. . . . " He appeared exhausted.

It was singular the way those two discussed—discussed "the situation" at three-thirty in the morning. Well, nobody wanted to be asleep that night, it seemed. Even in that obscure[37] street mobs went by, shouting and playing concertinas. She had never heard Mark discuss before—and she was never to hear him discuss again. He appeared to regard that girl with a sort of aloof indulgence; as if he were fond of her but regarded her as over-learned, too young, devoid[38] of all experience. And Marie[39] Léonie had watched them and listened with intentness. In twenty years these three weeks had for the first time showed her her man in contact with his people. The contemplation had engrossed her.

She could, nevertheless, see that her man was exhausted in his inner being, and obviously that girl was tried beyond endurance. Whilst she talked she appeared to listen for distant sounds. . . . She kept on recurring to the idea that punishment was abhorrent to the modern mind. Mark stuck to his point that to occupy Berlin was not punishment, but that not to occupy Berlin was to commit an intellectual sin. The consequence[40] of invasion is counter-invasion and symbolical occupation, as the consequence of over-pride is humiliation. For the rest of the world, he knew nothing of it; for his own country that was logic—the logic by which she had lived. To abandon that logic was to abandon clearness of mind: it was mental cowardice. To show the world Berlin occupied, with stands of arms and colours on her public places, was to show that England respected logic. Not to show the world that, was to show that England was mentally cowardly. We dared not put the enemy nations to pain because we shrank from the contemplation.

Valentine had said: "There has been too much suffering!"

He had said:

"Yes, you are afraid of suffering. . . . But England is necessary to the world. . . . To my world. . . . Well, make it your world and

it may go to rack and ruin how it will. I am done with it. But then
... you must accept the responsibility.[41] A[42] world with England
presenting the spectacle[43] of moral cowardice would[44] be a world
on a lower plane.... If you lower the record for the mile you
lower the standard of blood-stock. Try to think of that. If
Persimmon had not achieved what it did the French Grand Prix
would be less of an event and the trainers at Maisons Laffitte[45*]
would be less efficient. And the jockeys. And the stable lads. And
the sporting writers.... A world profits by the example of a stead-
fast nation...."

Suddenly Valentine said:

"Where is Christopher?" with such intenseness that it was like
a blow.

Christopher had gone out. She exclaimed:

"But you must not let him go out.... He is not fit to go out
alone.... He has gone out to go back...."

Mark said:

"Don't go...." For she had got to the door. "He went out to
stop the Last Post. But you may play the Last Post, for[46] me.
Perhaps he has gone back to the Square. He had presumably
better see what has happened to his wife. I should not myself."

Valentine had said with extraordinary bitterness:

"He shall not. He shall not." She had gone.

It had come through to Marie Léonie partly then and partly
subsequently that Christopher's wife had turned up at Christopher's empty house, that was in the Square a few yards away
only.[47] They had gone back late at night probably for purposes of
love and had found her there. She had come for the purpose[48] of
telling them that she was going to be operated on for cancer, so
that with their sensitive natures they could hardly contemplate
going to bed together at that moment.

It had been a good lie. That Mrs. Tietjens was a *maîtresse
femme*. There was no denying that. She herself was[49] engaged for

---

* Racecourse in the north-west area of Paris, a little over ten miles from the city centre.
  In Sisley Huddleston's 1927 book, *In and About Paris* (London: Methuen, 1927), dedicated to Ford, he refers to the seventeenth-century chateau there and notes that
  Maisons-Laffitte 'has an Anglo-American colony, largely composed of trainers and
  jockeys' (210). Apparently, Persimmon never raced in France at all and there was no
  race of this name, though it may be a popular reference to the Grand Prix de Paris,
  first run in 1863.

those others both by her own inclinations and the strong injunctions of her husband, but Mme Tietjens was certainly ingenious.[50]
She had managed to incommode and discredit that pair almost
as much as any pair could be incommoded and discredited,
although they were the most harmless couple in the world.

They had certainly not had an agreeable festival on that
Armistice Day. Apparently one of the officers present at their
dinner of celebration had gone raving mad; the wife of another
of Christopher's comrades of the regiment had been rude to
Valentine; the colonel of the regiment had taken the opportunity to die with every circumstance of melodrama. Naturally all
the other officers had run away and had left Christopher and
Valentine with the madman and the dying colonel on their hands.

An agreeable *voyage de noces*.... It appeared that they had
secured a four-wheel cab in which, with the madman and the
other, they had driven to Balham—an obscure suburb, with
sixteen celebrants hanging all over the outside of the cab and two
on the horse's back—at any rate for a couple of miles from
Trafalgar Square. They were not, of course, interested in the interior of the cab; they were merely gay because there was to be no
more suffering. Valentine[51] and Christopher had got rid of the
madman somewhere in Chelsea at an asylum for shell-shock
cases; but[52] the authorities would not take the colonel, so they
had driven on to Balham, the colonel making dying speeches
about the late war, his achievements, the money he owed
Christopher.... Valentine had appeared to find that extremely
trying. The man died in the cab.

They had had to walk back into Town because the driver of
the four-wheeler was so upset by the death in his cab that he could
not drive. Moreover, the horse was foundered. It had been twelve
midnight before they reached Trafalgar Square. They had had to
struggle through packed crowds nearly all the way. Apparently
they were happy at the accomplishment of their duty—or their
benevolence. They stood on the top step of St. Martin's Church,
dominating the square,* that was all illuminated and packed and

---

* In *Provence* 23 Ford would write of 'the only Great View in London or the British
Empire': 'from the third step of the left-hand entrance-staircase of the National
Gallery', looking from there across Trafalgar Square. He mentions St Martin's (the
present St Martin-in-the Fields, designed by James Gibbs, was completed in 1726) two
pages later (25).

roaring, with bonfires made of the paving wood and omnibuses, and the Nelson Column going up and the fountain-basins full of drunkards, and orators and bands. . . . They stood on the top step, drew deep breaths and fell into each other's arms. . . . For the first time—though apparently they had loved each other for a lustre* or more. . . . What people!

Then, at the top of the stairs in the house in the Inn, they had perceived Sylvia, all in white!. . .

Apparently she had been informed that Christopher and that girl were in communication—by a lady who did not like Christopher because she owed him money. A Lady Macmaster. Apparently there was no one in the world who did not dislike Christopher because they owed him money. The colonel and the lunatic and the husband of the lady who had been rude to Valentine . . . all! all! Right down to Mr. Schatzweiler, who had only paid Christopher one cheque for a few dollars out of a great sum and had then contracted a nervous breakdown on account of the sufferings he had gone through as a prisoner of war. . . .

But what sort of a man was that Christopher to have in his hands the fortunes of a woman?. . . Any woman!

Those were practically the last words her Mark had ever spoken to her, Marie Léonie. She had been supporting him whilst he drank a tisane she had made in order that he might sleep, and he had said gravely:

"It is not necessary that I should ask you to be kind to Mademoiselle Wannop. Christopher is incapable of looking after her. . . ." His last words, for immediately afterwards the telephone bell had rung. He had just before[53] seemed to have a good deal of temperature, and it had been whilst his eyes were goggling at her, the thermometer that she had stuck in his mouth gleaming on his dark lips, and whilst she was regretting letting him be tormented by his family that the sharp drilling of the telephone had sounded from the hall. Immediately the strong German accent of Lord Wolstonmark† had, with its accustomed disagreeableness, burred

---

* A period of five years. A *lustrum* was a purification ceremony performed by the censors of Rome every five years.

† Ford may not have had a specific figure in mind but one tempting possibility is Lord Milner (1854–1925), who was not only born in Germany but in Giessen, where Ford had spent the best part of a year in 1910–11, in his misguided attempt to secure a 'German divorce'. Though Ford often blamed Joseph Chamberlain and President

in her ear. He had said that the Cabinet was still sitting and they desired to know at once the code that Mark used in his communications with various ports. His second in command appeared to be lost amongst the celebrations of that night. Mark had said with a sort of grim irony from the bedroom that if they wanted to stop his transport going out they might just as well not use cypher. If they wanted to use a twopenny-halfpenny economy as window-dressing for the elections they'd have to have they might as well give it as much publicity as they could. Besides, he did not believe they would get into Germany with the transport they had. A good deal had been smashed lately.

The Minister had said with a sort of heavy joy that they were not going into Germany: and that had been the most dreadful moment of Marie Léonie's life; but with her discipline she had just simply repeated the words to Mark. He had then said something she did not quite catch: and he would not repeat what he had said.* She said as much to Lord Wolstonmark, and the chuckling accent said that he supposed that that was the sort of news that would rattle the old boy. But one must adapt oneself to one's day; the times were changed.

She had gone from the instrument to look at Mark. She spoke to him; she spoke to him again. And again—rapid words of panic. His face was dark purple and congested; he gazed straight before him. She raised him; he sank back inertly.

She remembered going to the telephone and speaking in French to the man at the other end. She had said that the man

---

Kruger for bringing about the Boer War, Milner actually played a large part in doing so. Appointed in 1915 as President of the Board of Agriculture and Fisheries, he was drafted into Lloyd George's war council in December 1916. Instrumental in the Anglo-French appointment of Marshal Foch as co-ordinator of allied armies in the west, he then replaced Lord Derby as secretary of state for war on 20 April 1918, which took him out of the war cabinet. In favour of a negotiated armistice to end German militarism, Milner was criticised for not taking a harder line on unconditional surrender. His relations with Lloyd George deteriorated and he took no part in the 1918 elections. Replaced by Winston Churchill, he went to head the Colonial Office in December 1918.

* The 'something' said but not quite caught is a recurrent Fordian usage. In *The Good Soldier* Edward Ashburnham mutters something that Dowell 'did not catch' (in the manuscript, it was 'Girl, I will wait for you there'). He then cuts his throat with 'quite a small pen-knife' (162). In *No More Parades*, during the crucial conversation between Campion and Tietjens, marked by heroic instances of misunderstanding and inattention, Tietjens has to drag his attention back to the General and confess: 'I didn't catch, sir!' (III.ii).

at the other end was a German and a traitor; her husband should never speak to him or his fellows again. The man had said: "Eh, what's that? Eh . . . Who are you?"

With appalling shadows chasing up and down in her mind, she had said:

"I am Lady Mark Tietjens. You have murdered my husband. Clear yourself from off my line, murderer!"

It had been the first time she had ever given herself that name; it was indeed the first time she had ever spoken in French to that Ministry. But Mark had finished with the Ministry, with the Government, with the nation. . . . With the world.

As soon as she could get that man off the wire she had rung up Christopher. He had come round with Valentine in tow. It had certainly not been much of a *nuit de noces* for that young couple.

PART II

CHAPTER I

SYLVIA TIETJENS, using the[1] persuasion of her left knee, edged her chestnut[2] nearer to the bay mare of [3] the shining general. She said:
"If I divorce Christopher, will you marry me?"
He exclaimed with the vehemence of a shocked hen:
"Good God, no!"
He shone everywhere except in such parts of his grey tweed suit as would have shown by shining that they had been put on more than once. But his little white moustache, his cheeks, the bridge but not the tip of his nose, his reins, his Guards' tie, his boots,[4] martingale, snaffle, curb, fingers, finger-nails—all these gave evidence of interminable rubbings.... By himself, by his man, by Lord Fittleworth's stable-hands, grooms.... Interminable rubbings and supervisions at the end of extended arms. Merely to look at him you knew[5] that he was something like Lord Edward Campion, Lieutenant-General retired, M.P., K.C.M.G.[6]* (military), V.C.,[7] M.C., D.S.O....
So[8] he exclaimed:
"Good God, no!" and using a little-finger touch on his snaffle-rein, made his mare recoil from Sylvia Tietjens' chestnut.[9]
Annoyed at its mate's motion, the bad-tempered chestnut with the white forehead showed its teeth at the mare, danced a little and threw out some flakes of foam. Sylvia swayed backwards[10] and forwards in her saddle and smiled down into[11] her

---

* Knight Commander of the Order of St Michael and St George. The honours and decorations are given in the wrong order here: the Victoria Cross should precede all others and the DSO should precede the MC. In *A Man Could Stand Up* – III.i McKechnie may be a little crazy but he recites them in the right order.

husband's garden.

"You can't, you know," she said, "expect to put an idea out of my head just by flurrying the horses...."

"A man," the general said between "Come ups"[12] to his mare, "does not marry his ..."

His mare went backwards a pace or two into the bank and then a pace forwards.

"His what?" Sylvia asked with amiability. "You can't be going to call me your cast mistress.* No doubt most men would have a shot at it. But I never have been even your mistress.... I have to think of Michael!"

"I wish," the general said vindictively, "that you would settle what that boy is to be called.... Michael or Mark!" He added: "I was going to say: 'His godson's wife.' ... A man may not marry his godson's wife."

Sylvia leant[13] over to stroke the neck of the chestnut.

"A man," she said, "cannot marry any other man's[14] wife.... But if you think that I am going to be the second Lady Tietjens after that ... French prostitute...."[15]

"You would prefer," the general said, "to be India...."[16]

Visions of India went through their hostile minds. They looked down from their horses over Tietjens's in West Sussex, over a house with a high-pitched, tiled roof with deep windows of[17] the grey local stone. He nevertheless saw names like Akhbar Khan, Alexander of Macedon, the son of Philip, Delhi, the Massacre at Cawnpore....† His mind, given over from boyhood to the contemplation of the largest jewel in the British Crown,‡ spewed up those romances. He was member for the West Cleveland Division§

---

* Cf. Tietjens to Levin in *No More Parades* I.ii and note. 'Cast' as in rejected: the term 'cast mistress' was not uncommon in seventeenth- and eighteenth-century drama.

† Probably Mohammed Akbar Khan, son of Dost Mohammed, active in the Afghan War of 1839–42, and particularly in the slaughter of thousands of soldiers and civilians under the command of General William Elphinstone; Alexander the Great, son of Philip II of Macedonia – India was the furthest point of his march of conquest in 326 BCE; during the Indian Mutiny, the British recaptured Delhi in September 1857; earlier, at Cawnpore, the British had surrendered to Nana Sahib, who then massacred his prisoners.

‡ Queen Victoria was proclaimed Empress of India in 1877.

§ In the 1918 'Coupon Election' Sir Park Goff, Conservative, defeated the sitting Liberal Herbert Samuel in the Cleveland constituency, while Middlesbrough West was won by Trevelyan Thomson (Liberal). In the world of *Parade's End*, Campion's standing for the seat after the war has been prepared for in *No More Parades* II.ii.

and a thorn in the side of the Government. They *must* give him
India. They knew that if they did not he could publish revelations as to the closing days of the late war. . . . He would naturally
never do that. One does not blackmail even a Government.

Still, to all intents, he *was* India.*

Sylvia also was aware that he was to all intents and purposes
India. She saw receptions in Government Houses, in which,
habited with a tiara, she too would be INDIA. . . . As someone
said in Shakespeare:

> "*I am dying, Egypt, dying. Only*
> *I will importune death a while until*
> *Of many thousand kisses the poor last*
> *I lay upon thy lips . . . .*"†

She imagined it would be agreeable, supposing her to betray
this old Pantaloon‡ India, to have a lover, gasping at her feet,
exclaiming: "I am dying, India, dying. . . ." And she with her
tiara, very tall. In white, probably. Probably satin!

The general said:

"You know you cannot possibly divorce my godson. You are a
Roman Catholic."

She said, always with her smile:

"Oh, *can't* I?. . . Besides it would be of the greatest advantage
to Michael to have for a stepfather the Field-Marshal
Commanding. . . ."[18]

He said with impotent irritation:

"I wish you would settle whether that boy's name is Michael
or Mark!"

She said:

"He calls himself Mark. . . . I call him Michael because I hate
the name of Mark. . . ."

---

* On this 'habit of thinking of nations in terms of their figureheads and leaving the
populations concerned entirely out of account', see Goldring, *The Nineteen Twenties*
35, where he quotes from a twenties comedy. '"Have you heard," says one of the characters, "Dolly has promised to give us India – isn't it grand?"' The Prime Minister has
earlier agreed to make the speaker's husband Viceroy of India.

† *Antony and Cleopatra* IV.xvi.19–22. This is Antony's dying speech, having stabbed
himself.

‡ A buffoon, a stock character in the Italian *commedia dell'arte*, a foolish old man.

She regarded Campion with real hatred. She said to herself that[19] upon occasion she would be exemplarily revenged upon him. "Michael" was a Satterthwaite name—her father's; "Mark,"[20] the name for a Tietjens eldest son. The boy had originally been baptized and registered as Michael Tietjens. At his reception into the Roman Church he had been baptized "Michael Mark." Then had followed the only real deep humiliation of her life. After his Papist baptism the boy had asked to be called Mark. She had asked him if he really meant that. After a long pause—the dreadful long pauses of children before they render a verdict!—he had said that he intended to call himself Mark from then on. . . . By the name of his father's brother, of his father's father, grandfather, great-grandfather. . . . By the name of the irascible apostle of the lion and the sword. . . . * The Satterthwaites, his mother's family, might go by the board.

For herself, she hated the name of Mark. If there was one man in the world whom she hated because he was insensible of her attraction it was Mark Tietjens who lay beneath the thatched roof beneath her eyes. . . . Her boy, however, intended, with a child's cruelty, to call himself Mark Tietjens. . . .

The general grumbled:

"There is no keeping track with you. . . . You say now you would be humiliated to be Lady Tietjens after that Frenchwoman. . . . But you have always said that that Frenchwoman is only the concubine of Sir Mark. I heard you tell your maid so only yesterday. . . . You[21] say one thing, then you say another. . . . What is one to believe?"

She regarded him with sunny condescension. He grumbled on:

"One thing, then another. . . . You say you cannot divorce my godson because you are a Roman Catholic. Nevertheless, you begin divorce proceedings and throw all the mud you can over the miserable fellow. Then you remember your creed and don't go on. . . . What sort of game is this?" . . . She regarded him still ironically but with good humour across the neck of her horse.

He said:

"There's *really* no fathoming you. . . . A little time ago—for

---

* Mark the Evangelist is often represented as a lion; he is also the patron saint of Venice, and 'the lion of St Mark' is sometimes depicted holding a sword and a book.

months on end, you were dying of ... of internal cancer, in short. . . . "

She commented with the utmost good temper:

"I didn't want that girl to be Christopher's mistress. . . . You would think that no man with any imagination at all *could* . . . I mean with his wife in that condition. . . . But, of course, when she insisted. . . . Well, I wasn't going to stop in bed, in retreat, all my life. . . . "

She[22] laughed good-humouredly at her companion.

"I don't believe you know anything about women," she said. "Why should you? Naturally Mark Tietjens married his concubine. Men always do as a sort of death-bed offering. You will eventually[23] marry Mrs. Partridge if I do not choose to go to India. You think you would not, but you would. . . . [24] As for me, I think it would be better for Michael if his mother were Lady Edward Campion—of India—than if she were merely Lady Tietjens the second of Groby, with a dowager who was once a cross-Channel fly-by-night. . . . " She laughed and added: "Anyhow, the sisters at the Blessed Child said that they never saw so many lilies— symbols of purity*—as there were at my tea-parties when I was dying. . . . You'll admit yourself you never saw anything so ravishing as me amongst the lilies and the tea-cups with the great crucifix above my head. . . . You were singularly moved! You swore you would cut Christopher's throat yourself on the day the detective told us that he was really living here with that girl. . . . "

The general exclaimed:

"About the Dower House at Groby. . . . It's really damned awkward. . . . You swore to me that when you let Groby to that American[25] madwoman I could have the Dower House and keep my horses in[26] Groby stables. But now it appears I can't. . . . It appears . . . "

"It appears," Sylvia said, "that Mark Tietjens means to leave the Dower House at the disposal of his French concubine. . . . Anyhow, you can afford a house of your own. You're rich enough!"

---

* Not only of purity. In *The Heart of the Country* Madonna lilies are omens of death (*England* 158), and when Maisie Maidan is found dead, 'The stem of a white lily rested in her hand' (*The Good Soldier* 56). The lily was also closely associated with the Aesthetic movement.

The general groaned:

"Rich enough! My God!"

She said:

"You have still—trust *you!*—your younger son's settlement. You have still your general's pay.[27] You have the interest on the grant the nation made you at the end of the war. You have four hundred a year as a member of Parliament.* You have cadged on me for your keep and your man's keep and your horses' and grooms' at Groby for years and years. . . ."

Immense dejection covered the face of her companion. He said:

"Sylvia. . . . Consider the expenses of my constituency. . . . One would almost say you hated me!"

Her eyes continued to devour the orchard and garden that were spread out below her. A furrow of raw, newly-turned earth ran from almost beneath their horses' hoofs nearly vertically to the house below. She said:

"I suppose that is where they get their water-supply. From the spring above here. Cramp the carpenter says they are always having trouble with the pipes!"†

The general exclaimed:

"Oh, Sylvia. And you told Mrs. de Bray Pape that they had no water-supply so they could not take a bath!"‡

Sylvia said:

"If I hadn't she would never have thought of cutting down[28] Groby Great Tree. . . . Don't you see that for Mrs. de Bray Pape people who do not take baths are outside the law? So, though she's not really courageous, she will risk cutting down their old trees. . . ." She added: "Yes, I almost believe I do hate misers, and you are more next door to a miser than anyone else I ever honoured with my acquaintance. . . ." She added further: "But I should advise you to calm yourself. If I let you marry me you will

*   Members of Parliament received £400 per annum from August 1911; this continued until October 1931, when the figure was reduced to £380. It returned to its former level in July 1935 and only increased thereafter.

†   Of life at Coopers Cottage, Stella writes: 'The pipe which brought our water from the spring would freeze and burst' (*Drawn From Life* 84).

‡   This recalls an earlier lie in connection with another Tietjens household. In the opening chapter of *Some Do Not . . .* Tietjens asks how his breaking up the marital establishment is viewed and Macmaster answers that it's considered that Lowndes Street did not agree with Mrs Satterthwaite: 'Drains wrong.'

have my Satterthwaite[29] pickings. Not to mention the Groby
pickings till Michael comes of age, and the—what is it?—ten
thousand a year you will get from India. If out of all that you
cannot skimp enough to make up for house-room at my expense
at Groby you are not half the miser I took you for!"

A[30] number of horses, with Lord Fittleworth and Gunning,
came up from the soft track outside the side of the garden and on
to[31] the hard road that bordered the garden's top. Gunning sat
one horse without his feet in the stirrups and had the bridles of
two others over his elbows. They were the horses of Mrs. de Bray
Pape, Mrs. Lowther and Mark Tietjens. The garden with its
quince-trees, the old house with its immensely high-pitched roof
such as is seen in countries where wood was once plentiful,[32] the
thatch of Mark Tietjens' shelter and the famous four counties,
ran from the other side of the hedge out to infinity. An aeroplane
droned down towards them, many miles away.[33] Up from the road
ran a slope covered with bracken, to many great beech trees,
along a wire hedge.* That was the summit of Cooper's Common.†
In the stillness the hoofs of all those horses made a noise like that
of desultorily approaching cavalry. Gunning halted his horses at
a little distance; the beast Sylvia rode was too ill-tempered to be
approached.

Lord Fittleworth rode up to the general and said:

"God damn it, Campion, ought Helen Lowther to[34] be down
there? Her ladyship will give me no rest for a fortnight!" He
shouted at Gunning:[35] "Here you, blast you, you old scoundrel,
where's the gate Speeding complains you have been interfering
with?" He added to the general: "This old villain was[36] in my
service for thirty years, yet he's always counter-swinging the
gates in your godson's beastly fields.‡ Of course a man has to
look after his master's interests, but we shall have to come to

---

* Not in *OED* but perhaps simply a barbed wire barrier (recently and horribly familiar
to combatants on the Western Front). Barbed wire was originally known as 'thorn wire
hedge', according to Frank Horsfall, Jr, in 'Horticulture in Eighteenth-Century
America', *Agricultural History*, 43.1 (January 1969), 159–68 (160).
† Another clear echo of life at Coopers Cottage: 'our common at Bedham', Stella writes
(*Drawn From Life* 70).
‡ This complaint is expanded upon in the deleted passage reproduced in the Appendix:
'But that blasted cunning fellow Gunning would make all his master's field- and path-
gates cant inwards; so they swung to. And made the latches difficult to lift with a crop.
Latches ought to open at a touch and gates to stand as they swung.'

some arrangement. We can't go on like this." He added to Sylvia:

"It isn't the sort of place Helen ought to go to, is it? All sorts of people living with all sorts ... If what you say is true!"[37]

The Earl of Fittleworth gave in all places the impression that he wore a scarlet tail-coat, a white stock with a fox-hunting pin, white buckskin breeches, a rather painful eyeglass and a silk top-hat attached to his person by a silken cord. Actually he was wearing a square, high, black, felt hat,[38] pepper-and-salt tweeds and no eyeglass. Still, he screwed up one eye to look at you, and his lucid dark pupils, his contracted swarthy face with its little bristling[39] black-grey moustache, gave him, perched on his immense horse, the air of a querulous but very masterful monkey.

He considered that he was out of earshot of Gunning and so continued to[40] the other two: "Oughtn't to give away masters before their servants.... But it *isn't* any place for the niece of the President of a Show that Cammie has most of her money in. Anyhow she will comb my whiskers!" Before marrying the Earl, Lady Fittleworth had been Miss Camden Grimm. "Regular Aga ... Agapemone,* so you say.[41] A queer go for old Mark at his age."

The general said to Fittleworth:

"Here, I say, she says I am a regular miser.... You don't have any complaints, say, from your keepers that I don't tip enough? Tell her, will you? That's the real sign of a miser!"

Fittleworth said to Sylvia:

"You don't mind my talking like that of your husband's establishment, do you?" He added that in the old days they would not have talked like that before a lady about her husband. Or perhaps, by Jove, they would have! His grandfather had had a....[42]

Sylvia was of opinion that Helen Lowther could look after herself. Her husband was said not to pay her the attentions that a lady had a right to expect of a husband. So if Christopher....

She took an appraising sideways glance at Fittleworth. That peer was going slightly purple under his brown skin. He gazed out

---

* Literally, 'abode of love' (Greek), and specifically the name of a religious community set up at Spaxton, near Bridgwater, Somerset, by the Reverend Henry James Prince in 1849. Dickens used the term in 'Arcadian London' in 1860. Prince's successor, the Reverend John Hugh Smyth-Pigott, ran a similar community at Clapton, London. The word is generally used with implications of impropriety or excess. In *No More Parades* II.i Sylvia reflects that 'This whole war was an agapemone....'

over the landscape and swallowed in his throat. She felt that her time for making a decision had come. Times changed, the world changed; she felt heavier in the mornings than she had ever used to. She had had a long, ingenious talk with Fittleworth the night before, on a long terrace. She had been ingenious even for her; but she was aware that afterwards Fittleworth had had a long[43] bedroom talk with his Cammie. Over even the greatest houses a certain sense of suspense broods when the Master is talking to the Mistress. The Master and the Mistress—upon a word, usually from the Master—take themselves off, and the house-guests, at any rate in a small party, straggle, are uncertain as to who gives the signal to retire, suppress yawns even. Finally the butler approaches the most intimate guests and says that the Countess will not be coming down again.

That night Sylvia had shot her bolt. On the terrace she had drawn for the Earl a picture of the ménage[44] upon whose roof she now looked down.[45] It stretched out below her, that little domain, as if she were a goddess dominating its destinies. But she was not so certain of that. The dusky purple under Fittleworth's skin showed no diminution. He continued to gaze away over his territory, reading it as if it were in a[46] book—a clump of trees gone here, the red roof of a new villa grown up there in among the trees, a hop-oast with its characteristic cowl gone from a knoll. He was getting ready to say something. She had asked him the night before to root that family out of that slope.

Naturally not in so many words. But she had drawn such a picture of Christopher and Mark as made it, if the peer believed her, almost a necessity for a conscientious nobleman to do the best to rid his countryside of a plague-spot.... The point was whether Fittleworth would choose to believe her because she was a beautiful woman with a thrilling voice. He was terribly domestic and attached to his Transatlantic female, as only very wicked dark men late in life can contrive to be, when they come of very wicked, haughty and influential houses. They have, as it were, attended on the caprices of so many opera singers and famous professionals that when, later in life, they take capricious or influential wives, they get the knack of[47] very stiffly but minutely showing every sort of elaborate deference[48] to their life-partners. That is born with them.

So that the fate of that garden and that high-pitched roof was, in fact, in the hands of Cammie Fittleworth—in so far as great peers to-day have influence over the fates of their neighbours. And it is to be presumed that they have some.

But all men[49] are curious creatures. Fittleworth stiffened at queer places. He had done so last night. He had stood a good deal. It[50] had to be remembered that Mark Tietjens was an old acquaintance of his—not as intimate as he would have been if the Earl had had children, for Mark preferred houses of married people who had children. But the Earl knew Mark very well.... Now a man listening to gossip about another man whom he knows very well will go pretty far towards believing[51] what a beautiful woman will tell him. Beauty[52] and truth have a way of appearing to be akin;[*] and it is true that no man knows what another man is doing when he is out of sight.

So that in inventing or hinting at a ruinous, concealed harem, with consequent disease to account for Mark's physical condition and apparent ruin, she thought she was not going altogether too far. She had, at any rate, been ready to chance it. It is the sort of thing a man will believe ... about[53] his best friend even. He will say: "Only think.... All the while old X ... was appearing such a quiet codger he was really ..." And the words rivet conviction.

So that appeared to get through.

Her revelations as to Christopher's financial habits had not appeared to do so well. The Earl had listened with his head on one side, whilst she had let him gather that Christopher lived on women—on the former Mrs. Duchemin, now Lady Macmaster, for instance. Yes, to that the Earl had listened with deference, and it had seemed a fairly safe allegation to make. Old Duchemin was known to have left a pot of money to his widow. She had a very nice little place not six or seven miles away from where they stood.

And it had seemed natural to[54] bring in Edith Ethel for, not[55] so long ago, Lady Macmaster had paid[56] Sylvia a visit. It was about the late Macmaster's debt to Christopher. That was[57] a point about which Lady Macmaster was and always had seemed to be a

---

[*] Perhaps a properly sceptical modern variant on John Keats's 'Beauty is truth, truth beauty', in his 'Ode on a Grecian Urn'.

little cracky.* She had actually visited Sylvia in order to see if Sylvia would not use her influence with Christopher. To get him to remit the debt. Even in the old days Lady Macmaster had been used to worry Sylvia about that.

Apparently[58] Christopher had not carried his idiotcy[59] as far as might be expected. He had dragged that wretched girl down into those penurious surroundings, but he was not going to let her and the child she appeared to be going to have suffer actual starvation, or even too[60] great worry. And apparently, to satisfy a rather uneasy vanity, years before Macmaster had given Christopher a charge on his life insurance. Macmaster, as she well knew, had spunged[61] unmercifully on her husband, and Christopher had certainly regarded the money he had advanced as a gift. She herself had many times upbraided him about it; it had appeared to her one of Christopher's worst unbearablenesses.

But apparently the charge on the life insurance still existed and was now a charge on that miserable fellow's rather extensive estate. At any rate, the insurance company refused to pay over any money to the widow until the charge was satisfied.... And the thought that Christopher was doing for that girl what, she was convinced, he never would have done for herself had added a new impulse to Sylvia's bitterness. Indeed, her bitterness had by now given way almost entirely to a mere spirit of tormentingness—she wanted to torture that girl out of her mind. That was why she was there now. She imagined Valentine under the high roof suffering tortures because she, Sylvia, was looking down over the hedge.

But the visit of Lady Macmaster had certainly revived her bitterness as it had suggested to her new schemes of making herself a nuisance to the household below her. Lady Macmaster, in widow's weeds of the most portentous[62] crape, that gave to her at once the elegance and the direness[63] of a funeral horse, had really seemed more than a little out of her mind. She had asked Sylvia's opinion of all sorts of expedients for making Christopher loosen his grip, and she had continued her supplications even in correspondence. At last she had hit on a singular expedient....

* Probably more familiar now as 'cracked'. *OED* has 'Somewhat cracked in intellect; crazy'.

Some years before, apparently, Edith Ethel had had an affair of the heart with a distinguished Scottish Littérateur,[64] now deceased. Edith Ethel, as was well known, had acted the[65] Egeria* to quite a number of Scottish men of letters. That was natural; the Macmasters' establishment was Scottish, Macmaster had been a Critic and had had Government funds for the relief of indigent men of letters, and Edith Ethel was passionately cultured. You could see that even in the forms her crape took and in how she arranged it around her when she sat or agitatedly rose to wring her hands.

But the letters of this particular Scot had out-passed the language of ordinary Egerianishness. They spoke of Lady Macmaster's eyes, arms, shoulders, feminine aura. . . . These letters Lady Macmaster proposed[66] to entrust to Christopher for sale to Transatlantic collectors. She said they ought to fetch £30,000[67] at least, and with the ten per cent.[68] commission that Christopher might take, he might consider himself as amply repaid for the four thousand odd that Macmaster's estate owed him.

And this had appeared to Sylvia to be so eccentric an expedient that she had felt the utmost pleasure in suggesting that Edith Ethel should drive up to Tietjens's with her letters and have an interview—if possible with Valentine Wannop in the absence of Tietjens. This, she calculated, would worry her rival quite a little[69]—and even if it did not do that, she, Sylvia, would trust herself to obtain subsequently from Edith Ethel a great many grotesque details as to the Wannop's[70] exhausted appearance, shabby clothing, worn hands.

For it is to be remembered that one of the chief torments of the woman who has been abandoned by a man is the sheer thirst of curiosity for material details as to how that man subsequently lives. Sylvia Tietjens, for a great number of years, had tormented her husband. She would have said herself that she had been a thorn in his flesh. That was largely[71] because he had seemed to

---

* In Roman mythology, a goddess or nymph supposed to be the advisor and consort to Numa Pompilius, second King of Rome. Generally, a female advisor and patroness. In *A Man Could Stand Up* – I.i Lady Macmaster is described as 'Egeria to innumerable Scottish Men of Letters!' Perhaps a Fordian joke, implying that it is now 'well-known' because of that reference earlier in the series.

her never to be inclined[72] to take his own part. If you live with a person who suffers from being put upon a good deal, and if that person will not assert his own rights, you are apt to believe that your standards as gentleman and Christian are below his, and the experience is lastingly disagreeable. But, in any case, Sylvia Tietjens had had reason to believe that for many years, for better or for worse—and mostly for worse—she had been the dominating influence over Christopher Tietjens. Now, except for extraneous annoyances, she was aware that she could no longer influence him either for evil or for good. He was a solid, four-square lump of meal sacks too heavy for her hauling about.

So that the only real pleasure that she had was when, at night, in a circle of cosy friends, she could assert that she was not even yet out of his confidence. Normally she would not—the members of her circle would not have—made confidantes of her ex-husband's domestics. But she had had to chance whether the details of Christopher's ménage[73] as revealed by the wife of his carpenter would prove to her friends sufficiently amusing to make them[74] forget the social trespass she committed in consorting with her husband's dependents, and[75] she had to chance whether the carpenter's wife would not see that, by proclaiming her wrongs over the fact that her husband had left her, she was proclaiming[76] her own unattractiveness.

She had hitherto chanced both, but the time, she was aware, was at hand when she would have to ask herself whether she would not be better off if she were what the French call *rangée*[*] as the[77] wife of the Commander-in-Chief in India than as a free-lance woman owing her popularity entirely to her own exertions. It would be slightly ignominious to owe part of her prestige to a pantaloon like General Lord Edward Campion, K.C.B., but how restful might it not be! To keep your place in a society of Marjies and Beatties—and even of Cammies, like the Countess of Fittle-worth—meant constant exertion and watchfulness, even if you were comfortably wealthy and well-born—and it meant still more exertion when your staple capital for entertainment was the domestic misfortunes[78] of a husband that did not like you.

She might well point out to Marjie, Lady Stern, that her

---

[*] Settled, steady (French).

husband's clothes lacked buttons and the wife of his companion all imaginable chic; she might well point out to Beattie, Lady Elsbacher, that[79] according to her husband's carpenter's wife, the interior of her husband's home resembled a cave encumbered with packing cases in dark-coloured wood, whereas in her day . . . Or she might even point out to Cammie, Lady Fittleworth, to Mrs. de Bray Pape and Mrs. Lowther, that,[80] having a defective water-supply, her husband's woman probably provided him only with difficulty with baths. . . . But every now and then someone—as had been the case once or twice with the three American ladies—would point out, a little tentatively, that her husband was by now Tietjens of Groby to all intents and purposes. And people—and in particular American ladies— would attach particular importance before her to English Country[81] gentlemen who had turned down titles and the like. Her husband had not turned down a title; he had not been able to, for much as Mark had desired to refuse a baronetcy at the last moment he had been given to understand that he couldn't. But her husband had practically turned down a whole great estate, and the romantic aspect of that feat was beginning to filter through to her friends. For all her assertions that his seeming poverty was due to dissolute living and consequent bankruptcy, her friends would occasionally ask her whether in fact his poverty was not simply a voluntary affair, the result either of a wager or a strain of mysticism. They would point out that the fact that she[82] and her son at least had all the symptoms of considerable wealth looked like a sign[83] rather that Christopher did not desire wealth, or was generous, than that he had no longer money to throw away. . . .

There were symptoms of that sort of questioning of the mind rising up in the American ladies whom Cammie Fittleworth liked to have staying with her. Hitherto Sylvia had managed to squash them. After all, the Tietjens household below her feet was a singular affair for those who had not the clue to its mystery. She had the clue herself; she knew both about the silent feud between the two brothers and about their attitude to life. And if it enraged her that Christopher should despise the things that money could buy and that she so valued,[84] it none the less gratified her to know that, in the end, she was to be regarded as responsible for that silent feud and the renunciation that it had caused. It was her tongue that had set going the discreditable stories that Mark had once[85] believed against his brother.

But if she was to retain her power to blast that household with her tongue, she felt she ought to have details. She must have corroborative details. Otherwise she could not so very convincingly put over her picture of abandoned corruption. You might have thought that in her[86] coercing Mrs. de Bray Pape and her son into making that rather outrageous visit, and in awakening Mrs. Lowther's innocent curiosity as to the contents of the cottage, she had been inspired solely by the desire to torment Valentine Wannop. But she was aware that there was more than that to it. She might get details of all sorts of queernesses that, triumphantly, to other groups of listeners she could retail as proof of her intimacy with that household.

If her listeners showed any signs of saying that it was queer that a man like Christopher, who appeared like a kindly group of sacks, should actually be a triply crossed being, compounded of a Lovelace, Pandarus and a Satyr,* she could always answer: "Ah, but what can you expect of people who have hams drying in their drawing-room!" Or if others alleged that it was queer, if Valentine Wannop had Christopher as much under her thumb as she was said to have, even by Sylvia, that she should still allow Christopher to run an Agapemone in what was, after all, her own house, Sylvia would have liked[87] to be able to reply: "Ah, but what can you expect of a woman upon whose stairs you will find, side by side, a hairbrush, a frying-pan and a copy of Sappho!"

That was the sort of detail that Sylvia needed. The one item she had: The Tietjens, she knew from Mrs. Carpenter Cramp, had an immense fire-place in their living-room and, after the time-honoured custom, they smoked their hams in that chimney. But to people who did not know that smoking hams in great chimneys was a time-honoured custom, the assertion that Christopher was the sort of person who dried hams in his drawing-room would bring up images of your finding yourself in a sort of place where

---

* Richard Lovelace, Cavalier poet (and poetic lover); Pandarus, a Trojan archer mentioned in the *Iliad*, who – encouraged by Athena – breaks the truce between Greeks and Trojans by wounding Menelaus; Satyr, a spirit of the woods and hills, with tendencies towards bestial behaviour.

hams reclined on the sofa-cushions. Even that was not a proof to the reflective that[88] the perpetrator was a Sadic lunatic—but few people are reflective and at any rate it was queer, and one queerness might be taken as implying another.

But as to Valentine she could not get details enough. You had to prove that she was a bad housekeeper and a blue-stocking in order that it should be apparent that Christopher was miserable—and you had to prove that Christopher was miserable in order to make it apparent that the hold that Valentine Wannop certainly had over him was something unholy. For that it was necessary to have details of misplaced hairbrushes, frying-pans and copies of Sappho.

It had, however, been difficult to get those details. Mrs. Cramp, when appealed to, had made it rather plain that, far from being a bad housekeeper, Valentine Wannop did no housekeeping at all, whereas Marie Léonie—Lady Mark—was a perfect devil of a *ménagère*. Apparently Mrs. Cramp was allowed no further into the dwelling than the wash-house—because of half-pounds of sugar and dusters that Mrs. Cramp, in the character of charwoman, had believed to be her perquisites. Marie Léonie hadn't.

The local doctor and the parson, both of whom visited the house, had contributed only palely-coloured portraits of the young woman. Sylvia had gone to call on them, and making use of the Fittleworth ægis—hinting that Lady Cammie wanted details of her humbler neighbours for her own instruction— Sylvia had tried to get behind the professional secrecy that distinguished parsons and doctors. But she had not got much behind. The parson gave her the idea that he thought Valentine rather a jolly girl, very hospitable and with a fine tap of cider at disposal and fond of reading under trees—the classics mostly. Very much interested also in rock-plants as you could see by the bank under Tietjens's windows.... Their house was always called Tietjens's. Sylvia had never been under those windows, and that enraged her.

From the doctor Sylvia, for a faint flash, gained the impression that Valentine enjoyed rather poor health. But it had been only an impression arising from the fact that the doctor saw her every day—and it was rather discounted by the other fact that the doctor said that his daily visits were for Mark, who might be expected to pop off at any moment. So he needed careful watching. A little excitement and he was done for. . . . Otherwise Valentine seemed to have a sharp eye for old furniture, as the doctor knew to his cost, for in a small way, he collected himself. And he said that at small[89] cottage sales and for small objects Valentine could drive a bargain that Tietjens himself never achieved.

Otherwise, from both the doctor and the parson, she had an impression of Tietjens's as a queer household—queer because it was so humdrum and united. She really herself had expected something more exciting! Really. It did not seem possible that Christopher should settle down into tranquil devotion to brother and mistress after the years of emotion she had given him. It was as if a man should have jumped out of a frying-pan into—a duck-pond.

So, as she looked at the red flush on Fittleworth's face, an almost mad moment of impatience had overcome her. This fellow was about the only man who had ever had the guts to stand up to her. . . . A fox-hunting squire: an extinct animal!

The trouble was, you could not tell quite how extinct he was. He might be able to bite as hard as a fox. Otherwise she would be running down, right now, running down that zigzag orange path to that forbidden land.

That she had hitherto never dared. From a social point of view it would have been outrageous, but she was prepared to chance that. She was sure enough of her place in Society, and if people will excuse a man's leaving his wife, they will excuse the wife's making at least one or two demonstrations that are a bit thick. But she had simply not dared to meet Christopher: he might cut her.

Perhaps he would not. He was a gentleman and gentlemen do not actually[90] cut women with whom they have slept. . . . But he might. . . . She might go down there, and in a dim, low room[91] be making some sort of stipulation—God knew what, the first that came into her head—to Valentine. You can always make up some sort of reason for approaching the woman who has supplanted you. But he might come in, mooning in,[92] and suddenly stiffen into a great, clumsy—oh, adorable—face of stone.

That was what you would not dare to face. That would be

death. She could imagine him going out of the room, rolling his shoulders. Leaving the whole establishment indifferently to[93] her, closing only himself in invisible bonds—denied[94] to her by the angel with the flaming sword!...* That was what he would do. And that before the other woman. He had come once very near it, and she had hardly recovered from it. That pretended illness had not been so much pretended as all that! She had smiled angelically, under the great crucifix, in the convent that had been her nursing home—angelically, amongst lilies, upon the general, the sisters, the many callers that gradually came to her teas. But she had had to think that Christopher was probably in the arms of his girl and he had let her go when she had, certainly physically, needed his help.

But that had not been a calm occasion, in that dark empty house.... And he had not, at that date, enjoyed the favours, the domesticity, of that young woman. He hadn't had a chance of comparison, so the turning down had not counted.[95] He had treated her barbarously—as social counters go it had been helpful to her—but only at the strong urge of a young woman driven to fury: that[96] could be palliated. It hardly indeed affected her now as a reverse. Looked at reasonably: if a man comes home intending to go to bed with a young woman who has bewitched him for a number of years and finds another woman who tells him that she has[97] cancer, and then does[98] a very creditable faint from the top of the stairs and thus[99]—in spite of practice and of being[100] as hard as nails—puts her ankle out of joint, he has got to choose between the one and the other. And the other in this case had been vigorous, determined on her man, even vituperative. Obviously Christopher was not the sort of man who would *like* seducing a young woman whilst his wife was dying of internal cancer, let alone a sprained ankle. But the young woman had arrived at a stage when she did not care for any delicacies or their dictates.

No. That she had been able to live down. But[101] if now the same thing happened, in dim, quiet daylight, in a tranquil old

* This may refer to the expulsion of Adam and Eve in Genesis 3:24, where God 'placed at the east of the garden of Eden Cherubims, and a flaming sword which turned every way, to keep the way of the tree of life'. The archangel Uriel is named as the guardian in some apocryphal sources, though not in the canonical scriptures.

room ... that she would not be able to face. It is one thing to acknowledge that your man has gone—there is no irrevocability about going. He may come back when the other woman is insignificant, a blue-stocking, entirely un-chic. ... [102] But if he took the step—the responsibility—of cutting you, that would be to put between you a barrier that no amount of weariness with your rival could overstep.

Impatience grew upon her. The fellow was away in an aeroplane. Gone North. It was the only time she had ever *known* of him as having gone away. It was her only chance of running down those orange zigzags. And now—it was all Lombard Street to[103] a China apple* that Fittleworth[104] intended to disapprove of her running down. And you could not ignore Fittleworth.

---

* More often 'All Lombard Street to a China orange', to denote very long odds. OED offers instances of all Lombard Street 'to an egg-shell' and 'to nine-pence' (though a note was added to this, pointing out the general application of 'orange').

CHAPTER II

NO, you could not ignore Fittleworth. As a fox-hunting squire he might be an extinct monster—though, then again, he might not: there was no knowing. But as a wicked, dark adept with bad women, and one come[1] of a race that had been adepts with women good and bad for generations, he was about as dangerous a person as you could find. That gross, slow, earthy, obstinate fellow Gunning could stand grouchily up to Fittleworth, answer him back and chance what Fittleworth could do to him. So could any cottager. But then they were his people. She wasn't . . . she, Sylvia Tietjens, and she did not believe she could afford to outface him. Nor could half England.

Old Campion wanted India—probably she herself wanted Campion to have India. Groby Great Tree was cut down, and if you have not the distinction, if you rid yourself of the distinction, of Groby Great Tree just to wound a man to the heart—you may as well take India. Times were changing, but there was no knowing how the circumstances of a man like Fittleworth changed. He sat his horse like a monkey and gazed out over his land as his people had done for generations, bastard or legitimate. And it was all very well to regard him as merely a country squire married to a Transatlantic nobody and so out of it. He hopped up to London—he and his Cammie too—and he passed unnoticeably about the best places and could drop a word or so here and there; and for all the Countess' foreign and unknown origin, she had access to ears to which it was dangerous to have access—dangerous[2] for aspirants to India. Campion might have his war-services and his constituency. But Cammie Fittleworth was popular in the right places,[3] and Fittleworth had his hounds and, when it came even to constituencies, the tradesmen of a couple of counties. And was[4] wicked.

It had been obvious to her for a long time that God would one day step in and intervene for the protection of Christopher. After all, Christopher was a good man—a rather sickeningly good man.

It is, in the end, she reluctantly admitted, the function of God and the invisible Powers to see that a good man shall eventually be permitted to settle down to a stuffy domestic life ... even to chaffering over old furniture. It was a comic affair—but it was the sort of affair that you had to admit. God is probably—and very rightly—on the side of the stuffy domesticities.* Otherwise the world could not continue—the children would not be healthy. And certainly God desired the production of large crops of healthy children. Mind doctors of to-day said that all cases of nervous breakdown occurred in persons whose parents had not led harmonious lives.

So Fittleworth might well have been selected as the lightning conductor over the house of Tietjens. And the selection was quite a good one on the part of the Unseen Powers. And no doubt predestined. There was no accident about Mark's being under the ægis—if that was what you called it—of the Earl. Mark had for long been one of the powers of the land, so had Fittleworth. They had moved in the same spheres—the rather mysterious spheres of Good People—who ruled the destinies of the nation in so far as the more decorative and more splendid jobs were concerned. They must have met about, here and there, constantly for years. And no doubt Mark[5] had indicated that it was in that neighbourhood that he wanted to end his days simply because he wanted to be near the Fittleworths, who could be relied on[6] to look after his Marie Léonie and the rest of them.

For the matter of that, Fittleworth himself, like God, was on the side of the stuffy domesticities and on the side of women who were in the act of producing healthy children. Early in life he had had a woman to whom he was said to have been hopelessly attached and whom he had acquired in romantic circumstances—a famous dancer whom he had snapped up under the nose of a very Great Person indeed. And the woman had died in childbirth—or had given birth to an infant child and gone mad and committed suicide after that achievement. At any rate, for months and months, Fittleworth's friends had had to sit up night after night with him so that he might not kill himself.

Later—after he had married Cammie in the search for a

* Cf. the similar view expressed by Dowell near the close of *The Good Soldier* 160–1, with 'society' standing in there for God.

domesticity that, except for his hounds, he too had made[7] really almost stuffy—he had interested himself—and of course his Countess—in the cause of providing tranquil conditions for women before childbirth. They had put up a perfectly lovely lying-in almshouse right under their own windows, down there.

So there it was—and, as she took her sideways glance at Fittleworth, high up there in the air beside her, she was perfectly aware that she might be in for such a duel with him as had seldom yet fallen to her lot.

He had begun by[8] saying: "God damn it, Campion, ought Helen Lowther to be down there?" Then he had put it, as upon her, Sylvia's information, that the cottage was in effect a disorderly house. But he had added: "If what you say is true?"

That of course was distinctly dangerous, for Fittleworth probably knew quite well that it had been at her,[9] Sylvia's, instigation that Helen Lowther *was* down there. And he was letting her know that if it *was* at her instigation and if the house was really in her belief a brothel his Countess would be frightfully displeased. Frightfully.

Helen Lowther was of no particular importance, except to the Countess—and of course to Michael. She was one of those not unattractive Americans that drift over here and enjoy themselves with frightfully simple things. She liked visiting ruins and chattering about nothing in particular, and galloping on the downs and talking to old servants, and she liked the adoration of Michael. Probably she would have turned down the adoration of anyone older.

And the Countess probably liked to protect her innocence. The[10] Countess was fiftyish now, and of a generation that preserved a certain stiffness along with a certain old-fashioned broadness of mind and outspokenness. She was of a class of American that had once seemed outrageously wealthy and who, if in the present stage of things they did not seem overwhelming, yet retained an aspect of impressive comfort and social authority, and she moved in a set most of whose individuals, American, English, or even French, were of much the same class as herself.[11] She tolerated—she even liked—Sylvia, but she might well be[12] mad if from under her roof Helen Lowther, who was in her charge, should come into social contact with an irregular couple. You never knew when that point of view might not crop up in women of that date and class.

Sylvia, however, had chanced it. She had to—and in the end it was only pulling[13] the string of one more shower-bath. It was a shower-bath formidably charged—but in the end that[14] was her vocation in life, and, if Campion had to lose India, she could always pursue her vocation in other countrysides. She was tired, but not as tired as all that!

So Sylvia had chanced saying that she supposed Helen Lowther could look after herself, and had added a salacious quip to keep the speech in character. She knew nothing really of Helen Lowther's husband, who was probably a lean man with some dim avocation, but[15] he could not be very *impressionné*,* or he would not let his attractive young wife roam for ever over Europe.[16]

His Lordship gave no further sign beyond repeating that if that fellow was the sort of fellow Mrs. Tietjens said he was, her Ladyship would properly curl his whiskers. And, in face of that, Sylvia simply had to make a concession to the extent of saying that she did not see why Helen Lowther could not visit a show cottage that was known, apparently, over[17] half America. And perhaps buy some old sticks.

His Lordship removed his gaze from the distant hills, and turned a cool,[18] rather impertinent glance on her. He said:

"Ah, if it's only that ..." and nothing more. And she[19] chanced it again:

"If," she said slowly too, "you think Helen Lowther is in need of protection I don't mind if I go down and look after her myself!"

The general, who had tried several interjections, now exclaimed:

"Surely you wouldn't meet that fellow!" ... And that rather spoilt it.

For Fittleworth could take the opportunity to leave her to what[20] he was at liberty to regard as the directions of her natural protector. Otherwise he must have said something to give away his attitude. So she had to give away more of her own with the words:

* Perturbed, concerned (French).

"Christopher is not down there.[21] He has taken an aeroplane to York—to save Groby Great Tree. Your man Speeding saw him when he went to get your saddle. Getting into a plane." She added: "But he's too late. Mrs. de Bray Pape had a letter the day before yesterday[22] to say the tree had been cut down. At her orders!"

Fittleworth said: "Good God!" Nothing more. The[23] general regarded him as one fearing to be struck by lightning. Campion had already told her over and over again that Fittleworth would rage like a town bull at the bare idea that the tenant of a furnished house should interfere with its owner's timber.... But he[24] merely continued to look away, communing with the handle of his crop. That called, Sylvia knew, for another concession, and she said:

"Now Mrs. de Bray Pape has got cold feet. Horribly cold feet. That's why she's down there. She's got the idea that Mark may have her put in prison!" She added further:

"She wanted to take my boy Michael with her to intercede. As the heir he has some right to a view!"

And from those speeches of hers Sylvia had the measure of her dread of that silent man. Perhaps she was more tired than she thought, and the idea of India more attractive.

At that point Fittleworth exclaimed:

"Damn it all, I've got to settle the hash of that fellow Gunning!"

He turned his horse's head along the road and beckoned the general towards him with his crop handle. The general gazed back at her appealingly, but Sylvia knew that she had to stop there and await Fittleworth's verdict from the general's lips. She wasn't even to have[25] any duel of *sous-entendus** with Fittleworth.

She clenched her fingers on her crop and looked towards[26] Gunning.... If she was going to be asked by the Countess through old Campion to pack up, bag and baggage, and leave the house she would at least get what she could out of that fellow whom she had never yet managed to approach.[27]

The horses of the general and Fittleworth, relieved to be out of the neighbourhood of Sylvia's chestnut, minced companionably[28] along the road, the mare liking her companion.

* Innuendoes, insinuations (French).

"This fellow Gunning," his Lordship began.... He continued with great animation:[29] "About these gates.... You are aware that my estate carpenter repairs ..."[30]

Those were the last words she heard, and she imagined Fittleworth continuing for a long time about his bothering gates in order to put Campion[31] quite off his guard—and no doubt for the sake of manners. Then he would drop in some shot that would be terrible to the old general. He might even cross-question him as to facts, with sly, side questions, looking away over the country.

For that she cared very little. She did not pretend to be a historian: she entertained rather than instructed. And she had conceded enough to Fittleworth. Or perhaps it was to Cammie. Cammie was a great, fat, good-natured dark thing with pockets under her liquid eyes. But she had a will. And by telling Fittleworth that she had not incited Helen Lowther and the two others to make an incursion into the Tietjens' household Sylvia was aware that she had weakened.[32]

She hadn't intended to weaken. It had happened. She had intended to chance conveying the idea that she intended[33] to worry Christopher and his companion into leaving that country.

The heavy man with the three horses approached slowly, with the air of a small army in the narrow road. He was grubby and unbuttoned, but he regarded her intently with eyes a little bloodshot. He said from a distance something that she did not altogether understand. It was about her chestnut. He was asking her to back that ere chestnut's tail into the hedge. She was not used to being spoken to by the lower classes. She kept her horse along the road. In that way the fellow could not pass. She knew what was the matter. Her chestnut would lash out at Gunning's charges if they got near her[34] stern. In the hunting season it wore a large K[35]* on its tail.

Nevertheless the fellow must be a good man with horses: otherwise he would not be perched on one with the stirrups crossed over the saddle in front of him and lead two others. She did not know that she would care to do that herself nowadays; there had been a time when she would have. She had intended to slip down from the chestnut and hand it, too, over[36] to Gunning. Once she

* i.e., to warn other riders that the mare is a 'kicker'.

was down on the road he could not very well refuse. But she felt disinclined—to cock her leg over the saddle. He looked like a fellow who could refuse.

He refused. She had asked him to hold her horse whilst she went down and spoke to his master. He had made no motion towards her; he[37] had continued to stare fixedly at her. She had said:

"You're Captain Tietjens' servant, aren't you? I'm his wife. Staying with Lord Fittleworth!"

He had made no answer and no movement except to draw the back of his right hand across his left nostril—for lack of a hand-kerchief. He said something incomprehensible—but not conciliatory. Then he began a longer speech. That she under-stood. It was to the effect that he had been thirty years, boy and man, with his Lordship and the rest of his time with th' Cahptn.[38] He also pointed out that there was a hitching post and chain by[39] the gate there. But he did not advise her to hitch to it. The chestnut would kick to flinders any cart that came along the road. And the mere idea of the chestnut lashing out and injuring itself caused[40] her to shudder; she was a good horsewoman.

The conversation went with long pauses. She was in no hurry; she would have to wait till Campion or Fittleworth came back—with the verdict probably. The fellow when he used short sentences was incomprehensible because of his dialect. When he spoke longer she got a word or two out of it.

It troubled her a little, now, that Edith Ethel might be coming along the road. Practically she had promised to meet her at that spot and at about that moment, Edith Ethel proposing to sell her love-letters to Christopher—or through him.... The night before she had told Fittleworth that Christopher had bought the place below her with money he had from Lady Macmaster because Lady Macmaster had been his mistress. Fittleworth had boggled at that ... it had been at that moment that he had gone rather stiff to her.

As a matter of fact Christopher had bought that place out of a windfall.[*] Years before—before even[41] she had married him—he

---

[*] 'Then Ford had a windfall. He sold some film rights, and the money he received, plus some capital I withdrew from Australia, enabled us to buy "the" cottage, at Bedham': Bowen, *Drawn From Life* 69. See also Saunders, *Dual Life* II 78 ('It seemed like the magical reward of a fairy world') and *Nightingale* 116–17.

had had a legacy from an aunt, and in his visionary way had invested it in some Colonial—very likely Canadian—property or invention or tramway concession, because he considered that some remote place, owing to its geographical position on some road—was going to grow. Apparently during the war it had grown, and the completely forgotten investment had paid nine and sixpence in the pound. Out of the blue. It could not be helped. With a monetary record of visionariness and generosity such as Christopher had behind him some chickens must now and then come home—some visionary investment turn out sound, some debtor turn honest. She understood even that some colonel who had died on Armistice night and to whom Christopher had lent a good sum in hundreds had turned honest. At any rate his executors had written to ask her for Christopher's address with a view to making payments. She hadn't at the time known Christopher's address, but no doubt they had got it from the War Office or somewhere.

With windfalls[42] like those he had kept afloat, for she did not believe the old-furniture business as much as paid its way. She had heard through Mrs. Cramp that the American partner had embezzled most of the money that should have gone to Christopher. You should not do business with Americans. Christopher, it is true, had years ago—during the war—predicted an American invasion—as he always predicted everything. He had, indeed, said that if you wanted to have money you must get it from where money was going to, so that if you wanted to sell you must prepare to sell what they wanted. And they wanted old furniture more than anything else. That was why there were so many of them here. She[43] didn't mind. She was already beginning a little campaign with Mrs. de Bray Pape to make her refurnish Groby— to make her export all the clumsy eighteen-forty mahogany that the great house contained to Santa Fé, or wherever it was that Mr. Pape lived alone; and to refurnish with Louis Quatorze[44] as befitted the spiritual descendant of the Maintenon. The worst of it was that Mr. Pape[45] was stingy.

She was, indeed, in a fine taking that morning—Mrs. de Bray Pape. In hauling out the stump of Groby Great Tree the wood- cutters had apparently brought down two-thirds of the ball-room exterior wall, and that vast, gloomy room, with its immense lustres, was wrecked, along with the old school-rooms above it. As far as she could make out from the steward's letter Christopher's boyhood's bed-room had practically disappeared.... Well, if Groby Great Tree did not like Groby House it had finely taken its dying revenge.... A nice shock Christopher would get! Anyhow, Mrs. de Bray Pape had already pretty[46] well mangled the great dovecote in erecting in it a new power station.

But apparently it was going to mangle the de Bray Papes[47] to the tune of a pretty penny, and apparently Mr. Pape might be expected to give his wife no end of a time.... Well, you can't expect to be God's Vice-gerent* of England without barking your shins on old, hard things.

No doubt Mark knew all about it by now. Perhaps it had killed him. She hoped it hadn't, because she still hoped to play him some tidy little tricks before she had done with him.... If he were dead or dying beneath that parallelogram of thatch down among the apple boughs all sorts of things might be going to happen. Quite inconvenient things.

There would be the title. She quite definitely did not want the title, and it would become more difficult to injure[48] Christopher. People with titles and great possessions are vastly more difficult to discredit[49] than impoverished commoners, because the scale of morality changes. Titles and great possessions expose you to great temptations: it[50] is scandalous, on the other hand, that the indigent should have any fun!

So that, sitting rather restfully in the sunlight on her horse, Sylvia felt like a general who is losing the fruits of victory. She did not much care. She had got down Groby Great Tree: that was as nasty a blow as the Tietjenses[51] had had in ten generations.

But then a queer, disagreeable thought went through her mind, just as Gunning at last made again a semi-comprehensible remark. Perhaps in letting Groby Great Tree be cut down God was lifting the ban off the Tietjenses.[52] He might well.

Gunning, however, had said something like:

"Sheddn gaw dahn theer. Ride Boldro up to farm n put he in loose box." She gathered that if she would ride her horse to some

---

* Properly not hyphenated, though in practice it often is. Applied to priests and, specifically, to the Pope, it does mean representative of God or Christ. The Papist Ford may be punning on Popes and Papes here.

farm he could be put in a loose box and she could rest in the farmer's parlour. Gunning was looking at her with a queer intent look. She could not just think what it meant.

Suddenly it reminded her of her childhood. Her father had had a head gardener just as gnarled and just as apparently autocratic. That was it. She had not been much in the country for thirty years. Apparently country people had not changed much. Times change; people not so much.[53]

For it came back to her with sudden extraordinary clearness. The side of a greenhouse, down there in the west where she had been "Miss Sylvia, oh Miss *Sylvia!*"[54] for a whole army of protesting retainers, and that old, brown, gnarled fellow who was equally "Mr. Carter"[55] for them all, except her father. Mr. Carter had been potting geranium shoots and she had been a little teasing a white kitten. She was thirteen, with immense plaits of blonde hair. The kitten had escaped from her and was rubbing itself, its back arched, against the leggings of Mr. Carter, who had a special affection for it. She had proposed—merely to torment Mr. Carter—to do something to the kitten, to force its paws into walnut shells perhaps. She had so little meant to hurt the kitten that she had forgotten what it was she had proposed to do. And suddenly the heavy man, his bloodshot eyes fairly blazing, had threatened if she so much as blew on that kitten's fur to thrash her on a part of her anatomy on which public schoolboys rather than young ladies are usually chastised ... so that she would not be able to sit down for a week, he had said.

Oddly enough, it had given her a[56] queer pleasure, that returned always with the recollection. She had never otherwise in her life been threatened with physical violence, and[57] she knew that within herself the emotion had often and often existed: If only Christopher would thrash her within an inch of her life....[58] Or yes—there had been Drake.... He had half-killed her: on the night before her wedding to Christopher. She had feared for the child within her! That emotion had been unbearable!*

She said to Gunning—and she felt for all the world as if she

---

* Sylvia's sadomasochistic tendencies surface at several other points in the tetralogy, particularly in relation to the white bulldog that reminds her of Christopher and that she whips mercilessly: it dies shortly afterwards (*No More Parades* II.ii).

were trying a torment on Mr. Carter of years ago:

"I don't see why I need go to the farm. I can perfectly well ride Boldero down this path. I must certainly speak to your master."

She had really no immediate notion of doing anything of the sort, but she turned her horse towards the wicket gate that was a little beyond Gunning.

He scrambled off his horse with singular velocity and under the necks of those he led. It was like the running of an elephant, and, with all the reins bunched before him, he almost fell with his back on the little wicket towards[59] whose latch she had been extending the handle of her crop.... She had not meant to raise it. She swore she had not meant to raise it. The veins stood out in his hairy open neck and shoulders. He said: No, she didn'!

Her chestnut was reaching its teeth out towards the led horses. She was not certain that he heard her when she asked if he did not know that she was the wife of the Captain, his master, and guest of Lord Fittleworth, his ex-master. Mr. Carter certainly had not heard her years ago when she had reminded him that she was his master's daughter. He had gone on fulminating. Gunning was doing that too—but more slowly and heavily. He said first that the Cahptn would tan her hide if she so much as disturbed his brother by a look; he would hide her within an inch of her life. As he had done already.

Sylvia said that by God he never had; if he said he had he lied. Her immediate reaction was to resent the implication that she was not as good a man as Christopher. He seemed to have been boasting that he had physically corrected her.

Gunning continued dryly:

"You put it in th' papers yourself. My ol' missus read it me. Powerful set on Sir Mark's comfort, the Cahptn is. Threw you downstairs the Cahptn did, n give you cancer. It doesn show!"

That was the worst of attracting chivalrous attentions from professional people. She had begun divorce proceedings against Christopher, in the way of a petition for restitution of conjugal rights,* compounding with the shade of Father Consett and her conscience as a Roman Catholic by arguing that a petition for the restoration of your husband from a Strange Woman is not the

---

* The divorce court made a decree of restitution of conjugal rights in favour of Ford's wife Elsie in January 1910: see Saunders, *Dual Life* I 305.

same as divorce proceedings. In England at that date it was a preliminary and[60] caused as much publicity as the real thing to which she had no intention of proceeding. It caused quite a terrific lot of publicity, because her counsel in his enthusiasm for the beauty and wit of his client—in his chambers the dark, Gaelic, youthful K.C. had been impressively sentimental in his enthusiasm—learned counsel had overstepped the rather sober bounds of the preliminary aspects of these cases. He knew that Sylvia's aim was not divorce but the casting of all possible obloquy on Christopher, and in his fervid Erse oratory he had cast as much mud as an enthusiastic terrier with its hind legs out of a fox's hole. It had embarrassed Sylvia herself, sitting brilliantly in court. And it had roused the judge, who knew something of the case, having, like half London of his class, taken tea with the dying Sylvia beneath the crucifix and amongst the lilies of the nursing home that was also a convent. The judge had protested against the oratory of Mr. Sylvian Hatt, but Mr. Hatt had got in already a lurid picture of Christopher and Valentine in a dark, empty house on Armistice night throwing Sylvia downstairs and so occasioning in her[61] a fell disease from which, under the court's eyes, she was fading.[62] This had distressed Sylvia herself, for, rather with the idea of showing the court and the world in general what a fool Christopher was to have left her for a little brown sparrow, she had chosen to appear all[63] radiance and health. She had hoped for the appearance of Valentine in court. It had not occurred.

The judge had asked Mr. Hatt if he really proposed to bring in evidence that Captain Tietjens and Miss Wannop had enticed Mrs. Tietjens into a dark house—and on a shake of the head that Sylvia had not been able to refrain from giving Mr. Hatt, the judge had made some extremely rude remarks to her counsel. Mr. Hatt was at that time standing as parliamentary candidate for a Midland Borough and was anxious to attract as much publicity as that or any other case would give him. He had therefore gone bald-headed for the judge, even accusing him of being indifferent to the sufferings he was causing to Mr. Hatt's fainting client. Rightly handled, impertinence to a judge will gain quite a number of votes on the Radical side of Midland constituencies, judges being supposed to be all Tories.

Anyhow, the case had been a fiasco from Sylvia's point of view, and[64] for the first time in her life she had[65] felt mortification; in addition she had felt a great deal of religious trepidation.[66] It had come into her mind in court—and it came with additional vividness there above that house, that, years ago in her mother's sitting-room in a place called Lobscheid, Father Consett had predicted that if Christopher fell in love with another woman, she, Sylvia, would perpetrate acts of vulgarity.* And there she had been, not only toying with the temporal courts in a matter of marriage, which is a sacrament, but led undoubtedly into a position that she had to acknowledge was vulgar. She had precipitately left the court when Mr. Hatt had for the second time appealed for pity for her—but she had not been able to stop it. . . .[67] Pity! She appeal for pity! She had regarded herself—she[68] had certainly desired to be regarded—as the sword of the Lord smiting the craven and the traitor—to Beauty! And was it to be supported that she was to be regarded as such a fool as to be decoyed into an empty house! Or as to let herself be thrown down stairs!. . . But *qui facit per alium*† is herself responsible, and there she had been in a position as mortifying as would have been that of any city clerk's wife. The florid periods of Mr. Hatt had made her shiver all over, and she had never spoken to him again.

And her position had been broadcasted all over England—and now, here in the mouth of this gross henchman, it had recurred. At the most inconvenient moment. For the thought suddenly recurred, sweeping over with immense force: God had changed sides at the cutting down of Groby Great Tree.

The first intimation she had had that God might change sides had occurred in that hateful court, and had, as it were, been prophesied by Father Consett. That dark saint and martyr was in Heaven, having died for the Faith, and undoubtedly he had the ear of God. He had prophesied that she would toy with the temporal courts; immediately[69] she had felt herself degraded, as if strength had gone out from her.

Strength had undoubtedly gone out from her. Never before in her life had her mind not sprung to an emergency. It was all very

---

* See *Some Do Not . . .* I.ii. Sylvia recalls that occasion in *No More Parades* II.ii.

† He or she who acts through another. The usual Latin expression is *qui facit per alium fecit per se*: 'is herself responsible' expresses the latter part of it.

well to say that she could not move physically either backwards or forwards for fear of causing a stampede amongst all those horses and that therefore her mental uncertainty might be excused. But it was the finger of God—or of Father Consett who, as saint and martyr, was the agent of God. . . . Or perhaps God Himself was here really taking a hand for the protection of His Christopher, who was undoubtedly an Anglican saint. . . . The Almighty might well be dissatisfied with the other relatively[70] amiable saint's[71] conduct of the case, for surely[72] Father Consett might be expected to have a soft spot for her, whereas you could not expect the Almighty to be unfair even to Anglicans. . . . At any rate up over the landscape, the hills, the sky, she felt the shadow of Father Consett, the arms extended as if on[73] a gigantic cruciform—and then, above and behind that, an[74] . . . an August Will!

Gunning, his bloodshot eyes fixed on her, moved his lips vindictively. She had, in face of those ghostly manifestations across hills and sky, a moment of real panic. Such as she had felt when they had been shelling near the hotel in France, when she had sat amidst palms with Christopher under a glass roof. . . . A mad desire to run—or as if your soul ran about inside you like a parcel of rats in a pit awaiting an unseen terrier.

What was she to do? What the devil was she to do?. . . She felt an itch. . . . She felt the very devil of a desire to confront at least Mark Tietjens . . . even if it should kill the fellow. Surely God could not be unfair! What was she given beauty for—the dangerous remains of beauty!—if[75] not to impress it on the unimpressible! She ought to be given the chance at least once more to try her irresistible ram against that immovable post before . . . She[76] was aware. . . .

Gunning was saying something to the effect that if she caused Mrs. Valentine to have a miscarriage or an idiot child, Is Lordship would[77] flay all the flesh off er bones with is own ridin crop. Is Lordship ad fair done it to im, Gunning, isself[78] when e lef is missis then eight and a arf munce gone to live with old Mother Cressy! The child was bore dead.

The words conveyed little to her. . . . She was aware. . . . She was aware. . . . What was she aware of?. . . She was aware that God—or perhaps it was Father Consett that so arranged it, more diplomatically, the dear!—desired that she should apply to Rome for the dissolution of her marriage with Christopher, and that she should then apply to the civil courts. She thought that probably God desired that Christopher should be freed as early as possible, Father Consett suggesting to Him the less stringent course.

A fantastic object was descending at a fly-crawl the hill-road that went almost vertically up to the farm amongst the beeches. She did not care!

Gunning was saying that that wer why Is Lordship giv im th sack. Took away the cottage an ten bob a week that Is[79] Lordship allowed to all as had been in his service thritty yeer.

She said: "What! What's that?" ... Then it came back to her that Gunning had suggested that she might give Valentine a miscarriage.... Her[80] breath made a little clittering sound,* like the trituration of barley ears, in her throat;[81] her gloved hands, reins and all, were over her eyes, smelling of morocco leather; she felt as if within her a shelf dropped away—as the platform drops away from beneath the feet of a convict they are hanging. She said: "Could ..." Then her mind stopped, the clittering sound in her throat continuing. Louder. Louder.

Descending the hill at the fly's pace was the impossible. A black basket-work pony phaeton: the pony—you always look at the horse first—four hands too big; as round as a barrel, as shining as a mahogany dining-table, pacing for all the world like a *haute école* circus steed, and in a panic bumping its behind into that black vehicle. It eased her to see.... But ... fantastically horrible, behind that grotesque coward of a horse, holding the reins, was a black thing, like a funeral charger; beside it a top hat, a white face, a buff waistcoat, black coat, a thin, Jewish beard. In front of that a bare, blond head, the hair rather long—on the front seat, back to the view. Trust Edith Ethel to be accompanied by a boy-poet cicisbeo![†] Training Mr. Ruggles for his future condition as consort!

---

* 'To make a thin vibratory rattle; to cause to vibrate and rattle lightly' (*OED*). The word appears in the opening section of Joyce's *Finnegans Wake* ('with larrons o'toolers clittering up and tombles a'buckets clottering down'), which Ford could have seen in *transition* (1, April 1927). But he had used it himself in *A Call* (156) and, even earlier, in the 1906 collection, *Christina's Fairy Book*: 'I heard a little clitter-clittering noise', which, it transpires, is the noise a fairy sometimes makes. Quoted in Alison Lurie's 'Ford Madox Ford's Fairy Tales' (1980), conveniently reprinted in *Don't Tell the Grown-Ups: Subversive Children's Literature* (London: Bloomsbury, 1990), 74–89 (85).
† A married woman's male companion or gallant (Italian).

She exclaimed to Gunning:

"By God, if you do not let me pass, I will cut your face in half...."[82]

It was justified! This in effect was too much—on the part of Gunning and God and Father Consett. All of a heap they had given her perplexity, immobility and a dreadful thought that was griping[83] her vitals.... Dreadful! Dreadful!

She must get down to the cottage. She must get down to the cottage.

She said to Gunning:

"You damn fool.... You *damn* fool.... I want to save ..."

He moved up—interminably—sweating and hairy, from the gate on which he had been leaning, so that he no longer barred her way. She trotted smartly past him and cantered beautifully down the slope. It came to her from the bloodshot glance that his eyes gave her that he would like to outrage her with ferocity. She felt pleasure.

She came off her horse like a circus performer to the sound of "Mrs. Tietjens! Mrs. Tietjens," in several voices from above. She let the chestnut go to hell.

It seemed queer that it did not seem queer. A shed of log-parings set upright, the gate banging behind her. Apple-branches spreading down; grass up to the middle of her grey breeches. It was Tom Tiddler's Ground;[84]* it was near a place called Gemmenich on the Fourth of August, 1914!... But just quietude: quietude.

Mark regarded her boy's outline with beady, inquisitive eyes. She bent her switch into a half hoop[85] before her. She heard herself say:

"Where are all these fools? I want to get them out of here!"

He continued to regard her: beadily: his head like mahogany against the pillows. An apple-bough caught in her hair.

She said:

"Damn it all, *I*[86] had Groby Great Tree cut[87] down: not that tin Maintenon. But, as God is my Saviour, I would not tear

---

*   A place where a fortune can be easily picked up but also no man's land, from the children's game. Ford's strong sense of the changing boundaries between peace and war and the blurring of military and civilian spheres is relevant here, though he had used the phrase years before the war (see, for instance, *England* 111, 113).

another woman's child in the womb!"

He said:

"You poor bitch! You poor bitch! The riding has done it!"*

She swore to herself afterwards that she had heard him say that, for at the time she had had too many emotions to regard his speaking as unusual. She took, indeed, a prolonged turn in the woods before she felt equal to facing the others. Tietjens's had its woods onto which the garden gave directly.

Her main bitterness was that they had this peace. She was cutting the painter,† but they were going on in this peace; her world was waning. It was the fact that her friend Bobbie's husband, Sir Gabriel Blantyre—formerly Bosenheim[88]‡—was cutting down expenses like a lunatic. In her world there was the writing on the wall. Here they could afford to call her a poor bitch—and be in the right of it, as like as not!

---

* Cf. *Provence* 359, 'It was the riding that did it' – a rather ambiguous phrase.
† The painter is the rope that fastens a (usually small) boat to a ship or to the quay. Cutting the painter allows a silent departure. More figuratively, it is understood to mean effecting a separation or severing a connection and accomplishing release. *Brewer's Dictionary of Phrase and Fable* notes that the phrase was 'much used in the 19th century with reference to possible severance between Britain and her colonies'.
‡ For some examples of the many hasty name-changes notified to the *London Gazette* in the early weeks of the war (Rosenheim to Rose, Brueggemeyer to Bridges), see E.S. Turner, *Dear Old Blighty* (London: Michael Joseph, 1980), 97. Turner lists Ford as one of the writers 'who changed their names' but the context implies that he did so on the outbreak of war rather than in 1919, as was the case. See also Peel, *How We Lived Then* 42–3.

CHAPTER III

VALENTINE was awakened by the shrill overtones of the voice of the little maid coming through the open window. She had fallen asleep over the words: "*Saepe te in somnis vidi!*"* to a vision of white limbs in the purple Adriatic. Eventually the child's voice said:

"We only sez 'mem' to friends of the family!" shrilly and self-assertively.

She was at the casement, dizzy and sickish with the change of position and the haste—and violently impatient of her condition. Of humanity she perceived only the top of a three-cornered grey hat and a grey panniered skirt in downward perspective. The sloping tiles of the potting-shed hid the little maid; aligned small lettuce[1] plants, like rosettes† on the dark earth, ran from under the window, closed by a wall of sticked peas, behind them the woods, slender grey ash trunks going to a great height. They were needed for shelter. They would have to change their bedroom: they could not have a night nursery that faced the north. The spring onions needed pricking out: she had meant to put the garden pellitory into the rocks in the half-circle; but the operation had daunted her. Pushing the little roots into crevices with her fingers; removing stones, trowelling in artificial manure, stooping, dirtying her fingers would make her retch. . . .

She was suddenly intensely distressed at the thought of the lost coloured[2] prints. She had searched the whole house—all imaginable drawers, cupboards, presses. It was like their fate that, when

---

* Not quite Propertius, II, xxvi ('Vidi te in somnis fracta'). The same phrase appears in *A Man Could Stand Up* – I.i. Ford discusses the opening lines of Propertius' poem in *March* 184–5 (and see *Nightingale* 172).

† This is another example of 'parallel thoughts', the same image having occurred in Marie Léonie's reflections earlier; yet it may also refer back to *No More Parades* II.ii and the 'great octagonal, bluish salon where Lady Sachse gave her teas'. It is the scene of Levin's wedding-breakfast, precisely and overtly a 'parade', and Ford notes that the room is 'vaulted, up to a rosette in the centre of the ceiling'. He then mentions '[a] fattish, brilliantined personality, in mufti, with a scarlet rosette', standing beside the duchess. The contrast with the lettuce plants could hardly be more marked.

they had at last got a good—an English—client, their first commission from her should go wrong. She thought again of every imaginable, unsearched parallelogram in the house, standing erect, her head up, neglecting to look down on the intruder.

She considered all their customers to be intruders. It was true that Christopher's gifts lay in the way of old-furniture dealing—and farming. But farming was ruinous.* Obviously if you sold old furniture straight out of use in your own house, it fetched better prices than from a shop. She did not deny Christopher's ingenuity—or that he was right to rely on her hardihood. He had at least the right so to rely. Nor did she mean to let him down. Only . . .

She passionately desired little Chrissie to be born in that bed with the thin fine posts, his blond head with the thin, fine hair on those pillows. She passionately desired that he should lie with blue eyes gazing at those curtains on the low windows. . . . *Those!* With those peacocks and globes. Surely a child should lie gazing at what his mother had seen, whilst she was awaiting him!

And, where were those prints?. . . ³ Four parallelograms of faint, silly colour. Promised for tomorrow morning. The margins needed bread-crumbing. . . .† She imagined her chin brushing gently, gently back and forward on the floss of his head; she imagined holding him in the air as, in that bed, she lay, her arms extended upwards, her hair spread on those pillows! Flowers perhaps spread on that quilt. Lavender!

But if Christopher reported that one of those dreadful people with querulous voices wanted a bedroom complete?. . .

If she begged him to retain it for her. Well, he would. He prized her above money. She thought—ah, she knew—that he prized the child within her above the world.

Nevertheless, she imagined that she would go all on to the end

* As with the later references to pigs, this statement reflects aspects of Ford and Stella's lives at Bedham, recalled in Bowen's *Drawn from Life*, particularly 75–6.

† See Charles Holmes, 'Some Elements of Picture Cleaning', *Burlington Magazine*, 40.228 (March 1922), 132–4 (133), discussing the circumstances in which the use of water is dangerous (abrasion, cracked surface or porous canvas) and 'the amateur cleaner must be content with bread crumbs. The crumb of a white loaf worked gently for some time over the surface will gradually remove the greater part of the accumulated dirt.'

with her longings unvoiced.... Because there was the game....
His game ... oh, hang it, *their* game! And you have to think
whether it is worse for the unborn child to have a mother with
unsatisfied longings, or a father beaten at his ... No, you must
not call it a game.... Still, roosters beaten by other roosters lose
their masculinity.... Like roosters, men....* Then, for a child
to have a father lacking masculinity.... for the sake of some
peacock and globe curtains, spindly bed-posts, old, old glass
tumblers with thumb-mark indentations....

On the other hand, for the mother the soft feeling that those
things give!... The room had a barrel-shaped ceiling, following
the lines of the roof almost up to the roof-tree; dark oak beams,
beeswaxed—ah, that beeswaxing! Tiny, low windows almost
down to the oaken floor.... You would say, too much of the
show-place: but you lived into it. You lived yourself into it in spite
of the Americans who took, sometimes embarrassed, peeps from
the doorway.

Would they have to peek into the nursery? Oh, God, who
knew? What would He decree? It was an extraordinary thing to
live with Americans all over you, dropping down in aeroplanes,
seeming to come up out of the earth.... There, all of a sudden,
you didn't know how....

That woman below the window was one, now. How in the
world had she got below that window?... But there were so many
entrances—from the spinney, from the Common, through the
fourteen-acre, down from the road.... You never knew who was
coming. It was eerie; at times she shivered over it. You seemed to
be beset—with stealthy people, creeping up all the paths....

Apparently the little tweeny was disputing the right of that
American woman to call herself a friend of the family and thus
to be addressed as "Mem!" The American was asserting her descent
from Madame de Maintenon.... It was astonishing the descents
they all had! She herself was descended from the surgeon-butler
to Henry VII—Henry the Somethingth.† And, of course, from

---

*   This and the earlier comparison of roosters with both Rodin and Mark Tietjens in
    Marie Léonie's reflections are in calculatedly marked contrast to General Campion's
    exclaiming 'with the vehemence of a shocked hen' (II.i).
†   Perhaps Thomas Vicary (1490?–1561/2), who became Master of the Barber-Surgeons'
    Company and Sergeant-Surgeon to Henry VIII. He advanced the status of surgery in
    England and wrote the first anatomy textbook to be published in English. In Holbein's

the great Professor Wannop, beloved of lady-educators, and by ladies whom he had educated.... And Christopher was eleventh Tietjens of Groby—with an eventual burgomaster of Scheveningen* or somewhere in some century or other: time of Alva.† Number one came[4] over with Dutch William, the Protestant Hero!... If he had not come, and if Professor Wannop had not educated her, Valentine Wannop—or educated her differently—she would not have ... Ah, but she would have! If[5] there had not been any HE, looking like a great Dutch *treckschluyt*‡ or whatever you call it—she would have had to invent one to live with in open sin.... But her father might have educated her so as to have—at least presentable underclothes....

He could have educated her so as to be able to say—oh, but tactfully:

"Look here, you.... Examine my ... my *cache-corsets*....§ Wouldn't some new ones be better than a new pedigree sow?" ... The[6] fellow never had looked at her ... *cache-corsets*. Marie Léonie had!

Marie Léonie was of opinion that she would lose Christopher if she did not deluge herself with a perfume called Houbigant** and wear pink silk next the skin. *Elle ne demandait pas mieux*— but she could not borrow twenty pounds from Marie Léonie. Nor yet forty.... Because, although Christopher might never notice the condition of her all-wools, he jolly well would be struck by the ocean of Houbigant and the surf of pink.... She would give the world for them.... But he would notice—and then she might lose his love. Because she had borrowed the forty pounds.†† On

---

painting (probably completed by his workshop assistants after his death in 1543), Henry hands to Vicary the charter of the 1540 Act of Unification between the Company of Barbers and the Guild of Surgeons.

* A town in the Hague, to the north-west of Delft.

† The Duke of Alva or Alba (so-spelt in Borrow's *The Romany Rye* 20), Ferdinand Alvarez de Toledo, a general at 26, conquered the Netherlands and later established the 'Bloody Council' which drove thousands of Huguenot artisans into exile, many of them emigrating to England.

‡ The Dutch word *trekschuit* means a horse-drawn barge. George Borrow, to whom Ford often alludes, uses 'treck-schuyt' in *Lavengro* (London: Dent, 1961), 26.

§ Bodices (French).

** This Paris perfumery was founded in the 1770s: Marie Antoinette was a customer.

†† It was, of course, precisely forty pounds that Christopher borrowed from Marie Léonie at the end of I.vi in order to celebrate Armistice Night with Valentine and his regimental comrades.

the other hand, she might lose it because of the all-wools. And heaven knew in what condition the other pair would be when[7] they came back from Mrs. Cramp's newest laundry attentions. . . . You could never teach Mrs. Cramp that wool must not be put into boiling water!

Oh God, she ought to lie between lavendered linen sheets with little Chrissie on soft, pink silk, air-cushionish bosoms!. . . Little Chrissie, descended from surgeon-butler—surgeon-barber, to be correct!—and burgomaster. Not to mention the world-famous Professor Wannop. . . . Who was to become . . . who was to become, if it was as she wished it. . . . But[8] she did not know what she wished, because she did not know what was to become of England or the world. . . . But if he became what Christopher wished he would be a contemplative parson farming his own tithe-fields and with a Greek Testament in folio under his arm. . . . A sort of White of Selborne. . . . Selborne was only thirty miles away, but they had had never the[9] time to go there. . . . As who should say: *Je n'ai jamais vu Carcassonne.* . . . [*]
For, if they had never found time, because of pigs, hens, pea-sticking, sales, sellings, mending all-wool under-garments, sitting with dear Mark—before little Chrissie[10] came with the floss silk on his palpitating soft poll and his spinning pebble-blue eyes: if they had never found time now, before, how in the world would there be time with, added[11] on to all the other, the bottles,[12] and the bandagings and the bathing before the fire with the warm, warm water, and feeling and the slubbing[†] of the soap-saturated flannel on the adorable, adorable limbs? And Christopher looking on. . . . He would never find time to go to Selborne, nor Arundel, nor Carcassonne, nor after the Strange Woman. . . . Never. Never!

He had been away now for a day and a half. But it was known between them—without speaking!—that he would never be away for a day and a half again. Now, before her pains began he could . . . seize the opportunity! Well, he had seized it with a

---

[*] Cf. *A Man Could Stand Up* – I.i: 'Never see Carcassonne, the French said', as Valentine reflects on the possible significance of having missed the historic moment of the war's ending.

[†] 'Slub' is used again later but *OED* has 'To draw out and twist (wool, cotton, etc.) after carding, so as to prepare it for spinning' and 'To cover or plaster with mud', neither of which seems quite right. The sense is clearly a very generous, wet lathering.

vengeance.... A day and a half! To go to Wilbraham sale! With
nothing much that they wanted.... She believed ... she
believed that he had gone to Groby in an aeroplane.... He had
once mentioned that. Or she knew that he had thought of it.
Because the day before yesterday when he had been almost out
of his mind about the letting of Groby, he had suddenly looked
up at an aeroplane and had remained looking at it for long,
silent.... Another woman it could not be....

He had forgotten about those prints. That was dreadful. She
knew that he had forgotten about them. How could he, when
they wanted to get a good, English client, for the sake of little
Chrissie? How could he? How could he? It is true that he was
almost out of his mind about Groby and Groby Great Tree. He
had begun to talk about that in his sleep, as for years, at times, he
had talked, dreadfully, about the war.

"*Bringt dem Hauptmann eine Kerze*.... Bring the Major a
candle," he would shout dreadfully beside her in the blackness.*
And she would know that he was remembering the sound of picks
in the earth beneath the trenches. And he would groan and sweat
dreadfully, and she would not dare to wake him.... And there
had been the matter of the boy, Aranjuez', eye. It appeared that
he had run away over a shifting landscape, screaming and holding
his hand to his eye. After Christopher had carried him out of a
hole.... Mrs. Aranjuez had been rude to her at the Armistice
night dinner.... The first time in her life that anyone—except
of course Edith Ethel—had ever been rude[13] to her. Of course you
did not count Edith Ethel Duchemin, Lady Macmaster!... But
it's queer: your man saves the life of a boy at the desperate risk of
his own. Without that there would not have been any Mrs. Aranjuez: then Mrs. Aranjuez is the first person that ever in your life
is rude to you. Leaving permanent traces[14] that made you shudder
in the night! Hideous eyes!

Yet, but for a miracle there might have been no Christopher.
Little Aranjuez—it had been because he had talked to her for so
long, praising Christopher, that Mrs. Aranjuez had been rude to
her!—little Aranjuez had said that the German bullets had gone

---

* This is the still-recurring nightmare of voices speaking beneath his bed that Tietjens
has earlier suffered in A Man Could Stand Up – II.i.

over them as thick as the swarm of bees that came out when
Gunning cut the leg off the skep with his scythe!... Well, there
might have been no Christopher. Then there would have been
no Valentine Wannop! She could not have lived.... But Mrs.
Aranjuez should not have been rude to her. The woman must
have seen with half an eye that Valentine Wannop could not live
without Christopher.... Then, why should she fear for her little,
imploring, eyeless creature![15]

It was queer. You would almost say that there was a Provvy who
delighted to torment you with: "If it hadn't been that ..."[16]
Christopher probably believed that there was a Provvy or he
would not dream for his little Chrissie a country parsonage....
He proposed, if they ever made any money, to buy a living for
him—if possible near Salisbury.... What was the name of the
place?... a pretty name.... Buy a living where George Herbert
had been parson....*

She must, by the by,[17] remember to tell Marie Léonie that it
was the Black Orpington labelled 42 not the Red 16 that she had
put the setting of Indian Runners under. She had found that Red
16 was not really broody, though she had come on afterwards. It
was queer that Marie Léonie had not the courage to put eggs
under broody hens because they pecked her, whereas she, Valentine, had no courage to take the chickens when the settings
hatched, because of the shells and gumminesses that might be in
the nests.... Yet neither of them wanted courage.... Hang it
all, neither of them wanted courage, or they would not be living
with Tietjenses.[18] It was like being tied to buffaloes!†

And yet ... How you wanted them to charge!

Bremersyde.... No, that was the home of the Haigs.... Tide
what will and tide what tide, there shall be Haigs at Bremersyde....‡ Perhaps it was Bemersyde!... Bemerton, then. George
Herbert, rector of Bemerton, near Wilton, Salisbury.... That

---

* Valentine's struggle to recall the name 'Bemerton' echoes Christopher's similar
  struggle in *A Man Could Stand Up* – II.ii and furnishes one of the most striking examples of this affinity between characters of phrase or image.
† Cf. *Some Do Not* ... I.vii, where Tietjens wonders: 'But why was he born to be a sort
  of lonely buffalo: outside the herd?' See also *No More Parades* II.ii.
‡ The lines are often ascribed to the thirteenth-century Thomas of Erceldoune, also
  called Thomas the Rhymer: 'Tyde what may whate'er betide, / Haig shall be Haig of
  Bemersyde.'

was what Chrissie was to be like.... She was to imagine herself sitting with her cheek on Chrissie's floss-silk head, looking into the fire and seeing in the coals, Chrissie, walking under elms beside ploughlands. *Elle ne demandait*, really, *pas mieux!*

If the country would stand it!...

Christopher presumably believed in England as he believed in Provvy—because the land was pleasant and green and comely. It would breed true. In spite of showers of Americans descended from Tiglath Pileser[*] and Queen Elizabeth, and the end of the industrial system and the statistics of the shipping trade, England with its pleasant, green comeliness would go on breeding George Herberts with Gunnings to look after them.... Of course with Gunnings!

The Gunnings of the land were the rocks on which the light-house was built—as Christopher saw it. And Christopher was always right. Sometimes a little previous. But always right. Always right. The rocks had been there a million years before the lighthouse was built: the lighthouse made a deuce of a movable flashing—but it was a mere butterfly. The rocks would be there a million years after the light went for the last time out.[†]

A Gunning would be, in[19] the course of years, painted blue, a Druid-worshipper, a[20] Duke Robert of Normandy,[‡] illiterately burning towns and begetting bastards—and eventually—actually at the moment—a man of all works, half-full of fidelity, half blatant, hairy. A retainer you would retain as long as you were prosperous and dispensed hard cider and overlooked his pecca-dilloes[21] with women. He would go on....

The point was whether the time had come for another Herbert of Bemerton. Christopher thought it had: he was always right; always right. But previous. He had predicted the swarms of Americans buying up old things. Offering fabulous prices. He was right.

---

[*]   Tiglath-Pileser III was the empire-building king of Assyria from 745 to 727 BCE, mentioned in 2 Kings 15:29. 'Tiglath Pileser' was also the title of an early story by Rudyard Kipling (the horse is so-named). Ford strongly admired Kipling's early work.

[†]   In Virginia Woolf's 1919 novel *Night and Day*, which Ford reviewed in 'Thus to Revisit: I', *Piccadilly Review* (23 Oct. 1919), 6, Woolf writes of the Hilbery forebears: 'and when they were not lighthouses firmly based on rock for the guidance of their generation, they were steady, serviceable candles, illuminating the chambers of daily life'.

[‡]   William I of England was the illegitimate son of Robert, Duke of Normandy – also known as 'Robert le diable' (Robert the devil) – and his mistress Herleva of Falaise.

The trouble was they did not pay when they offered the fabulous prices: when they did pay they were as mean as . . . she was going to say Job. But she did not know that Job was particularly mean. That lady down below the window would probably want to buy the signed cabinet of Barker of 1762* for[22] half the price of one bought in a New York department store and manufactured yesterday. . . . And she would tell Valentine she was a blood-sucker, even if—to suppose the ridiculous!—Valentine let her have it at her own price. On the other hand, Mr. Schatzweiler[23] talked of fantastic prices. . . .

Oh, Mr. Schatzweiler, Mr. Schatzweiler, if you would only pay us ten per cent. of what you owe us I could have all the pink fluffies, and three new gowns, and keep the little old lace for Chrissie—and have a proper dairy and not milk goats. And cut the losses over the confounded pigs, and put up a range of glass in the sunk garden where it would not be an eyesore. . . . As it was . . .

The[24] age of fairy-tales was not, of course, past. They had had windfalls: lovely windfalls when infinite ease had seemed to stretch out before them. . . . A great windfall when they had bought this place; little ones for the pigs and old mare. . . . Christopher was that[25] sort of fellow; he had sowed so many golden grains that he could not be always reaping whirlwinds. There must be some halcyon days. . . .

Only it was deucedly awkward now—with Chrissie coming and Marie Léonie hinting all day that, as she was losing her figure, if she could not get the grease stains out of her skirt she would lose the affections of Christopher. And they had not got a stiver. . . .† Christopher had cabled Schatzweiler. . . . But what was the use of that?. . . Schatzweiler would be finely dished if she lost the affections of Christopher—because poor old Chris could not run any old junk shop without her. . . . She imagined

---

* In *A Man Could Stand Up* – III.i 'the model cabinet by Barker of Bath' is specified. Here, 'the signed cabinet' and, later, 'the Barker cabinet' with 'its green, yellow and scarlet inlays'. 'Barker of Bath' is normally understood to refer to Thomas Barker (1769–1847), a painter and lithographer, clearly born too late for this to tally. His father, Benjamin, was also an artist: born c.1720, he died in 1793. He was known at one time for decorating japanned ware (glossy black varnish) but worked mainly in South Wales until the early 1770s, when he moved to Bath. The phrasing allows for the 'Barker' to be responsible for the decoration of the cabinet rather than its creation.

† A tiny sum: formerly a Dutch penny.

cabling Schatzweiler—about the four stains on the skirt and the necessity for elegant lying-in gowns. Or else he would lose Christopher's assistance. . . .

The conversation down below raised its tones. She heard the tweeny maid ask why if the American lady was a friend of the family she did not know Er Ladyship theere?. . . Of course it was easy to understand: These people came, all of them, with letters of introduction from Schatzweiler. Then they insisted that they were friends of the family. It was perhaps nice of them—because most English people would not want to know old-furniture dealers.

The lady below exclaimed in a high voice:

"That Lady Mark Tietjens! That! Mercy me, I thought it was the cook!"

She, Valentine, ought to go down and help Marie Léonie. But she was not going to. She had the sense that hostile presences were creeping up the path[26] and Marie Léonie had given her the afternoon off. . . . For the sake of the future, Marie Léonie had said. And *she*[27] had said that she had once expected her own future to offer the reading of Aeschylus beside the Aegean sea. Then Marie Léonie had kissed her and said she knew that Valentine[28] would never rob her of her belongings after Mark died!

An unsolicited testimonial, that. But of course Marie Léonie would desire her not to lose the affections of Christopher. Marie Léonie would say to herself that in that case Christopher might take up with a woman who *would* want to rob Marie Léonie of her possessions after Mark died. . . .

The woman down below announced herself as Mrs. de Bray Pape, descendant of the Maintenon, and wanted to know if Marie Léonie did not think it reasonable to cut down a tree that over-hung your house. Valentine desired to spring to the window: she sprang to the old panelled door and furiously turned the key in the lock. She ought not to have turned the key so carelessly: it had a knack[29] of needing five or ten minutes[30] manipulation before you could unlock the door again. . . . But she ought to have sprung to the window and cried out to Mrs. de Bray Pape:[31] "If you so much as touch a leaf of Groby Great Tree we will serve you with injunctions that it will take half your life and money to deal with!"

She ought to have done that to save Christopher's reason. But she could not: she could not! It was one thing living with all the tranquillity of conscience in the world in open sin. It was another, confronting elderly Americans who knew the fact. She was determined to remain shut in there. An Englishman's house may no longer be his castle—but an Englishwoman's castle is certainly her own bedroom. When once, four months or so ago, the existence of little Chrissie being manifest, she had expressed to Christopher the idea that they ought no longer to go stodging along in penury, the case being so grave: they ought to take some of the Groby money—for the sake of future generations. . . .

Well, she had been run down. . . . At that stage of parturition, call it, a woman is run down and hysterical. . . . It had seemed to her overwhelmingly the fact that a breeding woman ought to have pink fluffy things next her quivering skin and sprayings of say, Houbigant, all over her shoulders and hair. For the sake of the child's health.

So she had let out violently at poor wretched old Chris, faced[32] with the necessity for denying his gods, and had[33] slammed to and furiously locked that door. Her castle had been her bedroom with a vengeance then—for Christopher had been unable to get in or she to get out. He had had to whisper through the keyhole that he gave in: he was dreadfully concerned for her. He had said that he hoped she would try to stick it a little longer, but, if she would not, he would take Mark's money. Naturally she had not let him—but she *had* arranged with Marie Léonie for Mark to[34] pay a couple of pounds more a week for their board and lodging, and as Marie Léonie had perforce taken over the housekeeping, they had found things easing off a little. Marie Léonie had run the house for thirty shillings a week less than she, Valentine, had ever been able to do—and run it streets better. Streets and streets! So they had had money at least nearly to complete their equipments of table linen and the layette. . . . The long and complicated annals!

It was queer that her heart was nearly as much in Christopher's game as was his own. As house-mother, she ought to have grabbed after the last penny—and goodness knew the life was strain enough. Why do women back their men in unreasonable romanticisms?* You might say that it was because, if their men had their masculinities abated—like defeated roosters!—the women would suffer in intimacies. . . . Ah, but it wasn't that! Nor was it merely that they wanted the buffaloes to which they were attached to charge.

It was really that she had followed the convolutions of her man's mind. And ardently approved. She disapproved with him of riches, of the rich, of the frame of mind that riches confer.[35] If the war had done nothing else for them—for those two of them— it had induced them, at least, to install Frugality as a deity. They desired to live hard, even if it deprived them of the leisure in which to think high! She agreed with him that if a ruling class loses the capacity to rule—or the desire!—it should abdicate from its privileges and get underground.

And having accepted that as a principle, she could follow the rest of his cloudy obsessions and obstinacies.

Perhaps she would not have backed him up in his long struggle with dear Mark if she had not considered that their main neces- sity was to live high. . . . And she was aware that why, really, she had sprung to the door rather than to the window had been that she had not desired to make an unfair move in that long chess game. On behalf of Christopher. If she had had to see Mrs. de Bray Pape or to speak to her it would have been disagreeable to have that descendant of a king's companion look at her with the accusing eyes of one who thinks: "You live with a man without being married to him!" Mrs. de Bray Pape's ancestress had been able to force the king to marry her. . . . But that she would have chanced: they had paid penalty enough for having broken the rules of the Club. She could carry her head high enough: not obtru- sively high, but sufficiently! For, in effect, they had surrendered Groby in order to live together and had[36] endured sprays of obloquy that seemed never to cease to splash over the garden hedges.

No,[37] she would have faced Mrs. de Bray Pape. But she would hardly, given Christopher's half-crazed condition, have kept herself from threatening Mrs. Pape with dreadful legal conse-

* Perhaps a nod to Stella, who had backed Ford's 'unreasonable romanticism' in launching the *transatlantic review* in 1924. It cost her a significant proportion of her capital. When they separated, they agreed on a figure owed to her by Ford of £2,704: Saunders, *Dual Life* II 329.

quences if she touched Groby Great Tree. That[38] would have been to interfere[39] in the silent Northern struggle between the brothers. That she would never do, even to save Christopher's reason—unless she were jumped into it!.... That Mark did not intend to interfere between Mrs. Pape and the tree she knew—for when she had read Mrs. Pape's letter to him he had signified as much to her by means of his eyes.... Mark she loved and respected because he was a dear—and because he had backed her through thick and thin. Without him ... There had been a moment on that dreadful night ... She prayed God that she would not have to think again of that dreadful night.... If she had to see Sylvia again she would go mad, and the child within her.... Deep, deep within her the blight would fall on the little thread of brain!

Mrs. de Bray Pape, God be thanked, provided a diversion for her mind. She was speaking French with an eccentricity that could not be ignored.

Valentine could see, without looking out of the window, Marie Léonie's blank face and the equal blankness with which she must have indicated that she did not intend to understand. She imagined her standing, motionless, pinafored and unmerciful before the other lady, who beneath the three-cornered hat was stuttering out:

"Lady Tietjens, mwaw, Madam de Bray Pape, desire coo-pay la arbre.... "

Valentine could hear Marie Léonie's steely tones saying:
"On dit 'l'arbre,' Madame!"

And then the high voice of the little maid:
"Called us 'the pore,' she did, your ladyship.... Ast us why we could not take example!"

Then a voice, soft for these people, and with modulations:
"Sir Mark seems to be perspiring a great deal. I was so free as to wipe ... "

As,[40] above, Valentine said: "Oh, Heaven!" Marie Léonie cried out: "Mon Dieu!" and there was a rush of skirts and pinafore.

Marie Léonie was rushing past a white, breeched figure, saying:
"Vous, une étrangère, avez osé...."*

_____

* 'You, a stranger, have dared ...' (French).

A shining, red-cheeked boy was stumbling slightly from before her. He said, after her back:

"Mrs. Lowther's[41] handkerchief is the smallest, softest . . ." He added to the young woman in white: "We'd better go away. . . . Please let's go away. . . . It's not sporting. . . ." A singularly familiar face; a singularly moving voice. "For[42] God's sake let us go away. . . ." Who said "For God's sake!" like that—with staring blue eyes?

She was at the door frantically twisting at the[43] great iron key; the lock was of very old hammered iron work. The doctor ought to be telephoned to. He had said that if Mark had fever or profuse sweats, he should be telephoned to at once. Marie Léonie would be with him; it was her, Valentine's, duty to telephone. The key would not turn; she hurt her hand in the effort. But part of her emotion was due to that bright-cheeked boy. Why should he have said that it was not sporting of them to be there? Why had he exclaimed for God's sake to go away? The key would not turn. It stayed solid, like a piece of the old lock. . . . Who was the boy like? She rammed her shoulder against the unyielding door. She must not do that. She cried out.

From the window—she had gone to the window intending to tell the girl to set up a ladder for her, but it would be more sensible to tell her to telephone!—she could see Mrs. de Bray Pape. She was[44] still haranguing the girl. And then on the path, beyond the lettuces and the newly sticked peas, arose a very tall figure. A very tall figure.[45] Portentous. By some trick of the slope figures there always appeared very tall. . . . This appeared[46] leisurely: almost hesitant. Like the apparition of the statue of the Commander in Don Juan, somehow.* It appeared to be preoccupied with its glove: undoing its glove. . . . Very[47] tall, but with too much slightness of the legs. . . . A woman in hunting-breeches! Grey against the tall ash-stems of the spinney. You could not see her face because you were above her, in the window, and her head was bent down! In the name of God! . . .

---

* Don Juan sees in a graveyard the statue of a nobleman ('the Commander') whose daughter he tried to ravish and whom he later killed in a duel. He invites the statue to dinner and it accepts, seizes Juan and drags him down to Hell. The story features in a play by Molière, Le Festin de pierre (The Stone Feast, 1665), also in Mozart's Don Giovanni.

There wafted over her a sense of the dreadful darkness in the
old house at Gray's Inn on that dreadful night.... She must not
think of that dreadful night because of little Chrissie deep within
her. She felt as if she held the child covered in her arms, as if she
were looking upwards, bending down over the child. Actually she
was looking downwards.... Then she had been looking
upwards—up the dark stairs. At a marble statue: the white figure
of a woman: the Nike ... the Winged Victory. It is like that on
the stairs of the Louvre. She must think of the Louvre: not Gray's
Inn. There[48] were, in a Pompeian anteroom, Etruscan tombs,
with guardians in uniform, their hands behind their backs.
Strolling about as if they expected you to steal a tomb!...

She had—they had—been staring up the stairs. The house had
seemed unnaturally silent when they had entered. Unnaturally.... How can you seem more silent than silent. But you *can*!
They had seemed to tiptoe. She had, at least. Then light had
shone above—coming from an opened door above. In the light
the[49] white figure that said[50] it had cancer!

She must not think about these things!

Such rage and despair had swept over her as she had never
before known. She had cried to Christopher, dark, beside her:
that the woman lied. She had not got cancer....

She must not think about these things.

The woman on the path—in grey riding things[51]—approached
slowly. The head still bent down. Undoubtedly she had silk
underthings beneath all that grey cloth.... Well, *they*—Christopher and Valentine—gave her them.

It was queer how calm she was. That of course was Sylvia Tietjens. Let it be. She had fought for her man before and so she could
again; the Russians should not have ... The old jingle ran in her
calm head.... *

But she was desperately[52] perturbed: trembling. At the thought
of that dreadful night. Christopher had wanted to go with Sylvia
after she had fallen down stairs. A good theatre fall, but not good
enough. But she had[53] shouted: No! He was never going with

---

* 'We've fought the Bear before and so we will again; / The Russians shall not have
Constantinople.' This is the chorus of 'Macdermott's War Song', written by G.W.
Hunt (1878). 'The earliest patriotic song that the writer ever sang or heard sung': *A
History of Our Own Times* 5. Cf. *A Man Could Stand Up* – II.ii.

Sylvia again. *Finis Sylviae et magna....** In the black night ...
They had gone on firing maroons.[54] They could be heard![55]

Well, she was calm. The sight of that figure was not going to
hurt the tiny brain that worked deep within her womb. Nor the
tiny limbs! She was going to slub the warm, soap-transfused
flannel onto those little legs in the warm of the great hearth....
Nine hams up that chimney! Chrissie looking up and
laughing.... That woman would never again do[56] that! Not to a
child of Christopher's. Not to any man's child, belike!

That had been that woman's son![57] With a girl in white
breeches!...[58] Well, who was she, Valentine, to[59] prevent a son's
seeing his father. She[60] felt on her arm the weight of her own son.
With that there she could confront the world![61]

It was queer! That woman's face was all blurred.... Blubber-
ingly! The features swollen, the eyes red.... Ah, she had been
thinking, looking at the garden and the stillness: "If I had given
Christopher that I should have kept him!" But she would never
have kept him. Had she been the one woman in all the world he
would never have looked at her. Not after he had seen her, Valentine Wannop!

Sylvia had looked up, contemplatively—as if into the very
window. But she could not see into the window. She must have
seen Mrs. de Bray Pape and the girl, for it became apparent why
she had taken off her glove. She now had a gold vanity box in her
hand: looking in at the mirror and moving her right hand swiftly
before her face.... Remember: it was *we* who gave her that gold
thing. Remember! Remember it hard!

Sudden anger came over her. That woman must never come
into their house-place, before whose hearth she was to bathe the
little Chrissie! Never! Never! The place would be polluted. She
knew, only by that, how she loathed and recoiled from that
woman.

She was at the lock. The key turned.... See what emotion at
the thought of harm to your unborn child can do for you! Subcon-
sciously her right hand had remembered how you pressed the key
upwards when you made it turn....[62] She must not run down the

*   'The end of Sylvia and a great thing too', perhaps. If it is a quotation this has not yet
    been traced.

narrow stairs. The telephone was in a niche on the inner side of the great ingle. The room was dim: very long, very low. The Barker cabinet looked very rich, with its green, yellow and scarlet inlays. She was leaning sideways in the nook between the immense fireplace and the room wall, the telephone receiver at her ear. She looked down her long room—it opened into the dining-room, a great beam between. It was dark, gleaming, rich with old beeswaxed woods.... *Elle ne demandait pas mieux* ... the phrase of Marie Léonie occurred constantly to her mind.... She did not ask better—if only the things were to be regarded as theirs! She looked into the distant future when things would spread out tranquilly before them. They would have a little money, a little peace. Things would spread out ... like a plain seen from a hill. In[63] the meantime they had to keep all on going.... She did not, in effect, grumble at that ... as long as strength and health held out.

The doctor—she pictured him, long, sandy and very pleasant, suffering too from an incurable disease and debts, life being like that!—the doctor asked cheerfully how[64] Mark was. She said she did not know. He was said to have been profusely sweating.... Yes, it was possible that he might have been having a disagreeable interview. The doctor said:[65] "Tut! Tut! And yourself?" He had a Scotch accent, the sandy man.... She suggested that he might bring along a bromide. He said: "They've been bothering you. Don't let them!" She said she had been asleep—but they probably would. She added: "Perhaps you would come quickly!" ... Sister Anne! Sister Anne! For God's sake, Sister Anne!* If she could get a bromide into her it would pass like a dream.

It was passing like a dream. Perhaps the Virgin Mary exists....

---

*   In Perrault's version of 'Bluebeard', the young wife has posted her sister on the wall to watch out for their brothers. As she is threatened with murder, she calls to her sister Anne with increasing urgency to ask whether they are in sight yet. See *The Complete Fairy Tales*, a new translation by Christopher Betts (Oxford: Oxford University Press, 2009), 109–12, and the Introduction to this volume. Rudyard Kipling wrote of a young woman's 'hundred Sister Anne glances up the road', in *From Sea to Sea* (London: Macmillan, 1900), II, 45. It was to Kipling's prose work of this period that Ford referred most positively. The phrase also occurs in Violet Hunt's *Their Lives* (London: Stanley Paul, 1916). Of Mrs Radmall, Hunt writes: '"Sister Anne!" she would cheerfully observe to Christina's back' (130). The book includes Ford's 'Preface', written 'Somewhere in Belgium' and signed 'Miles Ignotus' ('the Unknown Soldier'), dated September 1916.

If she does not we must invent her to look after mothers who could[66] not ... But she could! She, Valentine Wannop!

The light from the doorway that was open onto the garden was obscured. A highwayman in skirts with panniers stood in the room against the light. It said:

"You're the saleswoman, I guess. This is a most insanitary place, and I hear you have no bath. Show me some things. In the Louie Kaators[67] style." ... It guessed that it was going to refurnish Groby in Louis Kaators[68] style. Did she, Valentine, as saleswoman, suppose that They—her employers—would meet her in the expense. Mr. Pape had had serious losses in Miami. They must not suppose that the Papes could be bled white. This place ought to be pulled down as unfit for human habitation and a model workman's cottage built in its place. People who sold things to rich Americans in this country were sharks. She herself was descended spiritually from Madame de Maintenon. It would be all different if Marie Antoinette had treated the Maintenon better. She, Mrs. de Bray Pape, would have the authority in the country that she ought to have. She had been told that she would be made to pay an immense sum for having cut down Groby Great Tree. Of course the side wall of the house had fallen in. These old houses could not stand up to modern inventions. She, Mrs. de Bray Pape, had employed the latest Australian form of tree-stump extractor—the Wee Whizz Bang. . . . * But did she, as saleswoman but doubtless[69] more intimate with her employers than was necessary, considering the reputation of that establishment ... did she consider? . . .

Valentine's heart started. The light from the doorway was again obscured. Marie Léonie ran panting in. Sister Anne, in effect! She said: "Le téléphone![70] Vite!"

Valentine said

"J'ai déjà téléphoné. . . .[71] Le docteur sera ici dans quelques minutes. . . . Je te prie de rester a côté[72] de moi!". . . I beg you to remain beside me! Selfish![73] Selfish! But there was a child to be born. . . . Anyhow Marie Léonie could not have got out of that door. It was blocked. . . . Ah!

* In the Great War a 'whizzbang' was 'a high-velocity, low-trajectory shell that made a shrill approach noise and then a sharp explosive report'. See John Laffin, A Western Front Companion (Stroud: Alan Sutton Publishing, 1997), 72.

Sylvia Tietjens was[74] looking down on Valentine. You could hardly see her face against the light.... Well, it did not amount to more than that.... She was looking down because she was so tall; you could not see her face against the light. Mrs. de Bray Pape was explaining what spiritual descent from grands seigneurs[75] did for you.

She[76] was bending her eyes on Valentine. That was the phrase. She said to Mrs. de Bray Pape:

"For God's sake hold your *damned* tongue. Get out of here!"

Mrs. de Bray Pape had not understood. For the matter of that neither did Valentine take it in. A thin voice from a distance thrilled:

"Mother! ... Mo ... ther!"

She—IT—for it was like a statue.... Marvellous[77] how she had made her face up. Three minutes before it had been a mush!... It[78] was flawless now; dark-shadowed under the eyes! And sorrowful! And tremendously dignified. And kind!... Damn! Damn! Damn!

It occurred to Valentine that this was only the second time that she had ever seen[79] that face....[80] Its stillness now was terrible![81] What was she waiting for before she began the Billingsgate* that they were both going to indulge in before all these people?... For[82] she, Valentine, had her back against the wall! She heard herself begin to say:

"You have spoilt ..."[83] She could not continue. You cannot very well tell a person that their loathsomeness is so infectious as to spoil your baby's bathing-place! It is not done!

Marie Léonie said in French to Mrs. de Bray Pape that Mrs. Tietjens did not require her presence. Mrs. de Bray Pape did not understand. It is difficult for a Maintenon to understand that her presence is not required!

The first time that she, Valentine, had seen that face, in Edith

---

* Foul language, vituperation – since the seventeenth century, according to Eric Partridge, *A Dictionary of Slang and Unconventional English* (London: Routledge, 8th edn, 1984), after the famous London fish market. Ford uses the expression in writing to Stella at Christmas 1926, telling her of a reviewer who had received 'a letter full of the most incredible Billingsgate' from Jessie Conrad: *Ford/Bowen* 274. Cf. Valentine's reference to Edith Ethel Duchemin breaking down 'into shrieked coarsenesses of fishwives' in *Some Do Not ...* II.v, and having 'the nature of a female costermonger' in *A Man Could Stand Up –* I.iii.

Ethel's drawing-room, she had thought how kind . . . how[84] blind-
ingly kind it was. When the lips had approached her mother's
cheek the[85] tears had been in Valentine's eyes. It had said—that
face of a statue!—that it must kiss Mrs. Wannop for her kindness
to Christopher. . . . Damn it, it might[86] as well kiss her, Valentine, now! . . . There would have been no Christopher to-day but
for her!

It[87] said—it was[88] so perfectly expressionless that you could
continue to[89] call it "it"—it said, coldly and without halt,[90] to
Mrs. de Bray Pape:

"You hear! The lady of the house does[91] not require your presence. Please go away!"

Mrs. de Bray Pape was explaining[92] that she had been telling
the saleswoman that she intended to refurnish Groby in the Looie
Kaators[93] style.[94]

It occurred to Valentine that this position had its comicalities:
Marie Léonie did not know that woman; Mrs. de Bray Pape did
not know her, Valentine. They[95] would miss a good deal of the
jam! . . . But where was the jam! Jam yesterday, jam to-
morrow. . . .* That figure had said "Mrs. Tietjens!" In sarcasm,
then? In delicacy?

She[96] caught at the telephone shelf; it was dark. The baby[97] had
moved within her. . . . It wanted her to be called "Mrs. Tietjens!"
Someone[98] was calling "Valentine!" Someone else was calling
"Mother!" A softer voice said: "Mrs. Tietjens!" What things they
chose to say! The first voice was Edith Ethel's!

Dark! . . . Marie[99] Léonie said in her ear: "Tiens toi debout, ma
chérie!"†

Dark, dark night; cold, cold snow—Harsh, harsh wind, and
lo!—Where shall we shepherds go, God's son to find?‡

Edith Ethel was reading to Mrs. de Bray Pape from a letter.
She[100] said: "As an American of culture, you will be inter-

---

* Lewis Carroll, *Alice Through the Looking-Glass*, Chapter 5: apparently a Latinist's
  delight since 'i' and 'j' are interchangeable in classical Latin and *iam* means 'now'. 'The
  word *iam* is used in the past and future tenses, but in the present tense the word for
  "now" is nunc.' Thus elucidated by Martin Gardner in *The Annotated Alice: The Definitive Edition* (Harmondsworth: Allen Lane, The Penguin Press, 2000), 206.
† 'Stand upright, my dear!' (French).
‡ 'Deep, deep snow; / Wild, wild wind; / Dark, dark night: and lo! / Where shall we shepherds go, / God's son to find?' This is the first verse of 'The Shepherds' Song' by Selwyn
  Image. See his *Poems and Carols* (London: Elkin Mathews, 1894), 35.

ested.... From the great poet!" ... A gentleman held a top-hat
in front of his face, as if he were in church. Thin, with dull eyes
and a Jewish beard! Jews keep their hats on in church....

Apparently she, Valentine Wannop, was going to be
denounced before the congregation! Did they bring a scarlet
letter.... They were Puritans enough, she and Christopher. The
voice of the man with the Jewish beard—Sylvia Tietjens had
removed the letter from the fingers of Edith Ethel.... Not much
changed, Edith Ethel! Face a *little* lined. And pale. And suddenly
reduced to silence—the voice of the man with the beard said:

"After all! It does make a difference. He is virtually Tietjens of
..." He began to push his way backwards, outwards. A man trying
to leave through the crowd at the church door. He turned to say
to her oddly:

"*Madame* ... eh ... Tietjens! Par*don!*"[101]

Attempting[102] a French accent.

Edith[103] Ethel remarked:

"I wanted to say to Valentine: if I effect the sale personally I
do not see that the commission should be payable."

Sylvia Tietjens said: They could discuss that outside. Valentine was aware that, some time before, a boy's voice had said:
"Mother, is this sporting?" It occurred to Valentine to wonder if
it was sporting of people to call her "Mrs. Tietjens" under Sylvia
Tietjens' nose. Of course she had to be Mrs. Tietjens before the
servants. She heard herself say:

"I am sorry Mr. Ruggles called me Mrs. Tietjens before you!"

The eyes of the statue were, if possible, doubly bent on her!

It said drily:

"An the King will ha'e my heid I carena what ye do wi' my ..."
It was a saying common to both Mark and Christopher....[104]
That was bitter. She was reminding her, Valentine, that she had
previously enjoyed Tietjens' intimacies—before her, Valentine!

But the voice went on:

"I[105] wanted to get those people out.... And to see ..." It
spoke very slowly. Marmoreally. The flowers in the jug on the
fald-stool* needed more water. Marigolds. Orange.... A woman
is upset when her child moves within her. Sometimes more,

---

* Here, a folding or camp stool.

sometimes less. She must have been very upset: there had been a lot of people in the room; she knew neither how they had come nor how they had gone. She said to Marie Léonie:

"Dr. Span is bringing some bromide.... I can't find those ..."

Marie Léonie was looking at that figure: her eyes stuck out of her head like Christopher's. She said, as still as a cat watching a mouse:

"Qui est elle? C'est bien la femme?"

It looked queerly like a pilgrim in a ballet, now, that figure against the light—the long legs slightly bent gave that effect. Actually this was the third time she had seen it—but in the dark house she had not really seen the face.... The features had been contorted and thus not the real features: these were the real features. There was about that figure something timid. And noble. It said:

"Sporting! Michael said: 'Be sporting, mother!'... Be[106] sporting...." It raised its hand as if to[107] shake a fist at heaven. The hand struck the beam across the ceiling: that roof was so low. And dear! It said: "It was Father Consett really.... They can all, soon, call you Mrs. Tietjens. Before God, I came to drive those people out.... But I wanted to see how it was you kept him...."

Sylvia Tietjens was keeping her head turned aside, drooping. Hiding a tendency to tears, no doubt. She said to the floor:

"I say again, as God hears me, I never thought to harm your child.... His child.... But any woman's.... Not harm a child.... I have a fine one, but I wanted another.... Their littleness.... The riding has done it...." Someone[108] sobbed!

She looked loweringly* then at Valentine:

"It's Father Consett in heaven that has done this. Saint and martyr: desiring soft things! I can almost see his shadow across these walls now it's growing dark. You hung him: you did not even shoot him, though I *say* you shot him to save my feelings.... †

And it's you who will be going on through all the years...."

She bit into a small handkerchief that she had in her hand,

---

*   'Gloomily, sullenly, threateningly' (*OED*).

†   In *Some Do Not* ... Sylvia tells Tietjens that Father Consett 'was hung on the day they shot Casement'. Roger Casement was tried for high treason and hanged – not shot – by the British authorities in 1916 (see *Some Do Not* ... II.i and note; *No More Parades* II.i). Sylvia has experienced an earlier 'vision' of Father Consett in *No More Parades* II.ii.

concealed. She said: "Damn[109] it, I'm playing pimp to Tietjens of Groby—leaving my husband to you!...."[110]

Someone again sobbed.

It occurred to Valentine that Christopher had left those prints at old Hunt's sale in a jar on the field. They had not wanted the jar. Then Christopher had told a dealer called Hudnut[*] that he could have that jar and some others as against a little carting service.... He would be tired, when he got back, Christopher. He would have, nevertheless, to go to Hudnut's: Gunning[111] could not be trusted. But they must not disappoint Lady Robinson....

Marie Léonie said:

"C'est lamentable qu'un seul homme puisse inspirer deux telles passions dans deux telles femmes....[112] C'est le martyre de notre vie!"

Yes, it was lamentable that a man could inspire two such passions in two women. Marie Léonie went to look after Mark. There was no Sylvia Tietjens. They[113] say joy never kills. She fell straight down onto the ground, lumpishly![114]

... It was lucky they had the Bussorah[†] rug, otherwise Chrissie ... They must have some money....[115] Poor ... poor....

---

[*] There was a Mrs Richard Hudnut who wanted Jean Rhys to ghost-write a book 'on Reincarnation and Furniture'. Max Saunders tells this story and comments that 'Ford's use of the name in *Parade's End* for a furniture dealer is an appropriate joke'. See Saunders, *Dual Life* II 286–7 on the Hudnuts.

[†] Probably more familiar as Basra, in south-eastern Iraq, its second largest city and main port. The British capture of Basra in November 1914 was the first significant action on the Mesopotamian Front in the Great War.

CHAPTER IV

MARK TIETJENS had lain considering the satisfaction of a great night he had lately passed. Or perhaps not lately: at some time.

Lying out there in the black nights, the sky seemed enormous. You could understand how somewhere heaven could be concealed in it. And tranquil at times. Then you felt the earth wheeling through infinity.

Night birds cried overhead: herons, duck, swans even: the owls kept closer to the ground, beating along the hedgerows.[1] Beasts became busy in the long grass. They rustled busily; then paused for long. No doubt a rabbit ran till it found an attractive plantain. Then it nibbled for a long time without audible movement. Now and then cattle lowed, or many lambs—frightened by a fox maybe....

But there would be nevertheless[2] long silences.... A stoat would get onto the track of the rabbit. They would run, run, run brushing through the long grass, then out into the short meadow and round and round, the rabbit squealing. Loudly at first.

In the dim illumination of his night-light, dormice would climb up the posts of his shelter. They would remain regarding him with beads of eyes. When the rabbits squealed they would hunch themselves together and shiver. They knew it meant S-t-o-a-t[3] = stoat! Their turn soon!

He despised himself a little for attending to these minutiae— as if one were talking down to a child.... On his great night the whole cattle of the county had been struck with panic; you heard them crashing down through the hedges and miles down into the silent valleys.

No! He had never been one to waste his time and mind on small mammals and small birds.... The Flora and Fauna of Blankshire!... Not for him. It was big movements interested him: "wherein manifesteth itself the voice of God!" ... Very likely that was true. Transport. Panic in cattle over whole counties. In people over whole continents.

Once, years—oh, years and years—ago, when he had been
aged twelve and on a visit to Grandfather, he had taken a gun to
Redcar sands from Groby, over the moors, and with one shot he
had brought down two terns, a sandpiper and a herring gull.*
Grandfather had been so delighted with his prowess—though
naturally the shot had been a fluke—that he had the things
stuffed, and there they were in Groby Nursery to this day. The
herring gull stiff on a mossy rock; the sandpiper doing obeisance
before it, the terns flying, one on each side. Probably that was the
only memorial to him, Mark Tietjens, at Groby. The younger
children had been wont to refer with awe to "Mark's bag" for long
years afterwards. The painted background had shewn Bambor-
ough⁴ Castle† with lashings of foam and blue sky. It was a far cry
from Redcar to Bamborough—but that was the only background
the bird-stuffing chap in Middlesbrough⁵ could paint for sea-
birds. For larks and the like he had a cornfield in the Vale of York;
for nightingales, poplar trees.... Never heard that nightingales
were particularly partial to poplars!

.... Nightingales disturbed the majesty of great nights. For
two months out of the year, more or less, according to the nature
of the season. He wasn't decrying the beauty of their voices.
Hearing them you felt like seeing a good horse win the St. Leger.
No other things in the world could do it—just as there was no
place in the world like Newmarket Heath on a breezy day.... But
they limited the night. It was true that nightingales deep down
in the spinney near where Gunning's hut must be—say a quarter
of a mile away—could make you think of great distance, echoing
up through the deep woods. Woods dripping with dew beneath
the moon.... And air-raids not so long ago! The moon brought
air-raids and its shining was discouraged.... Yes, nightingales
made⁶ you think of distance, just as the night-jar for ever crepi-
tating from twilight to dawn seemed to measure a fragment of

---

* Mark's lucky shot recalls the episode at Pent Farm when Ford fired at a rat 'from an
  incredible distance' and the 'great old grey rat crossing a road collapsed feebly'. He
  adds: 'That was ever afterwards scored to the writer as an immense feat of marksmanship, often referred to. If anyone talked of shooting Conrad would say: "Ah, but you
  should have seen Ford's rat! ..."' Ford himself was convinced that 'the rat was dying
  of old age before it was fired at, the bullet never reaching it' (*Joseph Conrad* 41).
† Located in the village of Bamburgh, on the Northumberland coast, not far from Lindisfarne and close to the border with Scotland.

eternity.... But only fragments! The great night was itself eternity and the Infinite.... The spirit of God walking on the firmament.

Cruel beggars, nightingales: they abused one another with distended throats all through the nights. Between the gusts of gales you could hear them shouting on—telling their sitting hens that they—each one—were the devils of fellows, the other chap, down the hill by Gunning's hut, being a bedraggled, louse-eaten braggart.... Sex ferocity.

Gunning lived in a bottom, in a squatter's cottage, they said. With a thatch like Robinson Crusoe's bonnet.* A wise-woman's cottage. He lived with the wise-woman, a chalk-white faced slattern.... And a granddaughter of the wise-woman whom, because she had a cleft palate and only half a brain, the parish, half out of commiseration, half for economy, had nominated mistress in the school up the hill. No one knew whether Gunning slept with the wise-woman or the granddaughter; for one or the other he had left his missus and Fittleworth had tanned his hide and taken his cottage from him. He thrashed them both impartially with a hunting thong every Saturday night—to learn them,[7] and to remind them that for them he had lost his cottage and the ten bob a week Fittleworth allowed such hinds as had been in his service thirty years.... Sex ferocity again!

> "And how shall I thy true love know from another one?
> Oh, by his cockled hat and staff and by his sandalled shoon!"†

An undoubted pilgrim had suggested irresistibly the lines to him!... It was naturally that bitch Sylvia. Wet eyes she had!... Then some psychological crisis was going on inside her. Good for her.

Good for Val and Chris, possibly. There was no real knowing.... Oh, but there was. Hear to that: the bitch-pack giving tongue! Heard ye ever the like to that, sirs? She had had

---

*   This could refer to a good many illustrated edition of Defoe's novel, but Joseph Finnemore (1860–1939) and Walter Paget (1863–1935) are both plausible candidates.
†   'How should I your true love know / From another one? – / By his cockle hat and staff, / And his sandal shoon': *Hamlet* IV.v.23–6. Cf. Joyce, *Ulysses* 63: 'My cockle hat and staff and his my sandal shoon'.

Groby Great Tree torn down.... But, as God was her maker, she would not tear another woman's child within her.... [8]

He felt himself begin to perspire.... Well, if Sylvia had come to that, his, Mark's, occupation was gone. He would no longer have to go on willing against her; she would drop into the sea in the wake of their family vessel and be lost to view.... But, damn it, she must have suffered to be brought to that pitch.... [9] Poor bitch! Poor bitch! The riding had done it.... She ran away, a handkerchief to her eyes.

He felt satisfaction and impatience. There was some place to which he desired to get back. But there were also things to be done: to be thought out.... If God was beginning to temper the wind to these flayed lambs* ... Then ... He could not remember what he wanted to think about.... It was—no, not exasperating. Numb! He felt himself responsible for their happiness. He wanted them to go rubbing along, smooth with the rough, for many long, unmarked years.... He wanted Marie Léonie to stay with Valentine until after her deliverance and then to go to the Dower House at Groby. She was Lady Tietjens. She knew she was Lady Tietjens, and she would like it. Besides, she would be a thorn in the flesh of Mrs.... He could not remember the name....

He wished that Christopher would get rid of his Jewish partner so as to addle a little brass. It was their failing as Tietjenses[10] that they liked toadies.... He himself had bitched all their lives by having that fellow Ruggles sharing[11] his rooms. Because he could not have borne to share with an equal, and Ruggles was half Jew, half Scotchman. Christopher had had, for toadies, firstly Macmaster, a Scot, and then this American Jew. Otherwise he, Mark, was reconciled with things. Christopher, no doubt, was wise in his choice. He had achieved a position in which he might—with just a little more to it— anticipate jogging away to the end of time, leaving descendants to carry on the country without swank.

Ah.... It came to his mind to remember, almost with pain. He had accepted nephew Mark as nephew Mark: a strong slip. A

---

*   Laurence Sterne, A *Sentimental Journey* (1768): 'God tempers the wind, said Maria, to the shorn lamb.' Apparently derived from a French proverb: God spares from further misfortune those that have already suffered.

good boy. But there was the point ... the point!... The boy had the right sort of breeches.... But if there were incest....

Crawling through a hedge after a rabbit was thinkable. Father had been in the churchyard to shoot rabbits to oblige the vicar. There was no doubt of that. He did not want rabbits.... But supposing he had mis-hit a bunny and the little beast had been throwing gymnastics on the other side of the quickset? Father would have crawled through then, rather than go all the way to the lych-gate and round. Decent men put their mis-hits out of their agony as soon as possible. Then there was motive. And as for not putting his gun out of action before crawling through the quickset.... Many good, plucked men had died like that.... *And father had grown absent-minded!*... There had been farmer Lowther had so died; and Pease of Lobhall; and Pease of Culler-coats. All good plucked* farmers.... Crawling through hedges rather than go round, and with their guns at full cock! And not absent-minded men.... But he remembered that, just[12] now, he had remembered that father had grown absent-minded. He would put a paper in one of his waistcoat pockets and fumble for it in all his other pockets a moment after: he would push his spectacles up onto his forehead and search all the room for them; he would place his knife and fork in his plate and, whilst talking, take another knife and fork from beside it and begin again to eat.... Mark remembered that his father had done that twice during the last meal they had eaten together—whilst he, Mark, had been presenting the fellow Ruggles's account of Christopher's misdeeds....

Then it would[13] not be incumbent on him, Mark, to go up to his father in Heaven and say: Hullo, sir. I understand you had a daughter by the wife of your best friend, she being now with child by your son....[14] Rather ghostly[15] so to[16] introduce yourself to the awful ghost of your father.... Of course you would be a ghost yourself. Still, with[17] your billycock hat, umbrella and racing-glasses, not an[18] awful ghost!... And to say to your father: "I understand that you committed suicide!"

Against the rules of the Club.... For I consider it no grief to be going there where so many great men have preceded me.

---

* Plucky, courageous. *OED* cites Thackeray's use of it in *Vanity Fair* as one example.

Sophocles that, wasn't it?* So, on his authority, it was a damn
good club. . . .

But he did not have to anticipate that *mauvais quart d'heure!*†
Dad quite obviously did not commit suicide. He wasn't the man
to do so. So Valentine was not his daughter and there was no
incest. It is all very well to say that you care little about incest.
The Greeks made a hell of a tragic row about it. . . . Certainly it
was a weight off the chest if you could think there had been none.
He[19] had always been able to look Christopher in the eyes—but
he would be able to do it better than ever now. Comfortably! It
is uncomfortable to look a man in the eyes and think: You sleep
between incestuous sheets. . . .

That then was over. The worst of it rolled up together. No
suicide. No incest. No by-blow at Groby. . . . A Papist there. . . .
Though how you could be a Papist and a Marxian Communist
passed his, Mark's, comprehension. . . . A Papist at Groby and
Groby Great Tree down. . . . The curse was perhaps off the family!

That was a superstitious way to look at it—but you must have
a pattern to interpret things by. You can't really get your mind to
work without it. The blacksmith said: By hammer and hand all
art doth stand!. . .‡ He, Mark Tietjens, for many years interpreted
all life in terms of Transport. . . . Transport, be thou my God. . . .
A damn good God. . . . And in the end, after a hell of a lot of
thought and of work, the epitaph of him, Mark Tietjens, ought
by rights to be: *"Here lies one whose name was writ in sea-birds!"*§
. . . As good an epitaph as another.

He must get it through to Christopher that Marie Léonie
should have that case, with[20] Bamborough and all, in her
bedroom at Groby Dower House. It was the last permanent record
of her man. . . . But Christopher would know that. . . .

---

* A couple of passages at the close of *Oedipus at Colonnus* resemble, but do not match,
these lines. More likely is a passage in Plato's *Phaedo* (63b), where Socrates discourses
on his willing acceptance of death and the prospect of finding himself 'among good
men': *The Last Days of Socrates*, trans. Hugh Tredennick and Harold Tarrant
(Harmondsworth: Penguin, 2003), 123.
† Literally a bad quarter of an hour: a brief, unpleasant experience (French).
‡ Cf. *England* 178; *Critical Essays* 119.
§ John Keats's epitaph for himself was 'Here lies one whose name was writ in water', as
reported by Joseph Severn, his companion during his last months in Rome: Andrew
Motion, *Keats* (London: Faber & Faber, 1997), 564. Ford alluded rarely to Keats but
his final comments, though brief, are strikingly positive (*March* 770–1).

It was coming back. A lot of things were coming back.... He could see Redcar Sands running up towards Sunderland, grey, grey. Not so many factory chimneys[21] then, working for him, Mark Tietjens! Not so many! And the sandpipers[22] running in the thin of the tide, bowing as they ran; and the shovellers turning over stones and the terns floating above the viscous sea....

But it was great nights to which he would now[23] turn his attention. Great black nights above the purple moors.... Great black nights above the Edgware Road, where Marie Léonie lived ... because, above the blaze of lights of the old Apollo's front, you had a sense of immense black spaces....

Who said he was perspiring a great deal? Well, he *was* perspiring!

Marie Léonie, young, was bending over him.... Young, young, as he had first seen her on the stage of Covent Garden ... In white!... Doing[24] agreeable things to his face with a perfume like that of Heaven itself!... And laughing sideways as Marie Léonie had laughed when first he presented himself before her in his billycock hat and umbrella!... The fine, fair hair! The soft voice!

But this was silly.... That was nephew Mark with his cherry-red face and staring eyes.... And this was his light of love!... Naturally. Like uncle, like nephew. He would pick up with the same type of woman as his uncle. That made it certain that he was[25] no by-blow! Pretty piece against the apple-boughs!

He wanted great nights, then!—Young Mark, though, should not pick up with a woman older than[26] himself. Christopher had done that, and look!

Still: things were takking oop!... Do you remember the Yorkshireman who stood with his chin just out of the water on Ararat Top as Noah approached. And: "It's boon to tak oop!" said the Yorkshireman.... It's bound to clear up!

A great night, with room enough for Heaven to be hidden there from our not too perspicacious eyes.... It was said that an earthquake shock imperceptible to our senses set those cattle and sheep and horses and pigs crashing through all the hedges of the county. And it was queer: before they had so started lowing and moving Mark was now ready to swear that he had heard a rushing sound.

He probably had not! One could so easily self-deceive oneself! The cattle had been panicked because they had been sensible of the presence of the Almighty walking upon the firmament. . . .

Damn it all: there were a lot of things coming back. He could have sworn he heard the voice of Ruggles say: "After all, he is virtually Tietjens of Groby!" . . . By no fault of yours, old cock! But now you will be cadging up to him. . . . Now there speaks Edith Ethel Macmaster! A lot of voices passing behind his head. Damn it all, could they all be ghosts drifting before the wind! . . . Or, damn it all, was he himself dead! . . . No, you were probably not profane when you were dead.

He would have given the world to sit up and turn his head round and see. Of course he *could*, but that would give the show away! He credited himself with being too cunning an old fox for that! To have thrown dust in their eyes for all these years! He could have chuckled!

Fittleworth seemed to have come down into the garden and to be remonstrating with these people. What[27] the devil could Fittleworth want? It was like a pantomime. Fittleworth, in effect, was looking at him. He said:

"Hello, old bean. . . ." Marie Léonie was looking beside[28] his elbow. He said: "I've driven all these goats out of your hen-roost." . . . Good-looking fellow Fittleworth. His Lola Vivaria had been a garden-peach. Died in child-birth. No doubt that was why he had troubled to come. Fittleworth[29] said: Cammie said to give Mark her love for old time's sake. Her dear love! And as soon as he was well to bring her ladyship down. . . .[30]

Damn this sweat. With its beastly tickling he would grimace and give the show away. But he would like Marie Léonie to go to the Fittleworths'.[31] Marie Léonie said something to Fittleworth.

"Yes, yes, me lady!" says Fittleworth. Damn it, he did look like a monkey as some people said. . . . But if the monkeys we were descended from were as good-looking . . . Probably he had good-looking legs. . . . How beautiful upon the mountains are the feet of them that bring good tidings to Zion. . . .* Fittleworth[32] added earnestly and distinctly that Sylvia—Sylvia Tietjens—*begged*[33] Mark to understand that she had not sent that flock of idiots

---

* Isaiah 52:7: 'How beautiful upon the mountains are the feet of him that bringeth good tidings … that saith unto Zion, Thy God reigneth!'

down here. Sylvia also said that she was going to divorce his, Mark's, brother and dissolve her marriage with the sanction of Rome.... So they would all be a happy family down there, soon.... Anything Cammie could do.... Because of Mark's unforgettable services to the nation....[34]

Name[35] was written in ... Lettest thou thy servant* ... divorce in peace!

Marie Léonie begged Fittleworth to[36] go away now. Fittleworth said he would, but joy never kills! So long, old ... old friend!

The clubs they had been in together.... But[37] one went to a far better Club than ... His breathing was a little troublesome.... It was darkish, then light again.

Christopher was at the foot of his bed. Holding a bicycle and a lump of wood. Aromatic wood: a chunk sawn from a tree. His face was white: his eyes stuck out. Blue pebbles. He gazed at his brother and said:

"Half Groby wall is down. Your bedroom's wrecked. I found your case of sea-birds thrown on a rubble heap."

It was as well that one's services were unforgettable!

Valentine was there, panting as if she had been running. She exclaimed to Christopher:

"You left the prints for Lady Robinson in a jar you gave to Hudnut the dealer. How could you? Oh, how could you? How are we going to feed and clothe a child if you do such things?"

He lifted his bicycle wearily round. You could see he was dreadfully weary, the poor devil. Mark almost said:

"Let him off: the poor devil's worn out!"

Heavily, like a dejected bull-dog, Christopher made for the gate. As he went up the green path beyond the hedge, Valentine began to sob.

"How are we to live? How are we ever to live?"

" Now I must speak," Mark said to himself.[38]

---

* An allusion to *Nunc Dimittis*, the Song of Simeon, based on the words of Luke 2:29: 'Lord, now lettest thou thy servant depart in peace ...' Ford writes of Nancy Rufford in *The Good Soldier* 145: 'It seemed to her that for one short moment her spirit could say: "*Domine, nunc dimittis....* Lord, now lettest thou thy servant depart in peace."' Ernest Rhys recalled Ford bringing D.H. Lawrence to a party at which Lawrence read his poems to the company. Rhys had to tell him to have a rest: on appealing later for 'one more lyric', Ford 'took him under his arm and marched him off murmuring wickedly, "Nunc, nunc dimittis."' Quoted, Sanders, *Dual Life* I 299.

He said:

"Did ye ever hear tell o' t' Yorkshireman . . . On Mount Ara . . . Ara . . ."

He had not spoken for so long. His tongue appeared to fill his mouth; his mouth to be twisted to one side. It was growing dark. He said:

"Put your ear close to my mouth . . . ." She cried out. He whispered:[39]

" ''Twas the mid o' the night and the barnies grat
And the mither beneath the mauld heard that. . . .'*

An old song. My nurse sang it. . . . Never thou let thy child weep for[40] thy sharp tongue to thy goodman. . . . A good man! Groby[41] Great Tree is down. . . ." He[42] said: "Hold my hand!"

She inserted her hand beneath the sheet and his hand[43] closed on hers. Then it relaxed.

She nearly cried out for Marie Léonie.

The tall, sandy, much-liked doctor came through the gate. She said:

"He spoke just now. . . . It has been a torturing afternoon. . . .[44] Now I'm afraid . . . I'm afraid he's . . ."

The doctor reached his hand beneath the sheet, leaning sideways.[45] He said:

"Go get you to bed. . . . I will come and examine you. . . ."

She said:

"Perhaps it would be best not to tell Lady Tietjens that he spoke. . . . She would like to have had his[46] last words. . . . But she did not need them as much as I."

THE END[47]

PARIS, *7th June*–AVIGNON, *1st August*–ST. LAWRENCE RIVER, *24th September*–NEW YORK, *12th November.*–MCMXXVII.[48]

---

* 'The Ghaistly Warning', a translation by Robert Jamieson of a Danish ballad, was printed in the 'Appendix' to Walter Scott's *The Lady of the Lake* (1810). That version reads: 'Twas lang i' the night, and the barnies grat: / Their mither she under the mools heard that.' Nelly Dean sings it to Hareton Earnshaw in Emily Bronte's *Wuthering Heights* (1847).

TEXTUAL NOTES

Conventions Used in the Textual Notes

The textual endnotes use the following abbreviations and symbols:

UK First United Kingdom edition of *Last Post* (London: Duckworth and Company, 1928)
TS Typescript of *Last Post*
US First American edition of *Last Post* (New York: Albert & Charles Boni, 1928)
Ed Editor
< > Deleted passages.
[ ] Conjectural reading (or editorial comment that a passage is illegible)
↑ ↓ Passage inserted above a line; often to replace a deleted passage.
↓ ↑ Passage inserted below a line; often to replace a deleted passage.

Most of the textual notes compare a passage from UK with the corresponding passage from TS, and where appropriate, with other witnesses. In these notes the abbreviation for the witness is given in bold typeface. Where witnesses agree, their abbreviations are listed, separated by commas. Semi-colons are used to separate the different quotations. The first quotation is always from UK; it is followed by the corresponding segment(s) from the typescript and/or other witness(es). With segments longer than a single word in UK, the first and last words are identical in all versions, to enable ready comparison. In the example:

UK, TS long and thin in; **US** long in

the UK and TS both print 'long and thin in' but the US edition prints 'long in'.

Deletions in the manuscript are quoted within angled brackets; insertions are recorded between vertical arrows, beginning with an up-arrow if the word is inserted from above the line or with a down-arrow if inserted from below. Thus:

UK was; **TS** <had> ↑was↓ **AR**; **US** had

indicates that where UK prints 'was', in the corresponding passage in the typescript, the word 'had' has been deleted, and 'was' inscribed above, a revision not carried over to US.

The abbreviation **Ed** is only used where the editor adopts a reading different from all the witnesses. This is mainly used only for grammatical corrections.

The abbreviation **AR** stands for 'Autograph Revision', indicating a hand-written revision to a typescript.

Discursive notes (which don't compare versions) are differentiated by not using bold face for the witness abbreviations.

The symbol ¶ is used to indicate a paragraph break in a variant quoted in the textual endnotes. For verse quoted in the footnotes, a line break is indicated by '/'.

Textual Notes for Dedicatory Letter

1 **UK** as being my; **TS** as ↑being↓ my **AR**; **US** as my
2 **UK** godmother in the United States—though; **TS** godmother ↑in the United States↓—though **AR**; **US** godmother in this country—though
3 **UK** at least of the tribe; **US** of the tribe at least
 TS has autograph line indicating change of word order (US to UK in this instance).
4 **UK** Save, that; **TS** <But>↑Save↓, that **AR**; **US** But, that
5 **UK, TS** it has always seemed; **US** it seemed
6 **UK** though Valentine and Tietjens were; **TS** though ↑Valentine and↓ Tietjens were **AR**; **US** though Tietjens and Valentine were
7 **UK, US** that they set; **TS** that ↑they↓ <he> set **AR**
8 **UK, TS** we all are and; **US** we are all and
9 **UK, TS** of time have; **US** of my life have
10 **UK, TS** Tory, omniscient; **US** Tory, genuinely omniscient
11 **UK** what he would; **TS** what <Marwood><he [?]> would; **US** what X— would
12 **UK** some satisfaction; **TS, US** some satisfactions
 TS/US reading adopted; plural to agree with preceding 'worries'.
13 **UK, TS** that longevity.... ¶ But; **US** that longevity that ... ¶ But

Textual Notes for I.i

1 Emended from 'PART ONE' for consistency, bringing it into line not only with the other volumes but with the second part of this volume, already headed with Roman numerals ('PART II').
2 **UK, TS** thatch; the; **US** thatch shelter; the
3 **UK** French crab-apple! The; **US** French crab apple! The; **TS** French crab! The
4 This last sentence is an autograph addition to TS.
5 **UK** unusual, vivacity, all; **TS, US** unusual vivacity, all
 TS/US reading adopted, to eliminate clearly superfluous comma.
6 **UK, TS** came; **US** led
7 **UK, US** an unbuttoned blue; **TS** an <open> ↑unbuttoned↓ blue **AR**
8 **UK, US** the oaken posts; **TS** the <supporting> ↑oaken↓ posts **AR**
9 **UK** right sort. ¶ Is; **TS** right ↑sort↓. **AR** ¶ Is; **US** right kidney. ¶ Is
10 **UK, TS, US** clap-nests; **Ed** clap-nets

'Clap-nest' is not in *OED*. It seems probable that both editions followed TS, assuming it to be dialect, but no instance of this has been traced.

11 **UK** his own thought. ¶ Old; **TS** ↑his meditations.↓ **AR** ¶ Old; **US** his own thoughts: ¶ Old
   In TS the whole sentence – from 'The man' to 'meditations' – is an autograph addition.

12 **UK, US** things. He knew all about fox-hunting; **TS** things. ↑He knew all about↓ Fox-hunting **AR**

13 **UK, TS** wouldn't. *From henceforth*; **US** wouldn't from henceforth

14 **UK, US** *circumciséd*; **TS** *circumscribed*

15 **UK, TS** family in Crutched Friars; **US** family somewhere in a Crutched Friars
   US may have assumed that TS refers to one of the communities founded by the order of mendicant friars introduced from Italy into England in the thirteenth century, who gave their name to this part of London.

16 **UK, US** the raspberry canes; **TS** the <strawberry> ↑raspberry↓ canes

17 **UK, TS** He; **US** Mark

18 **UK** turned him round he looked down-hill at the house. Rough, grey stone! ¶ Half-round, he; **TS** turned him round he looked down hill at the house. ↑Rough, grey stone!↓ [Half-round, he **AR**; **US** turned his bed round he looked down on the house. Rough, grey stone. ¶ Half round, he
   TS has autograph 'n.p.' in right-hand margin reinforcing the open square bracket.

19 **UK, US** counties; **TS** countries;

20 **UK, US** half round; **TS** half-round
   UK is inconsistent, hyphenating the first instance; US consistent in not hyphenating; TS adopted as also agreeing with first UK instance in this sentence.

21 **UK, TS** up the grass-slope to the hedge on the road-side. Now; **US** up a steep grass-bank to the hedge on the main roadside. Now

22 **UK, US** across the tops of the hay-grass, over; **TS** across the grass, over

23 **UK, TS** developing his possible interests. He; **US** finding possible interests for him. He

24 **UK, TS** didn't; **US** did not

25 **UK, TS** above and beyond; **US** above, beyond

26 **UK, TS** five, unspeakably; **US** five in a sailor's suit—unspeakably

27 **UK, TS** long and thin in; **US** long in

28 **UK, TS** his fault; **US** his, Mark Tietjens', fault
   This addition to US seems intended to remove possible ambiguity.

29 **UK** given the nation the transport it needed; they should have found the stuff. They; **TS** given <them all> ↑the nation↓ the transport <they> ↑it↓ needed; they should have found the stuff. They; **US** given the nation the Transport it needed: the nation should have found the food. They

30 **UK, TS** protruding wrists on pipe-stem arms; **US** wristbones that protruded on pipe-stems

31 **UK, TS** the nation's transport; **US** the Transport

32 **UK, TS** made; **US** built up

33 **UK, TS** official, from; **US** official: he had built it up, from

34 **UK, TS** thirty-five years before; **US** thirty years ago
   US reading has been preferred since UK would point to the novel's 'present'

as 1932, four years after its publication. See the Introduction for more on this.

35 **UK, TS** him; he; **US** him, for he

36 **UK** They let him read all; **TS** They ↑let him↓ read <him> all **AR**; **US** They helped him to read all

37 **UK, TS** pond up the hill continued; **US** pond continued

38 **UK, TS** churning boisterously the water; **US** churning the water, up the hill, boisterously

39 **UK, TS** and; **US** or

40 **UK, TS** thumb, then examined his thumb. Looking; **US** thumb. Looking

41 **UK, TS** for maggots, no doubt; **US** for traces of maggots

42 **UK, TS** war-starvation; **US** starvation

43 **UK, TS** they were presumably not; **US** presumably they were not

44 **UK, TS** sharp, brushing blows with; **US** with sharp, brushing blows of

45 **UK, TS** That was part of their consideration again! They; **US** They

46 **UK, TS** passers-by; **US** passengers

47 **UK, TS** would have preferred to let it grow high so; **US** would really have preferred to let it grow so high

48 **UK, TS** knew....; **US** thought for!

49 **UK, TS** the; **US** in

50 **UK, TS** *he* was; **US** he, Mark, was

51 **UK, US** up! ... Marie Léonie—formerly Charlotte!—knew [though US omits exclamation mark]; **TS** up! ... ↑Marie↓ Léonie <Augustine> ↑—formerly Charlotte!—↓knew **AR**

52 **UK, TS** them; **US** that precious couple

53 **UK, TS** though she had undoubtedly seen them peering; **US** she had certainly seen them peer down

54 **UK, TS** a shelf; **US** a broad shelf

55 **UK, TS** him! A; **US** him! He had always sought after larger quarry! ... A

56 **UK, TS** ghost-like, was on this [though TS omits comma] shelf. A thin, under-vitalized being that you never saw. It; **US** was ghost-like on his shelf. It

57 **UK, TS** He had always thought; **US** He thought

58 **UK, TS** bird: a; **US** bird—or perhaps that was because there were so many Americans about there, though he never saw them.... A

59 **UK, TS** thin; **US** slim
This change in US appears to be prompted by 'thin-billed' in close proximity.

60 **UK** the twilight; **TS** the <deep> twilight; **US** the deep twilight
TS deletion does not carry across to US despite obvious repetition: 'deep twilight of deep hedges'.

61 **UK** He only knew of Americans because of a book he had once read—a; **TS** He only knew of Americans because <i>↑o↓f <that>↑a↓ **AR** book he had once read – a; **US** Nearly all he knew of Americans came from a book he had once read—about a

62 **UK, TS** in shadows and getting into trouble with a priest. ¶ This; **US** in hedgerows and getting into trouble with a priest.... But no doubt there were other types. ¶ This

63 **UK, TS** bird, obviously Puritan; **US** obviously Puritan bird

64 **UK, TS** the bottle-tit, the great-tit; **US** the great-tit, the bottle-tit

65 **UK, TS** its upper and lower mandible; **US** its upper mandible with its lower
66 **UK, US** flitted, noiseless, into; **TS** flitted noiselessly into
67 **UK, TS** He could hear her; **US** He knew that by the sound of her
68 **UK, TS** figured; **US** printed
69 **UK, TS** cotton, and breathed heavily, holding; **US** cotton, holding
70 **UK, US** *Ce qu'ils ont fait de toi!*
   This is an autograph addition to TS.
71 **UK, US** scorn for both language and people of her adopted country. ¶ Her; **TS** scorn for language and people. ¶ Her
72 **UK, US** rush; **TS** flood
73 **UK** on Friday. In; **TS** on <a> Friday. In; **US** on a Friday. In
74 **UK** sculptor Monsieur Casimir-Bar; **TS** sculptor ↑, Monsieur↓ Casimir-Bar **AR**; **US** sculptor Casimir-Bar
   Autograph correction to TS not carried over to US.
75 **UK, US** been honoured by; **TS** been <decorated> ↑ennobled↓ by **AR**
   Neither TS revision nor the word emended carried on to UK or US editions.
76 **UK, US** value that had distinguished democrats; **TS** value ↑that had distin-guished↓ <of the> democrats
   Typed addition carried on to US.
77 **UK** home to her as; **TS** home ↑to her↓ as **AR**; **US** home as
   Addition to TS not carried on to US.
78 **UK,** debris; **US, TS** débris
79 **UK, US** the transition she; **TS** the <tradition> ↑transition↓ she **AR**
   This autograph correction appears to be in a different hand, possibly Stella Bowen's.
80 **UK** cleanly; **TS, US** clean
81 **UK, US** had really exhibited; **TS** had <really> exhibited
82 **UK, US** was admittedly a man of honour and sensibility and reputed; **TS** was <admittedly a man of honour and sensibility and> reputed
83 **UK, TS** Elle; **US** *Elle*
   The italicised form is not used consistently even in Marie Léonie's reflec-tions, so UK followed here despite the two previous instances being italicised.
84 **UK, US** observed; **TS** seen
85 **UK, TS** to the condition; **US** to what had used to be the condition
86 **UK, US** Léonie; **TS** Riotor
87 **UK** Priest as such the; **TS** Priest ↑as such↓ the **AR**; **US** Priest the
88 **UK, TS** he; **US** priests
89 **UK** reserve. Yet she; **TS** reserve. <Elle on the other hand – >↑Yet↓ she **AR**; **US** reserve. On the other hand—she
   Deletion in TS not carried over to US.
90 **UK, US** sort who had; **TS** sort ↑who↓ had **AR**
91 **UK, US** whole gratuitously to; **TS** whole ↑gratuitously↓ to
92 **UK, TS** had; **US** has
93 **UK** The last year he had gone racing; **TS** Last year he; **US** During the last year when he had gone racing he
   US merely elaborates what is a crucial change from TS to UK; see the Intro-duction.
94 **UK, TS** Groby; **US** the house
95 **UK, US** air of a Greek woman who; **TS** air ↑of a Greek woman↓ who

96 **UK, TS** umbrella and with his; **US** umbrella, his
97 **UK** saving; **TS, US** savings
  TS/US reading adopted: apparent UK compositor's error.
98 **UK, US** because his gifts; **TS** because <her> ↑his↓ gifts **AR**
99 **UK, TS** strength; **US** vigour
100 **UK, US** the dark glance; **TS** the ↑dark↓ glance
101 **UK, TS** proud, vigorous, alert; **US** proud, alert
102 **UK, US** fit had; **TS** fit <itself> had **AR**
103 **UK, US** Quarter stood very high: she; **TS** Quarter ↑stood very high↓ <was [?] >: she
104 **UK, TS** High Permanent Official; **US** High Official
105 **UK, US** the other end; **TS** the ↑other↓ end
106 **UK** companion for long, without; **TS** companion ↑for long↓ without **AR**; **US** companion, until lately without
107 **UK** they considered as now in; **TS** they <now> considered as ↑now↓ in **AR**; **US** they considered as in
  Autograph revision in TS not carried over to US.
108 **UK** almost incontrovertible. For; **TS, US** almost controvertible. For

Textual Notes for I.ii

1 **UK, TS** *bonne bouche*; **US** *hors d'oeuvre*
2 **UK** with minute attention that would; **TS** with minutes and attention that would; **US** with minuteness and attention. It would
  TS appears to be a simple mistyping; the US alteration seems intended to avoid the repetition of 'that'.
3 **UK, US** with race-horses had; **TS** with <racing> race-horses had
4 **UK, US** had been used to pay her over her predictions; **TS** had <paid> ↑been used to pay↓ her over her < [?] > predictions
5 **UK, TS** those; **US** these
6 **UK, TS, US** Seattle; **Ed** Scuttle
  As discussed in the Introduction, there is a strong case for thinking that Ford's TS error was carried over to both UK and US.
7 **UK, US** droned overhead; **TS** droned <slowly> overhead
8 **UK, US** the reverse with; **TS** the <same> reverse with
9 **UK, TS** newspaper-frame; **US** newspaper
10 **UK, US** that daily excited; **TS** that <continually> daily excited
11 The rhetorical questions in this paragraph are consistently provided with question marks, in both UK and TS (as is the next sentence, which seems not to require one), apart from this one, so US has been adopted and question mark added.
12 TS's very appropriate exclamation mark, supported by US, restored here in place of UK's question mark.
13 **UK, TS** it, in; **US** it be, in
14 Question mark was added to US and that reading has been adopted here.
15 **UK, US** the cost of the sacrifice; **TS** the ↑cost of the↓ sacrifice
16 **UK, TS** been his behaviour **US** been Monsieur Christophère's behaviour
17 **UK, TS** And; **US** An
18 **UK, US** the; **TS** his

19 **UK, TS** debris; **US** débris
20 **UK, US** seen advancing through the; **TS** seen < in [?]> ↑advancing through↓ the
21 **UK, TS** singular; **US** strange
   US alteration seems intended to avoid the repetition of 'singular'.
22 Both **TS** and **US** follow with a line break here.
23 **UK, TS** pie **US** pipe
24 **UK, TS** places **US** place
25 **UK** grand-father and grand-mother; **TS** grandmother and grand-mother; **US** grandmother and grandfather
26 **UK** would have lived similarly with; **TS** would equally have lived; **US** would have lived with
27 **UK, TS** and she; **US** and by now she
28 **UK** and yet others; **TS** and another; **US** and another. Many more!
29 **UK, US** demanderais pas mieux; **TS** demanderais mieux
30 **UK** that; **TS, US** thet
   TS/US reading adopted, in line with usage elsewhere, both in UK and TS.
31 **UK, TS** not self-indulgence; **US** not the self-indulgence
32 **UK, TS** again going on duty; **US** going on duty again
33 **UK** if lesions there were; **TS, US** if there were
34 **US** and **TS** follow with a line break here.
35 **UK, TS** had begun; **US** began
36 **UK** not; **TS, US** nor
   TS/US reading adopted to correct obvious error.
37 **UK** inquire; **TS, US** enquire
38 **UK** inquiries; **TS, US** enquiries
39 **UK** Government's; **TS** Governments; **US** Government
40 **UK, US** represented the England; **TS** represented England
41 **UK** serious *collage par excellence*; **TS** ↑serious↓ *collage* <*serieux*> par excellence **AR**; **US** *collage sérieux* par excellence
42 **UK** they as a *ménage*, were; **TS** they ↑as a ménage↓ were **US** they were as a *ménage*
   Emended TS reading adopted; UK has one comma where either two commas or none seem called for.
43 **UK, TS** immensely; **US** very
44 **UK** was; **TS** <had> ↑was↓ **AR**; **US** had
45 **UK, US** birds, extremely busy on; **TS** birds ↑extremely busy↓ on
46 **UK, TS** him; **US** Rodin
47 **UK, US** Un *vrai de la vraie*; **TS** Un *vrai de la vrai*
48 **UK** Monsieur, the; **TS, US** Monsieur the
   TS/US reading adopted, to remove clearly superfluous comma.
49 **UK** had inserted one too many suspension dots, according to Duckworth's own convention.
50 **TS** follows with a line break here.
51 **UK** she had slumbered; **TS, US** she slumbered
52 **UK, TS** a priest, a lawyer and a lawyer's clerk; **US** two priests, an official, a lawyer and a lawyer's clerk
53 **UK, TS** a month; **US** three weeks or a month
54 **US** begins new paragraph here.
55 **UK** jail-bird; **TS, US** gaol-bird

56 **UK, TS** her sister-in-law; **US** her legitimate sister-in-law

Textual Notes for I.iii

Note: The character 'Helen Lowther', as the name is given in both UK and US, appears consistently in TS as 'Helen Luther'. Stella Bowen still refers to 'Luther' in her letter to Ford of 14 October 1927. The change must, then, have occurred at proof stage. There are six instances of 'Luther' in this chapter alone; they are not noted separately.

1 **UK, TS** mark; a foreign Frenchy, bad; extraordinarily; **US** mark; a foreign Frenchy. That was bad. She was extraordinarily
TS deletes the final two letters of the original 'foreigner'.

2 **UK** regarded Marie Léonie with; **TS, US** regarded her with

3 **UK, TS** Governors; **US** Governor
US appears to be a correction, Cramp's only 'governor' seeming to be Christopher Tietjens, and so has been adopted.

4 **UK** More 'nundred yeers; **TS, US** Moren n undred years
TS has a typed vertical line after 'Moren' which resembles an exclamation mark but may simply have been unintended.

5 **UK** stalls. The Cahptn ad ad im, Cramp; **TS** stalls, the Cahptn ad n ad im, Cramp; **US** stalls, the Cahptn ad; n ad im, Cramp

6 **UK** for; **TS, US** fer

7 **UK, TS** Atchison; **US** Atchinson

8 **UK, US** glorious; **TS** glarious
UK and US assume a mistyping; it may be (though 'a' and 'o' are far apart on the keyboard); it may also, of course, be an attempt to reproduce local pronunciation, as in 'tarkin' for 'talking'.

9 **UK, TS** didn't; **US** did

10 **UK, TS** didn't; **US** did

11 **UK, US** nor rag-dolls nor apples. Smacked; **TS** nor ↑rag-dolls nor↓ apples. Smacked

12 **UK, US** knick-nacks; **TS** knock-nacks.
TS may be mistyping or further example of Cramp's idiosyncratic English. The usual form is either 'knick-knack' or 'nick-nack', but UK/US allowed to stand as a modified example of such idiosyncrasies. US ends the sentence here.

13 **UK** Kingsnorth; **TS, US** Kingsworth
TS/US reading adopted to maintain consistency with earlier instances.

14 **UK, US** Cramp; **TS** Scramp
One of several TS errors suggesting that some passages may have been typed from dictation.

15 **UK, TS** tale if; **US** tale about that if

16 **UK, US** riding side-saddle in; **TS** riding <astride> side-saddle in

17 **UK, TS** horses and sat staring, a little further up the road, down; **US** horses, a little further up the road, and sat staring down

18 **UK, TS** folk. They have; **US** folk. But they have

19 **UK, TS** you could milk; **US** you could sell milk
US reading adopted here: the idea of the sale without inherent rights requires 'sell'.

20 **UK, US** continued; **TS** maintained
 This change is clearly made, presumably at proof stage, to avoid a fourth use
 of 'maintained' in three lines.
21 **UK, TS** long the; **US** long in the
22 US differs from both UK and TS by having no extra line break here.
23 **UK, TS** From the; **US** Down through the garden by the zig-zag path that
 dropped right away from the
24 **UK, US** the bright red cheeks; **TS** the ↑bright red↓ cheeks
25 US and TS have 'De' here and capitalise the word once more before
 conforming to UK.
26 **UK** carburetters; **TS, US** carburettors
 TS/US form more familiar now but early spellings were so inconsistent,
 particularly in the first quarter of the century, that UK has been left to stand.
27 TS omits this word.
28 **UK** Croogers; **TS, US** Crugers
 Corrected in line with TS/US reading.
29 **UK** high the; **TS, US** high, the
 UK has extra space between the two words where a comma should clearly
 be, so TS/ US reading has been adopted.
30 **UK** flowers turning; **TS** flowers <that were> turning **AR**; **US** flowers that
 were turning
31 **UK, TS** homes; **US** houses
32 **UK, US** they so much as have; **TS** they <even> ↑so much as↓ have
33 **UK, TS** Lewis; **US** Louis
34 **UK** healthy with all that … ; **TS** healthy with … **US** [omits whole
 sentence].
35 **UK** hay; **TS** <u>hay</u>; **US** *hay*
 The word seems to require especial emphasis, so TS/US reading has been
 adopted.
36 **UK** foot; **TS, US** feet
 The inconsistency (foot/feet) is in TS and US, so UK adhered to.
37 **UK, US** hill. *Vox adhæsit.…* "His; **TS** hill. ↑*Vox adhæsit.…* ↓ "His
38 **UK, US** dry; **TS** dray
39 **UK, TS** forcing and forcing and forcing him; **US** forcing and forcing him
40 **UK, US** de Bray; **TS** Ray
41 **UK** never set any store by Fittleworth; **TS** never ↑set any store by↓ Fittleworth **AR**; **US** never taken much stock of Fittleworth
42 **UK, TS** correspondence; **US** corresponding
43 **UK, US** Dressing up as a housemaid and looking; **TS** Dressing up and
 looking
44 **UK, TS** dimned; **US** dimmed
 UK/TS corrected in line with US reading.
45 **UK** Italians say; **TS, US** They all say
46 **UK** pick? **TS, US** pick!
 UK seems a little awkward and the TS/US reading more appropriate here,
 so the latter has been adopted.
47 **UK, US** know of what; **TS** know what

Textual Notes for I.iv

1 **UK** "Waverley,"; **TS**, <u>Waverley</u>; **US** *Waverley*
   TS/US reading adopted in line with normal usage.
2 **UK, TS** had ever read; **US** had read
3 **UK, TS** vegetable beds. Marie; **US** vegetables. Marie
4 This is the last word on TS p.52, on the same line as the end of the previous sentence and thus implying no intention to begin a new paragraph. It is also the first word on p.53 which does, however, begin a new paragraph. US follows in this.
5 **UK, TS** disability; **US** disease
6 **UK, US** kind.... "I am; **TS** kind. She had written "whom" when you usually write "who".... "I am
7 **UK, US** Mr. Pape; **TS** Mr de Bray Pape
8 **UK, TS** part of California. Valentine; **US** part of the United States. Valentine
   US corrects what may well be an intended 'error' in Mark's reflections.
9 **UK** over Mrs. Pape's letter; **TS** over <the letter> ↑Mrs Pape's letter↓ **AR**; **US** over the letter
10 **UK, US** Mr. Pape; **TS** Mr de Bray Pape
11 **UK, US** a Pape Quality; **TS** a De Bray Pape Quality
12 **UK, TS** knowledges; **US** knowledge
13 **UK** those fellows with queer collars who; **TS** those <other> fellows ↑with queer collars↓ **AR** who; **US** those other fellows who
14 **UK** disposing of typewriters; **TS, US** disposing of smuggled typewriters
15 **UK, US** knick-knack; **TS** nick-nack
   TS version is acceptable but UK/US retained as consistent with other uses.
16 **UK, TS** He had; **US** He himself had
17 **UK, TS** place—if; **US** place by now—if
18 **UK** Scarborough; **TS, US** Scarboro'
19 **UK, TS** Scutt's; **US** Scott's
20 **UK, TS** hired the family; **US** hired descent from the family
21 **UK, TS** son of one of the people; **US** son of the people
22 **UK, TS** they; **US** *they*
   Emphasis does seem effective here, so US reading adopted.
23 **UK** man unadvisedly to; **US** man, unadvisedly, to; **TS** man ↑unadvisedly↓ to
24 **UK** there! **TS, US** there:
   TS/US adopted to correct apparent error.
25 **UK** when Sylvia had run away from him! TS omits these words, ending the sentence with 'grief....'
26 **UK** him. The boy asked; **TS** him. <He> ↑The boy↓ **AR** asked; **US** him. He asked
27 US ends sentence here.
28 **UK** recognized, indeed, the; **TS** recognised indeed the; **US** recognized the
   US avoids the awkward repetition of 'indeed', so is adopted here.
29 **UK, US** descendants by his sons. The; **TS** descendants↑ by his sons↓. The
30 **UK, TS** debateable; **TS** debatable
   This spelling (dated to the close of the nineteenth century by the *OED*) has been retained since TS agrees with UK and (debatably) it is not wholly inap-

propriate to Mark.
31 **UK, US** The fellow had; **TS** The \<boy\> ↑fellow↓ had **AR**
32 **UK, TS** not care; **US** not much care
33 **UK, TS** the first minute. He; **US** the beginning. He
34 **UK** at; **TS, US** of
35 **UK, US** had no business with; **TS** had \<nothing to do\> ↑no business↓ with
36 **UK** towards twelve-thirty next day, walked; **TS, US** towards twelve-thirty, walked
37 **UK** disturbedly from; **TS, US** disturbedly, from
Necessary comma added in accordance with TS and US.
38 **UK, TS** he himself might; **US** he, Mark, himself, might
39 **UK, TS** he; **US** Christopher
40 **UK** swallowing his; **TS** swallowingat his; **US** swallowing at his
41 **UK** that very likely she had; **TS** that she no doubt had **US** that she, very likely had
42 **UK, TS** condition. On the one or two interviews he had had with; **US** condition. During the one or two interviews he had had years ago with
US primarily lengthens the period of time since the last personal contact between Mark and Sylvia.
43 **UK** being God; **TS, US** being a God
44 TS begins a new page here with no obvious indent; US has no new paragraph at this point.
45 TS indicates new paragraph here with autograph note 'n.p.' in the right-hand margin but US does not follow.
46 TS indicates run-on, overriding the indentation for new paragraph; US retains new paragraph.
47 **UK** honourable, but … oh, lawless; **TS** honourable but…. oh, lawless; **US** honourable but lawless
48 **UK** temperament by; **TS, US** temperament on temperament by
49 Fourth dot added, in line with Duckworth's own convention.
50 Mark's thoughts are sometimes a little unfinished but a word does seem to be missing here (from all witnesses), probably 'house' or 'family'?
51 **UK, TS** young fellow into; **TS** young \<family\> ↑fellow↓ into **AR**; **US** young springald into
52 **UK, US** Tietjens'; **TS** Tietjenses
TS reading restored since plural form seems required.
53 **UK, TS** the boy who was the son; **US** the legal son
54 **UK** might. He, Mark, was; **TS, US** might be. He, Mark, was
55 **UK, US** see; **TS** saw
56 **UK, US** to her own temperament. That; **TS** to \<their\> her own temperament. That
57 **UK, TS** was it? What; **US** was the reason for this visit? What
58 **UK** wife—the Saint!—had; **US** wife,—the Saint!—had; **TS** wife, ↑– the Saint! –↓ had
59 **UK** old furniture **TS, US** old-furniture
TS/US adopted in accordance with reading elsewhere.
60 **UK** Oha **US** Aha
TS has what looks like '@ha', implying a deleted, rather than overtyped, first letter. I suspect that Ford merely omitted to capitalise the 'h'. At any rate, the US reading is perfectly acceptable and adopted here.

61 **UK, TS** well; **US** Well
　　UK and TS capitalise neither this instance nor the one a few lines later; US
　　capitalises the first and not the second.
62 **UK, TS** cedar. Offerings to; **US** cedar. Or maybe a thorn? Offering to
63 **UK, TS** was obviously unlikely that; **US** was impossible that
　　US revision seems designed to avoid third use of 'obviously' in as many lines.
64 **UK, US** moustaches; **TS** moustache
65 **UK, TS** Mark and; **US** Mark—they were such old friends—and
66 **UK** had a try, then another; **TS** had ano ther try, then another; **US** had
　　another try, then another
67 Suspension dot, missing in UK, now added, in line with Duckworth's own
　　convention.
68 Superfluous space removed before first suspension dot, in line with Duck-
　　worth's own convention.
69 **UK** b—y; **TS, US** B—y
　　The issue of swear words is particularly relevant to *No More Parades* but is
　　also discussed in the general Note on this Edition. US uses a dash here but
　　not in the second instance, so UK/TS has been retained in both instances.
70 **UK, TS** b—y; **US** bloody
71 **UK** it had been on; **TS, US** it was on

Textual Notes for I.v

1　**UK** Wolstonmark; **TS, US** Wolstonemark
2　**UK** him, Mark, up; **TS, US** him up
3　**UK** disappeared in the rejoicings, and; **TS** disappeared and; **US** disappeared
　　in the rejoicings in the sy— and
4　**UK** Wolstonmark; **TS, US** Wolstonemark
5　**UK, TS** himself. In; **US** himself, Already in
6　**UK, TS** about affairs—the affairs of; **US** about the affairs of
7　**UK, TS** menage; **US** *ménage*; **Ed** ménage
　　I have discussed the reasons for this decision in the Note on the Text.
8　**UK** idea of retiring, not only from the Office but the whole world, had; **TS**
　　idea ↑of retiring not only from the Office but the whole world↓ had **AR; US**
　　idea had
9　**UK, TS** them, and; **US** them! And
10 **UK** Wolstonmark; **TS, US** Wolstonemark
11 **UK,** bore; **TS** <tire> ↑bore↓ **AR; US** tire
12 **UK** wet
　　TS has a very faint but illegible autograph squiggle; US omits the word.
13 **UK** always; since; **TS** always ↓;↑ <and,> **AR; US** always; and since
14 **UK, TS** That would have been quite; **US** That for a long time had seemed
　　quite
15 **UK, TS** him and a; **US** him a
16 **UK, US** by fourteen years; **TS** by <eighteen> ↑fourteen↓ years
17 **UK, TS** seen; **US** known
　　'See' or 'seen' three times in successive lines presumably accounts for the US
　　revision.
18 **UK, US** who had got trepanned; **TS** who <gets> ↑had got↓ trepanned

19 **UK** society of all wrong uns; **TS, US** society of Jewish or Liberal cabinet minister's wives, all wrong uns

20 **UK, US** him … and; **TS** him … <But the day had> and **AR**

21 **UK, US** Club: ¶ Has; **TS** Club: ¶ <"Has it occurred to you that, since those two boys are killed, that fellow Christopher is practically heir to Groby? You have no legitimate children, have you?" Mark replied that he hadn't any bastards either.¶ It certainly had not occurred to him that Christopher must almost certainly come in to Groby. He could certainly [sic], too, understand his father's perturbation.> "Has **AR**
The deleted passage ends TS p.80; the next page and the one following it are both numbered 81, though the text is consecutive.

22 **UK** marry Papist Marie Léonie; **TS** marry ↑Papist↓ Marie Leonie **AR**; **US** marry Marie Léonie

23 **UK** sort of bad; **TS** sort ↑of↓ bad **AR**; **US** sort bad

24 **UK, TS** class if; **US** class. If

25 **UK, US** nor; **TS** or

26 **UK** needs get with child the daughter of their father's oldest friend, and; **TS** needs <seduce> the daughter of their father's oldest friend, <must needs> get <her> with child and **AR**
Autograph line encircles and links the phrase 'get <her> with child' to the space produced by the deletion of 'seduce' in the line above. US reproduces original TS version, before deletions.

27 **UK, TS** absolutely; **US** fiercely

28 **UK, TS** be as obstinate; **US** be obstinate

29 **UK, US** woman who wore white; **TS** woman <in> ↑who wore↓ white **AR**

30 **UK** He had got; **TS** He ↑had↓ got **AR**; **US** He got

31 **UK** wheat, under proper farming, should; **TS** wheat ↑under proper farming↓ should **AR**; **US** wheat should

32 **UK, TS** crimes; **US** crime

33 **UK, US** sown on exposed moors where; **TS** sown ↑on exposed moors↓ where

34 **UK** and Mark his horror at what Christopher; **TS** and Mark his horror at ↑what↓ Christopher **AR**; **US** and Mark had voiced his horror at what Christopher

35 **UK** Englishmen's; **TS, US** Englishman's
Obvious UK error corrected in accordance with TS/US.

36 **UK, US** the grate, a; **TS** the <great> ↑grate↓, a **AR**
Another indication that part of the novel may possibly have been typed from dictation.

37 **UK, TS** you, to; **US** you, and to
TS has a typed deletion of a word between 'you' and 'to', most likely 'and', but not decipherable.

38 **UK** agreed that; **TS, US** agreed indeed that

39 **UK, TS** over; **US** about

40 **UK, US** pay himself from; **TS** pay ↑himself↓ from

41 **UK** must reawaken to the necessity for exacting; **TS** must <return to> ↑reawaken to the necessity for↓ exacting **AR**; **US** must return to exacting

42 **UK** stormy; **TS, US** storm

43 **UK** secured? There had seemed to be several; **TS** secured<.>? There <were> ↑had seemed to be↓ several **AR**; **US** secured? There were several

44 **UK, US** that Christopher; **TS** that <his brother> Christopher

45 **UK, US** nevertheless privately desired; **TS** nevertheless ↑privately↓ desired

46 **UK, US** and that that was; **TS** and ↑that↓ that was

47 **UK** jail; **TS, US** gaol

48 **UK** job; innocuous too, if; **TS** job↑;↓<but> innocuous ↑too↓ if **AR; US** job but innocuous if

49 **UK** Mark thought that Christopher; **TS** Mark still thought that Chrsitopher; **US** Mark still thought that Christopher
While US follows TS (apart from its obvious mistyping) UK deletes 'still' which will be repeated later in the sentence, a decision presumably authorised by UK proofs.

50 **UK, US** exacts from; **TS** exacts <the deposit> from

51 **UK, US** was pretty; **TS** was <by then> pretty

52 **UK, TS,** for; **US** to

53 **UK, US** She had, however, surrendered; **TS** She ↑had however↓ surrendered

54 **UK** whether after an attempt at a divorce he married her or; **TS** whether ↑after an attempt at a divorce↓ **AR** he married her <after a divorce> or; **US** whether he married her after a divorce or

55 **UK** a Prime; **TS, US** a late Prime

56 **UK, TS** marriages; **US** marriage

57 **UK** before an English registrar; **TS** before <a> ↑an English↓ **AR** registrar; **US** before a registrar

58 **UK, TS** moral; **US** spiritual

59 **UK, TS** man and woman; **US** you and a woman

60 **US** begins new sentence here.

61 **UK** was good-natured; **TS** was <at least> good natured **AR; US** was at least good natured

62 **UK** had acquiesced in the justness of his; **TS** had <accepted> ↑acquiesced in the justness of↓ his; **US** had listened to his

63 **TS** has an open square bracket before the next word and 'n.p.' written in the right-hand margin. US follows original TS in not beginning a new paragraph here.

64 **UK** old-furniture millionaire; **TS** old-furniture <buying> millionaire; **US** old-furniture buying millionaire

65 **UK, TS** considerable admirer; **US** considerable an admirer
US variant adopted

66 **UK** soldiers; **TS** soldier↑s↓ **AR; US** soldier

67 **UK, TS** them; **US** him

68 **UK, TS** So, in; **US** In

69 **UK, TS** intelligences; **US** intelligence

70 **UK** had been; **TS, US** had at least been
UK deletion of the phrase avoids repetition of it, occurring in the same sentence, retained in US.

71 **UK** bill-discounting. Moreover, he; **TS** bill-discounting. <And> ↑Moreover↓ he **AR; US** bill-discounting. And he

72 **UK, TS** bedside that he had been occupying and; **US** bedside and

73 **UK** finished; you; **TS** finished↑;↓<and> you; **US** finished and you

74 **UK** of an afternoon about; **TS, US** of a day about
UK eliminates possible ambiguity about time of day and shortens the time available.

75 **UK** Mark had replied; **TS, US** Mark replied
76 **UK, TS** roused; **US** aroused
77 **UK, TS** satisfaction; **US** contentment

Textual Notes for I.vi

1 **UK** registered the dates of that period; days; **TS** registered ↑the↓ dates ↑of that period↓ <then> days **AR**; **US** registered dates; days
2 **UK, TS** before; **US** ago
3 **UK** "Spelden on Sacrilege,"; **TS, US** *Spelden on Sacrilege*
   TS actually underlines (for italics) but clearly a book title so US reading adopted, in line with normal usage.
4 **UK, TS** fellows; **US** families
5 **UK** bogy; **TS, US** bogey
6 **UK, TS** prophesy; **US** prophecy
7 **UK** Forty-Five; **TS** Forty Five; **US** 'Forty Five
8 **UK, TS** if; **US** supposing
9 **UK** Groby, and then, too, it
   Both TS and US end sentence after 'Groby'.
10 **UK, TS** they had had to; **US** they had to
11 **UK** before, rum or no rum. And; **US** before rum or no rum. And; **TS** before ↑rum or no rum↓. And **AR**
12 **UK** "Life of Johnson,"; **TS** <u>Life of Johnson</u>; **US** *Life of Johnson*
   TS/US reading adopted, in line with normal usage.
13 **UK, TS** damn; **US** damned
14 **UK** learned, too; **TS, US** learned too
   TS/US reading adopted; UK comma here seems clearly superfluous.
15 **UK, TS** 20th; **US** 29th
16 **UK, TS** 20th; **US** 29th
17 **UK** on to; **TS, US** onto
18 **UK** years. Father's father had; **TS** years. <His> ↑Father's↓ father had **AR**; **US** years. Grand-father had
19 **UK, TS** because his father had; **US** because Grand-father had
20 **UK, TS** as rather a dunce; **US** as a dunce
21 **UK** Tietjenses; **TS, US** Tietjens's
22 **UK** Tietjenses; **TS, US** Tietjens's
23 **UK** 1812; **US** 1810
   Last digit of the year in TS is illegible, but 1812 is correct.
24 **UK** Tietjenses; **TS, US** Tietjens's
25 **UK, TS** by blood; **US** by both name and blood
26 **UK, US** the worse off; **TS** the <better> ↑worse↓ off **AR**
27 **UK** wall. It; **TS** wall <of the house>. It **AR**; **US** wall of the house. They always quoted too the Italian saying about trees over the house. Obviously Christopher had told it to his son and the young man had told it to Mrs. De Bray Pape. That was why the saying had been referred to three times that day.... Anyway it was an Italian tree! It
28 **UK** ha-ha; **TS, US** haha
29 **UK, TS** consulting heir who; **US** consulting the heirs who
30 **UK, TS** greay; **US** grey

This appears to be a simple error (rather than an archaic or dialect spelling); both *Some Do Not ...* and *A Man Could Stand Up* – have John Peel's coat as 'grey'. US reading has been adopted.

31 **UK** Pape was, he; **TS** Pape ↑was↓ he **AR**; **US** Pape had got to he

32 **UK** to Cammy Fittleworth! She; **TS** to \<Sally Montreeor\> ↑Cammy Fittleworth↓. She **AR**; **US** to Cammie Fittleworth. She
US spelling of 'Cammie' adopted, consistent with all other instances in UK.

33 **UK, US** then Fittleworth was; **TS** then \<Montreeor\> ↑Fittleworth↓ was **AR**

34 **UK** Tietjenses; **TS, US** Tietjens's

35 **UK, TS** he expected; **US** he had expected
US reading adopted to place the expectation clearly before its vindication.

36 **UK, TS** except; **US** enough

37 **UK** to; **TS, US** as

38 **UK, TS** brother except; **US** brother back except

39 **UK, TS** and he will nurse you like a blasted soft woman—except; **US** and you will nurse him like a blasted soft worm—except
US reading adopted because it is Christopher – the nurse – who is the 'you' addressed at this point. Ford must have emended the US but not the UK proofs.

40 **UK** Bennett; **US** Bennet
TS has an autograph mark after the final letter of 'Bennet' which resembles but is not quite a second 't'. Samuel Johnson's friend was Bennet Langton. US reading adopted.

41 **UK, TS** crashes; **US** crash

42 **UK** with the Greek; **TS, US** with Greek

43 **US** begins a new paragraph here.

44 **UK, TS** parson; **US** person

45 **UK** day, if he; **TS** day when he; **US** day and when he

46 **UK** Wolstonmark; **TS, US** Wolsonmark

47 **UK, TS** the; **US** a

48 **UK** the; **TS** tha; **US** that
US reading adopted as better choice and as strongly indicated by TS, the terminal letter presumably simply missed.

49 **UK** jigamaree. Years before, Sir John had; **TS** jigamaree. ↑Years before↓ Sir John \<apparently\> had **AR**; **US** jigamaree. Sir John had

50 **UK** nirls; **TS** \<h\>↑g↓irls; **US** girls
Obvious error corrected in line with US.

51 **UK** and; **TS, US** an

52 **UK** icy. Mark had; **TS** icy. \<He\>↑Mark↓ had **AR**; **US** icy. He had

53 **UK, US** for a thousand pounds; **TS** for fifty thousand pounds
Fifty thousand pounds, while a gigantic sum, could be seen as representative of the huge stakes in this feud between the brothers; but, in *Some Do Not ...,* when Mark cancelled his father's security for Christopher's overdraft, he told the banker, Port Scatho, to make over from Mark's own account 'a thousand a year to my brother as he needs it. Not more than a thousand in any one year' (II.ii).

54 **UK** a; **TS, US** à
Corrected in line with TS/US.

55 **UK, TS** regiment; **US** régiment
Corrected in line with US.

56 **UK** d'Amour, monsieur, je; **TS** d'Amour, ↑monsieur,↓ je; **US** d'amour, monsieur, je
57 Both TS and US follow with a line break here.

Textual Notes for I.vii

1 **UK, TS** savours; **US** odours
2 **UK, US** cider; **TS** cyder
3 **UK, TS** rule—a rule so strong that it had assumed the aspect of a regulation—she; **US** rule she
4 **UK, TS** beings; **US** being
5 **UK** corner; **TS** cornere; **US** corners
6 **UK** hedge. He; **TS** hedge too. He; **US** hedge, too. He
7 **UK** "sparrers"; in London they called them that—just; **TS, US** "sparrers" as in London they called them—just
8 **UK** country; **TS, US** nation
9 **UK, TS** no; **US** No
  US adopted: ellipses indicate end of sentence at 'people!'
10 **UK** liquid; **TS** liquide; **US** liquids
11 **UK** and drink the rest from the cask; **TS** and drink the rest for the cask; **US** and bottle the rest of the cask
12 **UK, TS** casks; **US** kegs
13 **UK** an English lady; **TS, US** a lady
14 **UK** As; **TS, US** For
15 Both UK and TS have a full stop here; US reading adopted.
16 **UK, TS** as cart-wheel; **US** as a cartwheel
  US adopted: indefinite article clearly missed in UK and TS.
17 **UK** ought to be; **TS, US** should be
18 **UK, TS** Cap; **US** Cape
19 **UK, TS** takes; **US** take
20 **UK, TS** She; **US** Marie-Léonie
21 **UK** Cramp; **TS, US** Camp
22 **UK, TS** Aeschyle; **US** Aeschylus
23 **UK** orfn n orfn; **TS** orfn n orfen; **US** orfen 'n orfen
24 **UK, TS** women; **US** woman
25 **UK** Marie Léonie; **TS, US** she
26 **UK** Armistice; **TS, US** that
27 **UK, TS** street of that; **US** street that
28 **UK** girl-guide's; **TS, US** girl-guides'
29 **UK** against one another; **TS** one against ↑one↓ another; **US** one against another
30 **UK, TS** heart had contracted; **US** heart contracted
31 **UK, TS** fortunes; **US** fortune
32 **UK** Valentine; **TS, US** The girl
33 **UK, TS** allowances; **US** allowance
34 **UK, US** show; **TS** shew
  TS very frequently has 'shew' or 'shewn'; none of the six further instances in this chapter is noted.
35 **UK, TS** monsters; **US** assassins

36 **UK** you may run; **TS** you ↑may↓ run **AR**; **US** you must run
    The inserted word is very faint but almost certainly 'may'.
37 **UK** obscure; **TS** obscure [but fifth and sixth letters overtyped]; **US** obscene
38 **UK, TS** young, devoid; **US** young, and devoid
39 **UK, TS** experience. And Marie; **US** experience. Marie
40 **UK, TS** consequence; **US** consequences
41 **UK** you must accept the responsibility.; **TS, US** do you accept the respon-
    sibility! ...
42 This commences a new paragraph in US.
43 **UK, TS** spectacle; **US** spectacles
44 **UK** would; **TS** would [but 'will' heavily overtyped]; **US** will
45 **UK, TS** Laffitte; **US** Laffite
46 **UK, TS** Post for; **US** Post, for
    US reading adopted as preferable, allowing for that slight ambiguity ('*for* me'
    and 'as far as I'm concerned').
47 **UK** a few yards away only; **TS** a few yards away, only; **US** only a few yards
    away
48 **UK, US** purpose; **TS** purposes
49 **UK, US** She herself was; **TS** She was
50 UK, at the bottom of the page, actually omits the full stop.
51 **UK, TS** No doubt Valentine; **US** Valentine
    US reading adopted: 'No doubt' is clearly superfluous since the fact is stated
    immediately afterwards.
52 **UK, TS** cases; but; **US** cases. There he had remained ever since. But
53 **UK, US** just before; **TS** just before just before [last words and first words on
    successive pages]

Textual Notes for II.i

Note: TS still gives the name 'Helen Lowther' as 'Helen Luther', though both
UK and US editions have 'Lowther'. Instances in this chapter have not been
noted except when part of a more complex variant and, on one occasion, where
US has mistakenly followed TS; nor have the three instances of TS repeating
'Tietjens'' where 'Tietjens's' is intended.
1 **UK** using the; **TS** using <merely> the; **US** using merely the
2 **UK** her chestnut; **TS** her <bay> ↑chestnut↓ **AR**; **US** her chestnut bay
3 **UK, US** the bay mare of; **TS** the <horse> ↑bay mare↓ of **AR**
4 **UK, US** reins, his Guards' tie, his boots; **TS** reins, <leggings> ↑his Guards'
    tie, his↓ boots
5 **UK, TS** knew; **US** would know
6 **UK** retired, M.P., K.C.M.G.; **TS** retired, ↑ M.P↓ K.C.M.G. **AR**; **US** retired,
    K.C.M.G.
7 **UK, TS** V.C.; **US** M.P.V.C.
8 **UK** D.S.O.... ¶ So; **TS** D.S.O.... Some of that basketful he must have been;
    probably he was all....... So; **US** D.S.O.... So
9 **UK, US** chestnut; **TS** <bay> ↑chestnut↓ **AR**
    US does not begin a new paragraph after this line. TS has autograph mark
    indicating new paragraph,
10 **UK** swayed backwards; **TS** swayed <a little> backwards **AR**; **US** swayed a

little backwards

11 **UK** smiled down into; **TS** smiled down<wards> into **AR**; **US** smiled downwards into

12 **UK** Come ups; **TS**, **US** Comeups

13 **UK**, **TS** leant; **US** bent

14 **UK**, **TS** any other man's; **US** any man's

15 **UK** French prostitute ...; **TS** French ↑prostitute↓ <hairdresser's widow> ... **AR**; **US** French hairdresser's widow ...

16 **UK**, **TS** to be India; **US** to go to India

17 **UK** of; **TS**, **US** on

18 **UK** stepfather the Field-Marshal Commanding....; **TS** step<son>↑father↓ the Field Marshal .↑Commanding↓.... **AR**; **US** stepfather the Field Marshal...

19 **UK** said to herself that; **TS** said ↑to herself↓ that **AR**; **US** said that

20 **UK** name—her father's; "Mark,"; **TS** name,↑—her father's—↓ "Mark" **AR**; **US** name, "Mark,"

21 **UK** Mark. I heard you tell your maid so only yesterday.... You; **TS** Mark. ↑I heard you tell your maid so only yesterday↓ .... You **AR**; **US** Mark.... You

22 **TS** does not begin a new paragraph here though the previous page ends with a half-line.

23 **UK**, **US** You will eventually; **TS** You <would>↑will↓ eventually **AR**

24 **UK** you would not, but you would; **TS** you would not but you would; **US** you will not but you will

25 **UK** that American; **TS** that <damned> American **AR**; **US** that damned American

26 **UK** in; **TS** <o>↑i↓n; **US** on

27 **UK** your general's pay; **TS** your <Field Marshal'>↑general'↓s pay **AR**; **US** your Field Marshal's pay

28 **UK** have thought of cutting down; **TS** have <dared to cut>↑thought of cutting↓ down **AR**; **US** have dared to cut down

29 **UK** have my Satterthwaite; **TS**, **US** have Satterthwaite

30 **UK**, **US** for!" ¶ **A**; **TS** for!" ¶ <Lord Fittleworth with Gunning at his saddle-bow came along the road. He said: "God damn it, Campion, Helen Luther ought not to be down there. Her> ¶ **A**

31 **UK** on to; **TS**, **US** onto

32 **UK** was once plentiful; **TS** was ↑once↓ plentiful **AR**; **US** was plentiful

33 **UK** many miles away; **TS** twenty miles away; **US** miles away

34 **UK** Campion, ought Helen Lowther to; **TS** Campion, ↑ought↓ Helen Luther <ought not> to **AR**; **US** Campion, Helen Lowther ought not to

35 **UK**, **US** fortnight!" He shouted at Gunning; **TS** fortnight!" ↑He shouted at↓<And to> Gunning

36 **UK** old villain was; **TS** old <scoundrel>↑villain↓ was; **US** old scoundrel was

37 The last six words are an autograph addition to **TS**.

38 **UK** a square, high, black, felt hat; **TS** a white-grey Trilby hat; **US** a square, black felt hat

39 **UK** with its little bristling; **TS** with <grey whiskers and> bristling **AR**; **US** with grey whiskers and bristling

40 **UK**, **US** continued to; **TS** continued: <Ladyship will give me no rest...." He said to Gunning: "Here, you, blast you, where is this damned gate!" To the General: "This old scoundrel is always counterswinging the confounded

gates on Tietjens' beastly fields." To Sylvia: "It isn't the sort of place Helen Luther ought to go to, is it? All sorts of people living with all sorts...." He considered Gunning at his knee and held his tongue..... ¶ The Earl of Fittleworth gave always the impression that he wore a scarlet tail coat, white buckskin breeches, a rather painful eyeglass and a silk top-hat attached to his person by a silk cord. Actually he was wearing a white-grey Trilby hat, pepper and salt tweeds and no eyeglass. ¶ Having recovered himself he said to Gunning: ¶ "Here, you, go and stand by the beastly gate till I come...." He added> to

41 **UK** Agapemone, so you say; **TS** Agapemone, <they>↑so you↓ say **AR**; **US** Agapemone if what you say is true

42 **UK** had had a; **TS** had <kept > a **AR**; **US** had kept a

43 **UK**, **TS** long; **US** longer

44 **UK** menage; **TS** ménage; **US** *ménage*
   TS reading adopted here; I have discussed the reasons for this in the Note on the Text.

45 **UK** upon whose roof she now looked down; **TS** ↑upon↓ whose <garden she then dominated> ↑roof she now looked down↓ **AR**; **US** whose garden she then looked down on

46 **UK** were in a; **TS** were ↑in↓ a **AR**; **US** were a

47 **UK** wives, they get the knack of; **TS** wives, ↑they get the knack↓ of; **US** wives, of
   TS has signalled that the indicated clause be moved from the previous line; US follows the original order.

48 **UK** deference; **TS** deference<s>; **US** deferences

49 **UK** But all men; **TS** <And>↑But all↓ men **AR**; **US** And men

50 **UK**, **TS** had stood a good deal. It; **US** had stood a good deal in the way of allegations from her. It

51 **UK** far towards believing; **TS** far <in the way of> ↑towards↓ believing **AR**; **US** far in the way of believing

52 **UK**, **TS** him. Beauty; **US** him about that other man. Beauty

53 **UK** believe ... about; **TS** believe ↑.... ↓ about **AR**; **US** believe about

54 **UK** had seemed natural to; **TS**, **US** had come rather naturally to

55 **UK** Ethel, for, not; **TS** Ethel for, not; **US** Ethel for not
   TS reading adopted to remove extraneous comma (though TS comma after 'for' is very faint).

56 **UK** had paid; **TS** had <actually> paid; **US** had actually paid

57 **UK**, **US** Christopher. That was; **TS** Christopher. <It> ↑That↓ was **AR**

58 **UK** debt. Even in the old days Lady Macmaster had been used to worry Sylvia about that. ¶ Apparently; **TS** debt. ↑Even in the old days Lady Macmaster had been used to worry Sylvia about that↓ ¶ Apparently **AR**; **US** debt! ¶ Apparently

59 **UK**, **TS** idiotcy; **US** idiocy
   An old-fashioned but still acceptable usage.

60 **UK** even too; **TS** even <to suffer from> too; **US** even to suffer from too

61 **UK**, **TS** spunged; **US** sponged
   This UK/TS spelling was already very old-fashioned, though still used sporadically.

62 **UK**, **TS** portentous; **US** fantastic

63 **UK** direness; **TS**, **US** portentousness

Again, UK is very old-fashioned (and usually replaced by 'direfulness') but left to stand.

64 **UK, TS** Littérateur; **US** Litterateur
65 **UK** the; **TS, US** as
66 **UK** Macmaster proposed; **TS** Macmaster, in one of her own to Sylvia, had proposed; **US** Macmaster had proposed
67 **UK** £30,000; **US** $30,000
TS has a handwritten '£' written over what is already over-typed and may well have been '$'.
68 **UK** ten per cent.; **TS, US** 10%
69 **UK, TS** little; **US** bit
70 **UK, US** to the Wannop's; **TS** to Wannop's
71 **UK** flesh. That was largely; **TS** flesh, and that, largely; **US** flesh, largely
72 **UK, TS** never to be inclined; **US** never inclined
73 **UK, TS** menage; **US** *ménage*; **Ed** ménage
I have discussed the reasons for this decision in the Note on the Text.
74 **UK, TS** her friends; **US** them
US emendation adopted to eliminate repetition of 'her friends'.
75 **UK** dependents, and; **TS, US** dependants and
76 **UK, US** was proclaiming; **TS** was not proclaiming
77 **UK, TS** as the; **US** as was the
78 **UK, TS** misfortunes; **US** misfortune.
79 **UK, US** out to Beattie, Lady Elsbacher, that; **TS** out ↑to Beattie, Lady Elsbacher↓ that
80 **UK** Lowther, that; **TS, US** Luther that
81 **UK, TS** Country; **US** county
82 **UK** that the fact that she; **TS** that ↑the fact that↓ she **AR**; **US** that she
83 **UK** wealth looked like a sign; **TS** wealth <as a> **AR** ↑looked like a↓ sign; **US** wealth as a sign
84 **UK** the things that money could buy and that she so valued; **TS, US** things that she so valued
85 **UK** had once; **US** once had
TS originally used US order but autograph line indicates on TS that words should be reversed.
86 **UK** that in her; **TS, US** that her
87 **UK, US** Sylvia would have liked; **TS** Sylvia liked
88 **UK, TS** Even that was not a proof to the reflective that; **US** Even that to the reflective would not necessarily be proof that
89 **UK, TS** small; **US** minor
90 **UK, TS** actually; **US** usually
91 **UK** a dim, low room; **TS** a <dark>↑dim, low↓ room **AR**; **US** a dark low-ceilinged room
92 **UK, TS** come in, mooning in; **US** come mooning in
93 **UK** establishment indifferently to; **TS** establishment ↑indifferently↓ to **AR**; **US** establishment to
94 **UK** denied; **TS, US** closed
95 **UK, TS** so the turning down had not counted; **US** so that the turning down need not count
96 **UK, TS** fury: that; **US** fury. That
97 **UK, US** that she has; **TS** that <he> ↑she↓ has **AR**

98 **UK, TS** and then does; **US** and does
99 **UK** thus; **TS, US** then
100 **UK, TS** and of being; **US** and being
101 **UK, TS** That she had been able to live down. But; **US** That Sylvia had been able to bear. But
102 **UK, TS** un-chic; **US** unnoticeable
103 **UK, US** Lombard Street to; **TS** Lombard<y> ↑Street↓
104 **UK, US** Fittleworth; **TS** he

Textual Notes for II.ii

Note: Ford's TS still gives the character 'Helen Lowther' as 'Helen Luther', though both UK and US editions have 'Lowther'. None of the nine separate TS instances of 'Luther' in this chapter is indicated.

1 **UK** women, and one come; **TS** women↑, & one↓ come **AR**; **US** women, and come
2 **UK, TS** ears to which it was dangerous to have access—dangerous; **US** ears that could well be dangerous
3 **UK, TS** popular in the right places; **US** popular in high places
4 **UK, TS** And was; **US** And he was
5 **UK, TS** And no doubt Mark; **US** And Mark
6 **UK** be relied on; **TS** be <calculated>↑relied↓ on **AR**; **US** calculated on
7 **UK** he too had made; **TS, US** he had made
8 **UK, TS** begun by; **US** begun it by
9 **UK, TS** been at her; **US** been her
10 **UK** Countess probably liked to protect her innocence. The; **TS** Countess ↑probably↓ liked to <preserve>↑protect↓ her innocence. The **AR**; **US** Countess liked to preserve the innocence of young American women. The
11 **UK, TS** class as herself; **US** class, at least by marriage, as herself
12 **UK, TS** be; **US** get
13 **UK, TS** it was only pulling; **US** it could only be pulling
14 **UK, TS** but in the end that; **US** but that
15 **UK, TS** dim avocation, but; **US** avocation in a rather dim West. But
16 **UK, TS** Europe; **US** Europe, alone
17 **UK** known, apparently over; **TS, US** known, apparently, over
TS/US reading adopted for clarity.
18 **UK, TS** a cool; **US** a long, cool
19 **UK** And she; **US** And, at that, she
The bottom right-hand corner of typescript leaf 153 is blank and only the word 'And' visible; presumably a corner of the sheet of carbon paper was folded
20 **UK, TS** to what; **US** to do what
21 **UK, TS** there; **US** here
22 **UK** a letter the day before yesterday; **TS** a <[?]>↑letter the day before↓ yesterday **AR**; **US** a letter yesterday
23 **US** begins a new paragraph here.
24 **UK, TS** he; **US** Fittleworth
25 **UK, TS** have; **US** have have [corrected in subsequent reprints]
26 **UK, US** and looked towards; **TS** and <made[?]> ↑looked↓ towards **AR**

27 TS and US follow with an extra line break here.
28 **UK, TS** companionably; **US** friendlily
   The rather awkward 'friendlily' is prompted by the close proximity of UK's 'companionably' and 'companion'.
29 US has new paragraph here.
30 TS follows with an extra line break here.
31 **UK** put Campion quite; **TS** put <Fittleworth>↑Campion↓ **AR** quite; **US** put the general quite
   There is a question mark in the right-hand margin and the inserted 'Campion' is written in ink, which has smudged, and in what appears to be a different hand.
32 **UK, TS** weakened; **US** made an important concession
33 **UK, TS** intended; **US** wanted
34 **UK, TS** her; **US** its
35 **UK, TS** K; **US** "K"
36 **UK** it, too, over; **TS** it too over; **US** it over
37 **UK** towards her; he; **TS** towards ↑her↓; he **AR**; **US** towards doing so; he
38 **UK** th' Cahptn; **TS** th Cahptn; **US** the Cahptn
39 **UK, US** post and chain by; **TS** post ↑& chain↓ by **AR**
40 **UK, US** out and injuring itself caused; **TS** out ↑and injuring itself↓ caused
41 **UK, TS** before even; **US** even before
42 **UK** somewhere. ¶ With windfalls; **TS** somewhere. ¶ <No doubt>↑W↓<w>ith wind-falls; **US** somewhere. ¶ No doubt with windfalls
43 **UK** else. That was why there were so many of them here. She; **TS** else. ↑That was why there were so many of them here.↓ She **AR**; **US** else. She
44 **UK, US** Quatorze; **TS** Quinze
45 **UK, US** Mr. Pape; **TS** Mr <de Bray> Pape **AR**
46 **UK** had already pretty; **TS** had ↑already↓ pretty **AR**; **US** had pretty
47 **UK, TS** the de Bray Papes; **US** the Papes
48 **UK, TS** injure; **US** decry
49 **UK** discredit; **TS** injure; **US** decry
50 **UK, TS** temptations: it; **US** temptations—you may be excused if you succumb. It
51 **UK** Tietjenses; **TS** Tietjens's; **US** Tietjens'
52 **UK** Tietjenses; **TS** Tietjens's; **US** Tietjens'
53 **UK** change; people not so much; **TS** change; <probably they do>↑people↓ not ↑so↓ much **AR**; **US** change; probably people do not, much
54 TS has autograph insertions of the speech marks and the exclamation mark.
55 **UK, TS** Mr. Carter; **US** "Mr. Carter"
   US adopted to justify the word 'equally'; the quotation marks were presumably added to US at proof stage.
56 **UK** given her a; **TS** given ↑her↓ a **AR**; **US** given a
57 **UK, TS** and; **US** but
58 Fourth dot added in accordance with Duckworth's convention.
59 **UK** wicket towards; **TS** wicket <back> towards **AR**; **US** wicket back towards
60 **UK, TS** preliminary and; **US** preliminary measure and
61 **UK, TS** occasioning in her; **US** occasioning her
62 **UK** under the court's eyes, she was fading; **TS** under <her eyes> ↑the court's eyes↓ she was <dying> fading; **US** under the Court's eyes, she was now fading

63 **UK, TS** appear all; **US** appear in all
64 **UK** fiasco from Sylvia's point of view, and; **TS** fiasco ↑from Sylvia's point of view↓ and **AR**; **US** fiasco and
65 **UK** life she had; **TS** life <Sylvia> ↑she↓ had **AR**; **US** life Sylvia had
66 **UK, TS** trepidation; **US** fear
67 **UK, TS** it; **US** him
68 **UK, TS** herself—she; **US** herself as—she
69 **UK, TS** courts; immediately; **US** courts. Immediately
70 **UK** the other relatively; **TS, US** the relatively
71 **UK, TS** amiable saint's; **US** amiable Catholic saint's
72 **UK, TS** case, for surely; **US** case in which the saint of the other persuasion was involved. For surely
73 **UK, TS** on; **US** in
74 **UK** then, above and behind that, an; **TS** then <beside> ↑above and behind↓ that an; **US** then above and behind that an
75 **UK** beauty for—the dangerous remains of beauty!—if; **TS, US** beauty—the dangerous remains of beauty!—for if
76 **UK, TS** post before ... She; **US** post ... She
77 **UK, TS** woul; **US** would
US reading adopted: TS appears simple error, followed by UK.
78 **UK, TS** im, Gunning, isself when; **US** im. Gunning isself, when
The commas in TS are a little blotched but US has not registered any punctuation after 'Gunning' while inserting one after 'isself' where TS has nothing.
79 **UK, TS** is; **US** Is
US adopted to maintain consistency with previous line (and earlier instances in this chapter).
80 **US** begins new paragraph here.
81 **UK, TS** made a little clittering sound, like the trituration of barley ears, in her throat; **US** made in her throat a little clittering sound like the trituration of barley ears
82 **UK** half ....”; **TS** half ... B”; **US** half... !B”
TS appears a simple mistyping which US has followed while adding an exclamation mark.
83 **UK, TS** griping; **US** gripping
84 **UK, TS** Ground; **US** Grounds
85 **UK, TS** hoop; **US** loop
86 **UK, TS** I; **US** *I*
US reading adopted: context seems to require that emphasis.
87 **UK, TS** cut; **US** torn
88 **UK** Bosenheim; **US** Bosenheir
Terminal letter in TS is overtyped and ambiguous.

Textual Notes for II.iii

1 **UK, US** lettuce; **TS** lettice
2 **UK** of the lost coloured; **TS, US** of those coloured
3 **UK** those prints? ...; **TS** those prints ....; **US** those lost prints? ...
4 **UK, US** came; **TS** come

5 **UK, TS** would have! If; **US** would! If
6 This begins a new paragraph in US.
7 **UK** knew in what condition the other pair would be when; **TS** knew what condition the other pair would be when; **US** knew what condition the other pair would be in when
8 This begins a new paragraph in US.
9 **UK, TS** had had never the; **US** had never had the
10 **UK** before little Chrissie; **TS, US** before Chrissie
11 **UK** with, added; **TS** with added; **US** when, added
12 **UK, TS** other, the bottles; **US** other, there should be the bottles
13 **UK** had been ever rude; **TS, US** had ever been rude
   TS/US reading adopted to correct apparent compositing error.
14 **UK, TS** traces; **US** memories
15 **UK, TS** creature; **US** soldier boy
16 Apparently superfluous space in UK (but not US) after the third dot has been deleted.
17 **UK** by the by; **TS** by the bye; **US** bye the bye
18 **UK** Tietjenses; **TS, US** Tietjens's
19 **UK** A Gunning would be, in; **TS** A Gunning would be in; **US** Gunnings had been in
20 **UK, TS** Druid-worshipper, a; **US** Druid-worshipper, later, a
21 **UK, TS** his peccadilloes; **US** his blear-eyed peccadilloes
22 **UK, US** Barker of 1762 for; **TS** Barker ↑of 1762↓ for
23 **UK, US** Schatzweiler; **TS** Hartweiler
   While UK and US consistently have 'Schatzweiler', TS as consistently has 'Hartweiler'. The six later instances of 'Hartweiler' in this chapter have not been separately noted.
24 **UK** As it was.... ¶ The; **TS** As it was [TS omits ellipsis, encouraging US decision to run sentences into one another, and ends page here] ¶ The; **US** As it was the
25 **UK, TS** the; **US** that
   US adopted, seeming more definite than the definite article.
26 **UK** path; **US** paths
   The bottom right-hand section of TS leaf 177 is missing – apparently because the corner of the carbon paper was folded – so TS reading is not available.
27 **UK** she; **TS, US** *she*
   TS/US adopted, to clearly differentiate Valentine as speaker.
28 **UK** that Valentine; **TS, US** that she, Valentine,
29 **UK** knack; **TS, US** nack
30 **UK, TS** minutes; **US** minutes'
31 US follows with a new paragraph.
32 **UK** Chris, faced; **TS, US** Chris who was faced
33 **UK** gods, and had slammed; **TS** gods and has slammed; **US** gods and she had slammed
34 **UK, US** Marie Léonie for Mark to; **TS** Marie Leonie ↑for Mark↓ to
35 **UK** confer; **TS, US** confers
36 **UK, TS** and had; **US** and she had
37 **UK, TS** hedges. ¶ No; **US** hedges... in order to keep Christopher alive and sane! ¶ No
38 **UK, US** Tree. That; **TS** Tree and that would have been. That

39 **UK, TS** would have been to interfere; **US** would not have been jonnock.
   That would have been to interfere
40 **UK, TS** As; **US** Whilst
41 **UK, US** Lowther's; **TS** Luther's
42 This begins a new paragraph in US.
43 **UK, TS** frantically twisting at the; **US** frantically trying to twist the
44 **UK, TS** She was; **US** That lady was
45 **UK, TS** tall figure; **US** tall, thin, figure
46 **UK** This appeared; **TS, US** The figure appeared
47 This begins a new paragraph in US.
48 **UK, TS** There; **US** They
49 **UK, TS** light the; **US** light had been the
50 **UK, TS** that said; **US** that had said
51 **UK, TS** things; **US** clothes
   US revision probably due to the two uses of 'things' in the previous four lines.
52 **UK, TS** was desperately; **US** was also desperately
53 **UK, TS** she had; **US** she, Valentine, had
54 **UK, TS** They had gone on firing maroons; **US** Maroons had gone on firing
55 **UK** be heard!; **TS, US** hear!
56 **UK, US** never again do; **TS** never do
57 **UK** been that woman's son; **TS** been her son; **US** been Sylvia Tietjens' son
58 Missing suspension dot inserted, in line with Duckworth's own convention.
59 **UK** she, Valentine, to; **TS, US** she to
60 **UK, TS** father. She; **US** father? She
61 There is no terminal mark in UK; both TS and US end with an exclamation
   mark which is thus adopted.
62 Missing suspension dot inserted, in line with Duckworth's own convention.
63 **UK, US** In; **TS** On
64 **UK, TS** cheerfully how; **US** cheerfully on the telephone how
65 US follows with a new paragraph.
66 **UK, TS** could; **US** can
67 **UK** Kaator's; **TS, US** Kaators
   TS/US adopted to remove what seems a superfluous apostrophe.
68 **UK** Quatorze; **TS, US** Kaators
   TS/US adopted to maintain consistency with other instances.
69 **UK, TS** saleswoman but doubtless; **US** saleswoman, doubtless
70 **UK** téléphone; **TS, US** telephone
71 **UK** déjà téléphoné; **TS** deja telephoné; **US** dêja telephone
72 **UK** côté; **TS** cote; **US** coté
73 **UK** moi!" ... I beg you to remain beside mé! Selfish!; **TS** moi!" Selfish!; **US**
   moi!" ... "I beg you to remain beside me!" Selfish!
74 **UK** Sylvia Tietjens was; **TS** She was; **US** Sylvia was
75 **UK, TS** grands seigneurs; **US** *grands seigneurs*
76 **UK, TS** She; **US** Sylvia
77 **UK, TS** for it was like a statue.... Marvellous; **US** For it was more like a
   statue than a human being.... Marvellous
78 **UK, TS** been a mush! ... It; **TS** been... It; **US** been all ... be-blubbered! It
79 **UK, TS** she had ever seen; **US** she had seen
80 US omits ellipsis and begins new paragraph here.
81 US begins another new paragraph here.

82 **UK** began the Billingsgate that they were both going to indulge in before all these people? ... For; **TS** began the Billingsgate that they were ↑both↓ going to indulge in ↑before all these people↓ .... For **AR**; **US** began upon the Billingsgate they would both have to use before they parted? ... For

83 **US** begins a new paragraph here.

84 **UK, TS** kind ... how; **US** kind—how

85 **UK, TS** When the lips had approached her mother's cheek the; **US** Those lips had approached her mother's cheeks and the

86 **UK, TS** it, it might; **US** it all, she might

87 **UK, TS** There would have been no Christopher to-day but for her! ¶ It; **US** But for her there would have been no Christopher. ¶ *You must not say Damn it all. The war is over* ... Ah, but its backwashes, when would *they* be over? ¶ It

88 **UK, TS** said—it was; **US** said—that woman's voice was

89 **UK, TS** continue to; **US** continue appropriately to

90 **UK, TS** and without halt,; **US** [omits these words]

91 **UK, US** hear! The lady of the house does; **TS** hear! Mrs Tietjens does

92 **UK, TS** Pape was explaining; **US** Pape had been explaining

93 **UK** Louie Kaator's; **TS** Looie Kaators; **US** Louis Quatorze
    TS adopted to maintain consistency with earlier instances.

94 **UK, TS** she had been telling the saleswoman that she intended to refurnish Groby in the Louie Kaator's style; **US** she intended re-furnishing Groby in the Louis Quatorze style

95 **UK, TS** comicalities: Marie Léonie did not know that woman; Mrs. de Bray Pape did not know her, Valentine, They; **US** comicalities. Mrs. de Bray Pape did not know her, Valentine. Marie Léonie did not know who that figure was. ¶ They

96 **UK, TS** the jam! ... But where was the jam! [**TS** has 'jam?'] Jam yesterday, jam to-morrow.... [**TS** has 'tomorrow.....'] That figure had said "Mrs, Tietjens!" In sarcasm, then? In delicacy? ¶ She; **US** the jam.... Jam to-morrow, jam yesterday.... Where was the jam? ... That figure had said "The lady of the house." Delicately. *Quelle delicatesse!* ¶ But she did not appear denunciatory. She dropped sideways: pensive. Puzzled. As if at the ways of God. As if stricken by God and puzzled at his ways.... Well, she might be. ¶ She

97 **UK, TS** shelf; it was dark. The baby had; **US** shelf. The child had

98 **UK, TS** called "Mrs. Tietjens!" Someone; **US** called Mrs. Tietjens in its own house. This woman stood in the way. She could not give a father's name to the little thing. So he protested within her. Dark it was growing. Hold up there. ¶ Someone

99 **UK** calling "Valentine!" Someone else was calling "Mother!" A softer voice said: "Mrs. Tietjens!" What things they chose to say! The first voice was Edith Ethel's! ¶ Dark! ... Marie; **TS** calling "Valentine!" Someone else was calling "Mother!" A softer voice said: "Mrs. Tietjens!" The first voice was Edith Ethel's! ¶ Dark! Marie; **US** "Valentine!" ¶ A boy's voice called: ¶ "Mother! Mother!" ¶ A soft voice said: ¶ "Mrs. Tietjens!" ¶ What things to say in her child's hearing! ... Mother! Mother! ... Her mother was in Pontresina, complete with secretary in black alpaca.... The Italian Alps! ¶ Dark! ... Marie

100 **UK** reading to Mrs. de Bray Pape from a letter. She; **US, TS** reading from a letter to Mrs. de Bray Pape. She

101 **UK** door. He turned to say to her oddly: ¶ "*Madame* ... eh ... Tietjens! Par*don!*" **TS** door. <He produced oddly, a telegram and came back to hand it to her>. He <said>↑turned to say to her,↓ oddly <interrogative[?]¶ Madame Tietjens [?]>: "↑Madame ... eh... Tietjens!↓ Par*don!*" **US** door. He said to Valentine oddly interrogative: ¶ "Mrs.... eh Tietjens!" And then: "Par*don!*"

102 US begins a new paragraph here.

103 **UK** accent. ¶ Edith; **US** accent. ¶ Edith **TS** accent./ <Christopher was killed in an aeroplane ... No. [?] instalment nine hundred cabled bank! ... They would be able to have ... Oh, innumerable[?] things.> ¶ Edith

104 Missing suspension dot inserted, in line with Duckworth's own convention.

105 **UK** her! It said drily: ¶ "An the King will ha'e my heid I carena what ye do wi' my ..." It was a saying common to both Mark and Christopher ... That was bitter. She was reminding her, Valentine, that she had previously enjoyed Tietjens' intimacies—before her, Valentine! ¶ But the voice went on: ¶ "I; **TS** her! ¶ It said: ¶ "I; **US** her! ¶ The bitter answer came to her as if from stiff lips: ¶ "An the King will have my head I carena what he may do with my ..." ¶ It affected Valentine disagreeably—with a pang of jealousy. What it amounted to was that Sylvia said: "You have my man, so you may as well have his name." But by using a saying that Christopher used habitually—and that Mark had used habitually when he could speak—by using then a Tietjens family saying she asserted that she too had belonged to the Tietjens family, and, before Valentine, had been intimate with their sayings to the point of saturation. ¶ That statue went on speaking. ¶ It said: ¶ "I

106 **UK** Be; **TS, US** But

107 **UK, US** to; **TS** the

108 **UK** another .... Their littleness .... The riding has done it ...." Someone; **TS** another .... It's the littleness .... It's the riding has done it .... I'm a poor bitch ...." Someone; **US** another .... with its littleness .... It's the riding has done it ...." Someone

109 US begins a new paragraph here.

110 Superfluous suspension dot deleted, in line with Duckworth's own convention.

111 **UK** Christopher. He would have, nevertheless, to go to Hudnut's: Gunning; **TS** Christopher. <But> He would have ↑nevertheless↓ to go to Hudnut's, Gunning **AR**; **US** Christopher. But he would have to go to Hudnut's, Gunning

112 **UK** deux telles passions dans deux telles femmes; **TS** deux passion dans deux femmes; **US** deux passions pareilles dans deux femmes

113 **UK** There was no Sylvia Tietjens. They; **US** Sylvia Tietjens was gone. They
TS has lost part of the typed line due to the blank space in the carbon copy. 'There was no' has been written in before the typed 'Sylvia'. The initial typed 'T' has had to be supplemented by autograph 'ietjens.'

114 **UK** onto the ground, lumpishly! ¶ ... It; **TS** ont↑o the ground. Lumpishly!↓ **AR** ¶ ... It; **US** onto the floor. Lumpishly.... It
The words and phrases written into this three-line paragraph occur where no carbon copy seems to have been produced, though there are no signif-

icant differences from UK.

115 **UK** They must have some money; **TS** They had some money; **US** They had no money

Textual Notes for II.iv

1 **UK** hedgegrows; **TS, US** hedgerows
UK misprint corrected in line with TS and US.

2 **UK** would be nevertheless long; **TS** would nevertheless long; **US** would nevertheless be long

3 **UK** S-t-o-a-t; **TS, US** S . . t . . o . . at

4 **UK** The painted background had shewn Bamborough; **TS** The background had been Bamborough; **US** The painted background had been Bamborough
Both UK and US have the helpful addition of 'painted' but this is the only instance of UK using this spelling of 'show', having consistently emended the TS versions to 'show' or 'shown'. This suggests that Ford added the word in proof, finding 'been' a little inert, and that the UK compositor did not notice the anomaly. I have, though, left UK unaltered.

5 **UK** Middlesbrough; **TS, US** Middlesboro

6 **UK, US** Yes, nightingales made; **TS** Yes, <they> ↑nightingales↓ made

7 **UK** to learn them; **TS** to <teach> ↑learn↓ them **AR**; **US** to teach them

8 **UK** child within her.... ¶ He; **TS, US** child .... ¶ He

9 **UK, US** pitch; **US** extreme

10 **UK** Tietjenses; **TS, US** Tietjens's

11 **UK, TS** Ruggles sharing; **US** Ruggles years ago sharing

12 **UK, TS** he remembered that, just; **US** he had remembered ... just

13 **UK, TS** would; **US** need

14 These two sentences within quotation marks in US only.

15 All three witnesses have 'ghostly': possibly 'ghastly'?

16 **UK** ghostly so to; **TS, US** ghostly to

17 **UK** Still, with; **TS** Still, <not,>with; **US** Still, not, with

18 **UK** racing-glasses, not an; **TS** racing-glasses, ↑not↓ an **AR**; **US** racing-glasses, an

19 **UK** chest if you could think there had been none. He; **TS** chest ↑if you could think there had been none↓. He **AR**; **US** chest. He

20 **UK, TS** case, with; **US** case of stuffed birds with

21 **UK** chimneys; **TS, US** chimnies

22 **UK, TS** sand-pipers; **US** sandpipers
TS hyphenated due to a line-ending and UK followed this; US reading has been preferred here.

23 **UK, TS** now; **US** not

24 **UK, US** Garden ... In white! ... Doing; **TS** Garden ... ↑In white! ... ↓ Doing

25 **UK** that he was; **TS** that <this> ↑he↓ was **AR**; **US** that this was

26 **UK, US** a woman older than; **TS** an older woman than

27 **UK, TS** the garden and to be remonstrating with these people. What; **US** the orchard. What

28 **UK, TS** looking beside; **US** looking from beside

29 **UK, US** troubled to come. Fittleworth; **TS** troubled. Fittleworth

30 **UK,** ladyship down.... ¶ Damn; **US** ladyship down. ¶ Damn; **TS** ladyship..... ¶ Damn

31 **UK, TS** Fittleworth's; **US** Fittleworths'
US reading has been adopted here to correct obvious error.

32 US concludes the previous sentence with an exclamation mark and ellipsis and begins new paragraph here.

33 **UK** that Sylvia—Sylvia Tietjens—*begged*; **TS** that Sylvia *begged*; **US** that his sister-in-law, Sylvia, *begged*

34 **UK** do.... Because of Mark's unforgettable services to the nation....; **TS** do... And because of Mark's unforgettable services....; **US** do.... And because of Mark's unforgettable services to the country....

35 TS precedes with handwritten deletion of second, superfluous ellipsis; the resultant space has been read as signalling a new paragraph in UK, followed in US. TS reading has been restored.

36 **UK, US** begged Fittleworth to; **TS** begged <him> ↑Fittleworth↓ to

37 **UK** friend! ¶ The clubs they had been in together.... But; **TS** friend! [The clubs that they had been in together... But; **US** friend! The clubs they had been in together! ... ¶ But

38 **UK, TS** Mark said. ¶ He; **US** Mark said to himself. ¶ He
US reading adopted, to make clear that Mark has not yet spoken aloud.

39 **UK, US** He whispered:; **TS** He whispered: ¶ "Remember Christopher is half a saint... Of the Anglican persuasions!" ¶ He whispered:

40 **UK** thy child weep for; **TS** thy barny grat for; **US** thy barny weep for
TS to US to UK shows a consistent process of clarifying; clearly, Ford did not want to risk puzzling the reader with a dialect word at this climactic moment.

41 **UK** thy good man .... A good man! Groby; **TS** thy man .... Groby; **US** thy goodman .... A good man! Groby
In TS, 'thy man' is, rhythmically, very unsatisfactory; US 'goodman' is adopted because more appropriate: *OED* refers to the form as 'archaic' and 'Scottish', both of which seem right, as does its use by Sir Walter Scott.

42 US begins new paragraph here.

43 **UK, TS** his hand; **US** his hot hand

44 **UK, US** a torturing afternoon; **TS** a torture of an afternoon

45 **UK, TS** sideways; **US** down

46 **UK, TS** would like to have had his; **US** would have liked to have his

47 These words do not appear in the typescript, but at the bottom of the last page is written: 'Printed in Great Britain at the Chapel River Press Kingston Surrey', with the proof instruction: 'ital'.

48 **UK** PARIS, *7th June*–AVIGNON, *1st August*–ST. LAWRENCE RIVER, *24th September*- NEW YORK, *12th November*.–MCMXXVII.; **US** PARIS 7th July—AVIGNON & S. S. MINNEDOSA—NEW YORK 2d NOVEMBER 1927
Dates are not noted on TS.

APPENDIX

This appendix concerns the 47 typewritten leaves preserved separately from the bulk typescript of 200 leaves that corresponds to the published text of the novel. They have been numbered in pencil in the bottom right-hand corner by the librarian or archivist and, since the typed numbers at the top right-hand corners of these leaves are often duplicated and not always strictly sequential, I shall refer to the librarian's pencilled numbers for the sake of clarity.

Two brief sequences bookend the more substantial sections. The first two leaves (1–2) duplicate leaves 129a and 131 in the main typescript and correspond to the end of I.vii in the published text, from 'just before seemed to have a good deal of temperature' to the chapter's conclusion ('that young couple'), while the final four leaves (44–7) duplicate leaves 160–3 in the main typescript and correspond to part of II.ii in the published text, from 'For it came back to her with sudden extraordinary clearness' to 'as if strength had gone out from her': Sylvia's recollections first of the incident with the gardener when she was a girl and then of the court case.

The second section begins with a title leaf (3), 'LAST POST/ Part II.' but the first eight leaves correspond to the opening of II.i in the published volume, though the last leaf (11) contains only four lines on the page and ends in mid-sentence. The following thirteen leaves (12–24) begin mid-sentence and continue that material though perhaps three or four lines are missing at the point of juncture. These 21 leaves (4–24) lack a good many of the revisions made on the primary typescript that have found their way into UK.

There follow ten leaves that comprise two copies each of five leaves (25–34), followed by three copies of a sixth leaf (35–7). The five leaves (or pairs of leaves) show practically no revisions, and those few are typewritten. The second of the three copies of the sixth leaf has the equivalent of three complete lines erased by hand and three other autograph emendations. Then follow two copies of the next leaf (38–9), two single leaves (40, 41) and two copies of the final leaf (42–3) in the sequence, the second half of which is a variant of the first half of leaf 40.

This section is the only material from these leaves that was excluded from the published novel and follows on from the separation of Campion and Fittleworth from Sylvia (II.ii). While UK remains with Sylvia, this section leaves her fairly abruptly and remains with the two men.

We don't know why Ford cut this section but there were two likely reasons. Firstly, Fittleworth might emerge as an implausibly admirable feudal figure, a landlord remarkably concerned with the well-being of his tenants and neighbours, verging indeed on the figures in Tietjens' good-humoured reflections in *No More Parades* I.iv on his official religion: God the great English landowner, Christ 'an almost too benevolent land steward [. . .] knowing all about the estate down to the last child at the porter's lodge'. Secondly, Fittleworth's change of heart, his readiness to criticise not only Campion but Sylvia too, his willingness to defend Christopher even to the point of using his own and his wife's influence to damage Campion's prospects of 'getting' India – all this would throw out the balance of the book, the tensions of it, and would radically undermine another 'change of heart': Sylvia's. She has been, already and quite plausibly, unsettled by Fittleworth whom she cannot 'read', whose motives (and values) she cannot grasp. This is a significant factor in her retreat, but the two primary ones must, I think, remain a general weariness, a reluctant recognition that her world is waning; and the religious aspect of that change of heart, her 'vision' of Father Consett already prepared for and her adherence (however fitful and idiosyncratic) to her faith well established. The inclusion of this material would, in short, have made it too easy for Christopher, and he must go on as he is now – always with that rather abstracted expression, a little worried, a little fatigued, 'since the salvation of a world is a large order'.

Ford's typing has been faithfully reproduced, including the varying number of dots in his ellipses. Textual indications of

inserted or deleted text follow the conventions established in the
main text. Numerals indicate the divisions of the TS leaves.

[25–6] His Lordship said that, damn it, that was just what it was.
If that fellow was the sort of fellow Mrs Tietjens said he was her
Ladyship would properly curl his, Lord Fittleworth's whiskers, for
letting Helen go down into that sink of iniquity.

Sylvia, whilst the general choked, said that as she herself
intended to descend into that dangerous vicinity she did not see
why Helen Luther should not. She presumed the young woman
could look after herself.

Fittleworth said that it was not that. The general exclaimed:

"Surely you would not....." but his voice lost itself in other
noises made by his agitated throat.

Fittleworth exclaimed:

"Damn it all this fellow Gunning would wear out the patience
of ...." He beckoned the general towards him with his crop
handle. Their horses, relieved to be out of the neighbourhood of
Sylvia Tietjens' chestnut minced gently along the road. "This
fellow Gunning...." his Lordship began.... He continued with
great animation: "About these gates.... You know my estate
carpenter repairs all the gates in my country. Independent of
whether they are on my or my tenents' [sic] lands or any other
fellow's.... Hang it, your confounded nephew – godson – whatever he is to you.... Is he a Bolshevik...What the hell is he? He
appears to be like everybody else...."

He broke off because his horse jolted three paces in advance.
When the general caught him up he said:

"And a pretty penny repairing these blasted fellows' blasted
gates stands me in...." He added that he did not care whether
Christopher Tietjens was a Bolshevik or anything else. He did
not pretend to look after his tenents' [sic] morals or politics or
anyone else's in his district. But he did look after their unting. He
said unting always in reference to Mr Jorrocks[1] just as he said that

---

1   Jorrocks appears in several works by R.S. Surtees and probably influenced Dickens in
    his creation of *The Pickwick Papers*. *Jorrocks's Jaunts and Jollities* (collected edition
    1838) was followed by *Handley Cross* (1843) and *Hillingdon Hall* (1845).

his countess would curl his whiskers, although he wore no
whiskers. His father however had used that expression and had
worn whiskers. He took [27–8] in fact from tadition [sic] what he
wanted to take from tradition. His father had always objected to
gates that bumped the behinds as he called it of lady riders' horses
after they had gone through. A gate should not swing to in a
hunting country. His lordship paid an army of earth-stoppers, foot
huntsmen, spare-horse-men and fellows that looked like tramps.
They had to see that all field-gates were closed after members of
the hunt had gone through. The tenants' beasts of course must
not get out.

But that blasted cunning fellow Gunning would make all his
master's field- and path-gates cant inwards; so they swung to. And
made the latches difficult to lift with a crop. Latches ought to
open at a touch and gates to stand as they swung. And there were
more paths going through Tietjens' fields and timber than on any
other blasted place in our [sic] out of the estate...Of course gates
must be kept shut...But that fellow went round after the estate
carpenter and canted all the gateposts inwards, ramming stakes
down beside them. And wedged up the latches .... His Lordship
went on and on. Suddenly however he exclaimed:

"But all that does not make this confounded fellow – Mark's
brother – I mean, necessarily a Bolshevik...Damn it all what does
it all mean, Campion?"

The general said he would be confounded if he knew. Sylvia
said now one thing, now another, the one completely contra-
dicting the other. Of course she was justified in saying anything
she liked: she had been atrociously treated. But it made the issues
confused...Look at how atrocious it was of that fellow to get his
brother to buy property in just the neighbourhood that Sylvia
desired to frequent, considering her <intimacy> friendship with
the Fittleworths.

Fittleworth said:

"Stop there, you know. Mrs Tietjens never honoured me with
much of her friendship till her husband bought this place. It was
her husband bought the place, not old Mark. Old Mark has stayed
with me often enough and glad we always were to have him. But
Mrs Tietjens never, till lately. It was old Mark, [29–30] as far as
I understand it who put his brother up to buying the place. I

would not have sold to anyone else. I am not under the necessity of selling my land. But an outlying piece – to <satisfy> oblige an old friend. I don't mind that. So now you know."

The general said:

"Damn it all, Fittleworth, what do I know? .... What can any body know?"

The two old gentlemen rgarded [sic] each other like well-bred dogs. They were not friends. The general considered that the earl was not doing his duty by the country because he did not <atke an avtive> ↑take an active↓ part in politics on the part of the government that should make him commander in chief of the forces in the country of Hyder Ali.[2] The earl considered that, according to the traditions of his House a peer should not take an active part in politics. The earl therefore considered that the general, the son of a peer, was importunate: the general considered the earl as, if nota [sic] traitor to his extate [sic], then at least indifferent to the interest of his order.

But if they were not friends at least they did not snarl. They were of the same order if holding different views. They both considered, for instance, that a gentleman does not mix his liquors. You should not drink brandy after beer or whiskey after wine. As long as you do not do that and as long as you take a cold bath in the morning you are all right.

The general said:

"No, I do not suppose that my godson Christopher is a Bolshevist.... The awkward – the damnable – thing for a godson of mine is that, according to Sylvia, he seems to model himself after...after Jesus Christ, in short."

The earl regarded the immense view, a great part of which he owned. It spread out beneath their eyes under the hedgerow – at first the great copses and spinneys of beech, then plantations of fir, then ploughlands with farms at the intersections of hedgerows, then rolling country – four counties, ending in gentle undulations and purple hills.

[31–2] The earl regarded the view. The general exploded suddenly into extraordinary blasphemy at the thought that his

---

2   Hyder (or Haider) Ali was a soldier and ruler of Mysore in the late eighteenth century who waged war against the British.

godson should desire the Redeemer to be his model. He desired
to give all his goods to the poor – something of that sort. In the
name of God what was to become of the country if ......

The Earl pointed the stag-horn handle of his crook [sic] at a
square-towered church three miles away in the blue-grey woods.

"Well," he said, "What <u>is</u> to become of the country? I don't
know. All this is my country. But who's the deuce it will be after
me, God knows...."

"But to model yourself.....", the general exclaimed.

"You might do worse," his interlocutor asserted tentatively.
"Didn't someone say.... Our Lord, I daresay, say 'And he had
great possessions' ... I tell you they worry you out of your life. I'm
sometimes thankful Cammy has no children."

"But what", the General exclaimed, "is to become of the
country? How are we to save India and the Colonies?"

The Earl removed his eyes from the view and fixed them darkly
on the man beside him.

"I'm damned if I know", he said, "and I don't know that I'm
not damned if I care. The country – this land – is much what it
was when my grandfather owned. If he got up out of the grave
and came to look at it ↑he↓ would not see much difference. Nor
his grandfather before him. Nor his. Nor the Poindestres before
them......"3

"But if the right people", the general maintained, "are giving
up the job, what is to become of the country? What? What in the
name of the Almighty? For that's what is damnable. Sylvia says
that this degenerate oaf of a nephew [sic] of mine refuses – <u>refuses</u>,
mind you – to own or look after Groby. Do you know what Groby
is? You could put your place in a corner of it and not find it. And
they're chopping down the trees. And they won't let me have the
[33–4] Dower House for my hunting box.... Well, then?"

"Doesn't it occur to you", the peer said, "that they may not be
the right persons to look after property? I don't know. If old Mark
chooses to run an Agapemone at the age of sixty five – He's much
the same age as myself – I don't see why he should not.4 But you

3 Ford's 'The Old Story' (Cornell), probably an early version of *The Nature of a Crime*,
   has a narrator called Ambrose Poindestre (information from Max Saunders, who
   mentions the story in *Dual Life* I 212).

4 The internal evidence of the novel suggests that Mark is no more than fifty-five; see
   the Introduction.

cannot run a great estate on those terms. The right sort of person
to possess an estate is the right sort of person to run it. I daresay
I am: at any rate I have done it for a long time and no
complaints..... If your godson does not consider himself to be the
proper person to run his estate it is damn creditable of him if he
does not. And for the matter of that he seems to be a pretty creditable sort of person. At any rate he's a marvellous hand with a
horse. I asked him as a favour to take in the Countess's Flora for
a week and she was not the same mare afterwards."

The general exclaimed:

"Creditable! That fellow! My God, if Sylvia heard you!"

Lord Fittleworth said:

"That's all I have to say about it. It does not interest me much.
These people are here. They have a right to be. The Countess has
left cards on old Mark and his wife and Lady Mark left cards on
us. She same [sic] to a garden party when it was mostly tenants.
A fine woman. A damn fine woman; French and no worse for
that. And that's that. Live and let live is my motto. And
Cammie's. I daresay Cammie would leave cards on your godson's
light of love, if she saw her way to it...But that's different from
liking Helen Luther to go down there. American's [sic] apparently
ain't like us. Cammie would be afraid of what her connections
would say to her if they knew!"

[TS has line break here]

The general exclaimed:

"Hang it all. It's incomprehensible to me. There you are, a
great landowner; a man of the old school. I remember your father.
And you are as [35–7; two of the three copies of this leaf have no
emendations; the emended page is the one transcribed] indifferent to the well-being of your inferiors....."

Fittleworth said:

"Hang it all, Campion, if it comes to well-being how can I tell
they mayn't know as well or better than I what's good for them?
No, my motto is Never interfere and never interfere it will
continue to be. Besides: what do you want me to do?"

The general shook his head. He did not know. He would be
hanged if he knew.

"Dnounce [sic] your godson to the police? As a Bolshevik? In
order to gratify Sylvia <by making that girl have a miscarriage at

the visit of the police **AR**>? I'm not so green. Besides, old Mark has a stake in the country too. You say yourself he's a greater stake than me! And he<'s> ↑was always↓ a damn sight more of a public figure than I <am>. The police would <a deal sight> more likely listen to him than to me. I never made a speech but once in the House of Lords and then it was about Foot and Mouth Disease and I broke down because my language pained the Lord Chancellor. He looked like a cat that had swallowed a glass of lemon-juice, old Halsbury on the Woolsack....[5] All the same you are bound to have foot and mouth disease <o>↑i↓f you let Canadian cattle in alive. And there's an end of hunting, for I'm as ready to admit as any man that you can't have hounds running through tainted country.

The general said:

<"The country is going to the dogs anyhow if you have this sort of thing going on. Hang it all **AR**> ↑"↓If a bankrupt, discredited fellow like that is to be allowed to settle down in peace. In open sin! With the daughter of his father's best friend. Getting bastards and ...."

"Oh damn it, Campion", Fittleworth grinned, ↑with sudden fury **AR**↓ "You've trodden on the wrong toe this time. The country's all right if that's all that's wrong with it. Wasn't my own grandfather a bastard? And didn't William IV give the peerage to him to please his father who was the eleventh earl of the old line? You've come to the wrong shop to talk of that. The wrong shop! If I [38–9] could divert the peerage and the settled estates from that idle devil Wentworth to my Harry – and no offence to Cammie because she's no children – do you suppose I wouldn't do it.... No, you've come to the wrong shop. . ."

His lordship was quivering with anger. He thought slowly, but with passion.

"The whole thing," he said, "your whole confounded show is on a wrong basis. I don't know that I approve of selling all your goods and giving them to the poor. I shouldn't do it myself – but Our Lord recommends the course and I have not gone every Sunday to service in that church there – every Sunday morning,

---

5 Hardinge Giffard (1823–1921) was created Baron Halsbury in 1885 and appointed Lord Chancellor. He held the position again from 1886–92 and from 1895–1905.

child and boy and man for sixty years and then to deny that our
Lord is a good chap to follow, heaven help me. You've overshot
the mark and I'd advise you – you are nearly as old as I and ought
to have learnt some wisdom – I'd advise you to retrace your steps.
You're so damn under the thumb of Sylvia that you have lost all
sense of.... of..... proportion. I'd advise you to use all the influence you have with her to stop this show. Now. Here!" He
stopped to shorten his reins. The general stoutly maintained:
    "Sylvia has been damn badly used. That fellow...."
Fittleworth's horse tried on a little fit of impatience at the
waiting. The peer had to readjust his hat so he lost his train of
thought. He began upon another.
    "I've been damn in the wrong myself", he said. "Damnably! If
what you say is true.... And it is.... this Tietjens fellow is as much
a great landowner as myself. He's my equal and we ought to stand
together. You can't get away from that, you who are always blat-
ting about duty to your class. Then I have been wanting in my
duty. If that fellow chooses – does me the honour – to settle on
my land it's my duty to see that he lives in peace with his doxy
and all. He may not choose to spaffle his money but that does not
make him any less Tietjens of Groby to all intents and purposes
because old Mark's done for.... Then it's been damnably wanting
in hospitality in me to let Sylvia come down here and pin-prick
these people. That's what it's been and you know it.
    [40] "You mean," the general said with a certain stiffness, "that
we are not welcome...MY godson's wife and I are not welcome.
I may say that I approve of all her actions...." He was at that
moment Lord Edward Campion, Lieutenant General, M.P. and
so on.
    "Then I should advise you to give up approving, damn sharp!"
the Earl said. "Your welcome here is sound enough. Her ladyship
likes Sylvia or she would not be here. So do I. But it's time Sylvia
dropped it. I did not understand the lay of the land. Now I begin
to.... Well, you take a friendly word while it's still friendly. You
want India and you will be a damn good man in India. But you
stop monkeying between that man and his wife or you will burn
your fingers so you will not be able to sign G.O.C.i.C's Orders."
    Campion's moustache stood up; his mouth opened; he leaned
right back in his saddle, extending his stirrups to the full forward

cock of his legs.

He said:

"Excuse me Fittleworth, you're speaking as...."

"I'm speaking" Fittleworth said, "as myself. But I'm voicing a whole lot of people. I'll tell you the way Lady Fittleworth sees it – since last night. That fellow – the younger brother – has taken his punishment. There's every symptom that he wants to marry that gal. It's you who stop him – for the fun of the thing. You've dragged him through every sort of mud, private and public. . Well, that's his affair. But this is mine – and Cammie's. I'm not one to mince matters. As for her Ladyship she's straighter than I. She <will> can make more fuss in the Lord Chamberlain's Office.... say in the Lord Chamberlain's Office...You understand what I mean...."

The general began to grow white round the nostrils.

"This appears to be a threat, Fittleworth," he said.

"It means," Fittleworth said, "that if you and Sylvia do not stop tormenting those people while you are under my roof – and when you're elsewhere – Cammie will ask Sylvia to pack her bags. And it means that Lady Fittleworth will use [41] all her influence...And mine. . In say the Office...."

His Lordship who had begun to speak with harsh emotion here exclaimed:

"What the devil's that?"

A singular, varnished, black basket work chaise had approached them, emerging from the shadow of high beeches along the road. It contained a thin, graceful widow in extraordinarily deep weeds, who drove, a singularly emaciated man in a high silk hat, who wore a beard of a curly kind that singularly did not become him, and a hatless, very young man whose hair curled. Its slow progress was occasioned by a too obese cob whose skin and harness nevertheless shone.

The general said:

"I've hitherto regarded myself as the champion...." Fittleworth drew his horse alongside the hedge, but the pony-chaise stopped.

The emaciated man exclaimed:

"You would singularly oblige us, Lord Fittleworth, if you would assist us to get to Mark Tietjens'" He held his top-hatted head on one side and used his jaws with the air of a magpie that was eating something distasteful.

Fittleworth pointed with his crop.

"Tietjens' place is down there," he said, "But you won't be able to do much with him. I seem to know you."

"This," His interlocutor said, "is Lady Duchemin [?]" His voice took on an additional tone of distaste: "This is Mr Redfern, the poet...I myself am Ruggles...of the ...in short of the Lord Chamberlain's Office!"

[42–3] It's all right for a woman to avenge her wrongs: but only within limits. If a man of our class – your's too if you like though your father made his money in beer! – if a man of our class chooses not to live with his wife he doesn't and who's to interfere? He isn't anybody's <[tenant]> so his landlord can't. Nor yet the Archbishop of Canterbury, So his wife has to lump it. That's the way of our class and chance it. It's the way of old Gunning's class to [sic]: I don't know about the middle classes." [The remainder of this leaf repeats in part the beginning of leaf 40 but with certain differences]

"You mean," the general said with a certain stiffness, "that we are not welcome.... My godson's wife and I are not welcome....."

"Oh, damn it all your welcome is sound enough. Cammie likes Sylvia <well enough> or she would not be here. So do I. But it's time she dropped it. I didn't understand the lay of the <old> land. Now I do.... And let me tell you this, Campion. You want India and you will be a damn good man in India. But you stop monkeying between man and wife or you will burn your fingers so you won't be able to sign Orders.... And there's another thing [TS ends here]

SELECT BIBLIOGRAPHY

Works by Ford (whether as 'Hueffer' or 'Ford')

Ancient Lights and Certain New Reflections: Being the Memories of a Young Man (London: Chapman & Hall, 1911); published as *Memories and Impressions* (New York: Harper, 1911)

Between St. Dennis and St. George (London: Hodder & Stoughton, 1915)

A Call (1910) (Manchester: Carcanet, 1984)

The Cinque Ports (Edinburgh and London: William Blackwood and Sons, 1900)

The Correspondence of Ford Madox Ford and Stella Bowen, ed. Sondra J. Stang and Karen Cochran (Bloomington and Indianapolis: Indiana University Press, 1994)

Critical Essays, ed. Max Saunders and Richard Stang (Manchester: Carcanet, 2002)

Critical Writings, ed. Frank MacShane (Lincoln, NE: University of Nebraska Press, 1964)

England and the English, ed. Sara Haslam (Manchester: Carcanet, 2003) (collecting Ford's trilogy on Englishness with *The Heart of the Country* and *The Spirit of the People*)

The English Novel from the Earliest Days to the Death of Joseph Conrad (Manchester: Carcanet, 1983 [1930])

The Fifth Queen (London: Alston Rivers, 1906)

The Fifth Queen Crowned (Eveleigh Nash, 1908)

The Ford Madox Ford Reader, with Foreword by Graham Greene; ed. Sondra J. Stang (Manchester: Carcanet, 1986)

The Good Soldier, ed. Martin Stannard (Norton Critical Edition; New York and London: W. W. Norton & Company, 1995)

Great Trade Route (London: Allen & Unwin, 1937)

The Heart of the Country (London: Alston Rivers, 1906)

Henry James: A Critical Study (London: Martin Secker, 1914)

A History of Our Own Times, ed. Solon Beinfeld and Sondra J. Stang (Manchester: Carcanet, 1989)

'A House (Modern Morality Play)', *The Chapbook*, 21, March 1921 (London: The Poetry Bookshop, 1921)

It Was the Nightingale (1933), ed. John Coyle (Manchester: Carcanet, 2007)

Joseph Conrad: A Personal Remembrance (London: Duckworth, 1924)

Last Post (London: Duckworth, 1928) – the fourth and final novel of *Parade's End*

Letters of Ford Madox Ford, ed. Richard M. Ludwig (Princeton, NJ: Princeton University Press, 1965)

A Little Less Than Gods (London: Duckworth, 1928)

A Man Could Stand Up – (London: Duckworth, 1926) – the third novel of *Parade's End*

The March of Literature (London: Allen & Unwin, 1939)

The Marsden Case (London: Duckworth, 1923)

Mightier Than the Sword (London: Allen & Unwin, 1938)

A Mirror to France (London: Duckworth, 1926)

Mister Bosphorus and the Muses or a Short History of Poetry in Britain. Variety Entertainment in Four Acts... with Harlequinade, Transformation Scene, Cinematograph Effects, and Many Other Novelties, as well as Old and Tried Favourites, illustrated by Paul Nash (London: Duckworth, 1923)

New York Essays (New York: William Edwin Rudge, 1927)

No More Parades (London: Duckworth, 1925) – the second novel of *Parade's End*

No Enemy (1929), ed. Paul Skinner (Manchester: Carcanet, 2002)

On Heaven and Poems Written on Active Service, The Bodley Head (London: John Lane, 1918)

The Panel: A Sheer Comedy (London: Constable, 1912)

Portraits from Life (Boston and New York: Houghton Mifflin, 1937)

Pound/Ford: the Story of a Literary Friendship: the Correspondence between Ezra Pound and Ford Madox Ford and Their Writings About Each Other, ed. Brita Lindberg-Seyersted (London: Faber & Faber, 1982)

Privy Seal (London: Alston Rivers, 1907)

Provence: From Minstrels to Machine (1935), ed. John Coyle (Manchester: Carcanet, 2009)

Return to Yesterday (1931), ed. Bill Hutchings (Manchester: Carcanet, 1999)

Selected Poems, ed. Max Saunders (Manchester: Carcanet, 1997)

Some Do Not ... (London: Duckworth, 1924) – the first novel of *Parade's End*

The Spirit of the People (London: Alston Rivers, 1907)

Thus to Revisit: Some Reminiscences (London: Chapman & Hall, 1921)

War Prose, ed. Max Saunders (Manchester: Carcanet, 1999)
When Blood is Their Argument (London: Hodder & Stoughton, 1915)
When the Wicked Man (London: Jonathan Cape, 1932)
The Young Lovell: A Romance (London: Chatto & Windus, 1913)

Other Works

Borrow, George, *The Romany Rye* (London: Dent, 1969)
Boswell, James, *Life of Johnson*, ed. R.W. Chapman, rev. J.D. Fleeman (Oxford: Oxford University Press, 1980).
Bowen, Stella, *Drawn From Life* (London: Virago, 1984 [1941])
Cocker, Mark, and Richard Mabey, *Birds Britannica* (London: Chatto & Windus, 2005).
Goldring, Douglas, *The Nineteen Twenties: A General Survey and Some Personal Memories* (London: Nicholson and Watson, 1945)
Gordon, Ambrose, Jr, *The Invisible Tent: The War Novels of Ford Madox Ford* (Austin, TX: University of Texas Press, 1964)
Harvey, David Dow, *Ford Madox Ford: 1873–1939: A Bibliography of Works and Criticism* (New York: Gordian Press, 1972)
Joyce, James, *Ulysses* (London: The Bodley Head, rev. edn, 1969)
MacShane, Frank (ed.), *Ford Madox Ford: The Critical Heritage* (London: Routledge, 1972)
Mizener, Arthur, *The Saddest Story: A Biography of Ford Madox Ford* (London: The Bodley Head, 1972)
Morrell, Ottoline, *Ottoline at Garsington: Memoirs of Lady Ottoline Morrell 1915–1918*, ed. Robert Gathorne-Hardy (London: Faber & Faber, 1974)
Peel, C.S., *How We Lived Then, 1914–1918: A Sketch of Social and Domestic Life in England During the War* (London: John Lane, The Bodley Head, 1929)
Saunders, Max, *Ford Madox Ford: A Dual Life*, 2 vols (Oxford: Oxford University Press, 1996)

Further Critical Reading on *Parade's End*

Armstrong, Paul, *The Challenge of Bewilderment: Understanding and Representation in James, Conrad, and Ford* (Ithaca, NY, and London: Cornell University Press, 1987)
Attridge, John, "'I Don't Read Novels ... I Know What's in 'em": Impersonality, Impressionism and Responsibility in *Parade's End*', in

Impersonality and Emotion in Twentieth-Century British Literature, ed. Christine Reynier and Jean-Michel Ganteau (Montpellier: Université Montpellier III, 2005)

Auden, W. H., 'Il Faut Payer', *Mid-Century*, 22 (Feb. 1961), 3–10

Becquet, Alexandra, 'Modernity, Shock and Cinema: The Visual Aesthetics of Ford Madox Ford's *Parade's End*', in *Ford Madox Ford and Visual Culture*, ed. Laura Colombino, International Ford Madox Ford Studies, 8 (Amsterdam and New York: Rodopi, 2009), 191–204

Bergonzi, Bernard, *Heroes' Twilight: A Study of the Literature of the Great War* (Manchester: Carcanet, 3rd edn, 1996)

Bradbury, Malcolm, 'The Denuded Place: War and Ford in *Parade's End* and *U. S. A.*', in *The First World War in Fiction*, ed. Holger Klein (London and Basingstoke: Macmillan, rev. edn, 1978), 193–209

——'Introduction', *Parade's End* (London: Everyman's Library, 1992)

Brasme, Isabelle, 'Between Impressionism and Modernism: *Some Do Not . . .*, a poetics of the *Entre-deux*', in *Ford Madox Ford: Literary Networks and Cultural Transformations*, ed. Andrzej Gasiorek and Daniel Moore, International Ford Madox Ford Studies, 7 (Amsterdam and New York: Rodopi, 2008), 189–99

Brown, Dennis, 'Remains of the Day: Tietjens the Englishman', in *Ford Madox Ford's Modernity*, ed. Robert Hampson and Max Saunders, International Ford Madox Ford Studies, 2 (Amsterdam and Atlanta, GA: Rodopi, 2003), 161–74

Brown, Nicholas, *Utopian Generations: The Political Horizon of Twentieth-Century Literature* (Princeton, NJ: Princeton University Press, 2005)

Buitenhuis, Peter, *The Great War of Words: British, American and Canadian Propaganda and Fiction, 1914–1933* (Vancouver: University of British Columbia Press, 1987)

Calderaro, Michela A., *A Silent New World: Ford Madox Ford's Parade's End* (Bologna: Editrice CLUEB [Cooperativa Libraria Universitaria, Editrice Bologna], 1993)

Caserio, Robert L., 'Ford's and Kipling's Modernist Imagination of Public Virtue', in *Ford Madox Ford's Modernity*, ed. Robert Hampson and Max Saunders, International Ford Madox Ford Studies, 2 (Amsterdam and Atlanta, GA: Rodopi, 2003), 175–90

Cassell, Richard A., *Ford Madox Ford: A Study of his Novels* (Baltimore, MD: Johns Hopkins University Press, 1962)

——*Ford Madox Ford: Modern Judgements* (London: Macmillan, 1972)

——*Critical Essays on Ford Madox Ford* (Boston: G. K. Hall, 1987)

Colombino, Laura, *Ford Madox Ford: Vision, Visuality and Writing* (Oxford: Peter Lang, 2008)

Conroy, Mark, 'A Map of Tory Misreading in *Parade's End*', in *Ford Madox Ford and Visual Culture*, ed. Laura Colombino, International Ford Madox Ford Studies, 8 (Amsterdam and New York: Rodopi, 2009), 175–90.

Cook, Cornelia, 'Last Post', *Agenda*, 27:4–28:1, Ford Madox Ford special double issue (winter 1989–spring 1990), 23–30

Davis, Philip, 'The Saving Remnant', in *Ford Madox Ford and Englishness*, ed. Dennis Brown and Jenny Plastow, International Ford Madox Ford Studies, 5 (Amsterdam and New York: Rodopi, 2006), 21–35

Deer, Patrick, *Culture in Camouflage: War, Empire, and Modern British Literature* (Oxford: Oxford University Press, 2009)

DeKoven, Marianne, 'Valentine Wannop and Thematic Structure in Ford Madox Ford's *Parade's End*', *English Literature in Transition (1880–1920)*, 20:2 (1977), 56–68

Erskine-Hill, Howard, 'Ford's Novel Sequence: An Essay in Retrospection', *Agenda*, 27:4–28:1, Ford Madox Ford special double issue (winter 1989–spring 1990), 46–55

Frayn, Andrew, '"*This* Battle Was not Over": *Parade's End* as a Transitional Text in the Development of "Disenchanted" First World War Literature', in *Ford Madox Ford: Literary Networks and Cultural Transformations*, ed. Andrzej Gasiorek and Daniel Moore, International Ford Madox Ford Studies, 7 (Amsterdam and New York: Rodopi, 2008), 201–16

Gasiorek, Andrzej, 'The Politics of Cultural Nostalgia: History and Tradition in Ford Madox Ford's *Parade's End*', *Literature & History*, 11:2 (third series) (autumn 2002), 52–77

Green, Robert, *Ford Madox Ford: Prose and Politics* (Cambridge: Cambridge University Press, 1981)

Haslam, Sara, *Fragmenting Modernism: Ford Madox Ford, the Novel, and the Great War* (Manchester: Manchester University Press, 2002)

Heldman, J. M., 'The Last Victorian Novel: Technique and Theme in *Parade's End*', *Twentieth Century Literature*, 18 (Oct. 1972), 271–84

Hoffmann, Charles G., *Ford Madox Ford: Updated Edition* (Boston: Twayne Publishers, 1990)

Holton, Robert. *Jarring Witnesses: Modern Fiction and the Representation of History* (Hemel Hempstead: Harvester Wheatsheaf, 1994)

Hynes, Samuel, 'Ford Madox Ford: Three Dedicatory Letters to *Parade's End*, with Commentary and Notes', *Modern Fiction Studies*, 16:4 (1970), 515–28

—*A War Imagined: The First World War and English Culture* (London: The Bodley Head, 1990)

Judd, Alan, *Ford Madox Ford* (London: Collins, 1990)

Kashner, Rita, 'Tietjens' Education: Ford Madox Ford's Tetralogy', *Critical Quarterly*, 8 (1966), 150–63

MacShane, Frank, *The Life and Work of Ford Madox Ford* (New York: Horizon; London: Routledge & Kegan Paul, 1965)

— ed., *Ford Madox Ford: The Critical Heritage* (London: Routledge, 1972)

Meixner, John A., *Ford Madox Ford's Novels: A Critical Study* (Minneapolis: University of Minnesota Press; London: Oxford University Press, 1962)

Mizener, Arthur, *The Saddest Story: A Biography of Ford Madox Ford* (New York: World, 1971; London: The Bodley Head, 1972)

Monta, Anthony P., '*Parade's End* in the Context of National Efficiency', in *History and Representation in Ford Madox Ford's Writings*, ed. Joseph Wiesenfarth, International Ford Madox Ford Studies, 3 (Amsterdam and New York: Rodopi, 2004), 41–51

Moore, Gene, 'The Tory in a Time of Change: Social Aspects of Ford Madox Ford's *Parade's End*', *Twentieth Century Literature*, 28:1 (spring 1982), 49–68

Moser, Thomas C., *The Life in the Fiction of Ford Madox Ford* (Princeton, NJ: Princeton University Press, 1980)

Munton, Alan, 'The Insane Subject: Ford and Wyndham Lewis in the War and Post-War', in *Ford Madox Ford: Literary Networks and Cultural Transformations*, ed. Andrzej Gasiorek and Daniel Moore, International Ford Madox Ford Studies, 7 (Amsterdam and New York: Rodopi, 2008), 105–30

Parfitt, George, *Fiction of the First World War: A Study* (London: Faber & Faber, 1988)

Radford, Andrew, 'The Gentleman's Estate in Ford's *Parade's End*', *Essays in Criticism* 52:4 (Oct. 2002), 314–32

Saunders, Max, 'Ford and European Modernism: War, Time, and *Parade's End*', in *Ford Madox Ford and 'The Republic of Letters'*, ed. Vita Fortunati and Elena Lamberti (Bologna: Editrice CLUEB [Cooperativa Libraria Universitaria, Editrice Bologna], 2002), 3–21

—'Introduction', Ford Madox Ford, *Parade's End* (Harmondsworth: Penguin, 2002), vii–xvii

Seiden, Melvin, 'Persecution and Paranoia in *Parade's End*', *Criticism*, 8:3 (summer 1966), 246–62

Skinner, Paul, '"Not the Stuff to Fill Graveyards": Joseph Conrad and *Parade's End*', in *Inter-relations: Conrad, James, Ford, and Others*, ed. Keith Carabine and Max Saunders (Lublin: Columbia University Press, 2003), 161–76

—'The Painful Processes of Reconstruction: History in *No Enemy* and *Last Post*', in *History and Representation in Ford Madox Ford's Writings*, ed. Joseph Wiesenfarth, International Ford Madox Ford Studies, 3 (Amsterdam and New York: Rodopi, 2004), 65–75

Snitow, Ann Barr, *Ford Madox Ford and the Voice of Uncertainty* (Baton Rouge: Louisiana State University Press, 1984)

Sorum, Eve, 'Mourning and Moving On: Life after War in Ford Madox Ford's *The Last Post*', in *Modernism and Mourning*, ed. Patricia Rae (Lewisburg, PA: Bucknell University Press, 2007), 154–67

Stang, Sondra J., *Ford Madox Ford* (New York: Ungar, 1977)

Tate, Trudi, 'Rumour, Propaganda, and *Parade's End*', *Essays in Criticism*, 47:4 (Oct. 1997), 332–53

—*Modernism, History and the First World War* (Manchester: Manchester University Press, 1998)

Trotter David, 'Ford Against Lewis and Joyce', in *Ford Madox Ford: Literary Networks and Cultural Transformations*, ed. Andrzej Gasiorek and Daniel Moore, International Ford Madox Ford Studies, 7 (Amsterdam and New York: Rodopi, 2008), 131–49

Weiss, Timothy, *Fairy Tale and Romance in Works of Ford Madox Ford* (Lanham, MD: University Press of America, 1984)

Wiesenfarth, Joseph, *Gothic Manners and the Classic English Novel* (Madison, WI: University of Wisconsin Press, 1988)

Wiley, Paul L., *Novelist of Three Worlds: Ford Madox Ford* (Syracuse, NY: Syracuse University Press, 1962)

THE
FORD
MADOX
FORD
SOCIETY

Ford c. 1915   ©Alfred Cohen, 2000   Registered Charity No. 1084040

This international society was founded in 1997 to promote knowledge of and interest in Ford. Honorary Members include Julian Barnes, A. S. Byatt, Hans-Magnus Enzensberger, Samuel Hynes, Alan Judd, Bill Nighy, Ruth Rendell, Michael Schmidt, John Sutherland, and Gore Vidal. There are currently over one hundred members, from more than ten countries. Besides regular meetings in Britain, we have held conferences in Italy, Germany, the U.S.A, and France. Since 2002 we have published International Ford Madox Ford Studies; a series of substantial annual volumes distributed free to members. *Ford Madox Ford: A Reappraisal* (2002), *Ford Madox Ford's Modernity* (2003), *History and Representation in Ford Madox Ford's Writings* (2004), *Ford Madox Ford and the City* (2005), *Ford Madox Ford and Englishness* (2006), *Ford Madox Ford's Literary Contacts* (2007), *Ford Madox Ford: Literary Networks and Cultural Transformations* (2008), *Ford Madox Ford and Visual Culture* (2009), and *Ford Madox Ford, Modernist Magazines and Editing* (2010) are all still available. Future volumes are planned on Ford and France, on his pre-war work, and on *Parade's End* and the First World War. If you are an admirer, an enthusiast, a reader, a scholar, or a student of anything Fordian, then this Society would welcome your involvement.

The Ford Madox Ford Society normally organises events and publishes Newsletters each year. Future meetings are planned in Glasgow, London, the Netherlands and Germany. The Society also inaugurated a series of Ford Lectures. Speakers have included Alan Judd, Nicholas Delbanco, Zinovy Zinik, A. S. Byatt, Colm Tóibín, and Hermione Lee. To join, please see the website for details; or send your name and address (including an e-mail address if possible), and a cheque made payable to 'The Ford Madox Ford Society', to:

Dr Paul Skinner, 7 Maidstone Street, Victoria Park, Bristol BS3 4SW, UK.
Telephone: 0117 9715008; Fax: 0117 9020294 Email: p.skinner370@btinternet.com

Annual rates: **Sterling:** Individuals: £12 (by standing order; otherwise £15); Concessions £8; **Euros**: €15.00 (by standing order; otherwise €20.00); Concessions €8.50. **US Dollars:** Any category: $25

For further information, either contact Paul Skinner (Treasurer) at the above address, or Sara Haslam (Chair) by e-mail at: s.j.haslam@open.ac.uk
The Society's Website is at: **http://open.ac.uk/Arts/fordmadoxford-society**